# what came first

# CAROL SNOW

**B**

BERKLEY BOOKS, NEW YORK

**THE BERKLEY PUBLISHING GROUP**
**Published by the Penguin Group**
**Penguin Group (USA) Inc.**
**375 Hudson Street, New York, New York 10014, USA**
Penguin Group (Canada), 90 Eglinton Avenue East, Suite 700, Toronto, Ontario M4P 2Y3, Canada
(a division of Pearson Penguin Canada Inc.)
Penguin Books Ltd., 80 Strand, London WC2R 0RL, England
Penguin Group Ireland, 25 St. Stephen's Green, Dublin 2, Ireland (a division of Penguin Books Ltd.)
Penguin Group (Australia), 250 Camberwell Road, Camberwell, Victoria 3124, Australia
(a division of Pearson Australia Group Pty. Ltd.)
Penguin Books India Pvt. Ltd., 11 Community Centre, Panchsheel Park, New Delhi—110 017, India
Penguin Group (NZ), 67 Apollo Drive, Rosedale, Auckland 0632, New Zealand
(a division of Pearson New Zealand Ltd.)
Penguin Books (South Africa) (Pty.) Ltd., 24 Sturdee Avenue, Rosebank, Johannesburg 2196,
South Africa

Penguin Books Ltd., Registered Offices: 80 Strand, London WC2R 0RL, England

This book is an original publication of The Berkley Publishing Group.

PRINTING HISTORY
Berkley trade paperback edition / October 2011

Library of Congress Cataloging-in-Publication Data

Snow, Carol, date.
    What came first / Carol Snow.
    p.    cm.
    ISBN 978-0-425-24303-9
    I. Title.
PS3619.N66W47    2011
813'.6—dc22                2010054196

PRINTED IN THE UNITED STATES OF AMERICA

10  9  8  7  6  5  4  3  2  1

*For my mother, Peggy Snow*

# Acknowledgments

Thank you, yet again, to my wonderful editor, Cindy Hwang, for her sharp eye and smart insights on this, our fifth book together. I am grateful for the hard work of the many talented people at Berkley Books, with a special shout-out to Leis Pederson for her competence, responsiveness, and overall niceness.

Thanks to Stephanie Kip Rostan for representing my books, guiding my career, and being my friend. Everyone at the Levine Greenberg Literary Agency has been a delight to work with; I especially appreciate the efforts of Monika Verma, Miek Coccia, and Melissa Rowland.

As usual when writing a book, I had to hit up friends and family to fill in my sizable gaps in knowledge. Thank you to Ted Bacon for sharing legal expertise; Jill Smolinski for filling me in on the Hermosa Beach area; Rafael Suarez for providing Spanish translations; and Tracey Scott for getting and keeping those crazy chickens. My husband, Andrew Todhunter, not only supplied engineering lingo but was also kind enough to take me to lunch at Hooters. Thanks, honey. You're the best.

I am indebted to numerous friends who, over the years, have shared concerns about declining fertility and stories of assisted reproduction. I could never have written this book without them. For information about assisted reproduction in general and donorship in particular, I turned to the Internet. (While I will miss Laura, Wendy, and Vanessa, I'll be glad to get "sperm" off my history browser.) The Donor Sibling Registry website (www.donorsiblingregistry) was an invaluable resource for learning about the unique issues facing donor families.

Finally, thanks to my readers. I hope you like this one.

## Part 1

# JANUARY

# 1

## Laura

The chickens are getting restless.

It is just past sunrise on a chilly Saturday morning in January, and insomnia kept my brain whirring until after two A.M. Now all I want to do is stay buried under my hypoallergenic faux-down comforter and return to the dream that is already slipping away.

But the chickens have other ideas—assuming their primitive little brains are capable of anything that can be termed an idea. In their coop (which is far too close to my bedroom: poor planning on my part), the birds shriek and cry and say *bock-bock-bock,* their clucks growing more frantic as the sky grows lighter. Each morning it's the same, as if they've never seen the sun before— which is patently absurd. We live in Southern California; they see almost nothing *but* sunshine.

In the dream, I'd been kneeling next to a man on a black sand beach, both of us digging up giant clams with our bare hands, prying the shells open and eating the mollusks raw. And yes, I know that sounds like raunchy symbolism, but I'm just extremely fond of shellfish. The man was wearing a tuxedo. And I think he had a tiara on his head. But that was okay because he liked me and I liked him, and my nightly pseudo-erotic dreams are the closest things I've had to a date in five years.

Eyes shut, I turn away from the window. Alfredo, the cat, a twenty-pound Maine coon named for my son's favorite pasta sauce, slinks up from the foot of my bed, settles himself on the pillow next to me, and starts to purr. And then I remember: if you have an independent source of income, reliable domestic help, and an affectionate cat, you'll never need a man. I didn't even need a man to get pregnant. At least, not one that I ever met.

So screw the guy in the tiara.

I sense Ian before I hear him, as if the air softens and warms the instant he tiptoes into the room. "Mom! You awake?"

"I am now." I open my eyes and drink him in, my bony eight-year-old boy with his too-big front teeth, his army-green eyes, and his shaggy brown hair, still shot with leftover streaks of summer blond. He is the sweetest, smartest, most beautiful person I have ever known. There is no one in the world I would rather spend time with. Some days, I still can't believe he is mine.

But right now, I really wish he would go away.

Monday through Friday I get up at 6:15 A.M. so I can take a too-short shower, put on a conservative skirt, blouse, and control-top panty hose, and join Ian for a hot breakfast (eggs, usually) before heading off to my office in Santa Ana, where I practice estate law while downing countless cups of mediocre coffee. Carmen, our nanny/housekeeper, takes Ian to school.

Unless Ian has a soccer game or other activity, weekends are my time to sleep a little later, trying in vain to recover from my increasingly common insomnia before launching into household projects. Single parenthood can be exhausting at times, but I chose this life, and I wouldn't trade it for anything.

"Feed the chickens," I mumble. "Then let them free-range."

The chickens are quieter out of their coop; perhaps I can sneak in a little more sleep.

Ian puts his head next to mine on a tiny patch of pillow and reaches over my shoulder to stroke the cat. "You said we could sit outside this morning and watch the chickens lay eggs."

Ian has become obsessed with catching the chickens in the act of laying. It is vaguely disturbing.

"I said *some* morning. I didn't say today. It's cold out."

"Please, Mommy?"

These days, Ian only calls me Mommy when he wants to soften me up. But then, the chickens were Ian's birthday present from me last spring, so I deserve this.

I reach my arms around his angular body, luxuriating in his warmth and little-boy smell. "You win. But you need to put on a coat. And I need to make coffee. You want hot chocolate?"

"With whipped cream," he says. "And marshmallows."

I kiss his shaggy hair. "Anything for you."

It's not just an expression. I really will do—in fact, pretty much *do* do—anything for my son. During his cheetah phase, I took him to the San Diego Wild Animal Park. When he moved on to dolphins, we headed to Sea World. I have seldom turned down a request for a playdate, sleepover, or pool party, and we take a vacation every August. In the years before Ian received chickens and a coop for his birthday, he racked up a Wii, an iPod, a fully stocked saltwater aquarium, and Alfredo the cat. For Christmas I gave him a piano.

More than things, though, I give him time and love and attention. Although I practice law, we are not wealthy. I took myself off the partner track when I became pregnant and have been content with regular hours and a solid, steady income. We live in a three-bedroom ranch house in Fullerton, a pleasant suburban town in north Orange County, California. I drive a five-year-old Honda Accord. It is enough. No, it is more than enough.

Of course, I worry that I'm spoiling Ian, that he will suddenly turn bratty and ungrateful or that he will crumple in the face of life's disappointments. But here's the thing: the more I give him, the greater he shines with curiosity about the world, the more he trembles with appreciation for all living things.

So, yes, I will do anything for my son. Because I love him so very much. And because the sad truth is that the one thing he really wants, the only thing he's requested for every birthday and every Christmas since he was old enough to talk, is something I haven't been able to give him.

Ian wants a sibling.

# Vanessa

Today is my birthday, and ever since I woke up this morning, I've had this feeling. Eric is going to ask me to marry him tonight. I thought he might do it at breakfast, but he had to work the early shift today, so he was already gone when I got up. He left me a note on the counter, though: *HAPPY BIRTHDAY, V. HAVE AN AWESOME DAY & I'LL SEE YOU AT DINNER.*

Eric is good with stuff like that. You know, leaving me notes or buying me little things. He's going to be really romantic when he asks me to marry him, write me a poem or maybe even a song, which is something he used to do when we first started going out, before he gave up the guitar. I'm not sure about the ring. Part of me thinks he'll want to pick it out together, and part of me thinks that since he works at Costco, he could get a good deal on a diamond.

I have searched through all of his drawers and jeans pockets, but haven't found anything. He must want me to help pick out the ring. Or maybe I haven't looked hard enough.

This feeling I've got, that today is the big day, is different from how I felt last month at Christmas. That time, I thought he would slip a ring onto a branch of our tree, which was actually just a ficus strung with silver and gold garlands. It's different, too, from how I felt on New Year's Eve, when I decided he'd drop the ring into a glass of champagne and wait for me to notice it till after we'd toasted.

At eleven o'clock on New Year's Eve, I asked Eric, "Do you want to open the champagne?"

He said, "I didn't buy any champagne. Did you?" And then, when he figured I wasn't going to put out, he went to bed.

My hands shake as I turn the key to our apartment. It's different this time. I can sense it. Today is not just any birthday. It's my twenty-ninth. Meaning, if I'm going to get married before I turn thirty, I have to get engaged *right now*.

During the three years I've lived with Eric, every one of my high school friends has gotten married. *Every single one*. For a while there was a wedding like every weekend. I'm a regular in the T.J.Maxx dress department. Time after time, Eric and I drive out to Riverside just to have people tease me about catching the bouquet or to say, "You guys must be next" or whatever. I'll laugh like that's funny even though it's so not, and Eric will just look uncomfortable.

If he doesn't propose tonight, there's always Valentine's Day.

The apartment smells of tomatoes and garlic. Jason Mraz is playing over the speakers connected to Eric's iPod. Eric and I have totally different taste in music, but we both like Jason Mraz. Eric calls him a "Universal Donor" of music. I don't really get what he means by that, but whatever.

I love living with Eric, at least most of the time, but our apartment sucks. It's dark and small and doesn't have enough closet space. The dinky living room has dirty beige carpet, and it opens to a kitchen that has brown cabinets made of this plastic-y stuff that is supposed to look like wood but doesn't. Rents are high in

Redondo Beach. This was all we could afford. Eric likes to surf, so he doesn't want to move inland.

Eric is at the sink, filling a big pot with water. He dries his hands on a dish towel and meets me by the front door. He's wearing what he wears every night, a faded T-shirt and his oldest, softest jeans. Eric's not too tall, but his shoulders are square and his hips are slim. He looks good in jeans.

"Hey, birthday girl." He cups my face in his hands and kisses me. All of a sudden I'm not nervous anymore. Everything is going to be okay.

"Eggplant Parmesan?" I ask.

"Uh-huh." He kisses me again.

"My favorite."

"I know."

Eggplant Parmesan really is my favorite thing Eric makes. It is also the only thing Eric makes, unless you count Kraft Deluxe macaroni and cheese. Eric doesn't eat meat. Eric doesn't cook meat. Eric doesn't even like meat in the house.

I bury my face in his neck. He runs a pale, slim hand through my thick black curls. I almost say "I love you," but I hold it back. Eric shows his love in a million ways, but he's not big on the words. The pause between when I say "I love you" and the moment he says it back always feels a beat too long. He hardly ever says it first. We had a fight about it once, and he explained that for him, saying "I love you" is a special occasion kind of thing, and if we say it too often it won't mean anything anymore. I still don't get that, but I kind of have to go along with it. So tonight, I'll save my "I love you" for the Big Moment. If there is a Big Moment.

If Eric doesn't give me a ring tonight . . . I can't even stand to think about it.

He goes back to cooking, and I go off to change. Our bedroom has almost no floor room, even with the double bed shoved into a corner. The closet is so crammed that I can hardly see what is in there. Like the dresser, we share the closet, but most of it is my stuff. Eric has only one suit and one dress shirt, both from Goodwill. He wears them to weddings.

Not that I even care about our wedding. We can have something small and cheap. Maybe something in a park. Eric's job at Costco is steady, and the hours are good, but he doesn't make a lot of money. But we've been to so many weddings. A lot of people would be hurt if we don't invite them. And then there's the registry to think about . . .

*Stop.*

I peel off my lavender scrubs. They match our bedroom walls. Our bathroom is lavender, too, a slightly darker shade. Eric gave me these scrubs for Christmas (when he didn't give me a ring). He said, "I know purple is your favorite color."

I hate scrubs. Scrubs make me look fat. Not that I'm so little. My boobs are kind of big (I'm okay with that) and so is my butt (not so okay), but my waist is small and my legs are good. When I'm in scrubs, you can't see that. I don't even get why I have to wear them to answer the phone and file papers at Great Grins, the dental office where I'm the receptionist. It's not like any of the patients are going to spew blood or saliva on me.

"You going somewhere?" Eric asks when I come out in my favorite purple dress.

"I don't know. You taking me somewhere?"

"Do you want me to?" Uh-oh. I made him squirm.

"No! I was kidding. I'm right where I want to be."

Okay, so that's kind of a lie. It would be nice to be somewhere other than this ugly apartment. Before Eric, I used to love clubbing with my girlfriends. Plus there was this guy, back in Riverside, who used to take me to expensive restaurants and fancy nightclubs. And I liked it. Dressing up, riding in his shiny car, having people wait on me. I liked it enough that for a while I was able to ignore the bad things about this guy. Like his cologne, which was way too strong. Or his voice, which was way too loud. Or the way he'd go into the restaurant bathrooms all crabby and come out with a new, happy, hyper personality. Or that he didn't believe that being with just one woman was natural.

Eric doesn't take me out to restaurants much, but we'll go to the beach to look for dolphins, to farmers' markets to pick out fruit, or to festivals to listen to music. I almost never like the music, but that's beside the point. Eric doesn't need to spend money to make me feel special.

"You want to walk down to the beach after dinner?" he asks. The beach is a mile and a half away.

"It's kind of cold out," I say. "And it's getting dark."

He shrugs. "Okay. Whatever you want."

He has set the little glass table that I bought on sale at Pier 1 and opened a bottle of the pink wine that I love and he hates. I pour the wine and start drinking, faster than I should because I'm feeling nervous again.

Even though the living room is small, the carpet is ugly, and Eric's surfboard is the first thing you see when you walk in the room, I've made it as pretty as I could. I painted the walls pale yellow and put up big framed pictures of blue and purple flowers that I got real cheap when Linens 'n Things was going out of business, along with a beige slipcover for the couch, some throw pillows, and a fake ficus (that doesn't have a ring hiding in its branches—I checked).

I sit on the couch. "Dr. Sanchez took me out to lunch."

He looks up from tossing a salad. "Just you?"

"Of course not. Melva and Pammy were there, too. We tried out a new Mexican place. It was okay." Melva and Pammy are the hygienists. "Melva is pregnant again. Did I tell you?"

I know I told him, but I keep waiting for a more enthusiastic reaction.

"Yeah. I think so." So much for enthusiasm.

"And she's already saying she wants one more after this."

"Mm."

The phone rings, and I answer, thinking maybe someone's calling to wish me happy birthday. Like maybe my mother. Or my sister. But it's just some company offering to lower my credit-card payments. After I hang up, I drink some more wine and tell myself that I don't care that they forgot. Someday I'll have the kind of family I missed out on growing up, and I'll never forget a birthday. Never.

My nose feels a tiny bit numb already. I shouldn't drink on an empty stomach. Sometimes when I get tipsy I say stuff I probably shouldn't. Like this:

"I used to think I'd have kids at twenty-six, twenty-eight, and thirty. Guess that's not going to happen."

He doesn't say anything, not even "Mm" or "Oh."

I take another pink sip. Tasty. "I could still have one at thirty."

Still no response. He opens the oven, checks the eggplant, sets the timer.

"Is it too late?" I ask.

He turns around but doesn't meet my eyes. "No. It's not too late."

"I want to have children, Eric."

He nods, just a little bit. "I know you do."

Uh! Why am I doing this? One thing at a time. We can have a serious talk about children after we get engaged.

It's all Melva and Pammy's fault. At lunch they were all, "Is this the big night?" Pammy kept going on about ultimatums, and Melva was all about diamond sizes. Dr. Sanchez just looked totally, totally uncomfortable.

If Eric doesn't give me a ring . . . Oh God, I can't stand the suspense.

When he sets the salad bowl on the table in front of me, I say, "So—you wanna wait till after dinner to do presents?"

He freezes. "Um, I only got you one thing. I hope that's okay."

One thing! Yessssss!

"Of course it's okay! It's, it's . . . *awesome*. One big gift is much better than a bunch of little things."

"I don't know that I'd call it big, exactly." Eric shoves his hands into his pockets and smiles, looking just a little nervous.

Eric got me a tiny diamond. That's okay. It'll do the job.

"Dinner's got another ten minutes," he says. "Do you want your present now?"

The wrapping is really pretty—thick purple paper and a big white bow. But the box is the wrong size, the wrong shape.

I try to keep my voice neutral. "It looks like a CD."

"Open it."

Hands shaking, I peel back the tape slowly, carefully. This is going to hurt, and I'm not ready.

It looks like a CD because it is a CD. And not one from a store either. Eric's careful printing covers the white paper insert inside the plastic case.

"It's a custom mix," he says. "I burned it for you."

I just look at him.

"A whole bunch of new artists," he says. "And some older ones I hadn't heard before. Stuff we can both listen to. That I think we'll both like."

I keep looking at him.

"You don't like it."

I put the case on the table. "I guess I expected something else. That you'd do more than burn a CD."

There will be no ring for Valentine's Day either. I know that now.

"I didn't just burn the CD," he says. "I had to spend a lot of time listening to music. I had to think about what you liked, what I liked—how the qualities might combine and carry over to something we hadn't heard before. So then I bought the best ones from iTunes. I loaded everything onto your iPod, too."

There's nothing left to say. I push back my chair and run to the bedroom, slam the door.

He doesn't come after me right away. By the time he knocks, I've stopped crying, and I've swapped my purple dress for ratty old pajamas. I don't ever want to wear that dress again. It will always remind me of tonight.

"Dinner's ready," he says, standing in the open doorway.

"I'm not hungry."

He nods. We are quiet for a moment, until he speaks again. "I'm sorry you didn't like my gift."

"I wanted a ring, Eric!"

He lets out a deep breath. "I know you did." When he closes the door, it barely makes a sound.

#  Wendy

Tuesday-night scrapbooking is the highlight of my week, which speaks volumes about just how crappy my life has become. There are fourteen of us in the group, all stay-at-home mothers, but typically only five or six women show up on any given evening. I'm always there.

No one ever asks me to host. Scrapbooking involves cutting tools, and my son Harrison's preschool scissor incident looms large in the collective community memory. I'd like to say that he's outgrown his aggressive behavior now that he's in kindergarten, but he hasn't, any more than his twin sister, Sydney, has moved beyond SCREAMING AT THE TOP OF HER LUNGS EVERY TIME SHE DOESN'T GET WHAT SHE WANTS.

So: scrapbooking. I've been at it for just over a year, and I'm on my eighth volume, *Bath Time for Babies!* Thanks to the water theme, I'm going with blue: blue covers, blue pages, blue stickers. Blue is calming.

Wine is calming, too. It flows by the gallon at these things, Chardonnay, mostly, though we have a handful of Merlot drinkers. We all live in the same North Scottsdale housing development, so home is always a short drive (or stumble) away.

Annalisa Lemberger scored hostess duties tonight. Annalisa lives a street away in a beige stucco house identical to mine, right down to the forest-green front door and the yellow lantana planted along the concrete walkway. Years ago, before the twins, a few months after Darren and I had moved to Arizona from Chicago, I drove my groceries "home" to Annalisa's house. My garage door opener didn't work, of course, so I parked in the driveway and lugged my plastic sacks of food and toilet paper to the front door. I spent maybe ten frustrating minutes trying to turn my key in the lock before the woman who lived there (not Annalisa—she's new) called neighborhood security. The guard assured me that people in our development confuse houses all the time, but I burst into tears anyway and didn't stop crying till I'd spent a half hour in the darkness of my own garage.

The house mistake pushed me over the edge, but it wasn't the true source of my unhappiness. Before stopping at the grocery store, I'd had an appointment with a fertility specialist. With no success after three years of what we all referred to as "trying," I needed to face facts. I might never become pregnant.

The idea of a childless future plunged me into an instant depression. How could I ever lead a full life without a house full of little people to call my own?

Ha! If only I could have seen into the future!

"You're the first one here!" Annalisa chirps now, opening her green front door. She's started in on the Chardonnay already, a sparkly wine charm clinking at the base of her heavy, green-rimmed Mexican wineglass. She looks Scottsdale-perfect as always: tall, trim, and frosty blond, wearing a teal sweater set, cream trousers, and silver sandals with delicate heels.

"Actually, I thought this was my house," I quip. Annalisa loves my wrong-house story. (I never told her that it ended in tears.)

When she laughs, she shows off her superstraight, bright-white teeth. Annalisa always laughs at my jokes, even the predictable ones, so I like her even though I can't help thinking of her as Scottsdale Barbie.

As much as our houses resemble each other from the street, walking into Annalisa's is like entering a different world. My house has that "lived in" look: once-white carpet; stain-resistant couches that aren't; and a mishmash of tables and chairs, all showing the effects of two active five-year-olds. ("Active" sounds so much better than "out of control.") Everything in Annalisa's house looks like it was bought in one day at a Southwestern decorating superstore. Which it probably was.

If I were a positive-thinking kind of person, I'd appreciate that my house has more personality than Annalisa's. But I am not a positive-thinking kind of person. Personality is overrated. I'd switch homes in a minute.

In Annalisa's combo living/dining room (we use it as a toy room), Colbie Caillet croons all barefoot-folksy-feminine from the stereo while cinnamon-scented candles flicker on the end tables. I wouldn't dare light candles like that in my house. Even matches hidden on hard-to-reach shelves make me nervous.

In addition to wine, Annalisa has laid out a seven-layer dip, an artichoke spread, a cheese platter, and brownies. Why do the skinniest women always serve the fattiest food? For years, I've moaned about my inability to lose my "baby weight." I put on sixty-five pounds with Sydney and Harrison and lost twenty-three in the year after their birth. The rest has settled quite comfortably onto my stomach, belly, hips, thighs, and—shoot me now—back. Now that the kids are in school, I've got to admit that all that padding can no longer be classified as "baby weight." It is just plain old fat, and it's not going anywhere. Pass the artichoke spread.

I have just finished affixing a cactus wine charm to my glass when Annalisa's husband, Roger, comes clomping down the stairs with their two little blond girls, whose names I can never remember. One of the girls is a year older than the twins, and the other is a year younger. Or maybe she's two years younger. I can never remember that either. It doesn't matter. As a rule, I get along better with women who don't have children in the twins' class.

"Hiya! Good to see you again!" Roger booms, his voice echoing off the too-tall ceiling. He has no idea who I am.

"You, too," I say. "Taking the girls out?"

"Yup." He puts a hand on each blond head. "Movie date with Dad."

Roger is the other reason that I don't hate Annalisa even though she looks like an unnaturally proportioned plastic doll (I mean that in a good way). Roger is a beast. That's not to say that he's not a nice man, because as far as I can tell, he lets Annalisa do pretty much anything she wants. But Annalisa is younger than me, in her early thirties, and Roger has got to be sixty. And not a youthful sixty. I don't know what's going on with his face, but the skin is all red and saggy, and he has pores the size of sesame seeds.

"What are Darren and the twins doing tonight?" Annalisa asks.

"Just, you know. Having a quiet evening at home."

When I left, Darren was at his computer, lost in a Sims trance, while Harrison and Sydney chomped on dinosaur-shaped chicken nuggets in front of the Cartoon Network. By now they'll have finished eating and be engaged in hand-to-hand combat, but whoops! I've left my cell phone in the car, so if Darren tries to call me, I won't even know.

"That's *nice*," Annalisa, says. "Sometimes we moms just need to get out of the way so the dads can have their one-on-one time."

In Sims, Darren is a childless sports agent with a knack for Cajun voodoo—his powers recently imbued by the Sims Makin' Magic Expansion Pack, which his mother gave him for Christmas.

She never did like me, and not just because she spent so many years blaming her lack of grandchildren on my faulty female plumbing. When Darren's sluggish sperm were finally identified as a far bigger obstacle to pregnancy than my irregular ovulation, she hardened herself against me even more. Now she sends "the children" (never "Harrison and Sydney," never "my grandchildren") ten dollars each for their birthdays and Christmas. I've learned not to expect or want any more from her.

The doorbell rings. Annalisa puts down her already-empty wine-glass and opens the door to another frosty blonde, slightly shorter and not quite as pretty as herself (Scottsdale Skipper). Two more women arrive shortly after. Annalisa pours them wine and refills her own glass. We pull out our supplies: binders, papers, scissors, stickers, and photographs—so many, many photographs.

We coo and giggle over the images: bath time, beach time, birth-days, and Christmas. Such adorable children. Such dashing hus-bands.

Thank God they're not here.

# Laura

In the backyard, the screeching chickens rush to greet us, peering through the chicken wire like inmates in a prison yard longing for visitors. Oh, who am I kidding? They're not happy to see us. They just want to see what we've brought to eat.

"Check the gate," I tell Ian, placing our steaming mugs on the teak patio table. Not surprisingly, it's chilly outside, the grass drenched with dew. I push our chairs out of the shade of the house and into the sunshine.

After running to the side yard to make sure the chickens can't escape, Ian unlatches the coop and throws in leftovers from last night's meal: peas and tomatoes, pasta and bread. Carmen makes dinner Monday through Friday. Saturday and Sunday we either eat out or order in. It's not that I can't cook, but my time with Ian is limited, and I don't want to waste it in front of a stove.

Okay, truth: I can't cook. I make a mean hot chocolate, though. And I'm an ace with a can opener and a microwave.

As the chickens peck at the leftovers, Ian checks for eggs. The henhouse has two levels, which we refer to, jokingly, as the Great Room and the Loft. The chickens sometimes sleep in the Loft, but all of the laying takes place in the lower left corner of the Great Room. The chickens take turns sitting on the pile of eggs.

I can't help wondering what it feels like, day after day, to force something that big out of your body. Does it hurt them? Does it sadden them to have their eggs snatched away? Do they hold out hope that warm eggs will hold new life? Could I anthropomorphize poultry any more?

Ian is a master of doing nothing, of living in the moment and feeling the world pulse around him. Me, I'm a bit more restless, my brain an endless whir. Shivering at the table, I think, *The concrete needs to be sealed maybe I should get pavers too bad we don't have a swimming pool but there really isn't room the avocado tree is doing well not sure what's going on with the lemon must ask Carmen to talk to the gardener I hope the chickens were a good idea what happens if one dies will Ian fall apart?*

The chickens. They're supposed to help me relax. *Think about the chickens.*

There are five birds in all. The two big Rock Bards have black and white speckles and bright red crowns: very French country. They lay the most and the biggest eggs. Inasmuch as creatures that operate almost entirely on instinct and reflex can be assigned personality traits, the two Rhode Island Reds, brown with red crowns, are the friendliest. Finally, the one Americana—small, brown, and skittish, vaguely reminiscent of a tubby, earthbound hawk—would be a total write-off if not for its small and precious eggs. The eggs are green. And yes, we have been known to eat them with ham.

Ian named all the chickens. He swears the two Rock Bards, Salt and Pepper, are easy to tell apart (they're not) but that only he knows the difference between the two Rhodies, Rusty and Red. I refer to all four of them as the Chickens, even though Ian protests. He says that's like calling him the Kid. Thanks to her green eggs, Ian took inspiration from Dr. Seuss and called the Americana Sam.

We started out with six fluffy yellow chicks, two of each kind, all supposedly female. But at eight weeks, it was clear, at least to anyone who'd been examining pictures of bird genitalia on one of several Web sites devoted to backyard chickens, that one of the Americanas was a rooster.

"Why can't we keep him?" Ian asked.

"Because he would mate with the girl chickens." I've never shielded my son from the facts of life.

"So?"

"So roosters can get aggressive. Besides, we don't need the eggs fertilized, so there's no point." Of course, sex is easier to explain when it's something that other people do, without any uncomfortable images of Mommy and Daddy groping in the darkness.

"We couldn't keep the rooster even if we wanted to," I told Ian. "We're zoned for hens but not roosters. Roosters are too noisy."

After they finish eating, most of the chickens venture into the yard, stepping like ladies in high heels navigating an icy sidewalk. One Rhodie walks up the ramp to the henhouse and settles into the egg-laying corner.

Ian plops down into the chair next to me. "What do you think chickens think about?"

I run a hand over his hair. "Nothing. I think they think about nothing."

"Well, I think you're wrong."

The whipped cream and marshmallows have already dissolved into his hot chocolate, but Ian doesn't care. He sips the sweet brew, watches and waits. And waits. And waits.

"You have any homework this weekend?"

"No." A white foam mustache quivers above his lip.

"You sure?"

"I'm sure."

A third grader, Ian began a gifted program this year. The greater workload resulted in some initial growing pains; during his fall conference, his teacher expressed concern about missing and incomplete assignments. After the conference, I bought Ian a giant calendar and helped him devise a filing system. It has made a world of difference.

"Don't forget to practice piano before your lesson this afternoon."

"Mm."

Ian doesn't like it when I nag. Neither do I.

We go back to watching the chickens.

"I wish I had a different name," he says, eyes still on the chickens.

"Why? What's wrong with Ian?"

He shrugs. "I just wish I were called something else."

"Like what?"

"Jake," he says without hesitation.

"You wish I'd named you *Jake*?"

"Uh-huh."

"But why?"

"I just do."

We go back to watching the chickens.

"This is nice," he says.

"It sure is."

Unfortunately, since I lack Ian's gift for living in the moment, "nice" quickly shifts to "boring." When I can't take it anymore, I nip back into the house for my work laptop, along with a couple of throw blankets. Outside, I drape one blanket across Ian's lap and the other across my own, and then I boot up my laptop. I check my e-mail, delete some forwarded jokes from my stepfather, and answer a couple of work queries. On Yahoo, I read the day's top news and check the weather forecast for Orange County: sunny with a high of seventy-two. What a surprise.

Finally, I shift the screen out of Ian's view and log on to the

Donor Sibling Network. "DSN featured on Good Morning America!!" it says on the home page. In Dallas, seven blond children and their parents, along with a *Good Morning America* crew, met for a New Year's Eve potluck. Photos show two children from one single mother, three from another, and two from a lesbian couple. It's eerie how much the children look alike: all those wide pug noses, that straight pale hair. If you superimposed all of the children's photos over one another, you'd probably get a pretty good idea of what their sperm donor looked like as a child.

Maybe it's odd, but until a couple of years ago, I didn't think much about Donor 613, the man who supplied half of Ian's chromosomes. At the time of his deposit, he was twenty-three years old and in his first year of medical school, a five-foot-eight Caucasian with light brown hair and blue eyes. The donor's height, hair, and eye color seemed irrelevant. It wasn't until after I'd conceived that I realized they were exactly the same as mine (though I've been highlighting my mousy hair since I was in my twenties).

It was his enrollment in medical school that sold me. Getting in takes extreme intelligence and getting through takes self-discipline and drive. Most likely, the desire for a medical career indicates a compassionate nature. Do drive and compassion flow through the genes? Maybe not, but you never know. Ian has always been an exceptionally gentle and generous boy.

I bought three vials of 613's sperm from the Southern California Cryobank, conceived with the first, disposed of the rest. It never occurred to me that I might want more children, that I'd fall so in love with my son that I'd long to give him a playmate just like him.

I could use another donor, of course. But Ian has asked questions about 613 since he was old enough to understand the concept. Do I think his donor likes spaghetti as much as Ian does? Do I think he's the reason Ian's so good at piano? Any identity issues are apt to amplify as time goes on; bringing a new set of genes into the mix could only make things worse. It would be so much better to give Ian a full sibling with whom he could compare proclivities and talents.

Two years ago, I turned forty. Faced with my declining (and possibly expired) fertility, I called the bank only to learn they had no more vials from Donor 613. They suggested I check the Donor Sibling Network, an online registry that was set up to allow families with shared donors to contact one another. The first time I logged on, I posted a message on the bulletin board: *Anyone else conceive from Southern California Cryobank Donor 613?*

Since then, I've checked the Web site every day, hoping to discover my son's blood ties. I'd love to meet that child or those children, to see Ian form an instant bond with a complete stranger, a more-than-friend that he can have for life and who can perhaps give him a more complete sense of who he is and where he came from.

But more than that, I'd like to meet other women who purchased the sperm. To ask if maybe, just maybe, there might be a vial left in a freezer somewhere, waiting for me.

---

The Rhode Island Red's squawking grows louder, more frantic. Her head moves around, even as she stays planted on the laying spot.

"She's doing it, Mom! She's laying!"

On the other side of the yard, the other chickens go about their business, walking, pecking, clucking. The Rhodie screams like a seagull and suddenly grows quiet.

I log off the Web site and follow Ian to the coop, where he reaches under the chicken, searching for his treasure.

The bird stands up.

There is nothing there.

# Vanessa

From the bedroom, I can hear Eric cleaning up the kitchen and putting everything away. He's good about little things like that, even if he's bad about big things like marriage. Every time he crosses the living room, I think he's going to come see me in the bedroom. No way am I making the first move.

Unfortunately, my stomach didn't get the memo about playing hard to get. Finally I can't stand the hunger pains anymore, and I open the bedroom door. Eric sits on the couch, reading a library book and listening to music. He looks up and turns off the iPod. When he doesn't say anything, I hurry through the room and open the refrigerator. But now I don't know what to eat.

I burst into tears. "Is this it? Is it over?"

He puts down his book and comes to me. I sob in his arms. The fridge stays open, like our own personal cold front.

He says, "Shh, shh, shh." In a comforting way, not like "Shut up."

He heats a messy slice of eggplant Parmesan in the microwave. I sit on the couch, balance the plate in my lap, cry and eat at the same time, which turns out to be kind of dangerous when I almost choke on a piece of really hot cheese. Eric keeps his arm around me, just getting up once to bring me a box of tissues. The tissue box is purple. It is hard to find purple tissue boxes. Eric bought it just for me.

"Do you want to break up?" I ask when I can speak without gasping.

"No." He dabs my tears.

"But you don't want to marry me."

He's quiet for a while. "If I was going to marry anyone, I'd marry you. It's just. . . I know you want . . . I don't know if . . ." He's quiet again.

"*What?*"

"Being married, it seems so . . . final. Not that I want to be with anyone else, because I don't. But I haven't figured out what I want to do with my life. And the thing is, I don't even *want* to figure that out yet. I'm just not ready to limit my options."

"And marrying me . . . that would be limiting."

"Not the *you* part. The marriage part. I'm committed to you, and you're committed to me. We *know* that. What difference does it make whether we stand up in front of a roomful of people and someone hands us a piece of paper? I don't need that piece of paper."

"But I do." I put the plate on the coffee table and take another tissue.

Eric strokes my hair. We are quiet for a little while, and then he goes, "I was just thinking . . . when you were in the bedroom, I was thinking . . . what if we went to Eastern Europe?"

"You mean on vacation?" I know he doesn't mean on vacation, but a girl can hope. A year after we met, Eric dropped everything, including me and his music career, and went to Thailand, Indonesia, Vietnam, and a couple of Asian countries I'd never heard of. Everyone said I was crazy to wait for him, but when he came back, eleven months later, he asked me to live with him, which I stupidly thought was a natural step on the way to marriage. Three years later, I'm not so sure.

"We can stay as long as we want," he says. "It's kind of incredible, when you think of all the places I've been, that I've never even seen Slovakia or Hungary, or, God, *Bosnia*. Bosnia would be awesome. And if you came . . ." He stops stroking my hair and gazes into the distance like he's watching a movie of our imaginary lives.

"I have a job," I remind him. "We have an apartment."

"You can get another job when you get back. And you hate this apartment."

"I like my job. And I don't hate this apartment." Yes I do, but that's beside the point.

"We'd get jobs over there. I'll teach English like I did in Jakarta. And you can wait tables at a café or something."

"I am not going to wait tables!" Oh, crap—I'm crying again. "And I am not moving to Europe. For God's sake, Eric, I'm twenty-nine years old! I want children and a house. I want a driveway and a garage and a garbage disposal that works."

He sits there for a long time, and then he stands up and goes, "You want some tea?"

I shake my head and stay there on the couch, snuffling and gagging on my snot while he goes to boil water.

When he comes back, he sticks his tea on the table and exhales. Then he says it. "I don't want children. I don't want that kind of responsibility."

I swallow. My throat hurts. "You say that, but—"

"I say it because I mean it."

It isn't the first time he's said it. But before he's always been, like, "I can't imagine a child in my life right *now*." This time he sounds so certain. So final.

"Not ever?" I ask.

He shakes his head. "I'm so sorry."

At work the next morning, I'm hanging up my coat when Melva comes in wearing her pink Hello Kitty scrubs. When she sees me, she runs through the waiting room and around the corner to the reception desk, grabs my left hand, looks at my naked ring finger, and—

"*Shit.*" She keeps holding on with her soft chubby hands. Her rings on her left hand are gold and swirly, the diamonds small and sparking against her light brown skin.

"Tell me about it." I try to laugh, but I can't.

"*Asshole.*" She lets go of me and rests her hand on her pregnant belly as if to protect her fetus from its mommy's mouth.

"He's not." Even now, I feel like I need to defend him.

"Did you give him an ultimatum like me and Pammy told you to?"

I shake my head. My nose tickles. My eyes fill with tears, and I probably would have burst out crying if Dr. Sanchez hadn't walked in.

"Good morning, Melva. Vanessa."

"Morning, Dr. Sanchez." I try to smile, but I just can't.

He pauses at the front desk and glances at my left hand. His mouth tightens, and then he goes to his office and shuts the door. I wonder what his reaction would have been if I'd come in sporting a diamond. Probably not too different.

I started working at Great Grins two years ago. Six months before that, Dr. Sanchez's wife, Rosie, died from ovarian cancer. That's why the job was open—because it used to be hers. The old patient files have her pretty, rounded handwriting all over them. She picked out all the paint colors, turquoise for the waiting room, peach for Dr. Sanchez's office, sunshine yellow for examination rooms. No one dares suggest we change them, even though the walls are looking scuffed and sunshine yellow seems to put people on edge.

Pammy, the other hygienist, was good friends with Rosie, but she doesn't talk about her much because it makes her too sad. "So full of life," she'll say, shaking her head.

Dr. Sanchez was different before Rosie got sick, Pammy says. Not a barrel of laughs, exactly, but just calm and quiet. Content. Now he looks haunted, with dark circles under deep-set brown eyes. His nose is straight and long, his cheekbones sharp. His bald head is shaved, flecks of gray mixing with the black in the stubble.

Maybe he's not haunted. Maybe he's just tired. He's got three kids at home. In any event, Pammy says he'll never get over Rosie, which makes me sad but also jealous. Which I know is wrong. But I can't help thinking that no man will ever love me like that.

Which brings me back to Eric, of course.

Melva puts her hands on her hips. "Shit or get off the pot. You tell him that from me." Even the Hello Kitties on her scrubs look pissed.

My nose stings and I think I'm going to cry. But then I remind myself that Dr. Sanchez never cries in the office. If he can suck it up, I can too. Of course, he never smiles either, but that's understandable. He might want to call this place something other than Great Grins, though.

I take a deep breath and get to work. When Pammy comes in and checks my hand, I say, "Let's talk about it at lunch," and pick up the phone.

I'm not the only one having a cruddy day. The phone rings and rings all morning. Seems everyone has a dental emergency. Toothaches. Broken crowns. Exposed nerves.

Tell me about it.

Dr. Sanchez does two root canals and a filling. Melva and Pammy scrape plaque and polish molars. They're both so friendly and chatty. They can't help making small talk with the patients.

"How's your son, Mrs. Ghazarian?" Pammy says in the examining room closest to me. "He's in, what, fifth grade now?"

"Uh-huh."

"Still playing soccer?"

"Aah-ih-all."

"He is?"

"Uh-uh. Aah-ih-all."

"Baseball?"

The mouth vacuum whirs for a while. Mrs. Ghazarian speaks. "Basketball."

"Oh. Right."

Pammy goes back to picking at Mrs. Ghazarian's teeth. "Why did he quit soccer?"

Since it's nobody's birthday and not the last Thursday of the month (also known as Pizza Day), Pammy, Melva, and I have lunch without Dr. Sanchez, who usually runs some errands and then eats a sandwich at his desk, which is covered with pictures of his kids and his dead wife. Since we're paying for ourselves (and Pammy needs toilet paper), we eat at Target, where it doesn't matter that we look dumpy in our scrubs. Well, Melva and I look dumpy, anyway. And according to more than one patient, we look like sisters. I don't see it. Melva is Filipina. I'm half white, half Mexican. But we both have curly black hair and plenty of curves, so I guess that's kind of sister-ish. Red-haired Pammy is superskinny. No boobs. No butt. Her scrubs are so short that her white gym socks show above her pink Crocs.

"You want to talk about it?" Pammy asks me.

"Of course she wants to talk about it," Melva says. "Right?"

"I dunno." I take the bun and a couple of iceberg lettuce leaves off my grilled chicken sandwich, rip open a package of mayonnaise, pile on the fat.

"You should talk about it," Pammy says. She wears a simple gold band on her left hand.

I put the lettuce and bun back on the sandwich.

"There's not much to tell. Eric said he loves me." (Had he said that? I couldn't remember, but he must have.) "And he doesn't want to break up. But he doesn't want children. So I guess—that's it." My voice cracks. I put down the sandwich. I can't eat.

"Oh, for God's sake," Melva says. "That's what all guys say. They're all about freedom and getting drunk with the boys and shit. But then the minute they become dads, it's like, ohmigod, this is the best thing that's ever happened to me."

She pauses for a moment. "I never told you guys this before, but me and Brent got married because I was pregnant."

She's already told us this, like, three times before, but Pammy and I look all shocked because that's the reaction Melva wants. Last time we just nodded and she was all, "You act like it's no big deal!"

"That must have been really hard for you, Mel," Pammy says.

I squeeze her hand.

"It was hard," Melva says. "But look at me and Brent now! Having our third kid." She pats her tummy. "And we have a house and everything."

Pammy puts down her plastic soup spoon and leans toward me. "What if you had, you know. An accident." Pammy has been married for over twenty years to a high school science teacher named Dave, but they don't have any kids.

"I can't do that. It's not honest." It's not like I've never considered "forgetting" to take my birth control pills. But it would be asking for trouble. And it would be wrong.

"Screw honesty," Melva says, her mouth full of grilled cheese.

There's something that's been bugging me since last night—actually, it's bugged me for as long as Eric and I have been together.

"You know what really makes me crazy? Eric had this girlfriend before me. Paige."

I try to say her name without sneering, but I can't. Paige was a vegetarian, like Eric. Paige did yoga. Paige was getting her master's in child psychology. When Paige stopped by Eric's apartment one day, a couple of months after we'd started going out, I answered the door and she said, "Oh. Are you Eric's new housekeeper?"

"They went out for like two years, maybe longer," I say. "And Paige had a kid, a daughter, four years old. And Eric was *fine* with it. When I asked if that's why they broke up, he was like, no, I liked Ophelia. He even told her he would've broken up with Paige sooner because she cheated on him, but he gave her a second chance because he felt so sad about losing Ophelia."

Pammy stops drinking her Diet Coke. "She named her kid Ophelia?"

"Holy shit," Melva says between chews.

"So he'd be fine with a kid if it wasn't his?" Pammy says.

I nod and take a bite of my sandwich. It's not great, but not terrible. Kind of like my life, these days.

"That's fucked," Melva says.

I say, "At one point last night, I was actually thinking, What if Eric and I broke up and I went out with some other guy? And I got pregnant? And then I went back to Eric and was like, 'This baby is all my responsibility, but I want to be with you.'"

"I don't think that's a good idea," Pammy says.

Melva agrees. "The other guy could be a psycho. Or Eric might not take you back."

"At least I'd still have a baby. I'm getting older. I can't wait forever."

Something crosses Pammy's face. "That's true."

"Maybe if the guy was really hot . . ." Melva says.

"You could use a sperm bank," Pammy says. "Pick whatever kind of guy you want, no strings attached."

Melva and I stare at her, and then Melva starts laughing. "Oh my God. You should! Why settle for Eric when you can pick some hot guy out of a catalog?"

"What's wrong with Eric?"

"Nothing," Pammy says.

"He's kind of short," Melva says. "And pale. And his nose . . ."

"What's wrong with his nose?"

"It's kind of big, don't you think?"

"I like Eric's nose."

"Maybe a sperm bank isn't a good idea," Pammy says.

"It's a great idea," Melva counters. "Plus, some of those places? I've heard they've got guys who look like celebrities. So it's kinda like you're having George Clooney's baby or whatever. Though personally, I've never been into Clooney. I think I'd pick someone different. Like the Rock, maybe."

Pammy wrinkles her nose. "Not so great if you have a girl. Clooney's safer. Or Johnny Depp."

I say, "Eric's really smart. He went to college." I turn to Pammy. "Do you think his nose is big?"

"I've never even noticed Eric's nose," Pammy says. "I just think you don't want to wait too long deciding whether or not to get pregnant."

Melva and I wait for her to continue, to talk about herself and why she never had children. But she goes back to sipping soup with a plastic spoon, and we let it drop.

"The guy from *Twilight*," I say. "Not the vampire. The other guy."

"Huh?"

"That's who I'd pick."

# Wendy

Back when I was trying to get pregnant, so many people said so many unintentionally offensive things that it's hard to pick the line that stung the most.

There was the religious camp. "This is all part of God's master plan."

There were the fatalists. "If you're meant to get pregnant, you'll get pregnant."

And then there were those who believed that a little red wine and a back massage could solve anything. "Maybe you just need to relax."

But I'll never forget the mantra repeated most often, courtesy of my next-door neighbor and then-closest-friend, Sherry Plant. "Motherhood is not a Baby Gap ad."

What did she know? Pregnancy had come easy to Sherry. She dropped eggs on a monthly basis, while her Cro-Magnon husband, Lane, spewed speedy and abundant sperm. Maybe she was trying to make me feel better, telling me, in her obnoxious way, that having kids was hard, that my life might be nicer without them. But it didn't feel that way. It felt like she was holding her fertility over me.

From the beginning, ours was a friendship of convenience. Darren and I were pushing thirty when we traded in Chicago's subzero weather and two dead-end jobs (his with a small engineering firm, mine in Northwestern's academic records department) for a new life in Arizona. A large aerospace firm offered him a 50 percent pay raise, potential for advancement, and a cubicle with a view. We could finally afford to buy a home (with a pool, no less!) and get serious about starting a family. Getting away from my pain-in-the-ass mother-in-law, who still displayed pictures of Darren and his high school girlfriend at their senior prom, was just a bonus.

Sherry and I hit it off right away, though in retrospect I was so lost and lonely that I would have liked anyone. She told me where to get my oil changed, where to find used furniture, where to get my hair cut (a poor recommendation: I looked like a poodle). She sent me to her dentist, her ophthalmologist, and her obstetrician—who would later pass me on to a fertility specialist, but I didn't know that then.

About once a month, Darren and I would have dinner with Sherry, Lane, and their daughters. Nothing fancy: chili or barbecue or pasta. Lane would drink too much, Sherry would yell at her kids, and Darren would shoot me looks that said, *Can we go now?* He even gave me those looks when we were in our own house, which made no sense at all. At first I accused Darren of being antisocial (which he is). Later, after I'd tearfully confessed to Sherry that fertility problems were straining our marriage, only to have her tell me that motherhood wasn't a Baby Gap ad, I began making excuses for why we couldn't get together.

Baby Gap. Please. Weird thing was, I never even saw Sherry's daughters, Ashlyn and Brianne, in anything that even remotely resembled Gap clothes. Ashlyn, the younger one, liked sparkly things: rhinestone-studded jeans, sequined tops, glitter sneakers. If she didn't get her shiny clothes, she'd whine. Come to think of it, she'd whine even if she did get them.

My children would never be like that.

At last, after a long wait and some serious medical intervention, it happened: the miracle of life. My nausea was mild, my weight gain extreme. I didn't mind. By the time I was six months pregnant, the babies were so restless you could see my belly moving through my maternity clothes.

"Look!" I told Darren. "Our babies are dancing!" I put extra emphasis on the *our*.

He forced a smile that bordered on polite.

I grabbed Darren's hand and placed it on my churning belly. Immediately, one of the twins kicked him, straight on the palm. Darren yanked his hand away as if he'd been burned.

"Maybe he'll be a soccer player," I said, wishing Darren would put his hand back on my belly, even as I knew he wouldn't.

"Maybe."

Sherry Plant kept her distance during the pregnancy. When Harrison and Sydney were born (five weeks early but healthy), Sherry gave them two little outfits . . . from the Children's Place. She didn't mention Baby Gap once after I'd finally conceived. I wrote her a hurried thank-you note, which I slipped in her mailbox. By then, our friendship had completely run its course.

Forget about Sherry. Forget about Baby Gap. Almost immediately, it became clear that the twins hadn't been dancing in utero. They'd been fighting like two pit bulls confined to a very small pen. As infants, they couldn't bear to be cuddled—yet they'd scream if I put them down. Laid on their backs, they'd kick and claw at the air, their delicate features twisted with red fury. They treated baths as near drownings, diaper changes as attempted disembowelments.

I consoled myself with the pediatrician's colic diagnosis. It wasn't anything I had or hadn't done. It was just a stage. It would pass.

When the twins turned one, they began to hit—first just me and each other, though later they'd whale on pretty much anyone. The tantrums kicked in at one and a half, the biting at two. By the time she was three, Sydney could scream so long and so loud that she'd make herself vomit. Harrison would merely black out—terrifying, yes, but not nearly so repulsive.

It hasn't gotten any better. I'm starting to lose hope that it ever will. Within a month of starting kindergarten, the twins' teacher called in a school psychologist to assess their behavior. She said she "didn't want to put a label" on them—especially since the obvious label, attention deficit hyperactivity disorder, had been more or less ruled out the year before. The psychologist said that although Sydney and Harrison clearly displayed "antisocial tendencies" (which sounded like a label to me), we should take comfort in the fact that they had never killed or tortured any animals. Which is kind of like saying that my family should take comfort in the fact that I had never set fire to our house, but whatever. Bottom line, she said there were probably genetic factors at work, but "maybe they'll grow out of it."

Until then, I deal with their behavior in the only way I know how: by throwing my own tantrums, screaming, crying, locking myself in my room—and, yes, spending one evening a week wielding wine and glue sticks. But in spite of everything, I love my children with a fierceness I never knew I possessed. My heart lifts every time they draw me a picture and breaks each time they are excluded from a classmate's birthday party.

I don't know what Darren feels for the kids. Or for me. He tiptoes around the three of us like a castaway stranded among savages. Harrison and Sydney look nothing like him. They have my coloring—dark brown hair and eyes—but their faces are all their own, their eyes deep-set, their chins dimpled.

Now that they are halfway through kindergarten, the school psychologist doesn't know what to do with them. Their teacher has suggested private school. When I come to the classroom at the end of each day, the other parents refuse to meet my eyes.

Congratulations, Sherry Plant. You were right. My life most definitely does not resemble a Baby Gap ad.

---

I don't talk about any of this at scrapbooking. I concentrate on my scallop-edge scissors, my aqua paper accents, my Chardonnay. There are only five of us tonight. None of us know the others very well.

Scottsdale Skipper—her name is actually Tara—is making a poo book. Her son Liam is almost four and still crapping in his pants. Tara hopes the perfect scrapbook will change that. She's got pictures of Liam sitting on the potty and pictures of Liam brandishing his penis in front of the big-boy toilet. She's got him modeling his Superman underpants. But all of that is a lead-up to the money shot: an eight-by-ten glossy of a perfect log poo floating in the bowl. It doesn't even gross me out until Tara reveals, with a giggle, that the poo actually came from her husband.

We trade toileting stories for a while. (The twins trained themselves at two and two-and-a-half. For once, I can brag.) And then conversation turns to daytime talk shows.

"That surrogate couple was on yesterday," Annalisa says. "You know, there's that woman who got hired to carry twins? And after they were born, she handed them over to the adoptive parents? But now she and her husband want them back?"

"That is so selfish," Tara says, affixing a brown border.

"I don't know," Annalisa says. "The woman who hired the surrogate, you know, the one who was going to adopt, it turns out she's mentally ill. And she got arrested for drugs once. And the surrogate didn't even know that."

"That's terrible," Tara says.

"But whose egg is it?" the other woman asks. Tonight is the first time I've met her, and I've already forgotten her name. I think it's Mary-something. Mary Ellen, Mary Beth, Maryann—one of those.

"They used an egg donor," Annalisa says. "So neither one is really the mother."

"But didn't they use the father's sperm?" Mary-something asks.

"Uh-uh. That was from a donor, too. So there's four parents fighting over the kid, but none of them is even actually related."

"That's wrong," Tara says. "I'm sorry, but it is."

I'm tempted to ask Tara what she thinks is wrong. The fighting? The desire to have a baby at any cost? Or donorship in general? But I don't dare say anything. There was a while when Darren and I thought we'd need both donor sperm and donor eggs to have a baby. Maybe it would have been better that way: more equal.

"Did you see that thing on *Good Morning America*?" Annalisa asks. "About the kids who had the same sperm donor?"

I keep my eyes on the bath shot I'm trimming.

"Their moms found each other on some Web site, and they all met for the first time on New Year's Eve. In Texas, I think. The kids all looked alike. It was weird. And their parents said they even acted kind of alike, and that they all just bonded immediately, like, ten times faster than if they were strangers. And what was kind of neat was that a few of the kids have some kind of mild learning disability, and their moms said it's been really helpful for them to talk to each other about it."

"Was it just moms, or were there any dads?" Mary-something asks.

"Just moms. Two were single, and there was a lesbian couple."

"If people want to live a gay lifestyle, that's fine for them," Tara says. "But I think it's wrong to involve children."

"You know, I used to feel that way too," Annalisa says. "But then I saw this thing on the *Today* show, and—"

"Did they say what the Web site was called?" I interrupt.

# Laura

At the kitchen table Monday morning, a cup of strong coffee helps me multitask through my fatigue. I check my e-mail while nibbling on a homemade breakfast burrito. We eat well when Carmen's here.

Thanks to twice the recommended dose of Benadryl, I fell asleep shortly after midnight, but I awoke just after four, my head swirling with dream images of a man in a Speedo riding a horse while eating a Taco Bell beef chalupa. The Speedo was red. The chalupa was doused with fire sauce.

I blame it on the antihistamine.

Carmen hums a Spanish tune while unloading the dishwasher, which is jammed with the entire weekend's dishes. Like many working mothers, I once worried that my son would love his nanny more than me. But it turns out that there is plenty of love to go around. Carmen is part of the family. I can't imagine life without her, and neither can Ian.

Carmen has a family back in El Salvador: a grown son and daughter, both with young children of their own. More than twenty years ago, Carmen left her children in her mother's care and fled to the United States. Ten years passed before she obtained a green card and was able to visit them. She did what she had to do to provide for her family; she says she has never regretted leaving. Whenever I am feeling worn down by the pressures of work and single parenthood, I think of Carmen and just how easy I really have it.

I have sixteen new e-mails since I checked last night. Some of my colleagues were working very late; others started very early. I make it a policy not to use the computer when Ian is at the table because I don't want to set a bad example. But Ian is still upstairs in the bathroom; I woke him up fifteen minutes ago and checked the clothes he'd picked out for school. Ian has a tendency to dress without any regard for the season: shorts in January, sweatshirts in July.

I log on to the Donor Sibling Network, expecting a quick perusal of the site—followed by the familiar pang of disappointment. But finally, to my astonishment, someone has responded to my posting.

### RE:  Southern California Cryobank, Donor 613

I believe we had the same donor. I conceived twins, a boy and a girl. They are now five years old and healthy. We live in Scottsdale, Arizona. I would love to hear about your son and any behavioral issues you have had to deal with.


Best regards,
Wendy Winder


I can't believe it. All this time, Ian has had a biological half brother and a half sister only a few hundred miles away. I feel happy and excited and scared and anxious all at once.

I want to reply right away, but Ian's footsteps sound on the hallway. When he enters the kitchen, he goes right to Carmen.

Carmen squeezes him tight. *"Hola mi amorcito, como amenasaste?"*

Two children share Ian's blood.

*"Bien, nannita."* Yes, he has slept well.

Carmen and Ian say a few more things to each other in Spanish. I can't understand more than a few phrases in the language but am thrilled my son is fluent—though of course that's not what I'm thinking about right now.

Ian has a biological half brother and a half sister.

Ian slips into the chair next to mine and shoots me a sly grin. "No computer at the table, Mom."

"Sure thing, boss."

Two hundred miles away, two children are probably eating breakfast. Do they look like Ian? Do they sound like him?

I turn off the computer and slip it into my briefcase. I will open it back up and respond to the e-mail as soon as I get to the office.

Twins. She had twins. How could anyone get that lucky?

---

At the office, I stop by my secretary's desk, where I find her sucking some enormous coffee beverage through a straw. With her free hand, she pokes at her cell phone.

When she sees me, she chucks her phone into her bag, grabs her computer mouse, and clicks a couple of times.

"Hold my calls, please, Marissa."

She plunks the cup onto a pile of papers that shouldn't have condensation rings on them. "No problem. I've got raging PMS, so nobody better mess with me."

I blink at her.

"Team I?" she says. When I don't respond—how would one respond to that?—she says, "You know. Too much information?"

My brain clicks a few times, and then I get it. "TMI. Right. I mean, no—not too much information. Just—hold my calls."

I, along with the partner in the corner office next door, hired Marissa eight months ago, when our previous secretary, Carlene, went back to school to study phlebotomy. I wasn't any closer to Carlene than I am to Marissa, but at least she was quiet.

Marissa says, "You already got one call this morning. Dorothy Hepplewhite died. I set up a meeting with her son for a couple weeks from now so you can go over the trust."

That stops me short. Dorothy was one of my first clients, and one of my favorites. Widowed as a young mother, she had gone back to work full-time as an office manager while raising her children to be responsible and successful adults. When she first came to see me, over ten years ago, she was in her midfifties and had just received a diagnosis of early-stage kidney disease. While her death, following years of dialysis and an unsuccessful transplant, was far from unexpected, the news stings.

"Thank you," I tell Marissa, pulling myself together. "Find out if there's anyplace I can send a donation, will you?"

I shut myself into my small office. The furniture is standard issue: a shiny wood desk, two visitor chairs, file cabinet, and bookcase. Beyond vertical blinds, my one window looks out on the parking lot. The partners and some of the more senior associates have better furniture, more windows, mountain views. But they don't have Ian.

My computer takes far too long to boot up. Finally, I reread Wendy Winder's e-mail and begin to type.

**RE: RE: Southern California Cryobank, Donor 613**

Dear Ms. Winder,

I am so excited to hear that my son Ian (age 8, picture attached) has two

I stop typing. What am I supposed to call her kids? Biological half siblings? I don't want to frighten her away. And maybe I shouldn't be quite so enthusiastic. I try again.

**RE: RE: Southern California Cryobank, Donor 613**

Dear Ms. Winder,

Thank you for contacting me regarding my posting on Donor Sibling Network. All evidence indicates that our children share common genetic paternity

Ugh. Dreadful. I sound like a lawyer. Of course, I am a lawyer, but that's no excuse.

**RE: RE: Southern California Cryobank, Donor 613**

Dear Ms. Winder,

Thank you so much for contacting me. I cannot wait to hear more about your twins. My son, Ian, is eight years old and the light of my life. I am attaching a picture and would love to see what your children look like, as well.

Warmly,
Laura Cahill

Good enough. I add my work and mobile numbers and hit send.

# Wendy

*The light of her life?* Is she kidding? Is she deranged? Is she medicated? (And if so, where can I get some?)

Rationalization. That has to be it. Laura Cahill must be one of those "God doesn't give me more than I can handle" types. So she treats her child's off-the-wall behavior as a challenge rather than the nightmare it really is. Of course, one kid is a lot easier to manage than two.

Unless . . . oh God. What if "light of my life" is a euphemism for a kid with a disability? Maybe her Ian has autism or spina bifida or some other handicap that brings out either the best or the worst in people. He looks normal enough in his picture, but that doesn't mean anything.

That has to be it. There is no other reasonable explanation. Poor Laura Cahill. She is a stronger woman than I.

"Laura Cahill's office." The voice is professional but young. It catches me off guard. For some reason, I had assumed Laura Cahill was a stay-at-home mother like me.

"I was . . . I'm calling for Laura Cahill. What kind of office is this, exactly?"

"A law office. Sullivan, Zurheide and Poole."

"Oh. I didn't realize she . . ." I don't dare finish the sentence: *has a big job and makes pots of money.* Maybe her son isn't handicapped, after all. Maybe she just works so many hours that she hardly ever sees him.

"Can I speak to her?" I ask.

"May I ask what this is in regards to?"

Oh God. What am I supposed to say? *The same stranger fathered our babies?*

"Just tell her my name is Wendy Winder. She'll know what it's about."

I am in the bedroom. The kids are at school and Darren is at work, but I close the door anyway.

I'm starting to think Laura Cahill's kid isn't disabled. More likely, she just keeps him around so she can have a nice picture on her desk. She's probably like those celebrities who have day nannies and night nannies and weekend nannies and never, ever see their children.

God, that sounds good.

She comes on the line.

"Ms. Winder, this is Laura Cahill. Thank you so much for calling."

I sit on the edge of the bed. "No problem. I, um . . . Thanks for sending your son's picture. He's really cute."

"He *is* cute, isn't he?" She laughs. "I'm dying to see what your children look like. Do they look like Ian?"

"Around the eyes—maybe a little." I pop up from the bed and cross to the window. "Mostly, they look like me. Dark curly hair and brown eyes. Of course, they're a lot thinner than I am!"

I expect her to laugh. She doesn't. "Oh, I'm sure you look great," she says, which for some reason makes me feel even fatter, as if she could see me through the phone wearing my size-sixteen jeans (which are getting tight).

"What are your twins like?" she asks me. "Are they musical?"

"I don't know. We haven't given them lessons or anything. They're only five."

"You shouldn't let that stop you. Honestly, I wish I'd gotten Ian started sooner. He just started piano, and his teacher said he's got an incredible natural ability. She says if he just practiced more often he could be amazing."

"Uh-huh." In the yard below, our tiny pool—four feet deep, twenty feet long—reflects the bright spring sky. By July, the water will reach one hundred swampy degrees.

She pauses for an instant. "You said 'we.' So you have a . . . partner?" The way she says it, you'd think it was entirely optional for the mother of five-year-old twins to have a husband.

"Yes, I'm married," I say just as I realize that she was trying to figure out whether my partner was a man or a woman. Now, *that's* funny. I live in Scottsdale, Arizona, one of the most conservative cities in America. Of course my partner is a man. The only question is whether he is closer to forty or sixty.

Before things get awkward on the partner front, she goes back to talking about music. "Ian always loved music, even as a tiny baby."

"Mm," I say. When the twins were toddlers, I played classical music CDs in a desperate attempt to calm them down. The music seemed to agitate them even more. They especially hated Beethoven.

"I played flute all the way through high school," she continues.

"So maybe he's getting some of it from me. But I was never that great. So I keep thinking some of it must be coming from our donor."

*Our donor.* Wow. She just throws it out there, as if she were saying *our hairdresser* or *our dentist.*

I walk away from the window, back to the door. I lock it. Again: absurd. Nobody's even home. But it makes me feel better.

"About our—that," I say. "What I was kind of wondering—wondering a lot, actually—is about personality traits that may have been passed along. That's actually why I contacted you. Does your son have any behavior issues?"

"Like . . . what?"

"Hitting?"

"No."

"Kicking?"

"No"

"Okay . . . How about biting?"

"*Biting?* No. Definitely no."

She didn't need to say it like that.

"What about other forms of acting out? Uncontrolled crying, say? Or extended screaming?"

"Uh-uh."

"Verbal assaults? Tantrums?"

She is quiet for a long time. And then she throws me the boniest of bones.

"There was one time when Ian was three, three-and-a-half years old. We were at Target, and he wanted me to buy him some candy, and I said no. He threw such a fit that we had to leave the store. I was so afraid that he might be entering some horrible new phase, but he came down with a terrible cold that night, so I think he just wasn't feeling well."

"Oh." It's all I can manage.

"Are your kids more . . . high-spirited?"

*High-spirited?* I force a laugh. "You could say that."

"I actually worry about Ian sometimes," she says. "He's active and energetic, but there's just no aggression there. So I'm concerned that someday another kid, some bully, might pick on him and he won't be able to defend himself."

"Is there anything . . ." I can't say *wrong with him.* "Does Ian have any special challenges?"

It takes her a moment to realize what I'm suggesting.

"You mean, like a disability?"

"Yes."

"No."

"Oh." That sounded wrong, like I'm disappointed. I'm not. I wouldn't wish that on anyone.

She says, "Do your children have any . . . challenges?"

"Oh, no—they're fine. Just very physical. And emotional. And I guess you could say aggressive. I'd say aggressive. Yes, very."

"Kids go through stages," she says. "I'm sure it will pass."

"Yes, of course." Like maybe after they kill each other.

"Ian's had his stages too. And he's far from perfect, but I've always felt he's perfect for me. My only regret is that I only have him. That's actually the reason—part of it, anyway—why I wanted to get in touch."

"Sure," I say, as if I have the vaguest idea of what she's getting at.

She says, "I know it's a long shot. But do you have any more of 613's sperm?"

"Excuse me?"

"I've read that some people store their donor's sperm after their children are born. In proper cold storage, it can keep for years. So I was wondering—hoping—that maybe you still had some of Donor 613's. That maybe I could buy it from you."

"You want his sperm?"

"I want a child."

"You can have one of mine!" I blurt. And then: "Kidding. Ha ha. No, I don't. No sperm."

"Oh." She sighs.

"Sorry." And I am, even though I am probably saving her from a genetic personality disaster that could destroy her perfect life with her perfect son.

"If you ever hear of anyone else who used this donor, will you let me know?"

"Sure." I pause. "Though if this guy has fathered a lot of kids, they'll start filling prisons in about ten years. That ought to make them easier to track down."

She doesn't laugh. After a bit more awkward conversation, we say good-bye, and I promise to e-mail a photo of the twins. When we get off the phone, I pull up my favorite recent picture: Harrison and Sydney at Sea World last summer, gazing into a tank full of sharks, their brown eyes wide, their pink mouths curved into little, wondrous smiles.

I stare at the picture on the screen for maybe a full minute. They were so good that day: holding Darren's hands and mine, waiting in line without squirming, passing the gift shops without complaint.

Before they fell asleep in our hotel that night, Sydney said, "I'm glad you took us to see the dolphins."

And Harrison said, "Today was awesome."

Why can't they always be that way?

I burst into tears. I love my children so much it makes my chest hurt.

# 9

## Laura

That didn't go quite the way I anticipated. No, let me rephrase: that didn't go at all the way I anticipated. Here I was, expecting to feel this instant connection or at least a sense of kinship with Wendy Winder: to compare notes on our children's food preferences and developmental milestones and maybe to discover similarities in sleep habits and artistic inclinations. Of course I'd known chances were slim that she'd have kept a vial in cold storage. But it never occurred to me that she'd recoil at the idea of wanting more children, as if motherhood were a punishment and not a privilege.

I pick up the phone to tell Marissa she can stop holding my calls—and then I put it down again. Locating a leftover vial is the most obvious way to get more of 613's sperm. But it's not the only way.

Nine years ago, the Southern California Cryobank assured Donor 613 that they would keep his identity confidential. And they have. I respected his right to privacy then; I still do. However, what I respect and what I want have turned out to be two very different things. When I purchased the sperm, neither the Southern California Cryobank nor Donor 613 nor I anticipated the rapid evolution and availability of genetic tests. We certainly never imagined that it could be possible to track down a sperm donor using the information gathered from a simple cotton swab.

I pull up the Donor Sibling Network's Web site and click through until I find what I'm looking for. A few computer pecks later, and I'm staring at the home page of Helix Laboratories, a company that analyzes genetic data. On the home page, a bright yellow button says, "Order your Y-line test kit today!"

I've learned all kinds of things from the Donor Sibling Network Web site and its links. The secret to genetic identity lies in the chromosomes. Each of us carries twenty-three pairs; one of each pair comes from the mother, the other from the father. The twenty-third is the sexual marker, better known as the X and Y chromosomes. Everyone gets an X chromosome from the mother, but it is the father's contribution that determines gender. An X chromosome means a female, a Y chromosome a male.

Both X and Y chromosomes have genetic markers, sequences of DNA that vary from individual to individual. Every time an X chromosome gets passed along, its genetic markers get shuffled. The Y chromosome is different. Like surnames, it passes virtually unchanged from father to son.

In 2005, an American teenager made international news when he tracked down his donor using a cheek swab DNA test, a genealogical database, and a Web site that specialized in people searches. If he could do it, why can't I?

If I pay Helix Laboratories to perform a Y-line test on Ian's DNA, it will give me a string of numbers that are completely useless—unless they match another male in Helix's large database. Best-case scenario, Donor 613 would come from a large, heavily male family with an interest in genealogy. A partial match—say, 50 percent—between Ian and a man in the database would mean that the two shared an ancestor many generations ago: interesting from a genealogy stand-point, but not much help in tracking down the donor. However, if I could find a perfect Y-line match, odds are I'd have tracked down a very close relative: Ian's biological uncle, grandfather . . . or even father.

It is a long shot—and perhaps a gray area, ethically. But it's been many years since things seemed black and white in my world. I don't know if I will go through with testing Ian—but it wouldn't hurt to have a kit on hand. Just in case.

I click on the bright yellow order button. A few more clicks, and I've paid three hundred and fifty dollars for a kit, scheduled to ship in five to ten days. The sale complete, I slip my credit card back into my wallet and log off the site.

I pick up the phone. "I can take calls now, Marissa."

# Vanessa

Dr. Sanchez takes Fridays off, so it's just me in my pale pink scrubs, sitting at the front desk while Melva and Pammy clean teeth and force patients to talk with their mouths full of tools and fingers. Usually I use this time to do some filing, submit insurance claims, or stamp appointment reminder cards. Sometimes when I run out of stuff to do, I'll check eBay. Okay, true confession time, I go on eBay a lot. A couple weeks ago I got these sandals—purple with rhinestones and three-inch heels—for eight bucks. Including shipping! It wasn't until the package arrived that it hit me. I have no place to wear three-inch heels, with or without rhinestones.

That's okay. I'm really pretty happy just having a quiet life these days, hanging out in the apartment with Eric, not talking about the future. Not talking about anything. Yeah, it's awesome.

So, eBay. The baby section is amazing. I like to look at the fluffy little hats and tiny shoes and holiday outfits. Last month there was a plum taffeta dress, size eighteen months, with velvet trim and matching headband. Cutest thing ever.

I'm just looking, of course. Before I can buy baby stuff, I need something. What is it? Oh, yeah! *A baby*. Which means I need that other thing first. Let me think, let me think . . . Oh, right. A *man*.

I thought Pammy was crazy when she suggested a sperm donor. I mean, come on. My job's okay and I still can't believe that I get health insurance (plus dental, natch), but there's not much left over at the end of the month. Look at what my mom went through, raising me and my sister poor and alone after my dad died. No, look at what I went through, growing up without a father.

If only I'd gotten a college education like I planned—and like my high school math teachers told me I was smart enough to do. Then I could afford to give my kid a good life, even on my own. But just two semesters of community college put me into enough debt to scare me. Plus it was so hard, working full-time for just-above-minimum wage while taking classes whenever I could fit them in. I always thought I'd go back, but it hasn't happened.

Eric says a college education is overrated, but it's easy for him to say that because he has one. I wanted to study accounting. I would have had a really good job by now. One where I didn't have to wear scrubs to answer the phone.

So after I came up with all the reasons why I shouldn't have a kid on my own, I started to think about how maybe I should. I mean, if I have to choose between being a struggling single mom or not having kids at all, what do I pick?

I don't have to make that decision yet. Maybe Eric will come through. Or maybe me having a baby would change his mind, even if it's not his. I know Eric would be an amazing dad. That's what really kills me.

As for sperm donors, it doesn't hurt to look.

There's nothing on eBay, at least right now. But Google turns up a whole bunch of sperm bank sites, each with a long list of donors. Think about it. All these men, there for the picking! Well, not the actual men, of course, but for a few hundred bucks, they'll give me what my boyfriend of five years won't.

None of the sites have photographs, which kind of blows. Not that I necessarily need to find someone who looks like that *Twilight* guy, but I don't want my baby daddy to be a troll. Still, there's a lot more information here than you'd see on an online dating site. (Yeah, I'm speaking from experience. I had a couple of dry years, manwise.) There are questions that the donor guy answered. Even better, there are interviews. Someone sits down with the guys, talks to them, writes down their impressions. That way, if the guy's all "I love people," and the interviewer's all "He wouldn't make eye contact," you know you might end up with shifty-eyed babies.

Again, I'm just looking. Just curious. But between filling out a next-appointment card for one of Melva's patients and telling some lady on the phone that Dr. Sanchez wouldn't be back until Monday (and that he'll be out next Friday and the Friday after that and I don't know why dentists take Fridays off, they just do), I fell just a little bit in love with Donor 4317.

**PERSONAL:**

**Born:** 06/1987
**Education:** BA, American history
**Current occupation:** Realtor trainee

**PHYSICAL:**

**Height:** 6 feet
**Weight:** 160 lbs.
**Hair:** Dark brown, wavy

**Eye color:** Brown
**Complexion:** Fair/rosy
**Body type:** Slim/athletic
**Ethnic origin:** English, German, Dutch, French, Mexican
**Religion:** Was raised as a Jehovah's Witness, considers himself
spiritual but has no specific religious affiliation
**Book group/Rh:** O positive
**Baby photo available:** No
**Other defining features:** Resembles Rivers Cuomo, the lead
singer of the band Weezer

After that there was a family medical history that was way too
boring to read. Then I got to the good parts.

**SELF-DESCRIPTION, Donor 4317**

**Describe your personality:** I love to laugh and have a good time.
Also, I like to make other people laugh, so I am always telling jokes
and stories. I try to be a good listener. I have a lot of energy. I do not
like to sit around but would rather be out doing something athletic or
building something or helping someone. I am driven and ambitious
and willing to work hard for what I want in life.

**Describe your interests and talents:** People say I am a people
person because I am good at putting people at ease. I guess that is
just because I genuinely like people and like to help them out. I enjoy
being outside and especially like the ocean. I have been a diver for
many years and am just learning to windsurf. I love the feeling of
freedom when I am out on the waves. I am also good with my hands.
I can fix and build things.

**Describe your feelings and skills in the following areas:**

**Math:** I always did well in math but didn't pursue it past high school because I enjoyed reading and writing more.

**Mechanical:** I am very good at fixing things. I also like to make wooden things like shelves or even tables. I have a niece who loves dolphins, so last year for her birthday I carved one for her. It wasn't the greatest thing ever, but she really loved it, and the smile on her face is something I will always treasure!

**Athletics:** I played a lot of sports when I was young (baseball, basketball, soccer, swimming). I was on the high school swim team, which I really enjoyed. I ranked statewide in the backstroke.

**Creative:** My most creative thing is that I like to make things. I have always been good at drawing and painting and am great at clay and sculpture. My father taught me how to make things out of wood, and I still enjoy woodworking. At times I have thought of making a business out of selling wooden jewelry boxes, but I do not feel I have the time or resources to commit to it at this time.

**Describe your goals and ambitions:** I am working toward my real estate license. I like real estate because I can help people find the perfect homes for their families. Eventually, I would like to own my own real estate brokerage, which would provide financial security for me and the family I hope to have someday. Another big goal is to fall in love with a woman, get married, and have children together. I can't wait to be a dad!

**Explain your reasons for becoming a sperm donor:** I grew up in a loving family, so I know how much it means to have that. Donating sperm is something I can do to help people build the kind of family that will spread a lot of happiness. Having a family has always been a big dream of mine, so I want to help others achieve that same dream.

**What would you like to say to the people who receive your sperm?**
I am honored to have the opportunity to help you and your family. All I ask is that your child grows up with a lot of love and support to become the best person possible.

"What you looking at?" I hadn't heard Melva coming up behind me.

"Just trying to pick the father of my unborn child." I laugh. "Not really, just I was bored, so I looked up this site."

"Lemme see." Melva scoots me out of the way. I use the interruption as an excuse to get a cup of coffee from our tiny break room, which is really just a walk-in closet with a coffeemaker and minifridge. The coffee tastes gross from sitting too long, but I add sugar and cream. That helps.

Melva is still on the computer, muttering, "Maybe . . . he's kind of . . . nah . . . too much asthma in the family." She clicks the mouse and brings up a new donor.

"I like this one." I reach over her for the mouse and click back to the wood-carving, family-loving, real estate guy.

**INTERVIEWER IMPRESSIONS, Donor 4317**

The first thing I noticed about Donor 4317 was his beautiful smile, which just lights up the room. He has dark hair and eyes, full lips, and strong cheekbones. His love for physical activity is evident in his lean, muscular build. His manner is very open and friendly but not overbearing. He was happy to answer my questions but made it clear that he was also a good listener. More than once he joked, "But enough about what I think. What do you think about me?"

Donor 4317 enjoys being active. He told me that one of the reasons he pursued real estate was because he couldn't stand the thought of being stuck behind a desk all day. He was a competitive swimmer in high school and still loves the water. He has enjoyed scuba diving in the past, and he has just taken up windsurfing. Clearly, this is a man who loves a challenge and enjoys life.

Donor 4317 is an only child. He lives a short drive away from his parents and visits them once a week. He is very close to them but says he's always wished for a big family and is glad that through donating sperm he can help others achieve that dream.

Melva is unimpressed. "Who's Rivers Cuomo?"

"Dunno. Says he's in Weezer."

We do a quick image search on Rivers Cuomo, and my love for Donor 4317 fades, just a tiny bit. He's okay looking, but no *Twilight* guy.

My cell phone rings. It's Eric. Weird . . . I feel this stab of guilt, like I really had been checking out guys on a dating site. Then I feel another stab of guilt as I think, *Eric has no career, no ambition, and no desire for a family. Plus Melva's right: he's kind of short. No one would ever pick him for a donor.*

I press the talk button on my phone. "Hey, baby." I'd still choose him over 4317, if only he'd let me.

Melva rolls her eyes.

It's been over a week since my birthday. I haven't said anything more about marriage or children, and neither has Eric (of course). All I can do is pretend it never happened.

"You free tonight?" He speaks loudly to be heard over the background noise. Eric usually calls me from the parking lot outside the Hawthorne Costco.

"Yeah." I would never plan something without checking with Eric first, so he's got to know I'm free. For some reason, whenever he wants to go somewhere, he calls and asks like it's a date. I used to think that was really cute, like he's not taking me for granted. I don't think it's so cute anymore.

"It's my dad's birthday, and my mom wants us all to come for dinner."

"Uh . . . sure. Is there going to be a cake?"

"Of course not. She just wants us around."

"Oh, right."

"Angie's put together that photo album or scrapbook or whatever she was talking about at Christmas." Angie is Eric's sister-in-law. "It's supposed to be a surprise, but my mom said she knows about it but we all need to pretend she doesn't."

The scrapbook. The thought of it makes my stomach clench. When Angie asked me for recent pictures of Eric, I gave her some cute pictures of us at Hermosa Beach last summer.

She said, "No offense, but I really just want pictures of the family in the book, so I'm going to have to cut you out.

*No offense.*

When I was a kid, my best friend was this girl named Julie Castillo. Julie lived down the street with her two sisters and four brothers in a cramped three-bedroom bungalow that looked just like mine from the outside except mine was beige and hers was yellow, plus mine had scruffy grass in the small strip between the concrete sidewalk and front steps, while hers had plastic flowers planted in the dirt. Which I know is tacky, but I really loved them.

On the inside, the Castillos' house was nothing like mine. The house was alive with the smells of Mrs. Castillo's cooking—onions and tomatoes and peppers—and the shouts and laughter of the seven Castillo kids and their army of friends. In my house, the television did all the talking, and the air smelled like garbage that should've been taken out yesterday.

Every time I went in the Castillos' house, at least after my father died, I wished I were part of their family. When Eric and I started going out and I heard he was one of four kids, I thought, this is it—the family I've been waiting for.

But now I realize it doesn't work that way. I need to have a family of my own.

"You working right now?" I ask Eric.

"I'm on break. Hey. Are we running low on bean burritos? We just got in a new shipment."

My jaw tightens. "Have you checked the freezer lately? We've got like twenty burritos left from the last bag you brought home."

"Yeah, I know. I was kidding. Anyway. See you at home."

Melva is still on the computer even though there's an old lady in the waiting room. She clutches a big black bag on her lap and looks annoyed.

"Hi, Mrs. Guerrero. Have you been helped?"

The old lady purses her lips and shakes her head. Melva keeps her eyes on the computer screen, her mouth curled in a sneer. Mrs. Guerrero's English is shaky, and Melva speaks Spanish, so she used to be Melva's patient. But Melva said something to piss her off, so now Mrs. Guerrero will only let Pammy clean her teeth.

"Pammy will be ready for you in a minute," I tell her, speaking slowly.

She nods and continues to look annoyed.

Melva surrenders my chair. "Eric calling to propose?"

"Yeah, right. It's his dad's birthday, so we're going up to Glendale for dinner."

"You get his dad a present?"

"Don't have to. He's dead."

# Laura

Based on the photo she e-mailed, I disagree with Wendy Winder's assessment that her children look nothing like Ian; there is a definite resemblance around the eyes and also in the little girl's expression. The picture shows them gazing into a tank at Sea World, one of Ian's and my favorite weekend destinations. He has gazed at the tank in just the same way, and while I know the odds are nearly nonexistent, I can't help but wonder whether we've ever passed by his biological half siblings—and whether there are any other children going about their daily lives of school and sports and vacations who share his DNA.

As much as Wendy Winder complained about her twins (who can't be as bad as she made them sound), I keep thinking, *At least they have each other.* Ian just has me. And someday I'll be gone.

---

When I see Doug Hepplewhite's name on my schedule Friday morning, I steel myself for an onslaught of uncomfortable emotions. Doug is Dorothy Hepplewhite's son and trustee. For someone who deals with the grief-stricken on a regular basis, I still struggle to strike the proper tone. Some people want to spend the entire session talking about their loved one, which, considering my hourly rate, can put a small dent in their inheritance. Other survivors get right to business. My fondness for Dorothy only compounds the situation, and I don't want my personal sadness to add to her son's burden.

Doug Hepplewhite arrives on time, a woman at his side. I assume it is his wife, but I am wrong.

"Linda Hepplewhite Smith," she says, shaking hands. "Doug's sister."

"I'm so sorry about your mother," I tell them, the words inadequate as always. "She was a lovely person."

They nod. Doug Hepplewhite looks older than he did three months ago, when he came in to help his mother finalize her affairs. Already thin, he appears to have lost weight.

I pull out the trust and we get down to business. Dorothy Hepplewhite had no debt and modest assets. She has split her money evenly between her children, with a separate trust for her grandchildren. There is little confusion, and no controversy: only resignation and sadness. As I provide guidance regarding dissolution of her accounts and the sale of her home and car, her children sit next to each other in straight-backed chairs, holding hands, while Doug makes occasional notes.

It's the hand-holding that does me in.

"I know this is a really difficult time, but let me say that your mother would have been proud of your absence of acrimony." I flip a page. And burst into tears.

Doug Hepplewhite says, "Were you and Mother . . . close?"

Linda Hepplewhite Smith says, "Are you okay?"

I reach for a tissue. "So sorry. My apologies. Personal matter."

The two bereaved children, still holding hands, remain strong in the face of my inexplicable breakdown.

I dab my eyes, take a deep breath, and get back to closing out Dorothy Hepplewhite's life.

I am saddened by her passing, it's true. Beyond that, I can't help thinking, once again, *Ian just has me. And someday I'll be gone.*

The irony of my preoccupation with Ian's genetic ties does not escape me. I do, after all, have a family of my own, and to say that we're not close does not even begin to cover it. My mother lives with her second husband in Seattle, my father with his second wife in Reno. Not to be outdone, my brother, Mike, seven years my senior and a tenured history professor at UC Davis, lives in Northern California with wife number three. He always was an overachiever.

Early in life, Mike decided that he didn't want children, which probably factored into the breakup of his first two marriages. Nevertheless, last summer, on his third time at the plate, he wed a woman with two girls, aged three and five. As I wasn't invited to the wedding, I've never met any of them. Mike explained, "I'd really like to have you and Ian there, but if I invite you, I've got to invite Mom and Dad." Having been seated between my silent, seething parents at the first two weddings, I considered my exclusion to be a reprieve.

My mother and stepfather visit once or twice a year, usually on their way to someplace more interesting. My mother has asked Ian, her only grandchild, to call her Nancy "because Grandma sounds so old." My father has met Ian twice. At my stepmother's invitation, we flew out to Reno shortly after Ian's birth and didn't see them again until Mike's second wedding. When we said good-bye, my father shook Ian's hand.

"Who was that again?" Ian whispered once my father walked away.

Ian shows considerably more enthusiasm for his uncle Mike—as do I. We usually see him once or twice a year, either because he's visiting a nearby university or because he's between women and doesn't want to spend Christmas alone. Not surprisingly for someone who racks up wives so easily, Mike is warm, handsome, and charming. He'll talk to Ian for hours on end about whales, stars, *Star Wars,* or whatever else Ian is consumed with at any given time. Once Ian goes to bed, we'll laugh and talk for hours, trading crazy-parent stories and dour childhood memories that only we two can appreciate.

Every time Mike says good-bye, we promise to see each other more often. But life gets in the way. Or, more often, a wife gets in the way. Still, it's a comfort to me, just knowing Mike is out there.

---

Friday afternoon, I leave the office at 5:01 and pull into my drive-way thirty-seven minutes later. The weekend stretches ahead, long, lazy—and wet. A storm is expected to roll in this evening, with rain forecast through Sunday. I don't mind one bit. Ian has a basketball game tomorrow afternoon, a piano lesson on Sunday. Otherwise, we have nothing to do but make popcorn, watch movies, and feed the chickens. Bliss.

The house smells like cheese and tomatoes and cumin. A casserole, something Mexican, bubbles in the oven. Sometimes Carmen makes dishes we can eat through the weekend. I'm never sure whether she disapproves of my dependence on takeout or whether she can't bear the thought of us going two whole days without tasting her food. Probably a little of both.

A padded envelope sits on the kitchen island, surrounded by the rest of the day's mail. I drop my handbag on the counter, pick up the envelope, check the return address: Helix Laboratories. My pulse quickens.

I leave the envelope on the island and head down the hall. Carmen is in my bedroom, putting away laundry.

"Something smells delicious."

"Chicken enchilada casserole. Ian say he want it. But now he say he no home for dinner."

"What?"

Carmen closes a dresser drawer. The room smells like lemon polish. "Alex's mom, she call you?"

"No."

"She call, say tonight is birthday party for Alex. Sleepover."

"Tonight?"

Ian appears in the doorway, a duffel bag slung over one shoulder, a sleeping back over the other. "Mom, we gotta go. The party started already. And we need to get a present for Alex."

"But . . . what . . ."

"At school today, Alex asked if I was coming to his birthday party. He said he gave me an invitation, but he didn't."

"Isn't Alex the one who makes fart noises during class? I thought you didn't like him."

"That's Axel, not Alex. Alex is cool. Mom, we really gotta go."

"But, but . . . I thought you didn't like sleepovers. Remember that time you stayed over at Kevin's house? And his mom called me at midnight to get you because you were scared?" In all my life, I've never been so happy to be called at midnight.

"I wasn't scared. There were all these crickets in a cage for his lizards, and the crickets made so much noise I couldn't sleep. Mom, *we have to go!*"

Disappointment makes my stomach hurt. There will be no dinner together. No movie. Just me and a really big casserole.

On the way out, we pass through the kitchen. The padded envelope is still sitting on the island.

"Give me one minute." I grab the envelope and duck into the bathroom. It smells of the same lemon as my bedroom. I rip the envelope open, scan the directions, and emerge brandishing a cotton swab.

"Open your mouth. I need to scrape the inside of your cheek."

Ian has always been full of questions, and I expect him to demand a detailed explanation. I haven't decided whether to tell him the partial truth—that a DNA analysis can shed light on his ethnic background—or the whole truth: a Y-line DNA test could lead us to his donor. I was going break the news slowly, gauge his reaction carefully. Now there's no time.

But Ian is so anxious to get to the birthday party, he doesn't ask questions, just opens his mouth so I can get my sample and then hurries into the car, which is still warm from my drive home.

Later, much later, after I've tried watching a movie and reading a book, only to find myself pacing around the echoing house, I grab my purse and the Tyvek envelope containing the saliva-soaked swab. The rain comes down in sheets, but the post office is less than a mile away. A blue mailbox stands at the edge of the tiny parking lot.

The envelope falls with a thud.

---

Two weeks later, I receive an e-mail from Helix Laboratories. They tell me that Ian is a male of Northern European ancestry, which is not much of a surprise. And then, the big news: Ian's Y chromosome matches two individuals in Helix Lab's extensive database. By 37 and 42 percent.

In other words, we have failed to track down any close relatives. I have met another dead end. If I sign a release, Helix will add Ian's results to their public database, but I don't want to give up that kind of control.

*Per your request, we will notify you of any future Y-line matches of greater than 50%,* the e-mail tells me. A name might pop up a year from now. Or two. Or ten. By then it will be too late.

*Part 2*

# APRIL

# Vanessa

I'm so over Donor 4317. Something about him just never felt right. Plus, once I broke down and read all of his boring medical stuff, I saw that there was a ton of cancer in his family, and that's not something you want to mess around with.

Right now I'm torn between two lovers. Nonlovers. Whatever. First, we've got Donor 5429, just a few miles away from me at the Southern California Cryobank. He's six foot four with brown hair and hazel eyes. He does triathlons and plays the drums. And he cries at movies.

Eric? Never cries.

Bachelor Number Two's money shot is in cold storage on the other side of the country, at the Northern Florida Sperm Repository. But that's okay. No long-distance relationship issues there. They ship! My baby could be a jet setter before he's ever born!

Bachelor Number Two, aka Donor 81GH2, calls himself a "nerdy jock." How cute is that? Plus, he says he can't wait to have children of his own someday.

Sometimes I daydream about meeting 5429 or 81GH2. We'd fall in love, get married, and then, *finally*, have babies together. I wouldn't even mind about his other little donor children running around somewhere in the United States (or even Europe). I've never been a selfish person. And anyway, he wouldn't love those other kids. They'd be like distant cousins he'd never met.

I've decided that 5429 is named Lucas and 81GH2 is named Shane. Or maybe Crispin.

Eric doesn't know that I've been cruising sperm donors. I've been waiting for just the right moment to threaten to have someone else's baby. If that's not a wake-up call, I don't know what is. In the meantime, thinking about these guys, trying to imagine their voices, smells, and eyes, makes me feel more in control of my destiny.

---

Friday night we have dinner at Eric's mom's house. She lives in Glendale, which is north of L.A. In other words, the drive is a nightmare, especially on Fridays.

I don't know how it's become a thing, but practically every Friday, Eric calls and asks me if I'm doing something because his mom is cooking dinner. His mom's nice and all, but it kind of sucks that her dinners are the closest thing Eric and I have to dates.

Eric and I started going out a couple of years after his father died. Since my dad died when I was little, Eric and I had a bond, right from the beginning. Sometimes I wonder if that's the problem in our relationship. Maybe he associates meeting me with how bad it felt to lose his father. Or maybe the real problem is that he just doesn't love me enough.

Our first year together was really sweet, probably our best, now that I look back on it. Eric really talked to me then. About his family, his music, and his dreams. When he told me how much he wanted to quit his job and travel through Asia, I told him, "Go. If you don't do it now, you'll always regret it."

Sure, I was afraid I'd lose him, but I kept thinking about that old saying. You know, if you love something set it free, and if it's yours it'll come back. So when Eric came back a year later, I thought it meant that he was mine. Three years have passed since then. I'm twenty-nine years old and starting to think that I shouldn't base my life decisions on stuff I read on a poster.

Everyone's at Eric's mom's house tonight, Eric's brothers A.J. and J.J., along with their wives and kids. Eric has a sister, too, but she lives in Florida. I've only met her twice. Both times, she pretty much ignored me, but Eric said that it had nothing to do with me, she's just like that.

The house is a ranch, built in like the sixties, but Eric's parents renovated it in the nineties, so it's got high ceilings and granite countertops and stuff. The backyard is huge and has a pool and a built-in barbecue that doesn't work very well but looks nice. There's lots of trees and grass everywhere. My family never had much money, and I think it would have been amazing to grow up in the kind of house that Eric did, but he acts like it's no big deal, just like he thinks it's no big deal that his parents paid for college and he didn't even have to work or take out loans.

We're the last ones to arrive and most people are in the kitchen, drinking beer and wine, fussing with dinner, and eating chips and salsa and veggies and dip. Everyone's talking loudly because the huge-screen TV is blasting cartoons in the attached family room. On the floor, the kids play with plastic dolls, superheroes, and blocks.

Everyone says hi, and then Angie, who's married to A.J., tosses her flat-ironed hair and goes, "Wow, it's getting late. We thought maybe you weren't coming." She smirks, like she thinks she's so superior. Or maybe she's just trying to hide her braces. Or both.

She runs a stalk of celery through some sour cream dip and nibbles carefully so she doesn't break a bracket.

Every time I get really sad about me and Eric maybe not getting married, I think about how at least then I wouldn't have to see Angie anymore.

"Traffic bad?" Eric's mom asks. She's a tiny thing but she talks too loud even when the TV isn't on because her hearing's not so great.

Eric shrugs. "No worse than usual."

"It was bad," I say, trying to be casual but coming off like I'm talking back to Angie. Which I am. She lives three miles away. She could practically walk here.

"We have Costco stores here too, you know," Eric's mom says. "If that's where you're going to work."

Eric's mouth tightens, just a little bit. "Yeah, but you don't have the ocean."

I don't care that much about the ocean and wouldn't mind living in Glendale, which is prettier and cheaper than Redondo. Except then I'd be spending more than one day a week with Angie, so it's probably not worth it.

Angie and A.J. have three boys, all totally cute and sweet even though their mother is a witch. When the oldest, Ty, sees us, he makes this buzzing noise and runs right into Eric, head-butting his stomach. Ty's six and weighs nothing, but Eric goes, "Ugh!" and falls over. Ty's little brothers, Ryan and Hayden, think it's hysterical and jump all over Eric on the floor. Eric makes more "Ugh! Ugh! Ugh!" noises, for real this time because Hayden is bouncing on his stomach. The scene is so sweet it makes me want to cry.

Angie and I don't really look alike (God, I hope not), but since she's Colombian and I'm half Mexican, we have similar coloring. So I figure if Eric and I had children, they'd look kind of like Ty, Ryan, and Hayden. All three boys have skin that looks tanned instead of just brown, gold eyes, and streaky light brown hair that looks like Angie highlights it. I wouldn't put it past her, but I've checked their roots a whole bunch of times, and it's natural.

If Eric and I had kids together, would they get that golden skin with the streaky hair? What if I used a sperm donor with Eric's hair color? What would my kids look like then?

Eric, A.J., and J.J. look like brothers, but Eric's the most handsome because A.J. has really big nostrils and J.J. doesn't have much of a chin. Also, since Eric's the only one without a desk job, he's in better shape and usually kind of tan. Kara, J.J.'s wife, is blond and skinny, and so are their kids, Emma and Christopher.

As always, the kids eat first. Kara and Angie always make entirely separate meals. Kara (who's really nice, don't get me wrong) is all about organic this and antioxidant that and how little boys will grow breasts if you let them drink milk from cows that took hormones. Today her kids eat whole-wheat spaghetti with turkey Bolognese sauce, steamed broccoli, and nonfat milk.

Angie's kids get pizza rolls, french fries, and some orange drink that supposedly contains vitamin C and calcium. Angie says, "If you deprive kids, they'll end up craving stuff." Which makes her sound better than "I am too lazy to cook real food."

The kids take a long time to eat, and then Emma, who's three, has a major meltdown because Kara won't let her eat chocolate chip cookies that Angie just baked. Well—heated. They were the frozen dough kind that you just stick on a sheet. It's so late and I'm so hungry, I'm ready to cry for one of the cookies too. The chips and celery sticks are just not cutting it.

Finally, we plant the kids in front of a Monster Truck DVD and go into the dining room. There's a fresh lace cloth on the table, and Eric's mom has put out her china even though we're eating meat loaf. The first time I ate dinner here, I felt really scared. What fork do I use? Am I holding my water glass correctly?

Okay, I still feel that way.

Things are so different in the cramped Riverside house that my mother shares with my sister and her three kids. There are elbows on the table and Cheetos on the floor. Everyone eats when and wherever they want to. My mother yells about all the dirty dishes lying around, but everyone ignores her.

Aurora got pregnant for the first time when she was sixteen and I was fifteen. I couldn't believe she was so stupid. It was even stupider for her to get pregnant two more times, at eighteen and twenty-one. The last guy was the only one she married, and he only married her because of the baby, who was two months old at the time of the wedding. Shock of shocks, the marriage didn't last, but at least he gives her child support, at least when he's got a job.

I was never going to be stupid like that. Oh, no, I'd get an education, find a nice guy, get married, buy a house. I had everything figured out.

Now, at the lace-covered table in Glendale, I sit next to Eric, and Kara sits next to me. She's known Angie a lot longer, but I'm pretty sure she likes me better, and not just because I've never tried to feed her kids nonorganic cookies.

"You been doing anything for fun lately?" I ask her. Over celery sticks, we'd already talked about Emma's allergies and how Christopher was adjusting to first grade. Kara's a little crazy on the food front, but she's a really good mom.

"I've been too busy with the kids to do much," she said. "But I joined a book club," she says. "We just read *Eat, Pray, Love*."

"Did you like it?" I think Pammy read that book. Or maybe she saw the movie.

Kara wrinkles her nose. "I couldn't get beyond the *Eat* part. The author clearly suffers from an eating disorder. Otherwise, yeah, I've just been doing stuff with the kids, karate and whatnot. Plus I've been working on my family tree, going to surprise my parents at Christmas. I'm all the way back to the 1500s on my mother's side."

"In the United States?" I ask.

She blinks funny. Next to me, Eric clears his throat.

"What?"

"Nothing."

"What?"

Eric looks at me. Then at Kara. Then back to me. And finally at his plate. "Europeans didn't settle in America until the 1600s."

I adjust the cloth napkin in my lap. "Oh. Right. I knew that." Sort of.

"I planted tomatoes today," Eric's mother says (kinda loud). She is not trying to take attention away from my ignorance. With her bad hearing, she just has trouble following the conversation. Good news for me.

I dig into the meat loaf and keep my mouth shut for the rest of the meal.

---

Traffic moves quicker on the way home, but there are still lots of cars. The lines of taillights make me think of Christmas decorations. Which makes me think of how I didn't get a ring for Christmas. Which makes me think of how I didn't get a ring for my birthday either. The way things are going, I probably never will.

"I'm thinking about using a sperm bank," I announce. When Eric doesn't say anything, I make myself clearer. "To get pregnant."

He nods, just a little bit, eyes on the road.

"How would you feel about that?" I ask.

He takes a long time to answer. When he does, his voice is quiet. "If that's what you want, I think you should do it."

"What do you want?" I press.

"I want you to be happy."

"You know what would make me really happy?"

I wait for him to say "What?" So I can say, "Having your baby." But he knows where I'm going with this, so he doesn't say anything.

"I guess I didn't think you'd like the idea so much. You know, me having some other guy's kid."

"If it's what you want, you should go for it. I'd support you. Always."

"You would?" My heart lifts for like half a second.

Then he explains. "As a friend. A good friend. But you've got to understand, this would be your baby, not mine. The way things are between us now, our relationship—it would be over."

"But you went out with Paige!" I blurt. "How come it was okay that she had a kid?"

He sighs, like, *Oh God, why do we always have to talk about Paige?*

He says, "She had a daughter before I came in the picture, and we both understood that Ophelia was just hers. I thought Ophelia understood it too, but . . ."

"What?"

He shakes his head. "After Ophelia . . . I'll never again go out with anyone who has a kid. I can't do that to another child. Be there one day, and then gone, out of her life. First her father left her, then me."

"But it was Paige's fault. She cheated on you."

"I knew that and Paige knew that. But Ophelia didn't."

"Do you still love her?"

"I'll always love Ophelia."

I meant Paige. For some reason, this stings even more.

# Laura

Marissa is texting and giggling as I approach her desk, and I wish, for the millionth time, that my last secretary, Carlene, hadn't left. When she sees me, Marissa chucks her phone into her bag. I half want to say, *Just finish the damn text,* and am half glad that I can still command something resembling respect.

"Kim Rueben's secretary," I say. "What's her name?"

Kim Rueben, the only female partner at Sullivan, Zurheide and Poole, is a fierce, fearless, and unforgiving divorce attorney with a reputation for digging up mountains of dirt. No one messes with Kim. She scares me, and I'm not even married.

"Paulina?" Marissa's penciled eyebrows shoot up.

"I don't know. Is that her secretary?"

"Maybe? I mean, I know Paulina's name is Paulina, but I'm not sure who she works for. She's blond? Kind of pretty but with crooked teeth? Gets body odor when it's hot out?"

What does Marissa say about me when I'm not listening? Never mind; I don't want to know. (Why did you leave me, Carlene? *Why, why, why?*)

I say, "That's who, uh. That's her. I need you to check with Paulina, see if Kim's got five free minutes today."

"To meet with you?"

"No, to get her *toenails* done. *Yes,* to meet with me."

Marissa stares at me, not with horror, exactly . . . more with the concentration necessary to memorize every sarcastic word I've said so she can provide an accurate report to whomever she was texting.

———————

Following Helix Laboratories' disappointing news that Ian had no close Y-line matches among their clients, I spent much of February and March combing through other online genealogy databases, searching for chunks of numbers that matched Ian's.

Although I squinted at genetic codes till my head hurt, I couldn't find a perfect or even a partial match. On the bright side, the late-night mental strain did help me sleep.

A few days ago, I was on the verge of giving up (or perhaps of *considering* giving up) when, to my astonishment, I—technically Ian—received a message from Helix:

According to your profile, you wish to be notified of any Y-line matches greater than 50%. The following member's Y-line sample matches yours by approximately 100%, indicating a MRCA (Most Recent Common Ancestor) within two generations.

For a stunned moment, I thought the man Helix had identified, a forty-year-old named John Fergus, might be Donor 613. It soon struck me, though, that he was several years too old. More likely, he was the donor's brother or perhaps a first cousin.

It was too much to hope that Google searches and national address database perusals could reveal which of the hundreds of John Ferguses I found online was the right one. It was definitely too much to hope that I'd nail down a clear John Fergus with a younger brother born on the same day as Donor 613. For a good private investigator, however, tracking down that information should be routine.

———

At 10:14, I check in with Paulina, an attractive thirtyish blonde who smells just fine.

She says, "Kim's just finishing up a phone call. I'm about to make a Starbucks run. Can I get you a latte or something?"

"Thanks, but I don't need anything."

Paulina makes good-natured Starbucks runs for her boss. If I were the crying type, I might have shed tears. Sometimes when I'm swamped, I'll send Marissa to pick up lunch, but she makes me pay in so many ways that don't involve money.

Paulina's phone beeps. "Hi, Kim. Yeah, she's ready for you . . . Sure thing, I'm on my way out. Tall vanilla latte, yes? No whip?" After a pause, she laughs and says, "I'll see what I can do."

Paulina leads me into Kim's office, which has a large window with sweeping mountain views and a beautiful wood desk. Kim stands up and walks around her desk to greet me. I am tall for a woman, but she towers over me, and as we shake hands I feel weirdly small. As always, Kim looks impeccable and intimidating, with stylish, short dark hair, a tailored black suit, dove-gray silk shirt, and silver hooker heels that she somehow gets away with. One of those ageless women who looks like she could be anywhere between thirty and fifty, she is actually fifty-three. One of her repeat clients is a successful Orange County plastic surgeon, and he does good work.

"But no brownies," Kim tells Paulina with a chuckle. "Too rich."

"Mm-hm," Paulina says, flashing her boss a warm smile before heading out to the coffee shop.

"Paulina's feeding my chocolate addiction," Kim tells me. "Who needs a man when you can have truffles?"

Somehow, I suspect she's used that line a few times before. If the rumor mill is to be believed—and, really, I am so far out of the loop that by the time something gets to me, it hardly even counts as a rumor—Kim is sleeping with a spray-tanned junior associate gym rat named Bryce, but that doesn't mean she can't enjoy a bit of chocolate now and then.

Kim invites me to sit down with her. Not only does she have Paulina and a view, she has a leather couch and a coffee table with a big box of tissues. Divorce may be lucrative, but it is never pretty.

"I'm looking for a recommendation," I say. "I need a private investigator."

"For a client?" she asks.

"No."

Her ageless face placid, she waits for me to fill the silence with an explanation; as if I'd fall for that old trick.

"Is there anyone in particular you'd recommend?"

"Depends," she says. "Is this for surveillance?"

"No. More records research. Computer work, that sort of thing."

"Ah!" She stands up and heads for her beautiful wood desk, opens a drawer, and plucks out a business card. "I've had good luck with this guy. Dexter Savage. Former cop—they usually are—but he's more tech savvy than most."

I stand up and take the stark white card.

She walks me to the door. "Let me know if he doesn't work out. I've got some other names I can give you."

I brace myself to skirt any further inquiries of my business, and then I realize: she doesn't care.

———

As I don't want any of my dealings with him tied to my office, I call
Dexter Savage from my cell phone.

"Yeah?" Static crackles on the line.

"Am I speaking to Dexter Savage?"

"Yeah."

"My name is Laura Cahill. I got your number from Kim Rueben, a fellow attorney at my firm."

"Yeah."

"Uh . . . right. Kim spoke highly of your research expertise, and
so I'd like to retain your services. There's a man I'm trying to track
down. I know his date of birth and also his brother's full name and
date of birth. However, I've never met him and don't know his first
name."

The line crackles some more.

"Bad reception." The line goes dead.

I am redialing when the call comes through. Unknown number.

"Laura Cahill," I say.

"You got that information for me?" Dexter Savage says.

"I do." I give him John Fergus's name and birthday, along with
the information I have for Donor 613.

"Don't you want to know what this is about?" I ask.

"Depends. Do you want to tell me?"

I consider.

"Not really."

"Then I don't need to know." With that, he hangs up.

# 3
## Wendy

When Darren comes home from work and walks into the kitchen, he finds the kids and me in various states of hysteria, surrounded by a sea of pretzels. I am sitting on the floor, clutching my knees in an upright fetal position. Sydney lies facedown on the white ceramic tiles, pounding the ground. Tears puddle around her face. A pretzel, surprisingly intact, sticks to her forearm. Harrison is the only one standing. It is easier to kick the wall that way.

Just a typical Tuesday in the Winder household.

I bury my face in my knees. I am so ugly when I cry. I expect Darren to recoil from the scene and head for the safety of his computer and his virtual life as a single sports agent. He surprises me by putting a gentle hand on my back. He rubs up and down, up and down. His tenderness makes me cry even harder.

He says, "Maybe we should call a sitter and go out."

A couple hours later, we are in P.F. Chang's at Kierland Commons. The twins are home with Ashlyn Plant, Sherry and Lane's younger daughter. Darren made the phone call. He still likes Sherry even though she and I aren't friends anymore. He never liked Lane. Darren is a quiet engineer. Lane is a pharmaceutical sales rep with a nasty streak. During the year or so that the four of us hung out, Lane called Darren "Spock," "Kirk," and "Scotty." Which is totally stupid. Darren doesn't even like *Star Trek*. It would take too much time away from the Sims.

I am wearing my favorite dress, which just happens to be the only dress that fits me. It is from Chico's, black and long and simple, with a crew neck and three-quarter sleeves. Darren is wearing a sky-blue golf shirt with khaki shorts.

Last time we came to P.F. Chang's, a couple of years ago, maybe more, we had to wait over an hour for a table, but today we get seated right away—at a booth, no less. There's something to be said for a weeknight in a recession. If you only go out to dinner once a year, it's nice to have your choice of tables.

The darkness and the comfy bench seat make me unwind, just a little. We decide what to order and then keep looking at the menu because it gives us something to do. I'm too tired for alcohol, so I order a diet soda and about three thousand calories' worth of nouvelle Asian cuisine. I'll bring a lot of it home.

The waitress takes our menus. Darren and I make eye contact, and . . . that's it. My mind goes completely blank. Sitting here with Darren feels like a blind date that isn't going well. He puts his elbow on the table, his chin on his hand, and looks from the window to the ceiling.

"How's work?" I ask, finally.

He shrugs. "Fine."

"Are you still working on . . . that thing you were working on? With the, um, superalloy?" Surely I deserve credit for remembering this term.

"Uh-uh. We finished that a couple months ago."

I wait for him to say more. He doesn't. "What are you working on now, then?"

His eyebrows arch with skepticism. "Do you really want to know?"

"Of course." Once, years ago, I told Darren that the only people who find engineering interesting are other engineers. I've regretted my words ever since.

"Well . . . okay. We're trying to reduce the specific fuel consumption of our latest engine by changing the geometry of the turbine blades. The simulations of our latest design indicate we can probably achieve around a four percent improvement. Maybe more."

He was right. I don't really want to know.

A group of skinny young women walk by wearing denim skirts, shorts, and flip-flops. I tug at a sleeve.

"I'm overdressed."

"Nobody's looking at you," Darren says, realizing about three seconds too late that that was an incredibly hurtful thing to say. "I didn't mean . . ."

"I know." No, I don't.

The waitress brings our drinks. I consider asking for some rum to put in my Diet Coke. At this point in the awkwardness, it might be worth the headache. But I'd rather use the calories for something else. Like, say, ten Oreo cookies after everyone has gone to bed. Yeah, that'll make everything better.

I make another stab at conversation. "Ashlyn sure has grown up. I hardly recognized her."

Now thirteen, Ashlyn has traded her sparkly clothes for plain blue jeans and logo T-shirts. She has breasts, braces, and just enough acne to be noticeable. Even with all that metal, her smile is surprisingly sweet. I can't remember her smiling a single time during the year or so when her mother and I were best friends.

"She seems like a nice girl," I add.

"Mm." Darren drinks his beer.

"She was such a bratty little kid, but I guess she grew out of it. That kind of gives me hope. I mean, with Harrison and Sydney."

He doesn't respond.

"You're probably wondering about the pretzels," I blurt.

He frowns with confusion. "I figured the kids spilled the bag."

I shake my head, realizing, too late, that I could have left him with his assumption: The kids spilled the pretzels. I yelled. They cried. I broke down.

If only it were that simple.

"I gave them a snack at three. Oreos and milk and apples." I don't tell him that they refused to eat the apples. "And then an hour later, I was feeling hungry." I don't tell him that I'd eaten four Oreos at snack time.

"So I opened a bag of pretzels, which I've been trying to eat instead of chips because they have no fat. The kids were watching TV in the toy room, but they heard the bag rustle, so they came in and said, 'Give me some.'"

My throat tightens at the memory. I swallow hard.

"So I said no because they'd already had a snack and this would ruin their dinner. Sydney started screaming and Harrison tried to grab the bag out of my hands. Which really, really pissed me off. I told them to go to the corner for time out, but they wouldn't."

My voice is starting to rise. I take a deep breath.

"So then I told them to go to their rooms. But they wouldn't do that either. They just kept screaming, 'Give me! Give me!' Harrison started kicking the wall—even though he promised he wouldn't do that anymore after we had to repaint. It was so *loud,* and I was so tired, so I just . . ."

Oh God. Why did I start this?

"What?" he asks.

Maybe the story will seem funny. Maybe we'll laugh.

"I started throwing the pretzels at them. First one at a time and then whole handfuls. And I was yelling too, I was saying, 'You want pretzels? Here are your pretzels!'" I try to laugh. I can't. Darren stays quiet.

I continue. "They were so shocked that they just froze. So I stopped with the pretzels. We all stared at each other, and Harrison said, 'Mommy, you're mean.' That made me cry. Which made them cry. Which made me angry. So I started throwing pretzels again and kept at it till the entire bag was gone."

He still doesn't laugh. Of course not. There's nothing funny about it.

Oh shit. I'm crying again. Right here in P.F. Chang's.

He hands me his black napkin. The polyester can't absorb my tears. I fish in my purse, retrieve a mangled tissue, blot my eyes, blow my nose.

"I'm not very good at this," I say. "At being a mother."

"They're difficult."

"I keep thinking it'll get better, and it keeps not getting better." I start to cry again.

"It'll get better," Darren says with no conviction—or emotion—whatsoever.

"I talked to their teacher today." My tears are falling faster than I can blot them. "When I came to get the kids, she said, 'Can I have a word,' and the kids went outside to the playground. I knew it was going to be bad. No one says 'can I have a word' unless it's bad. She went on for a bit about how disruptive the kids are and how other parents have been complaining. And then she asked—get this—if we've ever considered Ritalin."

"Huh." He almost laughs. Or maybe pretend-laughs.

"Seriously. She said that like it was such a new idea. Like maybe we'd never thought of drugs before."

When the twins were four, I read everything I could about Ritalin, Adderall, and other stimulants used to treat ADHD. I talked it over with Darren, who, frankly, was no help at all. Finally, despite a million misgivings, I asked the pediatrician for a prescription and braced myself for an end to the insanity.

It didn't work. The doctor upped the dose twice—still no good. Then he tried a couple of other ineffective medications before saying, "Maybe they're just immature. Maybe they'll outgrow it." Then he referred us to a child psychologist who was far more expensive but no more useful.

"Their teacher suggested I try homeschooling," I say.

This time he laughs for real. "That's not gonna happen."

"You got that right."

The waitress picks this moment to deliver our appetizers. I wonder if the food has been ready all along, if she's been waiting on the edges for a break in my hysteria.

"Dumplings." I inhale the aroma. "Mm."

Back in college, Darren used to say, "I love to watch you eat." He thought it was funny that I took so much pleasure from food. Of course, I was thin, then. Well, thinner, anyway. I swear Darren could eat the same thing for dinner every night and not care. Before we had kids, I used to wish he could appreciate my cooking and our restaurant dinners. Now that the twins' oversensitive palates have led us to a life of spaghetti and chicken nuggets, Darren's unrefined palate is a relief.

We eat the dumplings and crispy green beans without talking. When our plates are empty, the waitress brings Mongolian beef and Kung Pao shrimp. I am so happy when I eat. There will be nothing left to bring home, but I just don't care. Right now I'm not thinking about my strained marriage or my difficult children. I'm too busy savoring the sensations of salt, sweet, sour, spicy, and the newest, hippest, coolest taste on the block, umami.

"Wendy? I thought that was you!"

Annalisa Lemberger interrupts me in mid-umami. In three-inch heels, she towers over us, her old and ugly husband at her side. Unlike Darren and me, their outfits not only match in level of formality, they are actually color-coordinated. Annalisa wears white slacks with her heels. Come to think of it, that's what she's worn every time I've ever seen her, though the length of her white pants varies with the season. Her shirt tonight is a sleeveless peach silk. Roger wears a short-sleeved linen shirt: cream with peach tropical flowers. His slacks are tan.

"Annalisa! Hi!" I think I have some peppers stuck in my teeth.

I introduce them to Darren. I call Annalisa "one of my scrapbooking friends," and then wonder if I should have simply called her my friend. It might be nice to see her outside of the group.

"Those crazy scrapbookers!" Roger says. "I say to Annalisa, I think it's just an excuse for you girls to drink wine and gossip!"

"And have I ever denied it?" She laughs. Her teeth are really, really white—even brighter than her pants, which I see now are actually cream.

I don't really want to be friends with Annalisa Lemberger.

"So is Tuesday y'all's date night too?" she asks.

"Not really. Just tonight." What's up with the y'all? She's not even from the South. Or is she? I've known Annalisa for over a year. I should really know that.

Annalisa puts her arm around Roger. "When we had kids, we made a promise to each other that we'd go out, just the two of us, once a week."

Roger kisses her on the cheek. Even in the dark restaurant, I can see his seedlike pores.

"Oh, yeah, it's great to have some alone time," I say. "It can just be hard leaving the kids and all."

"You need to get over that," Annalisa says. "You need to have time for yourselves as a couple. Like I say to Roger, if there's no *us*, there's no *family*."

Roger pats her on the butt. She stiffens, just a little, before gazing up at him. I check Darren to gauge his reaction. He is staring at Annalisa, taking in her shiny white teeth and blond hair and perky boobs.

Annalisa is no friend of mine, not even a scrapbooking friend.

"Give me a call sometime, Wendy," she says. "I'd love to get together for coffee."

"Definitely!"

Once Annalisa and Roger leave, we return to our food with grim determination. I'd say it doesn't even taste good anymore, but it does. Even Annalisa can't ruin Kung Pao shrimp for me.

"What'd you think of Annalisa?" I ask.

Darren shrugs. "She seems nice."

"Don't you think she's attractive?"

He raises his eyebrows. "She seems high maintenance."

"She is," I say, even though I've never seen any evidence of that.

---

The house is quiet when we get home. Too quiet. Did Ashlyn strangle the twins? (And if so, do we still have to pay her?)

Ashlyn is sprawled on the couch in the sitting area off of the kitchen, staring at her cell phone, pushing the keypad with her thumbs. When she sees us, she scrambles into a sitting position. She finishes her text and sticks the phone in her back pocket.

"Where are Harrison and Sydney?" I ask.

"In bed."

"Asleep?"

"Yeah. I mean, I guess."

"And they ate the pizza?"

"No, they didn't want it. I made eggs for myself because I'm lactose intolerant, so I can't eat pizza. And they said they wanted eggs too, so that's what I gave them."

"They hate eggs," I say.

"Really? Oh." She shrugs. Apparently, the twins don't hate Ashlyn's eggs. Or if they do, they ate them anyway.

Her cell phone whirs. She touches her back pocket but doesn't take the phone out.

I pull twenty dollars out of my wallet—then I add an extra ten. This gawky teenager is a miracle worker.

"Thanks." She shoves the bills into her front pocket without counting. When her cell phone whirs again, she pulls it out and checks the display.

"You can get that," I say.

"Nah." She puts the phone back in her pocket. "It's just my mother."

Once Ashlyn leaves, Darren and I tiptoe up the stairs and go into the twins' darkened rooms. They both sleep curled into tight fetal positions, usually with their hands balled into angry fists. Tonight, Harrison faces the wall, but Sydney's face, calm and angelic, tilts toward us in the doorway. Her dark curls tumble on the pillow; her hands lie together, as if in prayer.

"She looks like you," Darren whispers.

"She's prettier," I say. (She is.)

He shakes his head. "You're both beautiful." Something passes over his face: something sad.

Tears spring to my eyes. I can't remember the last time Darren called me beautiful. I know he's just saying it to be nice, but it still means something. I take his hand and squeeze.

He squeezes back. "Think I'll play on the computer for a little bit before bedtime."

He drops my hand. And just like that, I've lost him to his Sims world. How foolish to worry that Darren might be attracted to Annalisa. He has no interest whatsoever in real live people.

I have my own computer. It's in the kitchen, which means I can surf the Web, cook meals, and scream at my children—all at the same time! Right now I want to look up lactose intolerance. Maybe milk is responsible for the twins' violent mood swings. It seems like a long shot, but you never know.

There's an e-mail waiting from Laura Cahill. I haven't heard from her in months, but now I can ask if her perfect son has any trouble digesting milk. (If he does, would it mar his perfection? Or would she somehow see it as a good thing?)

That question will have to wait. Laura's message is brief, to the point, and nondairy in nature: *I think I found him.*

# Laura

My cell phone rings just as I am pulling into the garage and wondering how to keep my eyes open long enough to take Ian to his seven o'clock Cub Scout meeting. My insomnia has returned with renewed vigor. Ever since mailing Dexter Savage a five-hundred-dollar retainer (which seemed a bit steep), I've lain awake at night, considering all of the things that could go wrong, from learning that Donor 613 is untraceable to hearing that he is dead, the victim of a tragic accident or, worse, some horrible and potentially genetic disease.

I turn off my ignition, grab the phone, and check the display: *Dexter Savage*. Less than a week has passed since we first spoke; I never imagined he'd get back to me so fast.

He says, "I found your man."

That wakes me up. It isn't until after the shock has passed that it strikes me. *I found your man.* What a corny thing to say, like something out of a bad television series.

"And he's alive?"

He pauses. "Was that a possibility? 'Cause I woulda checked death records first."

"Not really, I just—"

"The birth date made it easy," he tells me. "Lots of guys named Fergus, but only two born on the same day as your guy, and one died in infancy. Got this name, checked it against your John Fergus, and whammo. We got a match. They're brothers."

"I see you deposited my retainer. Given that the search was faster than anticipated—"

"Said it was easy. Didn't say it was fast. You want I give you the information now or you want I e-mail it?"

"You can give it to me now." I retrieve my bag from the passenger floor and dig inside for a legal pad and pen. And then I take a deep breath.

"You ready?" he says.

———

At nine-thirty, Ian is fast asleep, worn out from planting a windowsill herb garden at his Cub Scout meeting. At least three times, I came close to telling him that I'd tracked down his donor but held myself back; I need more information before I can decide what, if anything, to tell my son.

Right now, there is only one person I can talk to about this, even though she's a virtual stranger: Wendy Winder. I shot her a quick and slightly cryptic e-mail before heading out to Cub Scouts, but I haven't heard back. Now I'm wide-awake, sitting at the kitchen table with a cup of lukewarm decaf, searching Google, LinkedIn, Facebook, MySpace, Yahoo . . . anything that might shed light on Donor 613. And yet, nothing does. There are too many people with his name. Even adding his city of residence to the search doesn't help.

It is still so odd to think he has *a name*. Odder still to think that he has a telephone number and address, now in my possession thanks to Dexter Savage.

I'll never be able to sleep tonight.

My e-mail chimes. Wendy Winder received my message, after all.

*Can you ask him if he's lactose intolerant? I'll be up for a couple of hours. Here's my cell number if you want to talk. . . .*

I stare at the screen. Once I've decided she must be joking (though I don't get the humor), I pick up the phone and dial her number.

"It's Laura."

"Hi."

"Hi."

There is an odd, weighted silence. I don't know where to begin.

"How did you find him?" she asks finally.

"DNA." It all spills out: the kit, the lab, the Y-line results, the database. I hadn't realized how much I wanted to talk about it. Needed to talk about it. Kim Rueben wasn't even curious. Neither was Dexter Savage.

I say, "Presumably, he wants confidentiality, and I respect that. He's probably married, maybe has children of his own. And it's entirely possible that he never told his wife about the sperm donations."

"Did you Google him?" Wendy asks.

"Oh, yeah. Plenty of hits, but I don't know which are him."

"But you're sure this is the guy?"

"No. I won't be sure until I call him. But I think so. The investigator sounded pretty confident."

"If you could ask about dairy . . ."

"Um . . ."

"It's just a thought I had." Her voice rises to a higher pitch.

"That maybe my children's behavior is somehow related to lactose intolerance. What about Ian? Has he ever had trouble with milk?"

"Milk? No."

"Oh. That's too bad. I mean—ugh. That came out wrong. You know what I mean. I hope. I'm just trying to figure out . . . Anyway. Will you send me an e-mail? After you talk to him? . . . And maybe ask about the lactose?"

"Uh—sure."

"When are you going to call him?"

"Tomorrow morning. From work."

"But he won't be at his home number then, will he?"

Oh my God. She is right. It is like my brain had been completely jumbled ever since I talked to the detective. I don't have his work number. Even if I did, he'd be a doctor by now, and doctors are notoriously difficult to reach. I can't leave a message on his answering machine or, even worse, with his wife, if he has one. But now that I know who he is, I can't bear to go another whole day without making contact.

I look at the clock. "Do you think nine-forty is too late to call someone?"

"Not if that someone is responsible for half of your son's DNA."

# 5

## Vanessa

I make lard-free frozen bean burritos for dinner. I mean, they're not still frozen, I heated them in the microwave, but—you know. We had the same thing for dinner yesterday. And the day before. Eric keeps getting them for practically free at work. I'm all for free food, but they take up so much freezer space that I can't even buy ice cream.

It's late. Eric went to Venice to hear some band at some farmers' market or street fair thing or whatever. He asked me to go with, but I wasn't in the mood. When he comes home, it's after eight. I've got everything ready to go, the burritos plus a bag of salad because I'm trying to eat healthy. And also because bean burritos don't really fill me up since there's no meat. But if I try to make up for the no-meat thing by eating more than one bean burrito, well—you know.

When Eric sees the empty plates on the counter, he goes, "You didn't eat yet?" He should have said, "Thanks for waiting."

I go, "No, I didn't eat yet. I was waiting for you."

And he's like, "You didn't have to."

So I'm all, "I wanted to. I like spending time with you and like talking and stuff." Which sounds lame and stupid, but whatever. It's true.

He says, "Oh. That's nice. I mean, thanks."

Once upon a time, in a galaxy far, far away, Eric and I used to talk. I mean, really *talk*. About our dads, and our favorite movies, and how when we were little we dreamed about jet packs and hover cars and flying to other planets. So I know we can feel close to each other. I just don't know how to get there.

We fill our plates in the kitchen and then take them to the couch. No discussion. The little glass table is reserved for birthdays and special occasions, like the day after a bad fight. Other nights, it's you, me, and the TV. Which is mostly okay. We're both beat after work, and it's good to just be together. Right?

Eric snags the remote first. Damn. My bad for not getting there first. He channel-surfs, channel-surfs, channel-surfs . . .

"Pick something," I say.

He lands on a car-chase scene, something old, from like before we were even born. Or, before I was born, anyway.

"No," I say.

A little more surfing and he gets to a black-and-white war documentary that would be boring even if it were in color.

"Nuh-uh."

He passes a home-decorating show, a dance show, and a sitcom, only to stop at a soap opera. In Spanish.

"You're just trying to piss me off," I say.

"I'm not!" He laughs. "I'm just working on my Spanish comprehension!"

Eric thinks it's terrible that my father didn't speak Spanish to me. I've tried to explain that he wanted me and my sister to be American, free of the prejudices he suffered, but Eric doesn't get it.

My dad came to America from Mexico when he was seven, but he always kept a little accent. At least, I think he did. As much as I try to hear his voice in my head, the memory is gone.

Eric hands me the remote. "You choose."

I click around a little bit, but there's nothing I like that he won't hate. With a firm move of the thumb, I turn the set off.

"Bold," he says.

All of a sudden the apartment seems really, really quiet. Well, except for the street sounds and the low thrum of a stereo from an apartment down the hall. And the plumbing noises. Every time someone upstairs flushes the toilet, the water rushes and clicks through pipes in our ceiling. It would be really nice to have a house.

"Dr. Sanchez brought his kids to work today," I say. See? I can still make conversation. "They're on spring break. But their nanny had to do something. So they hung out in his office and by my desk. The little one, Sofie, she's five, she drew a picture of me. I put it up on the wall at work."

Eric looks seriously fascinated by his burrito.

"You know their mom died, right?" I say.

He looks up from the burrito. "Uh-huh." Looks back at the burrito.

"I guess that's why I feel this, like, bond with them. Because I know what it's like to lose a parent when you're just a kid. So, at the end of the day, Sofie hugged me and asked Dr. Sanchez if she could come back. And I said anytime, I'll watch them, but Dr. Sanchez said the nanny's back tomorrow."

Finally, Eric speaks. "Maybe you should be a nanny."

He did *not* just say that.

I almost say, "Fuck you." Instead, I turn the set back on and flip over to the decorating show.

He stays through the show's end. Then he takes both our plates to the kitchen and goes off to the bedroom. A dating reality show comes on. Eric hates dating shows, even though I've told him that seeing all those skeevy losers on TV makes me appreciate him more.

Tonight, a slimy banker named Jeff is trying to decide who he likes better, a blond skank or a brunette skank. Normally, I'd root for the brunette, but the blonde is named Vanessa, so she's my girl.

Forty-five minutes into the episode, Jeff and the brunette (her name is Andrea, which they say like ON-dree-uh) are in the hot tub. Jeff is weirdly lacking in body hair. He must wax.

Jeff tells ON-dree-uh that he feels a real connection with her but that he likes my girl Vanessa too and he doesn't want anyone to get hurt. ON-dree-uh says, "Let's not think about tomorrow. Let's think about right now." She puts her arms around him and they start kissing. You can see tongue, which shouldn't be allowed on network TV. Kids could be watching.

The phone rings. It's probably another call about lowering credit-card payments. I really need to figure out how to get on that Do Not Call list.

"Hello?"

"I'm trying to reach Eric Fergus."

He is sitting on the bed, leaning against a bunch of pillows, reading a library book. When he sees me, he takes his iPod buds out of his ears.

I hold out the phone. "It's for you."

My stomach hurts, and not from eating too many burritos. I don't know how I know it, but I do. The woman on the other end of the line is no telemarketer.

# Laura

In the months since I sent Ian's DNA sample off to Helix Laboratories, I've envisioned meeting Ian's donor. I've imagined long conversations about his childhood and family background. But, fearful that I might jinx the outcome, I'd never taken the time to prepare questions or plan my approach.

After talking to Wendy Winder, I finally got down to it, thinking and writing rapidly, having decided that telephoning after ten o'clock would be unconscionable, a poor reflection of both my character and on my appreciation for social norms, but that if I could get through before 9:59, all would be okay.

*Talking points:*

1. *Identify self*
2. *Confirm identity: birth date; brother; sperm donation*
3. *Reassure and express thanks for selfless act*

4. *Provide info re: Ian's life (e.g., "I am sure you have wondered over the years . . .")*
5. *Inquire as to donation history. Any other banks? How many sessions?*
6. *Request paternity test*
7. *Close the deal*

---

One thing I foolishly neglected to take into account: the possibility that his wife might answer the phone. At the sound of her voice, my stomach clenches.

"Hello?" A television plays in the background.

"I'm trying to reach Eric Fergus." My voice sounds lower than usual.

She doesn't respond. In the moment it takes for her to pass along the phone, I jot an additional note at the top of my list: *Apologize re: time.*

"Hello?" On the other end, something crashes. A door slamming, perhaps?

I try to keep my voice steady. "My apologies for calling at this late hour. Am I speaking to Eric Fergus?"

"Yes."

I dive right in. "My name is Laura Cahill, and I'm an attorney in Orange County. Before we proceed, I have a few brief questions."

"Is this a survey?" he asks, interrupting my flow.

"No."

"And you're a lawyer? I'm sorry, I don't understand what—"

"I am an attorney, but this is not a legal matter. I only told you that for the purposes of identification." We haven't even made it past the second point on my list—the third if you count the apology regarding the time—and already my pajama top is damp under the arms.

I continue, "For the purposes of confirmation, were you born on May second, 1977?"

". . . Yes."

"And do you have an older brother named John Jameson Fergus?

He hesitates even longer this time before confirming. We haven't even gotten to the Big Question yet. Perhaps I should shift my talking points, prepare him for the shock that lies ahead.

"Dr. Fergus. Eric. Nine years ago I conceived a son through artificial insemination, and I have reason to believe that you were the donor."

When he doesn't respond, I forge ahead to reassurance: "There's no cause for alarm. I don't want to interrupt your life in any way, and I'm not looking for you to take any kind of role in my son's life."

*Express thanks for selfless act.*

"Before we go any further, let me tell you how grateful I am. Thanks to your selfless act, I was able to fulfill my dreams of motherhood and bring a beautiful, bright, loving child into the world."

Still nothing.

I clear my throat. "Dr. Fergus, can you please confirm that you donated sperm at the Southern California Cryobank sometime prior to January of 2003?"

He is silent.

"Well. Did you?"

"Oh my God."

"Is that a yes? . . . Hello?"

"*Shit.*"

"I will take, um . . . I'll take that as a yes. Of course we would need a DNA test to confirm your paternity, but based on the information I've acquired, it looks like we have a match."

"But . . . but . . . the bank promised that my identity would be kept secret. They said no one would ever know."

"The bank has maintained your confidentiality and has never identified you by anything other than your donor number, 613. I tracked you down using genetic testing. Your brother John was registered with an online genealogy site, and my son matched."

"Stupid family tree," he mutters.

This is not going as well as I'd hoped. *Reassure.*

"Please rest assured that I do not see you as my son's father, nor do I expect any kind of emotional bond or financial contribution."

"*God.* I'd hope not."

Shaken, I consult my talking points. "Over the years, I'm sure you've wondered whether any of your donations resulted in live births. You've undoubtedly tried to picture the children that exist as a result of your selfless act and wondered what their daily lives must be like."

"Actually—no."

"Never?"

"Never."

"I find that hard to believe."

"It's true."

"Well, would you . . . like to hear about my son? And our lives together?"

"Um, yeah. I guess." He guesses?

I take a deep breath. "Ian is eight years old, in third grade. He's in a gifted program."

"Ian? That's his name?"

"Yes."

"Okay."

"You sound like you don't like it."

"No. It's, you know. Fine."

I squeeze my eyes shut for just a moment, trying to regain my composure, trying to capture the essence of my little boy in a few sentences. Then I take a deep breath and start talking.

"Ian has a great sense of humor, and he loves animals. Just

started playing the piano. He's involved in Cub Scouts, soccer, and basketball." I'm starting to sound like a Christmas-card newsletter or perhaps a private school application.

"He's a delight," I say. "Just really fun to be around. Everyone likes him. I really don't . . . I can't imagine my life without him." I stop and swallow hard. If only Eric Fergus could meet Ian, he'd see how amazing he is, how great we are together. He helped us once. Surely he'd do it again.

*Reassure.*

"I've been practicing law for almost fourteen years now," I say. "While I am a single parent, I am on very solid footing, financially. Further, I've employed the same full-time nanny since Ian was born, which has provided consistency and security."

"I really gotta go," he says.

"Wait—"

"This is just a lot to process. I need time to . . . process."

"Just a few more minutes of your time. You have my word." I still have three more points to cover. "Dr. Fergus—"

"I'm not a doctor."

"But . . . on your donor information card . . ." Oh my God. Was he the wrong guy, after all?

"I started medical school. But I left to pursue . . . other options."

"Oh. Okay. I mean—there are plenty of ways to skin a cat. Or. You know." From the windowsill, Alfredo turns his head and blinks at me. There's no time to pursue this line of inquiry.

I ask, "By any chance, did you ever donate to any other banks?"

"Any other . . . Oh. God. No. I didn't . . . do it . . . for long. Just a few times. I'd kind of forgotten about it, to be honest. Well, lately I've been sort of reminded. But it was so long ago. And I never . . ."

*Ask for a paternity test.* "I've located a DNA testing company that has flexible hours and a location very convenient for you. Before we go any further, it probably makes sense to do a paternity test. All it takes is a cheek swab. We'd have results in less than a week."

"A paternity . . . oh. Right. I mean, no! Not . . . not yet. I don't know."

There is no way he is going to agree to another donation on the basis of this conversation. No way. I have to find a way to continue the dialogue, to show him that he has nothing to worry about. I have to talk to him face-to-face.

*Close the deal.*

"I know this has been a shock. Perhaps it's best if we talk about all of this face-to-face," I suggest. "You're in Redondo Beach, correct? I live in Fullerton, in north Orange County, so it's not that far."

"You want me to—? Holy shit. This is just—so out of nowhere."

"I'd meet you anytime. Anyplace. Entirely at your convenience. Again, I am not looking for any kind of ongoing involvement. But it would be healthy, I think. For both of us. To answer questions, tie up loose ends. Afterward, you'll never hear from me again."

As long as he leaves a sample with my doctor, I'm good to go.

"This is just . . . I'm having trouble getting my head around it."

"I know. I understand. And again, let me say, I don't want to interrupt your life in any way."

"Okay," he says.

"You'll meet me?"

"No! I just meant, okay, I understand. I don't think I can—"

"Right. Of course. Let me give you my contact information." I rattle off my home, cell, and work numbers, even as I'm pretty sure he's not copying them down.

I say, "If I don't hear from you, I'll give you another call."

"Oh."

After I hang up, I remain standing in the kitchen, by the phone, staring into space, trying to picture Eric Fergus's face.

*He is not Ian's father.*

Something moves at the edge of the doorway. I think it is the cat, but no; Alfredo has been in the room with me all along, sitting on the windowsill.

Ian, wearing blue pajamas patterned with rockets, steps out of the shadows.

"Was that my donor?"

I stare at him. How much did he hear? Finally, I nod.

"I want to meet him."

"Buddy, I don't think that—"

"I want to meet him!" His eyes shine with unspilled tears. Now that he knows I've tracked down his donor, he will always wonder about him. He would have wondered about him, anyway.

I cross the room and put my arms around my son's warm, bony body. I would die for this child a hundred times over.

"He's not sure. He's nervous. But if he agrees, you can meet him. You will."

# Vanessa

The instant I slam the door, I think, *That was stupid*. Now I can't hear what Eric says to Paige. 'Cuz I know that was her on the phone, sounding all superior. *I'm trying to reach Eric Fergus.* Instead of treating me like I'm the housekeeper, like when I answered the door all those years ago, now she's acting like I'm a secretary or maybe just a random housemate. Bitch.

It's all I can do not to cry. How dare she? Eric and I have been together for five years now (if you include the year he traveled to Asia), which is a lot longer than she had him. How can she have so little respect for Eric and me that she thinks she can come barging into our lives like that? *And how can he let her?*

I try to watch the TV show, but now I don't give a crap about reality-show Vanessa versus ON-dree-uh. All I care about is real-life Vanessa versus *Paige*. And her damned kid. Who's got to be pretty big by now. Not that it's the kid's fault, but . . . *Shit!* Now I'm crying!

I turn off the TV so I can hear when he stops talking.

I take a tissue from a pink box. Eric has stopped buying me purple tissues. I wipe my puffy eyes and blow my snotty nose. Oh, yeah, I am one sexy mama.

After maybe ten minutes, I can't hear anything through the door, even when I press my ear up against it. I turn the knob slowly and push.

He's still on the bed, the library book lying next to him. When he looks across the room, it's like he doesn't even see me because he's too busy thinking about *her*.

"What did Paige want?" My voice shakes.

"Huh?" He blinks at me.

"That was Paige, wasn't it?"

He squints like I'm speaking a different language.

"On the phone?" he asks.

"Yes. On the phone."

He blinks some more. "No."

I let out a ton of air. I hadn't even known I was holding my breath. I feel relieved for like half a second, but then I look at his face and think: *Ohmigod, another girl? Someone from even further back in his past? Or, someone new?*

"Who was that, Eric?"

It takes him a while to say anything. Finally, he goes, "A long time ago, back when I was in med school, there was this time when I needed money."

Okay, now I'm confused. I say, "Uh-huh." Because I don't know what else to say.

He goes, "My parents paid for college, but for med school I had to take out all these loans. I thought I could get a part-time job, but between classes and labs and studying, there just weren't enough hours in the day. I was barely sleeping as it was. I could've asked my parents for money, they would've given me some, but I felt like I should do this on my own. And this guy Larry, he's a neurologist in Portland now, I don't think you ever met him, he said he knew an easy way to get cash."

He rubs his hands over his face.

This conversation isn't going at all the way I expected it to. What comes to mind is upsetting, but not surprising. You can't open *People* magazine or sit through a half hour of E! without hearing about people getting hooked on Vicodin or Percocet. In medical school, Eric would have had access to all kinds of stuff.

"Did you sell drugs, Eric?"

His eyes widen. "No! Of course not."

I exhale. Even laugh a little. My boyfriend was never a dealer.

"I sold my sperm," he says.

He did not just say that.

When I can speak, I say, "So you were a . . ."

"Donor."

This should be funny. If it were happening to someone else it would be hysterical. All those hours I'd spent looking at the sperm donor sites—! Once of those men might have been Eric. If only I'd known his number, maybe I could have had his baby, after all.

This is so not funny. If only he'd made money selling Percocet instead. Or maybe semiautomatic weapons. Anything but this.

"Larry—my friend. We went to donate together, but he got turned down. Too short. I was at the very bottom limit."

"Who was that woman on the phone?" My gut hurts.

"She was someone who used it. Bought it."

"She had your child." I can barely say the words.

"No! He's not my child. He was conceived with my sperm, but he's not mine. And anyway, it's possible there was a screwup, we'd need a DNA test to confirm. But based on the information she gave me, it looks like the boy is . . ." His voice trails off.

"A boy. She had your son."

"He's not my—"

Suddenly I am more pissed off than I've ever been in my life.

"You let a complete stranger have your child, but you won't have one with me! *A complete stranger!* What is wrong with me? What is wrong with *you*? Do you have any idea how many kids you might have running around? I cannot fucking believe this!"

If I had anyplace to go, I would have taken off. But this is my home. I sit on the bed and sob.

Eric takes me in my arms and says, "I'm sorry I'm sorry I'm sorry." He says, "He's not my child. It's just some cells. I'll take the DNA test. Maybe he's not even mine."

He fetches the pink tissue box from the living room. He says, "Shh, Shh," and finally, "I love you."

# Wendy

I've switched to lactose-free milk and soy cheese (that didn't go over so well; Harrison said it smelled like dog farts), but it doesn't seem to make any difference. If anything, the twins are every crankier than usual because ice cream always bought me a good twenty minutes of peace, especially if I doused it in chocolate syrup.

To make things worse, Harrison has a new friend. Or maybe I should say a new "friend." Dodie is ten years old. He leaves the door open and tracks dirt on the carpet. He tells poop jokes and engages Harrison in battles fought with shoes, blocks, and plastic knives (the stainless ones are kept out of his reach). And, get this, Dodie is *invisible*.

"Harrison has an imaginary friend," I tell my mother when she calls for our twice-weekly chat.

"Really! That's so funny, because I was just talking to your sister, and Jade has an imaginary friend too! Tracey says the books say that's a sure sign of a creative mind!"

I roll my eyes. Sure. In addition to being beautiful, graceful, and highly, highly verbal, my four-year-old niece, Jade, is creative. Since my sister, Tracey, lives in Texas (with her handsome and successful husband), it's been two years since I saw perfect Jade, who, I must say, was a perfectly awful two-year-old. However, my mother assures me that was just a normal and necessary phase. Nowadays, little Jadey is an absolute delight!

No, really. My mother said that. My dad can be kind of moody and edgy, but my mother is straight out of a Disney movie. Either she's just got this really, really sweet nature, or she's been taking mood-altering drugs for the past forty years. Either way, I love her to death—and not just because every time my kids act out during her visits, she believes me when I say that they're: (a) coming down with something; (b) sensitive to any change in their routine; or (c) feeling sad because they know Gammie and Pop-Pop will be leaving soon.

My mother continues, "Tracey said Jade's imaginary friend is a princess who lives in a magic kingdom called Sha-sha. Isn't that precious? And she has two imaginary horses, one called Shimmer and the other Sparkle."

Upstairs, Something crashes. Harrison growls, "DODIE! LOOK WHAT YOU MADE ME DO!"

"What kind of person is Harrison's imaginary friend?" my mother asks.

I think: *A sociopath.* I say: "Just a kid."

---

It's beginning to feel like Donor 613—Eric Fergus—is my imaginary friend: real but not-real. I keep thinking about him. It's weird. In all these years, I've hardly ever tried to picture him or imagine the sound of his voice. But the other night the kids were watching TV and apparently something was hysterical, because they began laughing in their identical wheeze-snort way that has always made me smile, and I thought: *Does he laugh that way, too?* There are other things I wonder. Are his fingers long and slender like Sydney's? Does he share Harrison's fascination with insects? I'm assuming he doesn't share Sydney's princess preoccupation, but you never know.

Friday and Saturday pass without any word from Laura. Sunday evening, after Darren has settled in with *his* imaginary friends on the computer and the children have gone to bed (with less fuss than usual—maybe the lactose-free milk is making a difference after all), I call her home number, which she included when she e-mailed pictures (*lots* of pictures) of her son.

---

"Did you talk to Eric Fergus?" Saying his name out loud feels weird. Forbidden.

I am sitting at the built-in kitchen desk, which is covered with bills and announcements and kindergarten forms, several of which require my immediate attention.

Laura says, "I did."

"And? Is he our guy?"

"Yes. At least I think so." She doesn't sound excited. "We need a paternity test to confirm. I found a lab near him that would do the test, but he hasn't agreed."

"Does that mean he doesn't want to give you more of his . . . you know. Man juice?"

"I haven't asked him yet," she says, not even pausing to chuckle at my use of the phrase "man juice." "I . . . he hasn't gotten back to me. When I called Thursday night, a woman answered. His wife, I assume. And he sounded really uncomfortable. So I thought we could talk when he was alone. But now I think, maybe I screwed everything up. By calling out of the blue, I mean. I should have sent him a letter instead. I shouldn't have taken him by surprise like that."

I am shocked to hear Laura Cahill sound anything less than

self-composed. It makes me like her . . . even if she doesn't think "man juice" is funny.

"Are you going to call him again?" I ask.

"Oh, yeah. I'll give it a couple of days and try again. I don't give up easily." She laughs. (And that wasn't even funny.)

"Did you ask him about lactose?" I say.

"No, I, uh . . . didn't get around to that."

"What did he sound like?" I ask. In other words, *Who is this man?* What is it about him, about his genes, that made my children the way they are?

Laura says, "Just—normal. His voice was medium deep. No accent or anything."

"No. I mean, did he sound edgy? Irritable?"

Suddenly I'm irritable. I go to the freezer and rummage around.

"He sounded surprised," she says. "Like a guy who'd just been told he had a child he never knew about."

I freeze—and not just because I'm standing in front of an open freezer. "Three children."

"Excuse me?"

"*Three* children were born from his . . ." Don't say "man juice." "Donations. That we know about. Didn't you tell him about mine?"

So this Eric guy knows about perfect Ian but not my imperfect twins? Even though their very flaws were probably written in his DNA? While I know I have no right to be angry—Laura Cahill owes me nothing, after all—fury flood my veins . . . just as my hand lands on an unopened sleeve of Girl Scout Thin Mints. That gives me strength.

"Give me his number."

"What?"

"His number. I'll call him." I pull out the column of cold cookies and shut the freezer.

"I don't think that—"

"Give it to me. And that DNA place, the lab. For the paternity test. Give me that information too. You spent all this time tracking him down. You can't just let it go. No offense, but you've already blown your first impression, so give me a shot. Besides, there are questions I need answered."

"If his wife answers—"

"I'll say I have a wrong number."

---

Half a sleeve of frozen Thin Mints gives me the courage I need to call Eric Fergus. I take the phone to the backyard. Since the computer room—also known as Darren's Happy Place (at least by me, in the safety of my own mind)—faces the front of the house, Darren won't hear anything. Not that we ever open the windows, anyway; the temperature is too extreme. It hit ninety today, but the evening is chilly. One of the many weird things about Arizona: with no moisture in the air, once the sun goes down, the temperature drops *like that.*

Ketchup streaks darken the glass table next to the mesh safety fence that surrounds our tiny pool. For dinner I prepared a nutritious spread of chicken nuggets, oven fries, canned corn, and Gatorade, but no crumbs dirty the table or the concrete underneath. Desert birds are more thorough than an army of Dustbusters.

My hands shake as I push in the numbers Laura gave me. As feared, the wife answers. Screw the wrong-number business: I hang up and retreat to the kitchen. All is quiet upstairs.

Wait. Hold. Were there any more Thin Mints in the freezer?

Just like that, life is good again.

Thirty minutes and another half sleeve later, when my cookie intake has moved me from self-assured to self-loathing, I return to the outside table (wearing a jacket and carrying a sponge this time; birds are one thing, but I despise ketchup-sucking ants). *It is a far better thing I do than . . .* One ring. Two rings. Three rings—

"Hello?"

Damn. It's the wife.

I hang up. This reunion business must wait until tomorrow. I'm out of cookies.

I'm about to yank open the back slider when the phone rings in my distressingly chubby hand.

"You just called?" she says.

Crap! My first instinct is to hang up, but then I realize that she knows where to find me. I shut the door and take a step backward.

"Ex . . . cuse me?" I pace the concrete and do my best to sound like I don't know what she's talking about.

"Someone just hung up on me. I called star-sixty-nine and got this number."

Double crap! I hate star-sixty-nine!

"Oh! That." I force a laugh. "I was trying to call someone and I dialed the wrong number."

The moon is so bright, it's like daylight out here. It makes me feel exposed.

"You called twice," she says.

I don't bother trying to play stupid. "Yes. Sorry. I must have written it down wrong."

"Who were you trying to reach?"

"Somebody else. Nobody. A man." I resume my pacing.

"Eric?" she asks.

Whoa! I wasn't expecting that. I stop pacing.

"Um . . . maybe?"

"This is about the sperm thing, isn't it?"

My craftiness deserts me. "The, um . . . it's, um . . . Yes."

She doesn't say anything. There goes my brilliant first impression.

I sit at the glass table and keep my voice down, even though Darren, upstairs on the other side of the house with Sims friends, can't possibly hear me.

"I don't want to make any trouble," I say.

"Tell me about your son," she says.

"Just my son? Harrison's, um. He's very creative." And then I get it. "Oh. You're thinking of Laura. Ian's mother. I'm Wendy. With the twins. Though I guess Laura didn't mention them."

She doesn't say anything.

I say, "I'm married, so my kids have a dad. Not that I don't think it's not okay that Laura's not—whatever. I just don't want you to think I'm looking for anything on that front."

She still doesn't say anything.

"Hello?" I say to the dark desert air.

"Twins?" She starts to cry. Triple crap!

All of a sudden I feel horrible for this woman on the end of the phone. "Nobody's trying to take anything away from you! Not your husband or your family or, or—anything."

"He's not my husband! I don't have a family!" She cries harder.

I really, really, really want to hang up, to end this for both of us. There is some shuffling on the line, and then a new, deeper voice comes on.

"Um, hello?" It's him. *It's him!*

"Is this . . . Eric Fergus?" Without meaning to, I drop my voice to a whisper when I say his name.

"Yes." He doesn't sound so happy to be Eric Fergus right now, not that I can blame him.

"Congratulations. You're the donor of twins!"

I've never been real good at breaking things gently.

"Oh my God." His voice—which, as Laura told me, is medium deep and otherwise normal—turns hoarse. "So there are . . . so you're a different . . . I assumed you were . . ."

Nerves make me babble.

"I'm not Laura Cahill. She's the lawyer with the perfect child. Who called you Friday. I'm mommy number two. Wendy Winder.

Laura found me through—it doesn't matter. I'm the . . . my kids are not perfect. On the plus side, at least for you, I live in Arizona, so I'm not going to be running into you at the grocery store or anything. Speaking of which, have you ever had any issues with lactose?"

"With—what?" In the background, the woman is crying. Now I feel bad. More bad. Badder. But I can't let that stop me. I need answers. I take a deep breath and try again.

"Lactose. Dairy. When you drink milk, do you get, you know. Aggressive?"

"From milk? No. I don't really get aggressive from anything. Excuse me, I'm just, this is just . . . you've got two of my kids? I mean, kids from my, um . . ."

"Sperm. Yes. Assuming you are Donor 613. I bought my supply from the Southern California Cryobank, six years ago. Please. Just tell me. When you were a child—what were you like?"

"Um. Childish?"

That is so not helpful.

"Did you ever hit anyone?" I press.

"Well, yeah. Of course. I have two older brothers. They hit me, I'd hit them back. It was a survival-of-the-fittest thing. So your twins are . . ."

"Five. Girl and boy. Sydney and Harrison. What about other aggressive behaviors? Did you pinch, kick, bite? Spit? Maybe you banged your head against the wall?"

"So you bought my, um . . ."

"Man juice."

He laughs. Not with a whole lot of joy, but still. I've got to give him credit.

"Right," he says. "You bought my, uh, man juice, what? Six years ago?"

"Right."

"Because I donated . . . it wasn't that many times . . . but I donated three years before that. I guess I would've guessed it would all be gone by then."

"We tried another donor first—one IUI and two in vitros—and it didn't take. But your boys. One shot and—bingo. Twins. So thank you for that. Today you are a man. But like I was saying. I do have some questions. About your childhood, primarily. How about throwing things? Did you do any of that? I'm talking little objects. Toys, pencils . . . food. Did you break dishes? Did your mother have to hide the knives?"

"Of course not!"

The woman in the background has gone silent.

"Do any of your relatives have food allergies?" I ask.

"Do my . . . what?"

"Food allergies. Any family history?"

"I have no idea . . . So I, what you're saying is—I was your second choice?"

"You shouldn't dwell on that. Your boys got the job done, and that's what mattered."

He is quiet. I am quiet. Not good: I can't stand silence and tend to blurt out the first thing that comes to mind. Such as: "So. Have you ever been in prison?"

"No!"

God, I'm drenched. Sweat and fear and . . . excitement. It's all too much. I must have more questions. Oh my God. Of course! I'm supposed to be helping Laura.

I say, "Laura—the other mother—she wants to meet you. Just a brief little, you know, meeting."

"I'm sorry. I just can't."

"Maybe you can do a paternity test, at least? So we can at least know. You too. Surely you want to know? Maybe you'll get lucky. Maybe we've got the wrong guy."

"Okay," he says.

"Really?"

That was way too easy.

---

After I turn off the phone, I sit there shivering for a while, listening to a pack of coyotes yelping in the moonlight.

I feel weird—sort of numb. Eric Fergus's voice echoes in my head, but it is the voice of a stranger. He is nothing to me. Nothing to my family.

A light turns on upstairs. Darren has gone into our bedroom. I hurry into the kitchen, turn on the dishwasher, turn off the lights, check the front door.

I meet Darren, eyes weary from too many hours in front of the computer, coming out of the bathroom. He is wearing a T-shirt and cotton pajama pants. His breath smells of peppermint toothpaste.

I slip my arms around him. He stiffens for an instant and then embraces me. I inhale peppermint and fabric softener and Darren, his underlying scent the same as it was on the day we fell in love.

We stand there for a few moments, still except for our breathing. I close my eyes, remember the past. Finally, he releases me.

"Early day tomorrow," he says.

I nod.

He kisses the top of my head and climbs into bed.

# 9

## Laura

I still don't understand how Wendy Winder got Eric Fergus to agree to a paternity test. She sent me an e-mail late that night:

**RE: That thing we talked about**

He said he'd do it. The test. I gave him the info. He said he'd go by there tomorrow afternoon. So you might want to call them in the a.m. and make arrangements. Can you tell me what the results are? E-mail is usually best, but I can also talk between 9:30—11:30 a.m. on weekdays.

---

I responded, of course.

**RE: RE: That thing we talked about**

Dear Wendy,

I cannot overstate the extent of my appreciation. I hope it is not causing him any marital tension. I will make the necessary arrangements and advise you of the results.

Warmly,
Laura

———————

The next morning, I received her reply.

**RE: RE: RE: That thing we talked about**

Oh, he's not married. That was just his crazy girlfriend on the phone.

———————

Now, driving home from work a week later, I rehearse the conversation I plan to have with Eric Fergus.

"A genetic counselor from the DNA lab called me this afternoon to confirm your paternity of my son."

Too cold.

"I understand your ambivalence about the situation, but I hope you will greet the confirmation of your paternity as happy news."

Absurd. He will not be happy.

"Congratulations! You're the father of a bouncing eight-year-old boy!"

*No! He is not Ian's father!*

When I walk into the kitchen and see Ian sitting on the floor, clutching his knees and sobbing, I forget all about Eric Fergus.

"What . . ."

Carmen slumps on a kitchen chair near him, looking helpless. "The yardman. He leave the gate open."

Ian tilts his head up. Tears slick his red face; a grimace distorts his beautiful mouth. He doesn't cry much, but when he does, he makes no sound.

My chest tightens. "The chickens."

"Just one," Carmen says. "When he come home from school, Ian go outside, he let the chickens out of the coop, he give them food. Then we come back inside. We think the chickens are okay in the yard. We think the fence is closed."

"Is it just missing, or . . ."

Carmen shakes her head. "A car. The Davies boy—you know, the teenager down the street. He drive too fast." She shakes her head.

Glass sliders lead to the backyard. There's movement in the coop, but between the chicken wire and the shadows, I can't tell which chickens are there.

"Which one was it?"

"The brown."

"One of the Rhodies?"

Ian looks up, his red face streaked with tears. "Sam!"

"Oh, no!"

We've lost our only Americana, the plainest of the chickens but the source of our precious green eggs. I sink to the ground next to my little son and take him in my arms. His body convulses in a steady rhythm.

"I love her," he says, his voice barely audible.

"I know." Now I'm crying. And I never cry. I tilt my face so Carmen can't see.

"I love her!" he says again.

"I know."

"I tell the yardman," Carmen says. "I tell him, you no leave the gate open. Three times, four times, I tell him."

"I know you did," I say.

"That boy, he drive too fast," Carmen says.

"You can go now, Carmen." When I realize how that sounds, I force myself to look up and add, "It's after five-thirty, and I'm sure you want to get home. I know this day has been . . . stressful. Thank you. For everything you did today."

She goes off to the laundry room to retrieve her handbag. When she comes back, she looks toward the front door and then back at me. "There's someone you can call? The yardman, maybe?"

I shake my head with confusion. Does she really expect me to call the gardener to complain about the gate right now?

"You want it gone soon," she says. "Before it gets dark and someone else hits it."

"Want what gone?"

She points toward the front of the house—in the direction of the street. And then I understand.

"Oh my God. Is Sam still out there?"

She nods. "You want . . . you want me to . . ."

"No, Carmen. That's okay. You go home. I'll deal with it." For some reason, it feels like disposing of the dead chicken is something I need to do myself.

"Okay," she says, her relief obvious. She forces something like a smile. "Your dinner is in the oven. Fruit and green salad in the refrigerator."

"Thank you, Carmen." In a vain attempt to turn the conversation back to normal, I ask, "What are we having tonight?"

She bites her lip. "Roast chicken."

---

Ian insists on coming with me to get Sam. The body lies near the curb in front of our elderly next-door neighbor's house. The boy who hit Sam lives farther down the road.

I expect the body to be mangled and maybe even flattened, but it is worse than that. Blood and feathers stain the road. The chicken's head, only partially attached to its body, bends back at an unnatural angle. Guts spill from its abdomen.

I never liked skittish Sam for more than her eggs, but pity spikes my heart. I take a deep breath, thankful there is no rot-smell yet, and open a black trash bag.

Ian sniffles.

"You okay, buddy?"

He nods and hugs himself.

My hands shake and sweat against the black plastic. My stomach twists with revulsion. For the first time since my divorce, I think, *I wish I had a husband.*

The upside-down bag positioned over the chicken's body, I cradle the form through the plastic, lift, flip, and knot. My arms quiver. I force myself to breathe.

We trudge back to the house in silence. Steps from the trash can, it hits me: "Should we give her a funeral?"

Ian nods.

In the backyard, we choose a burial spot in front of the avocado tree. I place the bag on the scruffy grass and retrieve a shovel from the garage.

The clay soil, packed tight, resists my efforts. I heave from exertion. Ian takes a turn, but his skinny arms are even weaker than mine, and we can't dig a big enough hole.

We move to a softer, sunny spot where I sometimes plant tomatoes. Soon, we have a hole big enough to plant a shrub—or bury a chicken.

"Her sisters should be here," Ian says. "To say good-bye."

As he opens the coop, I say, "Is the side gate latched?"

He races to the side of the house; the gate is closed.

The chickens squawk at me, miffed to find me empty-handed. Ian, the black plastic bag, and I form a triangle around the hole while Salt, Pepper, Rusty, and Red go off in search of grubs.

"Do you think they miss her?" Ian asks.

"Not really. Chickens aren't like—"

"I think they do."

"You're probably right. Do you want to . . . say something? About what Sam meant to you?"

"You first," he says, tears dripping down his soft cheeks.

I say, "Sam was a good bird. She was curious and loved to peck around the yard. She gave us beautiful green eggs and we will miss her."

Eyes squeezed shut, Ian clasps his hands in front of him.

"You ready?" I ask.

He nods and sniffles and finally begins to speak. "Whenever I feel lonely, I come out here to talk to Sam. All the chickens are part of our family, but Sam was special. She listened. And now, and now . . ." He starts crying full force, which makes me cry to see him so distressed. "She was my sister," he says. "I lost my sister."

I'm not crying over the chicken anymore or even over Ian's sadness over losing the chicken. I'm crying because he just called a flea-ridden, pea-brained creature his sister.

The hole could have been bigger. After I've placed the trash bag at the bottom and covered it with dirt, a corner of black plastic peaks out. Using the shovel, I scrape some more soil on top until it forms a kind of mound.

Ian crowns the grave with a large rock. He kneels on the dirt and says, "Good-bye, Sam." His shoulders shake.

All of a sudden I get a vision of Ian years from now, gray-haired, standing all alone at my fresh gravesite, sobbing, with no one to share his grief. My imagination is being melodramatic, I realize. In all likelihood, Ian will share his life with a wife and children.

Then again, plenty of people stay single or divorce; look at me.

Ian stands up and brushes dirt from his knees.

"Let's go eat." I hold out my hand.

He takes it.

———

The house smells of roast chicken cooked about thirty minutes too long. I consider turning off the oven and taking Ian out to Del Taco, but I don't want to make a big deal out of our dinner. Ever since we got the chickens, I've been afraid he'd refuse to eat poultry, but he either hasn't made the connection or doesn't care.

I set the chicken on a platter on the counter and begin slicing. Ian comes up next to me.

"What is that?"

"Dinner."

A slice of perfect white meat falls on the plate. I insert the knife back into the bird.

"But what is dinner?"

"It's a . . . roast."

"Oh. Okay."

For what feels like the first time all day, I exhale.

———

With all the excitement, I almost forget about Eric Fergus. Ian doesn't. After we snuggle up on his bed for half an hour, reading, I turn off the light and tuck him in.

"Do you think Sam is in heaven?" he asks.

"I'm sure she is."

"Regular heaven or chicken heaven?"

"I think there's only one heaven. And she's up there, laying green eggs for the angels."

He nods. I kiss his forehead and start to leave.

"Mom?"

I stop at the door. "Yes?"

"Will I meet my donor when I go to heaven?"

"I . . . I . . ."

"Or do you only see people you know?"

"Your donor isn't dead, honey."

"I know. But someday he will be. And someday I will be."

"You have a long life ahead of you, buddy. A long, long life."

---

Eric answers in the middle of the first ring. "Hello?"

"You have to meet my son," I blurt, completely forgetting the things I'd planned to say. "I know it's uncomfortable and you wish we'd just go away. And maybe you wish you'd never donated in the first place. But the fact is, you did donate, and now there's this child, this boy, this amazing person. And he needs to see you. He needs to know that you're real. I can't let him—you can't let him— walk around for the rest of his life with all these unanswered questions about who he is, where he came from. You have to meet him."

There is a long pause.

"Which one of you is this?" he asks.

"Laura. Ian's mother."

"The lawyer."

"Yes."

"The other one has twins."

"Wendy. Yes."

He clears his throat. "I need to think about it."

"That's what you said last time."

"I'm still thinking."

I say, "I got the results. The paternity test. He's yours. Well, not yours, no, that isn't what I mean, but he's got half your DNA."

He doesn't respond.

"Look," I say. "My son just lost his pet chicken, and I just—he can't take another disappointment right now."

"You have chickens?"

"Five. Yes. Well—four now. So please. If you could just—"

"What happened?"

"With the chicken?"

"Yeah."

"It got hit by a car."

"Ouch."

"Um. Yes. Ouch indeed. So . . . you'll meet with us?"

"I didn't say that."

"But will you?"

He pauses. Sighs. "I gotta be honest with you. I really don't want to."

My jaw tenses. "Okay, then. I'll be honest with you. I really don't care."

He is very quiet. I wonder if I've gone too far.

"It would mean a lot to my son," I say.

He says nothing.

"We're not looking to bring you into our lives," I say. "We just have some questions. And he has a need to see you, to talk to you."

He is still quiet.

"It would be entirely on your terms," I say. "When you want. Where you want."

The line crackles slightly. Finally, he speaks. "What kind of chicken was it?"

"What kind of . . . oh. An Americana."

"Are those the ones that lay green eggs? My neighbor had one of those when I was a kid."

"Yes. That's it."

He reverts back to his silence, until, finally: "I could Skype your son."

"You mean—over the computer? Videoconferencing?"

"Yeah."

It would be hard to get a sperm sample that way, but it might be a good way for Ian to meet his donor without it being too close, too real.

I say, "How about tomorrow?"

# Vanessa

Pammy is so shocked she can't even eat. "Eric. Your Eric."

Melva can always eat, but she finishes chewing her bite of grilled stuffed chicken burrito (we're at Taco Bell) before she blurts, "Why would anyone want Eric's sperm when they can have the guy from *Twilight*?"

"You can't really get the guy from *Twilight*," I say, jabbing my Diet Coke with a straw.

"Close enough."

"The werewolf or the vampire?" Pammy asks. "I forget which one you liked."

"Did she get some kind of a discount?" Melva asks. "The mother?"

———

That night, Eric squeezes blue, bubblegum-flavored paste on his toothbrush. "I'll be home late tomorrow. Like, sevenish."

He puts the brush in his mouth and begins to scrub, his eyes straight ahead.

I try to hold his eyes in the mirror, but it is impossible. My stomach hurts.

I say, "Where are you going? Or . . . don't I want to know?"

He scrubs some more. Spits. "Probably not."

He turns on the sink and leans forward to get a mouthful of water from the faucet. He swishes the water around his mouth and spits again.

"I'll wait till you get home to eat dinner," I tell him.

---

I never thought things would turn out like this. The night I met Eric, I was at a bar in L.A. with my friend Tanya and her boyfriend Creepy Cris. Originally Tanya and I were going out in Santa Monica to talk, for the five-thousandth time, about what a jerk Cris was. She would make excuses for his jerkiness. I would tell her that she was too good for him. Blah, blah, blah.

This was getting old. In the year since they'd started going out, Creepy Cris had broken up with Tanya once, cheated on her twice, and been busted for a DUI. Still, if I had to choose between spending a night hearing about Cris or spending a night *with* Cris, I'd pick hearing.

At the last minute, Tanya had called to say she and Cris had had this really long, really amazing talk. He said he felt threatened by her girlfriends, which Tanya totally bought. So she goes, "I know it was just going to be me and you tonight, but is it okay if Cris comes with?"

That was so obviously my cue to say, "Don't worry about me! You guys need time alone! I'll eat donuts and watch reality TV." No way. It was Saturday night. We were going to Santa Monica. Cris was *not* going to mess things up for me.

He messed things up, anyway. Tanya said there was a really

awesome bar with live music near Cris's apartment in Culver City, and we should just go there instead of dealing with Santa Monica traffic. Translation: Cris couldn't drive anywhere because his license got suspended with the DUI, and this was the only place within walking distance.

Tanya and I worked together at Sears—she was in men's and boys', and I was in housewares. Tanya met Cris when he returned a dress shirt that had obviously been worn. I mean, come on—there was ketchup on the sleeve. Later he admitted that he'd worn it to his cousin's wedding, but that day Tanya had given him the benefit of the doubt. After that, she continued to give him the benefit of the doubt—and to cry to me about how she and Cris were meant to be together "if he could only see that."

"It's my girl's birthday," Cris told the waitress in the dark, stuffy, not-awesome bar, speaking loudly to be heard over the guy playing guitar on the little stage. Cris had his arm around Tanya. She giggled. It wasn't her birthday.

The guitar was okay for background music, kind of like what we played at Sears. I didn't even mind that the speakers were up too loud because it made it easier to tune out Cris.

"Happy birthday!" the waitress shouted to Tanya.

Tanya giggled some more.

"So what you got goin' on?" Cris asked. "You know, for birthdays. You got a free piece of cake, or maybe a special drink . . ."

"No. Sorry."

"Ah, come on . . . Please? For me?" Cris leaned back and spread his bulky, tattooed arms. Cris was a personal trainer. Tanya thought that was just So! Amazing!—even though it turned out that the gym was a really convenient place for him to pick up bimbos.

The waitress laughed. "I'll talk to the bartender. See if he can work something out."

"Awesome! You're *awesome*!"

The guy onstage stopped playing for a minute, and then he said,

"Here's something I wrote." He tested a couple of notes on the guitar and started playing a song that sounded exactly like the last one.

Cris yelled, "Rock on, dude!" He must have done some front-loading on the booze. We hadn't even gotten our first round yet.

The waitress brought Tanya this creamy drink with a chocolate liqueur. "Bartender calls it a liquid chocolate cake." Because they didn't have any candles, the bartender had stuck an umbrella in the drink. "So you could blow on that," the waitress told Tanya.

Cris said something about what else Tanya could blow. Of course he did. Then he asked the waitress for matches and set the umbrella on fire.

It could have been a lot worse. When the umbrella flared, Tanya and I screamed. The waitress threw a napkin on the flame and it went out. Cris laughed his stupid head off. The waitress stopped smiling at him.

Tanya said, "It's not funny," and burst into tears.

Cris said, "Oh, baby," and then asked the waitress for another free drink since this one was ruined. She said no.

When the guitar guy finished his song, Cris said, "Hey! Dude! Play 'Happy Birthday.' My girl's twenty-one today!"

The guitar guy ignored him, played another song, and then took a break. Tanya stopped crying and Cris stopped being loud. Instead he started whispering in her ear and kissing her neck.

When Cris and Tanya started making out, I just had to get away, so I took my drink and went to the bar. There were only a few stools, and it wasn't until I sat down that I realized I was next to the guitar guy.

"Happy birthday," he said. He was wearing a short-sleeved plaid shirt over a white T-shirt, faded jeans, and sneakers.

"It's not my birthday." I was wearing tight jeans and a shirt that showed off my boobs.

"Yeah, I know." He didn't look at my boobs. I couldn't decide whether I was flattered or insulted.

"It's not my friend's birthday either. Her boyfriend just said that."

"Why?"

"Because he's an asshole."

The guitar guy grinned. The smile lit up his whole face. I thought, *He's cute. Not my usual type, but maybe that's a good thing.*

Confession: one of the reasons I hated Cris so much was because he was my type. He had a great body, he was a flirt, he seemed charming until you got to know him. He reminded me of at least three ex-boyfriends. I kept telling Tanya. "He's not going to marry you. He's not going to change. Trust me, I've been there." But she wouldn't listen.

"I like your music," I told the guitar guy, even though I'd already forgotten what it sounded like.

"Yeah?"

"Yeah. I'm Vanessa, by the way."

"Eric."

"Hi, Eric."

"Hi, Vanessa."

We grinned at each other. Held each other's eyes. I thought, *I should feel nervous right now, but I don't.*

He asked how I knew Tanya, and I told him about Sears. He said he was getting tired of the music scene and was thinking about getting a regular job. Or maybe traveling. We talked about working with the public, how sometimes it was fun but that people could be real jerks.

We talked so long the bartender had to tell him to go back onstage. The next set, it was like he was singing just to me. It's not like anyone else was really listening, I guess, but he sang a couple of love songs and I just knew it: there was something between us.

When Eric finished it was after midnight. Tanya and Cris had long since stumbled out of the almost-empty bar. I felt bad for Eric, that no one seemed to be listening to him. When I said that to him, he just shrugged and said, "At this point, I'd be more surprised if anyone did pay attention."

We sat at a table and talked some more. He told me his father had died a couple of years earlier and he wasn't dealing with it very well. I told him mine had died when I was a kid and that you don't ever get over it, but at least you get used to it.

We stayed till last call. I thought he'd ask me to go home with him. I didn't know what I was going to say. But instead he just walked me to my car, which was parked down the street. He asked if I was okay to drive, and I said yeah.

He said good night and turned to go.

I said, "Wait." I was going to ask him if he wanted my phone number. Instead I kissed him. We held each other for a long, long time and then exchanged phone numbers. Later I asked him why he hadn't asked for mine in the first place. Was he just going to walk away and forget about me? He said he'd been planning to find me in the Sears houseware department the next day. He was going to buy some pots and pans and then ask if he could make me dinner. How weird: Eric's most romantic gesture is something he never actually did.

Five months later, we went to Cris and Tanya's wedding. Eric offered to play guitar for free, but they said thanks, they had a DJ. Six months after that, Eric flew off to Asia, and I thought I'd never see him again. And then he came back and I stupidly thought he was mine.

# 11

## Laura

At six o'clock, Ian and I are in the office, sitting in our twin desk chairs, staring at the computer screen. We've left our half-eaten grilled cheese sandwiches in the kitchen. Dinner was early, and neither of us was very hungry (though after last night I appreciated Carmen's stab at a meat-free meal).

"How will we know when he's online?" Ian asks.

"We'll hear a beep. And then a message will pop up asking if we'll accept a video call."

I've used Skype at work, and the program was easy to set up on our home computer (a Mac that Ian and I supposedly share but that we both tacitly recognize as his since I've got my laptop from work). After our discussion last night, Eric Fergus and I set each other up as contacts.

"What if he doesn't call?" Ian asks.

"He'll call. Well—he'll Skype, anyway."

"But what if he doesn't?"

"Then we'll Skype him."

I've prepared a list of questions, most dealing with family and medical history, but with a few "fun facts" type inquiries that Ian might enjoy, such as, "Did you have any pets when you were a kid?" And, "What did you want to be when you grew up?"

Which reminds me: if Eric Fergus dropped out of medical school, what career path did he ultimately take? I make a note to ask him.

But he doesn't call. Or Skype. Ian sits very, very still, staring at the screen. His Angels baseball shirt, two sizes too big, makes his frame look even slighter than it is. Without explanation, he changed into the shirt after dinner, before we settled in front of the laptop. Ian doesn't even like baseball (the shirt was a gift), but I think he has it in his mind that males bond over sports. Which I suppose they do.

At six-fifteen, I click Eric's name on my Skype screen and select the green "video call" button. Ian watches without speaking. The computer beeps four times before a message pops up on the screen: *call failed.*

At six-sixteen, I dial his home number.

The woman answers. I refuse to feel bad about the intrusion. Had Eric Fergus Skyped us when he said he would, we could have avoided any awkwardness. Besides, according to Wendy, they're not even married.

"He's not here," the girlfriend informs me.

My jaw tenses with anger, but I strive to keep my tone professional. "Mr. Fergus and I had a Skype call scheduled for six P.M., but I haven't been able to reach him."

"I'll tell him you called." She hangs up without a good-bye.

"What did they say?" Ian asks.

"He's running late. We might have to reschedule."

Ian's eyes get shiny. Oh God. First the chicken, now this.

At six-thirty, I try to draw Ian out of the office with the promise of chocolate chip mint ice cream.

Still in his office desk chair, he asks, "Can we call again?"

"Not today, buddy. Maybe tomorrow."

I scoop chocolate chip mint ice cream into two big bowls and carry them to the couch. Ian pads out of the office and sits next to me.

I hand him the remote: "Your choice."

I know he will pick the Disney Channel and he does—but not before getting back up to open the office door as wide as it will go so we can hear the beep if anyone Skypes us.

The computer remains silent.

# Vanessa

Eric gets home a little before eight, his beat-up black laptop case slung over his shoulder. I can barely look him in the eye. I feel so betrayed, like he's been out having sex with another woman. And, worse, like I told him it was okay.

"I didn't make anything for dinner." My voice catches in my throat.

"We have any burritos left?"

I so do not feel like making jokes. I don't smile.

He puts his laptop case on the floor next to the couch and steps closer to me. I keep my eyes on the ground and try not to cry.

And then he goes, "I think we should get married."

Stunned, I check his face. He is smiling, just a little bit.

"For real?" I ask.

He nods.

"I, I . . ." I'm supposed to feel happy. Ecstatic. This is the moment I've been waiting, hoping, and praying for. And yet . . .

"I don't understand."

"I had an epiphany tonight," he says.

"Um . . ."

"I realized something."

My shoulders stiffen. "I know what 'epiphany' means." (Sort of.)

"Sorry," he says.

"I just don't get—I mean, you go Skype your kid. And then you come back and you . . ."

"I didn't Skype him," he says. "And he's not my kid. I mean, he's got my DNA. But that doesn't make him mine."

I say, "That lady called. His mother. I thought you were just late."

He shakes his head.

"But why?"

He takes me in his arms. "Because it would hurt you too much. This whole situation has been hurting you too much. And I keep doing things that make you feel bad, and . . ."

I squeeze him tight and wait for tears to fall. But they don't. Is that because I'm not sad? Or because I'm not happy?

"I realized something tonight," he says, still holding me. "I was on my way to Starbucks for the Skype call. It didn't seem right to do it from home. But I was still feeling like shit because of what it was doing to you, and it hit me. I donated sperm when I was, what? Twenty-three? That's young but not really—my parents got married at that age. And now this kid, he's eight already. All this time has passed and I'm thirty-two and still waiting for my life to begin. And, yeah, maybe I'm not going to have the kind of big career I always thought I'd have, in medicine or music or whatever, but I've got a steady job and a wonderful woman—and this is my life. And I just need to accept that."

I take a step back. I'm still not crying. "So what you're saying is that you'll settle for me?"

His face turns red. "No. Oh God. This is the worst proposal ever. I just meant my career. I guess I felt like I had to know what

I was doing for my life before I . . . whatever. But if I wait till . . . whatever, it could be too late and you might be gone. And that would be the biggest mistake I ever made."

He is totally right: this proposal sucks. He's had five years to come up with the perfect words, the perfect setting, the perfect *everything*, and this is what I get?

"Maybe I should just shut up," he says.

"Not yet."

He looks at me blankly.

"Ask me," I say.

"What?"

"Ask me."

Finally, he gets it. It's not too late to do this right. It's not too late for anything.

He takes my hands and looks into my eyes. "Vanessa Rodriguez, will you marry me?"

"Yes. I will."

We kiss.

I do not cry.

Together, we go into the kitchen to heat burritos. The phone is lying on the counter, right where I left it after speaking to that woman. Laura. The single mother.

"You should meet the kid," I say.

"What?"

"The kid. That little boy. You should meet him. Otherwise, he's always going to wonder . . . and maybe you will too. It's better to just do it."

"You're sure?"

"Positive."

He kisses my forehead. "You're the best. You know that?"

"I don't have to know it. Just you do."

# 13
## Wendy

"But what does the bug man do?" Harrison asks, peering out the back slider. Outside, the exterminator, wearing a beige jumpsuit with a tank strapped to his back, sprays the bottom of the stucco wall that separates our yard from the neighbors'. We are three days into spring break, and Harrison has already scouted two black widows and one brown recluse spider in our yard. It is time for some serious pesticides, the more toxic, the better.

I say, "The bug man makes the yard clean."

"So the yard is nice for the bugs?"

"Exactly."

Harrison presses his palms against the glass. "I want to be a bug man when I grow up."

I pat him on the head. "I was kind of hoping you'd be a surgeon, but hey. Whatever makes you happy."

The phone rings.

"I'LL GET IT." Harrison lunges.

Sydney, wearing a Snow White gown and a lopsided tiara, comes tearing in from the toy room. "NO, I'LL GET IT!"

"I WILL!"

"NO, I WILL!" Sydney grabs the phone from the cradle.

"MINE!" Harrison grabs Sydney's arm.

"YOU GOT IT LAST TIME—AARGH!"

Snow White is down for the count. She drops the phone. Harrison picks it up and presses the answer button. Score!

"Hello?"

He pauses. Sydney whimpers.

"Yes."

He pauses again. Sydney begins to howl, softly at first . . .

"Yes."

. . . and then not so softly.

"What?" Harrison scowls. *"What?"* He scowls some more and then hands me the phone. "I can't hear her." He goes back to looking out the window.

I cover the phone's mouthpiece and go into the toy room. Sydney's howl—it's really more of a shriek at this point—travels, but it's better than in the kitchen, and I can't go outside with the exterminator here.

"Hello?"

"Wendy? This is Laura Cahill. I hope it's okay to call. You said between nine-thirty and eleven-thirty . . ."

"Laura! Hi. My kids are on break this week. But it's fine. We're not doing anything right now." Can she hear Sydney screaming? Does it matter?

"Did you . . . did the DNA results come back?" I ask.

"They did." I hear her inhale. "Eric Fergus is Donor 613."

I feel unexpectedly light-headed and not just because my eardrums hurt. "Wow. I'd kind of assumed he was, but having it confirmed . . ."

"I know."

We are quiet for a moment.

I say, "So was he thrilled?"

"Ecstatic." She snorts. "But he agreed to meet with us. Ian and me, I mean. We're having lunch on Saturday. I thought you'd want to know."

"I do. Thank you."

Eric Fergus is nothing to me or my family. So why are my hands so damp?

Laura says, "Is there anything you want me to ask him?"

"I don't know. Just the usual medical stuff, I guess. Ethnic background. That sort of thing."

"Of course."

"And also . . ."

"Yes?"

"Can you take his picture? The kids . . . they might ask questions someday. You know, if it comes out that their dad is not, you know. Anyway, if you could take a picture . . ."

"Of course."

# Laura

My left eye is twitching, and I can't find Ian's shoes. As much as I'd like to blame the shoes for the twitch, clearly it comes from getting only three hours (tops) of fitful sleep last night. But the missing shoes aren't helping.

While I crawl around the living room, Ian plays with his Nintendo at the kitchen table, skinny legs swinging. He looks so handsome, in khaki shorts and an olive-green polo shirt. I made him change after he came down to breakfast in soccer shorts and an oversize, faded Maui T-shirt: appropriate attire for a day at the park but not for a restaurant lunch.

"You only get one chance to make a first impression," I told him—thinking, *And a last impression too.*

So far I've located one green flip-flop, one tan flip-flop, and one black soccer slide. I peer under the couch.

"What about your sneakers? Do you know where they are?"

"Uh-uh." His thumbs work the Nintendo.

I crawl over to a chair, put my face to the ground—nothing.

I say, "You might have to wear your dress shoes."

"That would look dumb."

"Not if you wore them with long pants."

"That would look dumb too." He looks up from the Nintendo. "Can't we just go get another pair of flip-flops at Target?"

"We don't have time."

He shrugs and goes back to his game.

Darn it! I should have insisted Ian lay out his clothes last night, as he does on school nights. (Okay, truth: usually I choose the clothes, but I try to involve him in the process as much as possible.)

As much as I hate to bother her on the weekend, I call Carmen. Since Ian was wearing his sneakers when she left last night, she won't know where they are, but she might be able to provide some clues about the flip-flops. In the name of tidiness, Carmen has a tendency to throw Ian's shoes into the nearest toy bin.

Her phone rings three, four, five times and then goes to voice mail. I hang up, and just like that, an image hits me: a green flip-flop, mixed in a basket with Ian's action figures. I saw it when I tucked him into bed last night.

I race up the stairs to his room, and there it is, right between Batman and a Ninja Turtle (Leonardo, I believe). Back in the kitchen, I hand Ian the pair. The sage-green flip-flops match his shirt, which in turn matches his eyes. Does Eric Fergus have eyes like that? No, his eyes are blue. That's one of the few bits of information the sperm bank gave out.

I grab my purse and we are out the door, just as I notice the damage that crawling around on the floor did to my beige linen skirt and sleeveless white cotton blouse. Oh, well. There's no time for ironing.

Ian buckles himself into the backseat, choosing the side with the DVD player. The dashboard clock reads 10:45. We are scheduled to meet Eric Fergus in Hermosa Beach at eleven-thirty. We should have just enough time.

My BlackBerry is fully charged, but I plug it into the car charger, anyway. That will make it easy to reach in case traffic is so heavy that I need to call Eric Fergus to say we'll be late. His numbers, added to my contact list last night, seem inappropriately intimate, mixed in with the information of so many people from my day-to-day life. Of course, maybe I'm just feeling that way because of last night's dream date, which I managed to squeeze into my three hours of sleep.

In the dream, I stood in a dim, red-walled room. A buff, shirtless man in blue jeans faced me from the other side. His hair was light brown, his eyes were pale. He looked like the kind of guy you see on shopping bags and billboards: shiny, sculpted . . . perfect.

Without saying anything, we crossed the room, met in the middle, and kissed. With tongue. After a while, we fell (or melted) to the floor, and rolled around for a bit. And then, on the soft red floor, we did it. We consummated the dream date, which would have been fine—wonderful, really. After all, it's not like I'm seeing any action during my waking hours. Only problem was that when I woke up, my entire body flushed and tingling, I realized that the man in my dream was Eric Fergus.

---

"You nervous?" I ask Ian as we pull onto the 91 Freeway, working hard to keep my tone casual.

"No," he says from the backseat.

"Good. Because there's no reason to be." My armpits are already damp, and it's not even seventy degrees outside.

"Can we go swimming after lunch?" he asks.

"What? You mean in the ocean?"

"Yeah."

"No! The water's too cold, and the air . . . besides, you don't even have a swimsuit or a towel."

"Details." He heard me say this once. Normally, it's funny coming from him. Today I have to force myself to laugh. There's no reason for me to be nervous. It's just lunch, after all. If only I were half as laid-back as my son. Or as his donor.

"Perhaps it's best for us to meet on neutral territory," I suggested to Eric Fergus once he agreed to get together. "A restaurant? Maybe down at the beach?"

"Sure," he replied.

"Is that okay?" I asked. "Because I want this meeting to be as comfortable for you as possible."

"Yeah, it's fine."

"I was thinking a Saturday afternoon," I said. "Unless Sunday is better."

"Either works."

Once I'd decided on Hennessey's, a pub in Hermosa Beach known for its ocean views, I called him back to confirm—using his cell-phone number this time.

"So we're all set, then?" I asked.

"Yup."

"And you'll be there?"

"Yeah. Sure. Of course."

"Um. I don't mean to be . . . it's just . . . last time, the Skype call—my son was very disappointed." It needed to be said. He needed to understand that standing us up a second time was not an option.

When he didn't respond, I said, "I need your assurances that, barring some unforeseen complication—by which I mean something major—you'll be at the restaurant when you say you will."

"Yeah. Sure."

"Because your girlfriend said it was okay to meet us."

"Yeah."

That's what he told me: that he'd bailed on the Skype call because his girlfriend was upset about it, and that he was agreeing to lunch because his girlfriend said he should.

Now, on the drive to the beach, I am trying to picture Eric Fergus's controlling girlfriend when a tan SUV swerves in front of me. I hit the brakes and steer toward the next lane, just missing a little orange car.

"Jerk!" I pound the horn. Adrenaline courses through my veins with such force I fear it will drip out of my ears.

"Mom!" Ian scolds.

"Sorry, buddy. I shouldn't have—I just got . . . sorry."

My armpits have soaked half-moon sweat marks onto my white cotton blouse.

But it's okay! Really! *Everything will be okay.* Ian will remember to put his napkin on his lap and chew with his mouth closed. We will tell stories about our life together: the vacations, the family dinners, the chickens.

*As you can see, Ian and I have a healthy, autonomous relationship with no desire or need for ongoing contact with you. We just have one very small request . . .*

I'll hold off on asking for more sperm till we're done with the meal. It's not the kind of thing you discuss over food. Besides, by then we'll be more comfortable with each other. He'll have seen what a devoted mother I am and what a great kid Ian is: so sweet and funny and smart. Such a good student . . . at least most of the time.

To get my mind off of our lunch, I say, "So buddy, when we get home, we're going to get right to work on your times tables."

"Tomorrow," he says.

"Good idea," I say. "We'll go over them today, and then we can do it again tomorrow. Right?"

"Mm."

"You've got the test on Tuesday, remember. This time you're going to ace it. Right?" He hadn't aced it last time. Actually, he'd failed it, his paper coming home with a line for a parent's signature and a hastily drawn sad face.

"Can I watch a DVD?" he asks, his hand already poised over the play button.

"Yes. But when we get home . . ."

"I'll feed the chickens," he says.

"And do your times tables."

He laughs. "Oh, yeah."

---

Thanks to the carpool lane, we make wonderful time—until the lane ends and we're forced into the sluggish mass of cars.

I hate being late. There's no excuse for it. If we had just left the house fifteen minutes earlier, as originally planned. If I had only set Ian's clothes out last night. If only we didn't live in a place with such hideous traffic. If only, if only . . .

It's 11:34 by the time I find street parking near the Hermosa Beach Promenade: not terrible, but late nonetheless. I put the car in park, turn off the ignition, and throw the car keys in my purse in one fluid motion.

The DVD player turns off with the car. "Can I finish watching the scene?" Ian asks.

"Buddy, we're late!"

"It'll only take like a minute."

"No!"

By the time we cross the street and hurry past cafés and T-shirt shops that line the promenade, it is 11:38. Hennessey's Tavern is the last restaurant before you hit the sand. There is no one waiting by the door except the hostess, a pretty young woman with pierced nose.

"Three for lunch," I tell her. "We've got one more person coming; I don't think he's here yet."

She gathers menus. "Right this way."

I say, "The third member of our party is a young man. Well, youngish. Five foot eight. Brown hair. Blue eyes. If you see him, can you . . ."

"Of course."

"My last name is Cahill," I say. "If he asks."

As we follow her up green-carpeted stairs and onto the upstairs patio, Ian whistles (a new skill; he's very proud) and I scan the space for a lone diner. It is chilly today, and there are plenty of empty tables, so it doesn't take long to see that the only gentleman eating alone is at least seventy. Eric Fergus has not arrived.

The waitress leads us to a table pushed up against the Plexiglas railing. "If you'd like something bigger, I can seat you at a middle table."

I pull out my wicker chair. "Oh, no—we'll take the view." The panorama of the vast white sand, beach, the pier, and the Pacific Ocean is breathtaking, though I'm too nervous to enjoy it.

At 11:56, Eric Fergus still hasn't arrived. He isn't in the downstairs dining room either; I checked. Twice. The waitress has brought our drinks, unsweetened iced tea for me, a Sprite for Ian. It's freezing up here. I should have requested a table near a propane heater. But the patio has suddenly filled; all the warmer seats are gone.

"You cold?" I ask Ian.

"Uh-uh." Bent over the soda, he chews on his plastic straw and gazes at the ocean. The sun glints harsh diamonds on the water.

"Your eyes hurt?" I ask. "You want to borrow my sunglasses?"

"Uh-uh."

It is 11:59.

Music blares from loudspeakers overhead. It puts me on edge. Even more than I already am, that is.

My chair faces the stairs. Three blond women in denim come in, followed by a heavyset young couple with a chubby baby. Next to be seated is a young couple, dressed very casually: him in a ratty T-shirt, board shorts, and flip-flops, her in a short, low-cut sundress that lets it all hang out, as they say.

Ian looks away from the view. "Do you think he forgot?"

"No, of course not. He's—I'll call."

He answers on the second ring. "Yeah?"

"Eric? It's Laura. Laura Cahill."

"Hi."

"Hi." I wait for him to explain himself. When he doesn't, I say, "We expected you at eleven-thirty."

"Oh. Yeah? I couldn't remember if you said eleven-thirty or noon."

Breathe in. Breathe out. Do not yell.

"Are you coming?"

"I'm here. I didn't see you . . . oh, wait—"

Startled, I scan the patio. But, no—that can't be right. The only other person on the phone is the guy in the ratty T-shirt, the one with the half-naked girl. He is half out of his chair, peering around. When he sees me, he raises his hand in greeting. He gets up from the table, closes the phone, and heads toward us. The woman in the revealing sundress follows, her mouth grim.

There has been a terrible mistake. Maybe this is the wrong Eric Fergus. Or maybe the DNA company switched Ian's results with someone else. There is no way, *no way* that this scruffy guy is the overachieving medical student I chose to father my child. Of course, he doesn't look like the man in the dream (I realize, with a start, that I'd been expecting him), but he doesn't even look like Ian. He's attractive enough, but his features are sharp, almost hungry. Eyebrows, eyes, nose, mouth, chin: there isn't a single hint of my son on his face.

He's at the table now, standing right next to Ian, who stares at the man with a mixture of wonderment and anxiety. He crouches down, looks my son in the eye.

"Hi, I'm Eric. You must be Ian."

They look at each other. They bite their lips. They smile.

Their grins are identical.

# Vanessa

This was a horrible idea. Seriously, what was I thinking? *You should meet the kid. Because if you don't, you'll always wonder about him.* I actually said that!

Like now that Eric knows what the kid looks like and sounds like he'll never think about him again? Already I'm staring (I shouldn't stare) at the little boy's face (he's seriously cute) and trying to imagine what he'll look like at twelve and sixteen and twenty. Shit!

The mother looks up at me. "Hello."

Eric says, "This my girlfriend. Vanessa."

"Fiancée," I say.

The table is small and square, with one side pushed against the clear railing and wicker chairs on the other three sides. The little boy and his mother face each other. It's like we're interrupting their perfect little lunch. There's no room for us here. No room for me, anyway.

The little boy has streaky hair, a lot like Angie and A.J.'s oldest,

Ty, except this kid is lighter all around. Even his eyes are light—blue or green, it's hard to tell with the sun in my eyes.

I should have brought sunglasses. The mother has them. Of course she does.

Damn. She just said something to me, but the music is really loud. I go, "What?"

She goes, "Think of it as cozy." And she sort of smiles but not really.

I don't think I can say "What?" again without sounding like a moron. So instead I go, "Yeah."

She goes, "If you'd like."

Now I don't know what to say. It's like I've entered this whole other universe where nothing makes sense. I'm the queen of Stupid World. I break eye contact so I don't have to talk to her anymore. To make things worse, it's cold here in Stupid World.

It doesn't help that I'm hardly wearing any clothes. When I asked Eric where he was going to meet the kid, he said, "We're going to go to the beach and grab something to eat."

He didn't get that I was asking him so he'd invite me, but then, like a half hour before he left, he goes, "You want to come?"

Well, duh—of course I wanted to come. I mean, when else will I get a chance to feel so out of place? But I wasn't thinking about that then. I was just thinking about how bad it would feel if I got left behind.

I pretended to think about Eric's invitation, like I hadn't been waiting and waiting for it. "Yeah. Sure. Okay."

Like I had nothing better to do. Which I didn't, but whatever.

I threw on a bikini (not one of my smaller ones—I get credit for that) and a beach cover-up that fit perfectly last year. Now I'm thinking it must have shrunk in the wash. Or I got fatter. I'm voting shrinkage.

Anyway, it was all good until we got to the end of the promenade, but instead of going on to the sand Eric turned into this restaurant.

I said, "I thought we were going to the beach."

"Well, yeah—a restaurant at the beach."

"But I'm in my bathing suit! Didn't you notice?"

"You're in a dress. It looks nice. And, you know, maybe after lunch we can jump in the ocean."

For about ten seconds, I considered going back to the car, but then I figured that was retarded. But now that I'm standing here, having a nonconversation with the kid's icy mom (if I'm the queen of Stupid, she's the queen of Perfect), I wish I was in the car.

"Would you like me to get one for you?" the queen of Perfect asks.

"Uh, sure," I say—because I don't know her well enough to say, "I was distracted and the music's loud and I don't know what the hell you're talking about."

She stands up—damn, she's tall—and walks to the other table, takes a chair, and carries it over. She's dressed like a mom in an old black-and-white sitcom, in a tan skirt and white blouse and—swear to God—pearls. She's got one of those haircuts that's shorter in the back. The frosty front pieces come just to the edge of her jaw. She doesn't look like a real lawyer—more like one on a TV show who seems all prim and proper but then has dirty after-hours sex on her desk when everyone else has left for the night.

"There you go." She puts the chair down and gives me a tight sort-of-smile. Then I get it. She'd been suggesting I drag over a chair since my dumb-ass boyfriend obviously wasn't going to do it.

Is it too late to go back to the car?

Eric sees the chair, says, "Oh, thanks!" and sits down at the one that was already there. I squeeze into the new one, slightly back from everyone else, between Eric and the lawyer. The mother of his child. *One* of the mothers of his children.

The waitress comes barreling past us holding plastic baskets of food and almost rams right into me. "Excuse me, excuse me . . ." I pretend to scoot closer to the table, but there's just no room.

Eric and the little kid are talking.

"Chickens," Ian says. At first I think he's figuring out what he wants for lunch, but then he starts talking about names and personalities. He has chickens as pets. Got it.

That? Is weird.

The lawyer lady says, "The chickens have been a wonderful tool for fostering a sense of responsibility." No, seriously. She says that.

"Plus they're probably cool," Eric says to Ian.

Ian lights up. "They're awesome!" He's looking at Eric with big eyes and a bigger smile—Eric's smile. It's exactly the same.

And just like that I can't take it. I have to get out of here.

I stand up. The chair doesn't push back the way it should, and I stumble. "I've gotta pee." Score another one for the queen of Stupid. "I mean, the ladies' room. I'm going to go."

Eric glances at me and kind of smiles. The queen of Perfect looks at me like I just pissed on her petunias. I scoot the chair back.

The bathroom is downstairs. Shut into a stall, I sit on a toilet and hyperventilate. Then I pull out my phone and text Melva.

*Can u come get me?*

# Laura

My face hurts from trying to maintain a neutral expression, and perspiration soaks my blouse—not just under the arms now, but along my back and chest as well. I've never been much of a drinker, but I could really use a shot of tequila right about now. Maybe two.

I wasn't expecting the girlfriend—fiancée now, apparently. Even if I had known she was coming, I wouldn't have been prepared for such a distracted, sullen, half-naked young woman. All I did was offer to get another chair, and she looked at me like I was insane—or maybe condescending or stepping on toes.

Is that the kind of girl Ian will bring home someday?

Once the girl—Vanessa was her name—flees to the bathroom, it is easier to focus on Eric Fergus. He seems nice enough: easygoing, affable. Behind the scruffiness (you'd think he'd have shaved for the occasion), his face is kind. Handsome too. Well, handsome-ish, anyway. There's a magnetic quality to his blue eyes, which, I see now, with the sun shining on them, are speckled with green.

Ian says, "They like yogurt, but not peach flavored. Except for

Rusty. That's his favorite. They all like peas, and they like salad as long as it doesn't have ranch dressing on it. Which is too bad because ranch is the only kind of dressing I like!"

Eric seems genuinely intrigued by Ian's chicken stories. I hope he takes them as evidence of a happy, healthy home . . . one with room for another child.

The waitress comes to take our order. Without opening the menu, Eric asks, "You have macaroni and cheese? Or plain pasta, maybe?"

"No—sorry."

"How about grilled cheese? On sourdough?"

"We can do that."

I catch Eric's eye and motion toward the bathrooms—toward Vanessa. "You want to order for your . . ."

"She can do it when she comes back."

I hand the waitress my menu. "California citrus salad, please. And more iced tea."

She pokes her electronic pad with her electronic pen and gives Ian a big smile.

Ian sits up extra straight and speaks clearly, just as I've taught him. "May I please have the chicken fingers?"

"Of course!" The waitress's smile grows even bigger. She pokes at her electronic pad.

"Thank you," Ian says.

"You're very welcome!"

I beam with pride at my polite little son. Clearly, I have raised him right. Clearly, Eric Fergus made a good decision when he donated his sperm all those years ago.

Once the waitress leaves, I turn to Eric and prepare to launch into some of the questions I prepared last night.

He is staring at me with something like horror. No, it's not like horror—it *is* horror.

"Chicken?" he says.

Oh God.

"Chicken fingers aren't really chicken!" Ian says. "They're just called that! Chickens don't have fingers."

*Oh God.*

Eric stares at me. Everything rides on how I handle the chicken issue. Everything.

I fold my hands on the table in front of me. "Actually, buddy, I guess I always assumed you understood . . . the thing is . . ."

Confusion flickers across Ian's face until it hardens into a terrible kind of knowledge. *"Are chicken fingers . . . chicken?"*

"Uh—yes."

I look from Ian to Eric and back to Ian. I can still fix things—show Eric what a good mother I am.

I clear my throat. "You see, buddy, there are different kinds of eaters. Carnivores eat just meat. Herbivores eat just plants. And then there are omnivores, which eat both."

"I *know* that," Ian says.

A bead of sweat slithers between my breasts.

I say, "Humans are omnivores. That's where we are in the food chain. We need to eat both plants and animals—meat—to get the nutrients we need to live."

"I'm a vegetarian," Eric Fergus says, helpfully.

"You are?" Ian says.

"Do you work in the medical field?" I ask—abruptly, yes, but I am, after all, desperate to change the subject. Besides, I have a long list of questions to get through, a whole heap of rapport to build before I can ask for another sperm donation.

Eric blinks at me. "What do you mean?"

"It's tough to get into medical school. You must have had a strong science background. Biology and physiology and whatnot. So even though you decided not to be a doctor . . . I just wondered if you took some other medical path."

"Oh. Right." He shakes his head. "No."

"So, if you didn't, uh . . . what career path did you choose? If you don't mind my asking."

"I left med school to pursue my music."

"Really? That's so interesting because Ian—his piano teacher, she can't get over his natural talent. I always wondered if maybe you were . . . So now you're a professional . . . what do you play?"

"I played guitar. I don't anymore."

The waitress passes by, and Ian catches her eye. "Can I have a hamburger instead of chicken fingers?"

"Of course." She takes out her electronic pad and presses a button.

My head is buzzing. He dropped out of medical school. He abandoned his music. What does he do, exactly? I don't have to ask. When he sees my expression, he fills in the blank.

"I work at Costco."

"Are hamburgers made from ham?" Ian asks.

I say, "By Costco, you mean something like . . . branding? Or corporate management?"

"Cows," Eric tells Ian.

Ian yelps.

"Checkout," Eric tells me. He holds my eyes as he speaks, challenging me to disparage his career. His job.

"You knew hamburger came from cows," I tell Ian, my eyes still locked with Eric's.

"Sometimes I work the door," Eric adds. "Checking cards on the way in or receipts on the way out. But mostly I'm at the registers."

He knows what I'm thinking. I can tell by the way he holds my eyes and tightens his mouth. He's waiting for me to ask what happened, why he threw away such a promising future. He expects me to challenge him.

I tell myself that it doesn't matter. DNA is all about potential, not execution. He did, after all, get in to medical school, which means he excelled at college and aced his MCATs. So I know he's bright. I'm sorry for whatever life circumstances pushed him off track, but it doesn't affect me or my son.

Unless, of course . . .

"What can you tell me about your medical history?" I ask Eric.

"There's nothing much to tell." He takes a drink of water.

"Does it hurt the cows?" Ian asks. "When they die?"

"Any mental health or substance abuse issues?" I try to keep my tone matter-of-fact. Who goes from medical school to Costco?

"It can't feel good to the cows," Eric tells Ian. And then, to me: "Hard to say, really. I mean, did the hallucinogenic drugs spark my psychotic episodes? Or do schizophrenics seek out controlled substances in an attempt at self-medication?"

For a moment, the whole world goes still as a hundred horrid scenarios play out in my brain.

Seeing my expression, Eric Fergus bursts out laughing. "Kidding."

"So you didn't . . . there weren't any issues with . . ."

"No," he says. "I'm sane and sober. Always have been, more or less. Really."

"Oh my God. I can't . . ." Suddenly, realizing how ridiculous my reaction was, I burst out laughing.

"It's not funny that cows die!" Ian wails.

I reach across the table and ruffle his hair. "You're right, sweetie. It's not funny at all."

A busboy comes to refill our waters. I wipe a tear from under my eye. Eric is grinning. He is not at all what I expected, but I suddenly realize that I like him very much.

I say, "I wasn't just . . . by medical issues, I mainly meant anything genetic. You know, something to look out for in my son. So, I'd also be curious to hear about any diseases that run in your family."

He takes a drink of water, sets the glass on the table, and gazes at the ocean. "My father had a heart attack at fifty-seven."

"Was he okay?"

He shakes his head.

"I'm sorry. Was it . . ."

"Hypertension. High cholesterol. He was on blood pressure meds and antistatins. Even had an angiogram scheduled for the next month. But . . ." He shakes his head again. "He smoked for forty years, plus he was overweight. So I don't know how much is genetic, though his father died of a heart attack too. My cholesterol was fine, last I checked."

"What about your mother?"

"Mild osteoporosis. Cataracts. Both pretty common at her age. Plus she's got pretty significant hearing loss, though sometimes I think she hears more than she lets on but just doesn't want to deal with it." He half smiles.

"I prepared a list of questions. I hope you don't mind if I . . .?"

"Of course not. That's what we're here for, right?"

Well, not exactly. We're here so I can score more sperm, but I'd like the information too.

I reach into my bag and pull out two sheets of paper and a pen. We go through his dental history (a few cavities in childhood; orthodontia; all four wisdom teeth extracted). He details his ethnic background (Scottish, Irish, German). He provides an honest assessment of his athleticism (average at best, but he's always been active). He says that he reached his current height of five foot eight at nineteen, and that his tallest brother is five eleven.

"Any allergies?"

"I have a little hay fever," Eric tells me. "That's about it."

"And no behavior issues as a child? I wouldn't ask, but . . ."

He raises his eyebrows and then nods slightly, sensing that I don't want to discuss Wendy Winder in front of Ian.

He rests his chin on his hand and takes a moment to consider. "Every time I ask my mother what I was like as a child, she says she can't remember. So I guess I was pretty easy."

"She doesn't remember?"

"Middle child," he says. "Third of four. Half the time, she still gets my name wrong."

The waitress arrives with paper-lined brown baskets and sets one in front of each of us. Ian leans back from his burger as if he'd been served a platter of worms.

"Would you like more Sprite?" the waitress asks.

"Yes, please." He continues to look repulsed by his lunch.

When the waitress leaves, Eric looks toward the stairway. Oh, right: the fiancée. I'd actually forgotten about her.

"Do you think everything is okay?" I ask.

"Um . . ." He pulls out his cell phone, hits a couple of buttons, and holds it to his ear. After a pause, he shakes his head. "Voice mail."

"You want me to check the ladies' room?"

"You don't have to."

"No, it's fine."

It's not until the bathroom door has shut behind me that I realize that I've left my son with a complete stranger, genetics and good vibes be damned. What if the girlfriend's disappearance is all part of an elaborate kidnapping plot?

The bathroom is empty. Heart racing, I hurry back through the bar and up the stairs. Eric and Ian are still at our table on the patio. Of course they are. Ian's hamburger has been pushed to the side, replaced with a torn-off piece of Eric's grilled cheese sandwich.

Eric is on the phone. As I approach the table, he closes it and puts it in his pocket.

"She wasn't in the bathroom," I tell him.

"I know. She's . . . she had to . . ." He sighs. "She's fine."

# Vanessa

"Is she like a total cougar?" Melva asks. We're getting some static on the line.

"Not really. I don't know. Maybe."

"I bet she is," Melva says. "What is she, like fifty?"

"Not that old. Forty maybe. She's pretty. Tall. Skinny. Kind of blondish."

"Cougar."

The sun glints so sharply on the water, it hurts my eyes. After I called Melva from the restroom, I snuck out of the restaurant and came over to the beach. I was really careful: no way was I going to sit down someplace where Eric (that scum) and the baby mother (the cougar) and the little kid (Eric's *son*) could see from their nice little table.

Even though it's cold, there are people on the beach. There's a family next to me—I'm counting on their big umbrella to hide me—three little kids with a really fat mom in a bikini and a dad with a shaved head and a tattooed neck. He wears a white T-shirt and black shorts that fall below his knees, tall white socks, and black sneakers. The oldest kid—he's seven, maybe—holds out his hand. The father reaches into a pocket and gives him a few crumpled bills. The little boy takes it and runs toward the promenade with his younger brother.

"How long till you can come?" I ask Melva.

"I dunno. I'll leave as soon as Brent gets here." Melva is stuck at a Little League game in Torrance. Her oldest kid is playing T-ball. When I called her the first time, she said the game had just started, which meant Brent would be there any second and she'd leave right away. That's why I was kind of surprised, a half hour later, when she wasn't here. I figured she was stuck in traffic, but it turns out she hadn't left yet.

"Did Brent say when he'd be there?" I ask.

"He's not answering his phone. Asshole. He did this last week too. Said he forgot."

My eyes sting. I don't say anything.

"I'm really sorry, Nessa," Melva says—and I know she means it. "Brent promised he'd make the game. But lately he's just—shit. You want me to call Pammy? See if she can get you?"

"Her and Dave were going to the River this weekend."

"That's right. Shit. Dr. Sanchez lives in Manhattan Beach . . ."

I laugh, sort of. "No way I'm calling Dr. Sanchez."

"I bet he'd come."

"That's not the point."

"Well, if Brent doesn't show—and I think he will, seriously, he promised—I'll come as soon as the game's over."

"How long is that?"

"I dunno. An hour? Could be longer. These games are friggin' endless."

"Okay. Well, I'll be here."

When I was crying in the bathroom, escape seemed like the

perfect plan. Melva would come get me before Eric even noticed I was missing. We'd find a bar and order margaritas (well, I would, anyway), and I'd pour out my heart: how it felt to see Eric with this woman and her kid, how they looked like a family and I was just the trashy girlfriend who didn't belong and didn't even know what to wear to a restaurant. How all my life I've felt like I don't belong, but with Eric it felt like I could finally build a life. At last I could have someone all to myself. But it's too late. That little boy with Eric's smile—Eric already belongs more to him than he ever will to me.

Instead of pouring out my heart to Melva, I'm all alone on a cold beach, watching a gangbanger with his three kids. Even gangbangers have families. What is wrong with me?

My phone rings. I answer, thinking it's Melva, hoping she'll say that Brent has arrived and she's on her way.

"Where are you?" It's Eric.

"I'm, uh . . ."

In the distance, a dolphin jumps. The gangbanger's kids squeal.

"Are you okay?"

"I just had to get out of there," I say.

". . . You mean you *left*?"

"I just said that."

He is quiet.

"Eric?"

"Did you take the car?"

"Of course not. Melva's giving me a ride." I thought maybe he'd be upset that I'd left. Instead, he's just thinking of how he's going to get home.

He is silent.

"See you at home." I hang up fast so I don't have to listen to him not saying anything.

Next to me, the little boys return with their hands full of Popsicles, one for everyone.

———

When I was a little kid, I thought ice cream meant happiness. But not just any ice cream. It had to be one of those Popsicles that has a chocolate shell over vanilla ice cream and a solid hunk of dark chocolate inside. The first time I ate one, I was six years old and it was like a hundred and ten degrees outside. In Redondo, it hardly ever gets hot, but summers in Riverside were foul.

I was playing at my friend Julie's house, down the street. Julie's family was at least as poor as mine, so when I heard the ice cream truck roll by, bells playing "Pop Goes the Weasel," I couldn't believe that she asked her mother for money. I really, really couldn't believe that her mother gave her enough for both of us.

The van stopped as soon as the driver saw us.

"You can have anything," Julie told me.

The side of the truck was covered with colored pictures of ice cream: bars and Popsicles and cones. How could I pick just one?

"I'll have the same as you," I said.

When I unwrapped the Popsicle, I was bummed. It looked just like regular, boring chocolate over vanilla. But after I nibbled the brittle shell and licked the creamy vanilla, my teeth hit the chocolate hunk inside. To this day, when someone says, "It's what's on the inside that counts," I think of that Popsicle.

The next time I heard the ice cream truck playing "Pop Goes the Weasel," I was home with my mother and Aurora. The living room had an air conditioner in the window, so that's pretty much where me and Aurora spent our summers, lying on the worn brown carpet and watching TV.

My father must have been at work. He always had at least two jobs, changing oil or tires at an in-and-out auto place during the day and busing tables or doing dishes at some chain family restaurant at night. I hated that he was gone so much. When he was home, as tired as he was, he would hold me on his lap and tell stories about Mexico. He would slip me dimes and candies from his pockets. He would tell me he loved me. And then he'd slip off to bed, and when I got up the next morning, he'd be gone.

In my memory, my father is the handsomest man on earth, tall and powerful, with deep, dark eyes, glossy black hair, and a heart-stopping smile. But when I look at old photos, I see something different. His body was strong but square, like the whole world had been pressing down on his shoulders. His teeth were worn and crooked. His eyes looked so very, very tired. But they were beauti-ful. I was right about that.

"Pop Goes the Weasel" got louder as the ice cream truck got closer. I knew better than to ask my mother for money. Instead, I said, "When I was at Julie's house, her mother let us buy Popsicles."

My mother said, "So go live with Julie, then."

A couple of months later, she was waiting outside of school when Aurora and I got out. That was weird. Usually we walked home alone.

The Santa Ana winds blew hot, dusty air. I couldn't drink enough water that fall. I dreamed of swimming pools and sweet lemonade.

"Wanna go to Baskin-Robbins?" my mother asked.

Aurora and I were too surprised to say anything. Without wait-ing for our answer, my mother headed toward the closest strip mall. We followed her, amazed by our great luck.

Aurora got a dish of chocolate fudge or chocolate swirl or Rocky Road—something dark. I got a cone. Bubblegum ice cream. There were little bits of bubble gum inside. The more you licked, the bigger the wad got.

We sat at an outside table because my mother said she'd rather be too hot than too cold. She wasn't eating anything, wasn't even asking for bites of ours. We ate fast, afraid she'd change her mind and make us leave.

My bubblegum wad was medium big when she said it.

"Your father is dead. Car hit him. He was running across the street on his break, and—" She stopped talking. Tightened her mouth. Shook her head. That was all she was going to say about it, at least for now.

Just like that, my world turned black. The person who loved me best was gone. Later, my mother would have boyfriends, men who either didn't look at me at all or, when I got older, looked at me so long that I'd lock my bedroom door. But I'd never have another father whispering stories and sneaking me treats. Never.

But I was six years old. I didn't get it. Something terrible couldn't be happening while all that sugar swam in my mouth. When my mother stopped talking, I licked some more pink ice cream. I suctioned another bit of bubble gum from the surface, added it to my lump.

Aurora sat still, her spoon stabbing the side of her ice cream. She stared at my mother. And then she began to wail.

"Stop it," my mother commanded.

Aurora wailed louder.

"I said, *stop it*." My mother smacked Aurora's head, just above the ear. Not hard, but enough so Aurora jerked back, her hand still on her spoon, and knocked the ice cream on the ground.

I jumped up and pointed at the lump of chocolate, already turning to a puddle on the dirty concrete. "Should we save it?"

No one answered.

———

When I got older, most of the boys I liked were dark-haired, dark-eyed, mostly Hispanic. I wasn't a loser magnet like Aurora. Most of the guys I went out with were okay, if a little too slick, a little too flirty. None of them were kind and gentle like my father. None of them were happy just to sit and talk and *be* with me. They thought I should always be happy and laughing. They thought I should look good all the time, even if I was sick or sad or just tired. They liked me on my best days, but lots of days weren't my best, and that's when things would fall apart.

Then I met Eric and everything changed. Except maybe it didn't.

# Laura

Ian stands poised at the water's edge, ready to race the waves up the beach and back again.

A wave crashes at his ankles. Even from where I stand, farther up the sand, I can see his khaki shorts darkening at the hem. He twists his head to look at Eric and me, smiles, and holds his hands up as if to say, *What could I do?*

"He's a good kid," Eric says.

"He's a great kid." His green flip-flops dangle from my fingers.

I didn't plan it this way: time alone with Eric, the perfect opportunity to make my request. But when we reached the end of lunch, Ian suggested a walk on the beach. So here we are.

Ian follows the receding water down the slope, pauses for an instant, and tears back up the hill. Nearby, a woman snaps photos of a little red-haired girl in a pink bonnet.

"That reminds me," I say, reaching into my purse. "Wendy Winder, the other, you know . . ."

"I know."

"Right. She asked to see a photo of you. So if you don't mind . . . I mean, maybe you do mind. In which case . . ."

He shrugs. "Um, sure."

"Great." I pull out my compact camera and take his photo, realizing as I do so that I want the picture at least as much as Wendy does. I check the shot. He's squinting in the harsh midday light, but it will have to do.

I slip the camera back into my purse. "A lot of people thought I was crazy when I had Ian. When I chose to have him, I mean."

"Why?" Eric says.

"People kept telling me how hard motherhood is. How children can suck the life out of you."

"Someone actually said that?"

"My own mother," I admit. And then, to my surprise, I laugh. The statement has never struck me as amusing before.

I say, "And other people, some of whom I hardly even knew—coworkers and their wives—accused me of being selfish." No laughter this time: it still isn't funny. Besides, I hadn't intended to say this; it just slipped out somehow.

"These were people with children or without?" he asks.

"With. Traditional two-parent families. Mom stays home, Dad works. They said I wouldn't have enough time for a child. And that if I had a boy, he'd need a role model."

"You have any brothers?" Eric asks.

"One. Lives up north. We're not really close."

"What about your father?"

I shrug. "If it weren't for my stepmother, we'd never hear from him at all. But that's not to say Ian doesn't have any positive role models," I continue, trying to get the talk back on course. "His Cub Scout leader—his son and Ian are friends—he's been a really positive influence. As have his various sports coaches."

"From what I've seen, you're a really good mother," Eric says.

I check his face. The green specks in his irises sparkle in the sunlight.

"You don't end up with a kid like Ian unless you're doing something right," he adds.

"Thanks. Though I suppose genetics had something to do with it."

He grins. "From your side, maybe."

I clear my throat. This is it: my opening.

"The point I'm making is that although I was initially concerned with the challenges inherent in single parenthood, the endeavor has, in fact, been a success."

"I wasn't aware that you were making a point," Eric says.

I swallow hard. "I'm sorry. When I get nervous I tend to . . ."

"Sound like a lawyer?"

"Yes."

"Why are you nervous?"

Near the water, Ian squeals. He has failed to outrun a wave. His shorts are soaked, as is the bottom half of his shirt. He runs up the sand, laughing wildly.

"It was a big one!" he says.

"I see that."

He turns and heads back to the ocean.

"There's something I have to ask you," I tell Eric. "A request."

My phone rings. I grab it out of my purse and check the display: Carmen.

"Hi, Carmen."

"Ian's shoes in the closet, maybe?"

"What?"

"His shoes. You check the closet?"

Of course: I'd called her earlier.

I speak quickly. "One of his green flip-flops was in a toy basket. Don't worry. We found them."

Hands in pockets, Eric wanders toward Ian and the water.

Carmen and I say good-bye, but by the time I hang up, it is too late: Eric has reached Ian and is chasing the waves with him. The scene is almost painfully sweet. I resist the impulse to take their picture. And then I give in, furtively capturing the moment on my digital camera.

Eventually, they tire of the game and trudge back up the sand toward me.

"Why don't you build a sand castle?" I suggest to Ian. "Near the water, maybe."

He wrinkles his nose and shakes his head. He's not going anywhere. Looks like I'll have to make my request in front of him. Who knows? Maybe that will make it harder to refuse.

"I'll be forty-three in July," I tell Eric.

"Happy birthday."

"Well, yeah—it's a little early. But, um, according to my doctor, my odds of fertility are still, well, not good exactly, but good for my age."

"Eric?"

A trim man, dressed more for the golf course than the beach, has come up behind us. In his mid-to-late thirties, he is olive-skinned and dark-eyed, with a receding hairline and intense brown eyes.

For an instant, Eric looks confused. Then recognition clicks in. "Dr. Sanchez. Hey. I didn't recognize you without your white coat."

"I, uh—" The man looks at me, not entirely kindly, then back at Eric. "Melva called me. Said Vanessa needed a ride. But I guess . . ."

Just like that, I see her, a dot of purple against the white sand. She's a ways down the beach, beyond the volleyball nets and near a family with a beach umbrella, sitting on the sand, hugging her knees.

Eric says, "I thought she . . . I mean, uh—no. I got her. Thanks."

The man tightens his lips. "I'll just make sure she's okay."

He heads down the beach, shoulders hunched forward.

"Crap," Eric says.

"I'm sorry if this . . ."

"Lunch was a bad idea."

"No! Please don't say that." Ian stands next to me, looking up at Eric. "Maybe it was just a bad idea to . . ." I stop myself before I can say "bring her." I try again. "Maybe we should have eased into a meeting more gradually. And I suppose it's inevitable that this situation would arouse certain insecurities."

"I have to go," he says.

"Wait! There's just one thing I need to ask you. And then—well, here's the deal. Before I had Ian, I purchased three vials of your . . ."

"Right."

"But I threw two of them out. After Ian was born, that is. Because I didn't think I'd want another child. But now it turns out I do. Only I don't want to use a new donor because then I'll have two kids with identity issues. If they're full siblings, they have each other, and I just think it would make them more grounded. More secure. So what I was wondering was . . . can you give me some more?"

"You mean some more—"

"Yes."

"Oh. God."

"If you need some time to think about it . . ."

He shakes his head. "I don't."

"You—"

"I'm sorry. But I can't. I just—can't. It was nice meeting you, Laura. And you, Ian."

He hurries across the sand, away from us, toward the girl in purple.

# Wendy

The day was going so well.

And then it wasn't.

When I picked up the twins from kindergarten, they were smiling. Well, Sydney was, anyway. And Harrison was neither crying nor raging. So: score!

Their teacher, Mrs. Rath, whom I've taken to thinking of as Mrs. Stick-up-her-Rath, caught my eye before I had a chance to look away. But for once she didn't say, "Can I have a word?"

Instead, she nodded (slightly, but still) and said, "They did well today." And yes, okay, the clear implication was that tomorrow they'll probably be monstrous as usual, but so what? Today they did well!

To celebrate the victory, I took them for frozen yogurt. Because you know what? That lactose-intolerance thing is a load of crap. Harrison had chocolate yogurt with about fifteen toppings. Sydney had mint, peach, caramel, and pistachio mixed together with about sixteen toppings. I ordered nothing because right now I'm all about self-denial.

And then I ate most of Sydney's because she couldn't finish it and I hate waste. But it didn't count because it was from her dish and I didn't actually enjoy it.

At home, I let them unwind in front of semi-educational television and poured myself an icy glass of Diet Coke to sip while checking my e-mail. All week I'd been waiting for Laura's photos of Eric Fergus. Finally, here they were. I opened the photo attachments to see a beachy California guy on the sand, alone in one shot and with Laura's little boy in the other.

Her note was short: *An interesting lunch. Call me when you have time to talk.*

I saved the photos (filing them under "Friends and Family") and reached for the phone. That's when I noticed the answering machine light blinking.

*"Wendy? Hi! This is Annalisa Lemberger. From scrapbooking? I'm supposed to host tonight, but the girls have come down with a tummy bug—you know, that thing that's been going around? Starts with throw-up and then works its way down? So nasty. Hope you're all healthy over there! Anyway, sorry for such late notice, but I was really, really hoping you could have scrapbooking at your house instead . . ."*

I put my Diet Coke on the counter. I wept. And then I called Annalisa to say I'd be happy to host.

---

I spend the rest of the afternoon dumping toys into bins, shoving stuffed animals into closets, and semicleaning surfaces that haven't seen the light of day in years. Even without crap all over the floor, tables, and chairs, my house is dumpy. It needs a coat of paint. It needs new furniture. It needs pictures and window treatments and new carpet.

Since I have neither the time nor the money for any of those, at five o'clock I load the kids into the van and head to the grocery store to stock up on booze. If the ladies drink enough, they won't even notice the house.

Unfortunately, Harrison and Sydney used up all of their good behavior at school. Plus, five o'clock is the witching hour: blood sugar is low but it's not quite time for dinner.

"I don't wanna go to the store! I don't wanna get in my car seat!"

And then, when we pull into the Safeway parking lot? "I don't wanna get OUT of my car seat!"

I consider just leaving them in the car, but everyone knows that only very, very bad moms do that. A stranger might abduct them. Granted, the stranger would give them back after twenty minutes— a half hour, tops—but still.

Inside Safeway, I employ my most powerful parenting technique—bribery—with limited success. Four cookies, two Hershey bars, and a bag of Twizzlers later, I walk out of the store with six bottles of wine, a jug of premixed margaritas, some vodka, a veggie tray, and two extremely whiny children.

When we get home, Darren is upstairs in front of his computer. Of course he is.

I say, "You have to take them."

He says, "Huh?"

I say, "Scrapbooking is here. Tonight."

He says, "What?"

I say, "I'm hosting. It was supposed to be at Annalisa's house but her kids are puking, so now it's here. People are coming. Didn't you notice that the house was neater than usual? I spent three hours cleaning."

He squints at the door as if he can see around corners and down the stairs to the cleaner-than-usual common areas.

"People will be here in an hour," I say. "You need to stop playing Sims and get them out of here!"

"This isn't Sims. It's World of Warcraft."

"Mommy, I'm hungry!" Sydney hugs the door frame. Her voice has taken on the gurgling quality that generally precedes a crying jag. Her eyes glitter. In a bad way.

"Can't we just order a pizza?" Darren remains in his chair, top half twisted around to look at me, bottom half optimistically oriented toward the computer.

"I want pizza!" Harrison says.

"You can go out for pizza," I say. "Or to the McDonald's with the playland or whatever. But you've got to be out of the house. People are coming."

"McDonald's!" Sydney yells, loosening her grip on the door frame.

Harrison yells louder. *"I want pizza!"*

Oh, crap.

"I can't take them out when they're like this," Darren says.

"Then go downstairs and make them taquitos or something. You can go out after. Just as long as you're gone by seven. I have to get dressed, I have to do something with my hair, I've got to set out the food and booze . . ."

*"I don't want taquitos!"*

*"I want pizza!"*

"You can't just dump them on me like this," he says, his voice quiet.

*"Dump them on you?"* My voice is not quiet. "Who do you think takes care of them all day? Can't you act like a father for three lousy hours of your life?"

Okay. That? Was an extremely poor choice of words. And I would have backed down, apologized, whatever, but I'm so tired of doing all the work, of taking all the blame, of feeling like a single parent with a roommate.

I stare at Darren. Darren stares at me. And then Harrison takes two steps toward his sister and shoves her away from the doorway, into the hall.

Sydney howls. Darren springs from his chair and grabs Harrison from behind. Harrison kicks, misses his sister, takes out a lamp. Darren lets him go. Harrison punches the wall.

"*Stop!*" I'm shrieking. I didn't mean to lose my cool like that. But as long as I've started: "Stop! Stop! Stop!"

I cover my ears and squeeze my eyes shut. Once the tears start flowing, I can't get them to stop. Every time I break down like this, I think the twins might show a little empathy. Maybe they'll stop their tantrums to comfort me, but no.

Darren stands there, quiet and helpless—has any man ever been more passive?—waiting for our three flames to burn out. *If only he'd been able to give me children,* I think for the thousandth time. The kids might have inherited his meekness. He might have loved them more. He might still love me. If only, if only . . .

When the children stop crying, Darren grabs his keys. Sydney and Harrison follow him out of the house. The garage door rumbles and his car engine roars to life. Then the garage door closes and all is quiet.

I have twenty minutes to get ready.

My face is puffy. I don't want to see anyone or make pleasant chitchat or sort through pictures of my kids. But I have no choice. I pull on my all-purpose black dress. It's a little fancy for the occasion, but it will have to do. I run—well, yank—a comb through my dark curls and brush powder over my red face.

I'd planned to take the veggies out of their plastic tray and arrange them on a pretty platter, but there isn't time. I've just pulled off the lid and am setting out the bottles of wine (I forgot to chill the Chardonnay—damn!) when the doorbell rings. Seven o'clock on the dot: you've got to love those punctual types. I contort my face into a smile and open the door . . . to Sherry Plant.

"Sherry! Hi." She's put on a few pounds since we were friends, though not as many as I have, and since she stands a good half foot taller, she carries them better.

When she doesn't explain the reason for her appearance, I say, "I'm hosting my scrapbooking group tonight, so when the doorbell rang I thought it was . . . I mean . . . hi."

(What I really mean, of course, is: *I'm busy! Go away!*)

Her mouth twitches in a vague approximation of a smile. "That's why I'm here. Annalisa Lemberger invited me to join the group. It was supposed to be at her house tonight."

"Yes. I know." (Obviously.)

Wait. Annalisa and Sherry are friends? When did that happen? And why in the world would Sherry join my group? It can't be any more comfortable for her than it is for me. Why did she have to come tonight of all nights?

She carries a big black tote bag. It looks heavy. Her brown hair is the same as always: curly, layered, shoulder length, stuck in the eighties. She is wearing jeans, heels, a pink T-shirt, and too much foundation that she has neglected to blend at the jawline.

"Well, um . . . come in." There's no reason for me to feel so freaked out. Sherry and I wave to each other across our driveways all the time. (We also pretend not to see each other across our driveways all the time.) But is her joining the scrapbooking group— *my* scrapbooking group—an attempt to mend fences? Or does she just want to ruin the one good thing in my life?

There's no way I'm going to let her know how much she's rattled me. Not that it would take much; I've been rattled all afternoon.

As we pass through the living/dining-room-turned-toy-room, with its plastic bins against the walls and choo-choo train rug over the stained once-white carpet, I say, "I've completely remodeled the place since you were last here. I can give you my decorator's number, if you're interested."

She does not smile.

In the kitchen, I offer her wine, margaritas, and vodka with four different juices. She declines.

"Water?" I say.

"No thank you." She props her big black tote on the table and pulls out a binder, an envelope full of photos, paper, and markers.

"I didn't know you were into scrapbooking," I say.

She looks up. "Why would you?"

"I think I hear someone pulling up." I hurry out of the kitchen. In truth, I didn't hear anything, but if I spend one more moment alone with Sherry, I might attack her with one of my three pairs of scallop-edged scissors.

After an uncomfortable interval, the doorbell rings. I am actually glad to see Tara, who has moved on from her poo book to a chronicle of her family's yearly pilgrimage to Legoland.

"It's so nice that you agreed to host," Tara says as we exchange an awkward hug. "Being last minute and all." She is wearing white jeans, a turquoise T-shirt, and platform sandals.

"Oh, it's about time I had it at my house."

She tosses her blond hair. "Annalisa could have called you earlier. I mean, her kids have been sick since Monday. She did that to me in the fall, remember? Her sister or cousin or somebody was coming to town? But it wasn't until the day before scrapbooking that she thought to switch with me. Nice house!"

She grins at my ugly, high-ceilinged room.

"I can give you my decorator's number if you're interested."

She smiles. "Ooo, I'd love it, but I'm afraid that's not in the budget right now!"

Strike two.

In the kitchen, Tara makes a straight line to the booze.

"Margarita?" I suggest.

"Love one!"

It isn't until she's taken a (large) sip that she turns to Sherry. "Hi! I'm Tara!"

"Hi." Sherry stays seated.

"This is Sherry," I say, since she missed her cue. "She lives next door."

"You must be over here all the time, then," Tara says.

Sherry and I are quiet. Finally, she says, "We're both very busy."

The day Sherry and I met, I was planting a rosebush in our front yard (it died). Darren and I had just moved in a week or two earlier. Sherry walked over, introduced herself, and said, "I don't care what religion you are. I don't care about your politics. Just tell me you like to drink, and we'll get along fine."

Neither of us was much of a boozer, as it turned out, but in early days, if one of us was in a foul mood, the other would provide wine and appropriately misanthropic commentary.

"Don't you like Sherry?" I asked Darren after a barbecue during which he was unusually quiet (even for him).

"She's edgy."

"I'm edgy."

"You're edgy-funny. She's just mean."

Now that she's sitting at my kitchen table, frowning at old photos of Ashlyn and Brianne, she doesn't even seem edgy-mean. She just seems cranky.

The doorbell rings again (thank God). Three women, including Annalisa, come in at once. They are all wearing denim. When did scrapbooking get so casual? I am way overdressed.

I don't make my decorator joke. They won't get it.

"I didn't think I was gonna be able to come," Annalisa says. "But my Roger, bless his heart, he saw how frazzled I was and he goes, 'You go out and a have a good time. I'll hold down the fort.'"

"They have that stomach thing?" Mary-something asks (I think it's Marybeth, but I'm not sure). "Trevor's had diarrhea for a week. I've been giving him Gatorade, but it makes his poop turn funny colors."

It strikes me, for the five-hundredth time, that nobody ever tells you just how much motherhood revolves around bodily functions.

In the kitchen, Tara pops up and hugs everyone, even Debi, who's only come to scrapbooking three times over the past year. Sherry stays seated, daring anyone to say hello. She finally smiles when Annalisa sees her and says, "You made it!"

Sherry nods.

Annalisa says, "Y'all, this is Shelly. We met at Michaels when I was buying a new trimmer."

Debi asks, "Do you live around here?" as Mary-something says, "Hi, I'm Mary Jane." Thank God I didn't call her Marybeth.

Tara says, "What kind of trimmer?"

Sherry says, "Next door." Then she picks up a glue stick and jabs a gray sheet of paper. The frown line between her eyebrows deepens.

Everyone gets something to drink and stakes out a spot around the table. I fetch ice cubes for the Chardonnay drinkers: lukewarm wine doesn't cut it, especially in the desert. No one touches the veggie platter, but I choose to think it's because they're not hungry and not because it's such a lame excuse for munchies.

A couple of more women show up, drain the margarita pitcher, perch on stools, and spread their supplies out on the counter. I make more margaritas and refill my glass. The women talk over each other about vomit and diarrhea and whether Pedialyte is really any better than Gatorade.

The only spot left at the kitchen table is between Mary Jane and "Shelly." Crap. I put my binder-in-progress on the table. Mary Jane moves her stuff to make room. Sherry doesn't.

Having long since finished the *Bath Time for Babies!* scrapbook, I've moved on to miscellaneous memories, sorted by year. I recently completed *From Zero to One in Twelve Months* and *Two Are One* and am now working on *The Terribly Terrific Twos!*

Predictably, at two, Harrison and Sydney were more Terrifically Terrible than Terribly Terrific. Weirdly, that is the year I look back on most fondly. They were two! They were supposed to be terrible! I'd compare tantrum notes with other mothers, and I'd always win, which I foolishly put down to my children's strong-willed, independent natures.

Sherry is either doing a birthday book or several birthday pages. She trims pictures of Ashlyn and Brianne—wearing party hats and diving into cake—into ovals and stars and squares. (Nothing says "scrapbook rookie" like a dependence on shape templates.) In the photos, Sherry's girls are younger than when I first met them, their faces rounder, their eyes bigger. They only smile in a couple of shots. With their sour expressions, intense eyes, and dark coloring, they almost look like they could be related to Sydney and Harrison. Sherry's husband, Lane, is Greek, his grandfather's last name altered at Ellis Island.

For the first time in years, I think of the conversation that marked either the-beginning-of-the-end or the-end-of-the-end of our friendship. Over coffee one morning, long into my adventures in infertility, I told Sherry that Darren and I had agreed to use a sperm donor.

I thought she'd be happy for me. Instead, she said, "I think you're being really selfish."

"In what way?"

"You get to have a baby but Darren doesn't. You should just adopt. There are a lot of kids who need homes."

"It could take years to adopt."

"You could get an older child. Or a special-needs child. But to get pregnant by a stranger? It's like it's all about you and your ego that you have to have a kid with your genes."

"Your kids have your genes!"

"That's different. It was easy for Lane and me. We didn't waste thousands and thousands of dollars on medical treatments."

Darren was right: Sherry wasn't edgy. She was just mean.

Now, all these years later, Annalisa leans over the table to check out my pink page, which shows Sydney done up in her various Disney princess getups: Snow White, Cinderella, Ariel.

"Adorable!" Annalisa says. "And she looks just like you. I mean, look at that! Not a bit of your husband there!"

Sherry looks up from her page. "Why should there be?" Her voice is flat, her face hard.

I freeze. Everyone else pauses in their cutting and pasting to glance at Sherry. Tara raises her eyebrows and says, "*Some*one needs a glass of wine."

"I'm not drinking," Sherry says between her teeth.

"I meant me." Tara pops up from the table and clicks over to the counter, where the bottles, glasses, and veggie tray have been crowded together to make room for the late arrivals' scrapbook supplies.

For the first time ever, I like Tara.

Hands shaking, I select a photo of two-year-old Sydney smacking her brother with a star wand. After trimming with one of my scallop-edged scissors, I glue the picture onto the pink paper. Underneath, in gold ink, I write, *Sydney casts a spell on Harrison!*

# Vanessa

I'm pissed at Melva for calling Dr. Sanchez, and she's pissed at me for not going with him when he showed up.

"He had to call his nanny to come watch his kids and everything," Melva says.

"I never asked you to call him."

"What? You'd rather I just leave you stranded at the beach with no way to get home?"

"Eric was still there. Once he was done with . . . *them* . . . I was gonna call him."

We're eating lunch at Target again. Pammy needed tampons.

"What was she like?" Pammy asks, stirring her yogurt. "The mother."

"A cougar," Melva says. She has just finished her first burger and is moving on to her second. Whenever Melva is pregnant, she craves red meat. She says it's for the iron.

"You didn't even see her," I remind Melva.

She slaps the table. "I forgot there was a pizza party after the baseball game. And there was no way I could get out of it. I'm sorry, okay?"

I turn to Pammy. "The mother was a cougar."

We all burst out laughing. It is a huge relief. I can't afford to be pissed at Melva when I'm this pissed at Eric.

Not about the lunch. As he's reminded me like five times, that was my idea. But to go to the beach with them when he'd seen how upset I was? What the hell was that? And what about our engagement? I've tried talking to him about rings and vows and china patterns, and every time he changes the subject.

Once we got back from the beach and were speaking again, I explained. "I was okay with a lunch that was just a lunch. You know, to just meet and talk. But it felt like it was more than that. Like she wanted something more."

"She does. She wants my sperm." Just like that! All casual, like he's saying, *She wanted to borrow a pen.*

"*What?*"

"She wants another kid."

"Is she insane?"

"It's not that big a deal." He was looking at me like I was insane. Which was so unfair.

"Not that big a deal? Eric, are you serious? You're supposed to be having a kid with me, remember? *Me!* Except I've got no ring, and there's no wedding on the calendar. But now this complete stranger comes along and you're all, like, it's so not a big deal that she has one of your kids, now she can have another."

"He's not my kid. And I told her no."

"But you wanted to tell her yes, didn't you?"

He clenched his jaw like he was so annoyed and said, "You make it sound like I'm cheating on you and I'm not. I never have and I never will."

"So you're saying you feel nothing for that little boy?"

"It made me feel good. To know that I'd helped someone out, made a difference in someone's life—that means something."

"You didn't *make a difference* in someone's life, Eric, you *created* someone's life!"

"And I'm supposed to feel bad about that? I'm supposed to feel guilty? Did you *see* them together, Ian and his mom? They have this great rapport, this happy life . . . and part of that is because of what I did. When I think about what kind of difference I've made in the world, this is it. Helping Laura get pregnant was probably the best, most purely altruistic thing I've ever done."

We were quiet for a long, long time. My skin tingled with the tension. My gut hurt.

Finally, I said, "Fine. Sure. You wanna give this lady more of your sperm? You want to help *make a difference again*, you go do it."

"Thank you," he said. "Really. This means a lot. I'll call her tomorrow." He kissed the top of my head, went into the bedroom, and shut the door.

"I was being sarcastic," I told the empty air.

———

Now, in the Target café, I drop the bomb. "He's going to do it again. Donate sperm."

Melva almost chokes on her second burger.

"Even though you told him not to?" Pammy says.

"That's the thing," I admit. "I told him he could—but I was being sarcastic! I thought he'd get that."

"You and Eric have some serious communications issues," Melva says. "Can't you tell him you didn't mean it?"

Miserable, I shake my head. "It's too late. He already told her he'd do it, and today he's at some lab, getting tested for AIDS and hepatitis and whatever."

"Didn't you make him test for that before you, you know?" Melva asks.

"No. I knew he was . . . *God*."

"How old is she?" Pammy asks. "The mother."

"I don't know. Old. Forties, maybe?"

"She probably won't be able to get pregnant," Pammy says.

"I didn't mean forties is old," I say, too late.

"Pfft," Pammy says. "Of course it's old. Especially if you're trying to have a baby."

"Cougar," Melva says.

"Maybe you can go with him," Pammy says. "You know, when he donates. So it could be something you do together."

She checks my face.

"Or maybe not," she says.

# 21

## Laura

My office may not have much of a view, but it offers convenient ladies' room access. Ever since Eric Fergus called to say he would
donate after all, that has been an enormous plus, as I can gauge the
probable level of stall occupancy based on the number of women
passing my office. If Marissa thinks it odd that I've suddenly started
leaving my door open for an hour or so after lunch, she hasn't said
anything. Nor has she commented on the fact that I've begun visiting the restroom every afternoon between one forty-five and two-
fifteen, handbag slung over my shoulder. I have new appreciation
for Marissa's all-consuming fascination with her cell phone.

There are three stalls in the ladies' room; unfortunately, my
favorite, the one farthest from the door, is occupied. After shutting
myself into the first stall, I unzip my bag and pull out the ovulation
predictor kit, which is basically a pee stick not unlike a pregnancy
test. According to numerous Web sites, it yields the most accurate
results if used around two o'clock in the afternoon. Unwrapping
the stick from its package, I do my best to be quiet, but as I've dis-

covered over the last couple of weeks, there is no way to avoid the foil's crinkle, which I can only hope will be mistaken for a tampon wrapper.

Mercifully, the woman in the other stall flushes just as I begin the undignified task of peeing on the stick. For accurate results, the stick must lie flat, so while the woman washes her hands, I lay it on top of the toilet-paper dispenser, which I've covered with a torn piece of seat cover.

Then, I wait. The stick has two small boxes, one with a dark purple line, one without. Soon, whether I'm about to ovulate or not, a purple line will appear in the now-blank box, indicating the presence of luteinizing hormone, or LH. Up until now, the second purple line has been lighter than the comparison line, meaning the LH is at normal, low levels. It takes ten minutes to confirm a negative result. If Marissa has been paying attention to the length of my bathroom breaks, she must think I have intestinal issues.

A minute goes by. Two minutes.

If the second line on the stick is as dark or darker than the purple comparison line, it indicates a surge of LH, which in turn indicates that ovulation is imminent. It's no big deal if the results come up negative. There's no reason to experience that cold rush of disappointment. There's always tomorrow. And the day after that. And the next.

Three minutes have passed. Three and a half. Surely a little peek won't—

It's purple. Dark purple. Darker than I've ever seen. But is it as dark as the comparison line?

I wiggle up my panty hose, rearrange myself, and flush. Other days, I've simply thrown the negative test strip in the stall receptacle. Today I take it to the sinks, where the lighting is better. My heart races as I stare at the strip.

It's a match.

The door swings open, and Kim Rueben, the partner specializing in divorce, strides into the room and finds me holding my pee stick. In her hooker heels (copper today, and surprisingly chic with a cream suit), she has got to be six feet tall.

Feeling oddly guilty, as if I were caught holding a joint and not a pee stick, I swallow hard and wait for her to grill me.

Her eyes flick to my hands. "Hi, Laura."

"Hi, Kim."

She closes herself into a stall. I take a final look at the strip to make sure I read it correctly, and then I wrap it in paper towel and place it in the trash. It feels like I'm throwing away evidence.

Back at my office, I tell Marissa, who is checking Facebook on her phone, that I'm back and I'd like her to hold my calls.

She looks up. "Oh. Were you gone?"

I shut myself in my office and dial the Orange County Center for Reproductive Health, a fertility clinic in Irvine.

"We can see your husband tomorrow at eleven for the collection and you at three for the IUI," the nurse tells me.

"Isn't three o'clock too early? According to my research, the optimal time for intrauterine insemination is thirty-six hours after the LH surge, and that's only twenty-five."

She pauses. "Thirty-six hours from now would be, um . . ."

"Two o'clock in the morning. I understand that. But can't we go a little closer than that? Six P.M. tomorrow? Or maybe very early the next day?"

"No. Sorry. Would you rather wait until your next cycle?"

"No! Three o'clock will be . . . fine. I'll see you then. Actually, I'll be there for the eleven o'clock, as well." I pause before closing. "He isn't my husband, by the way. I barely even know the guy."

Eric doesn't answer his cell phone. When the voice mail picks up, I disconnect and dial his home phone, only to have it ring and ring. I try the cell again.

"Um. Yeah?"

"It's Laura Cahill, and I'm ovulating." Today, I have no prepared remarks, and my heart feels like it is going to climb right up my throat. It's amazing how awake I feel, considering I only slept about three hours last night.

He is silent for a moment, and then he laughs. "Um . . . okay . . ." His voice is froggy.

"Actually, that's not quite accurate. What I meant to say is that I'm surging. My hormones are surging. I am not ovulating yet, but I will be soon."

He cleared his throat. "Cool."

"Did I wake you?" According to my computer, it is now 2:20.

"No, I was, um . . . well, yeah. It's my day off, so I got up at like five and went surfing."

"That's, um, nice." Tuesday he surfs. Wednesday he donates sperm. Just a typical week.

I continue, "I've scheduled our appointments for tomorrow. For your donation and my insemination. You said you could make yourself available."

"Yeah, sure." He cleared his throat. "I'll just call in sick."

"Terrific."

Surfer. Slacker. Failed musician. This is the man I've chosen to father my child. Ah, well, it worked out well the last time.

I say, "Your results came in. Did they tell you? For HIV, hepatitis B, hepatitis C . . . and whatever else they tested. All negative. So we can move ahead. Thank you again. For getting the tests."

"Sure, no problem."

I give him directions to the clinic. "It's best if you're early. Say, fifteen minutes?"

"Sure," he says.

"Because you never know with traffic, and if you miss the appointment, I might have to wait until next month."

"Got it," he says.

———————

He's late. Or, late for being early, at any rate. Two minutes before eleven o'clock, I stand on the steps in front of a tall, shiny building in Irvine, the climbing sun stinging my eyes. The Orange County Center for Reproductive Health is on the fifth floor. It will take us at least three minutes to ride the elevator.

My obstetrician referred me to OCCRH last fall, when I told her that I was considering another child, ideally from the initial donor. A fertility clinic would have the necessary equipment for sperm washing and freezing. Plus, they would be prepared to address problems in the event that I had trouble conceiving. I've been here twice before, once for a physical exam to assess, as much as possible, my reproductive health, and again to discuss insemination options.

"My only real fertility issue is that I don't have a man," I joked to the doctor during the second visit.

His brow furrowed with concern. "At forty-two, you are by definition a low-odds, high-risk candidate."

I will no longer attempt humor with him. But no matter.

After Eric does his business in the bathroom today—assuming he shows up—his semen will be "washed." Washing uses centrifugal force to extract the sperm from the surrounding fluid, making it both sterile and more concentrated. If today's intrauterine insemination doesn't take, I'll have a couple more shots with frozen samples, though the odds of success will be cut in half.

I've been trying not to think too much about what comes next, but here it is. At three o'clock, the doctor will thread a catheter through my cervix and into my uterus. He says it won't hurt but will merely be uncomfortable—which, as anyone who has ever been to a doctor knows, means it will hurt. He will then inject Eric's washed sperm, which will have about a 12 percent chance of fertilizing my egg. Compared to my usual odds of zero, that's not so bad.

I am scrolling through my BlackBerry's contact list to find Eric's number when he comes bounding up the steps.

"Hey." He smiles, and a huge knot dissolves in my chest. With the sun in my eyes, I could almost mistake him for a cute, arty college kid. Partly, it's his style: longish hair tucked behind his ears; a faded, short-sleeved plaid shirt open over a T-shirt; faded Levi's; green Vans. Even more than that, though, it's the way he carries himself, his shoulders free of tension, his grin quick and easy, his thumbs looped into his front pockets. When I was in college, I never went in for the free-spirited arty types, though in retrospect maybe I should have.

Alone in the elevator, we stand shoulder to shoulder and stare at the glowing control panel.

"How was traffic?" I shoot him a side glance.

He shrugs. "No worse than usual."

"And your work—they were okay with you missing a day?"

He digs his hands deeper into his pockets. "People call in sick all the time. It's no big deal. They'll get someone else to fill the shift."

The shift. That's right: he'd be paid hourly. I had already promised to pay him the going rate for his sperm donation: three hundred dollars. Should I offer to cover the cost of his lost wages as well?

At the fifth floor, the elevator chimes and the doors open to a young, somber-looking couple holding hands. We change places with them. The elevator doors close, and they disappear.

At the check-in desk, Eric stands back while I tell the receptionist his name, and she hands me a clipboard with papers for him to fill out. It is a bit like taking Ian to the doctor, as long as you don't consider what we're here for.

"The bill goes to me," I tell her in a low voice. "Laura Cahill. My address is in the file."

Her face neutral, she makes a note.

Eric and I settle ourselves in matching blond-wood chairs with blue upholstered seats. Lake paintings cover the waiting room's greenish-blue walls. They are meant to be calming. They do not work.

"I feel like I should buy you a drink first," I blurt.

He looks up from the clipboard. "Gotta admit, I could use one right about now."

Across the room, a very pregnant woman sits next to a pudgy man, both wearing gold bands. She catches my eye and smiles. I smile back and cross my arms so she can't see my bare left hand.

When Ian was a baby I wore a ruby-and-gold ring my father (my stepmother, really) had given me when I graduated from high school. It didn't look like a wedding or even an engagement ring, but placed on the proper finger, it seemed to ward off disapproving stares. I haven't worn it in years, and not just because I didn't like feeling married to my stepmother. At a certain point, people just assumed I was divorced—which, of course, I am. I've never tried to pretend that my ex-husband was Ian's father, but if people make the connection, I don't go out of my way to correct them.

I reach into my leather bag, touch paper, hesitate.

"I brought the contract we discussed."

I'd e-mailed Eric a copy of the agreement, which laid everything out in crystal-clear terms (at least for anyone who reads legal documents all day). Once Eric made his deposit, he would be out of the picture entirely. Should the insemination result in a pregnancy, the embryo and resulting child would be mine and mine alone; Eric would have no rights or responsibilities.

"Do you want to sign it now, or . . ."

He looks up from the clipboard and hesitates. "We should probably just do it now. Because if we wait until after . . . well, you might not want to shake my hand."

It takes me a moment to realize what he just said. I slap my hand over my mouth. My shoulders shake with laughter.

The pregnant lady across the room looks at me funny, but I keep on laughing until there are tears in my eyes.

———————

Sometime later, a blond, heavyset nurse with a baby voice leads us into an examining room, where more lake scenes decorate powder-blue walls. One of the paintings features a moose; another shows two deer and a bunny.

"You can take a seat over there, Mrs. Fergus," the nurse tells me, pointing to a corner chair.

"We're not married," I say.

"Oh! Sorry. I didn't mean to assume anything."

"This is a private sperm donation. It should be in your notes." Still standing, I point at her clipboard.

"I'm sure it is," she chirps, without checking.

I settle into the corner chair. The nurse takes Eric's temperature and blood pressure—which is thankfully normal. I wouldn't want him having a heart attack in the middle of—you know.

"The doctor will be right in," the nurse tells us, and we smile and nod even though we know she's lying.

Eric remains perched on the examining table. "So," he says.

"So."

He swings his feet and drums his fingers. The paper on the examining table rustles as if a mouse were scampering across it.

He takes a deep breath and then exhales. "This is awkward."

"Extremely."

He tilts his head and squints at the wall. "Do you like the lake paintings?"

"No. They are generic and contrived. They should have just gone with ocean paintings. At least it would make sense, given that we're near the coast."

"Or they could have pictures of chickens," he says.

"Chickens?"

"Yeah. Sitting on eggs, waiting for them to hatch. That's what this place is about, right?"

"You sure do like chickens," I say.

"Have you thought about names?" Eric asks.

"For the chickens? Oh!" He means for the baby. I shake my head. "It's a little early. I don't want to jinx myself. If Ian had been a girl, I was going to call him Eleanor, but now I'm not sure."

"Eleanor?"

"You don't like it?"

"It's—you know. Whatever makes you happy." He mouths "Eleanor" with obvious distaste.

"What about Ian?" I ask. "The first time I told you my son's name, I got the impression you didn't like it."

"I never said that."

"Do you like it?"

He waits a beat too long and then says, "Sure."

"You're a terrible liar."

He bites his lip. "It's just a little, you know."

"What?"

"Nothing. It doesn't matter what I think."

"But what do you think?"

"It's just . . . a lot of vowels. But as long as you like it. And Ian likes it."

Ian wishes I'd called him something else.

"What about Jake?" I ask. "You like that?"

He sits up straighter. "*Jake*. Now, *that's* a name."

There is a rap on the door, and Dr. Goodman walks in. He is in his early sixties, with a generous shock of silver hair and Buddy Holly glasses. He wears a blue lab coat over a black henley shirt and khakis. His Nikes squeak against the floor.

"H'lo." He glances at us and then hunches over a file and flicks through some pages.

"The private sperm donation." It is a statement, not a question.

"Yes," I say. "Eric Fergus. Dr. Goodman." Eric holds out his hand, but Dr. Goodman continues to study his notes as if he's cramming for a test he knew was coming but hadn't taken the time to prepare for.

"The lab faxed over your results," he tells Eric, without looking up. "All good. Though as I told Ms. Cahill, I'd feel better if we were freezing your semen and waiting six months to test again for HIV."

"But you also said that my fertility is declining by the day," I reminded him. Given his chosen field, you'd think he'd be a little more diplomatic.

He looks at me. "It's a matter of pros and cons. So you recorded an LH surge yesterday, yes?"

"Yes."

"Okay, then. Assuming all goes well, we'll see you back here this afternoon for the IUI."

He turns to Eric. "So, Mr. Fergus, you are the father—or rather the donor—of Ms. Cahill's first child, correct?"

"Correct."

"And that has been confirmed by a DNA test?"

"Yes."

"Okay, then." Dr. Goodman sits on a stool. "Mr. Fergus, when was your last ejaculation?"

"Excuse me?"

"He wants to know when you last had sex," I say.

"I understood the question." Irritation tinges Eric's voice.

"Doesn't have to be intercourse," Dr. Goodman says. "Any ejaculation during the past forty-eight hours could compromise your sperm count."

"No one told me that," I say. "When I called to make the appointment, no one said anything about—"

"I have not ejaculated in the past forty-eight hours," Eric interrupts, flushing slightly.

"Excellent." Dr. Goodman makes a note on his chart. "And

Ms. Cahill, if the IUI is successful, this will be your second pregnancy, correct?"

"Third," I mumble.

He flips through some pages. "But only one live birth."

"My son. Yes." I keep my eyes on the nearest lake painting.

He stands up. "If you don't have any more questions, I'll send the nurse in. She'll arrange for the collection."

After Dr. Goodman leaves, Eric and I are silent. Finally, he says, "So you're getting IUI? I thought you might go for IVF." IUI is intrauterine insemination; IVF is in vitro.

"You've been reading up on it?"

"I did go to medical school for a year."

"Yes. Of course."

"Plus I'm good with Google."

"My ovulation is regular and predictable, so I thought I'd try this first."

"No hormone shots, even?"

"I don't want to risk multiples. I'm not exactly young . . ."

"You're not that old," he says.

I laugh. "Thanks."

I am feeling slightly less uncomfortable when the nurse reappears. "Ready to make your deposit?" she asks Eric.

"Uh, yeah," Eric says.

I am feeling uncomfortable again. "You want me to wait for you?"

"No, that's okay. But good luck later. With the—you know."

"Right. Thanks. And good luck with the . . . I guess that doesn't require much luck."

He grins. "Nah. It's all about skill."

I walk out of the office, take the elevator downstairs, cross the parking lot, unlock my car—and then it hits me. I can't leave, not when the first stage in the creation of my future child's life might be happening five floors above me. If I can't be part of the moment (and to be clear, I don't want to be), at least I should be nearby.

By the time I get back to the waiting room, the chubby white couple has been replaced by a thin Asian couple, along with two women who may or may not be together. Hope and anxiety mingle with the Muzak.

I sit near one of the women, a trim brunette in tailored slacks, heels, and a white blouse.

She catches my eye. "How long have you been trying?"

Since I don't know how to explain my situation, I say, "Since last year," which is as long as it took to track down Eric.

"Three years for me," she said.

"Good luck."

"You too."

I close my eyes and think: *twelve percent.*

---

All my life, I have been self-disciplined and goal-oriented. Things don't happen to me; I *make* things happen. And then, when I was thirty years old, three years out of law school and two years married, I got pregnant by mistake.

It was ten o'clock at night when I took the test. I had just gotten home from work; my panty hose lay crumpled on the bathroom floor. Rob, my husband, was still at his (different) law office: par for the course. I placed the test stick on a piece of toilet paper to show him when he got home, washed the pee off my hands, and called his office number.

"Robert Purdy's office." He always answered that way after his secretary left. He said it was so he could screen his calls, but I secretly believed he couldn't bear the idea that people might think he answered his own phone, even late at night.

"It's me. Can you come home?" I wanted to show him the stick.

"Is something wrong?"

"No. It's just—I have something to tell you." Blood pounded in my ears. I had no idea how Rob would take the news. At this point,

I wasn't even sure how I felt about it, but it seemed like something we should process together.

He said, "So tell me." Computer keys clicked in the background.

"I'd rather do it in person."

He sighed. "I should be out of here by, I don't know. One, maybe? I'm working on an acquisition, they need everything done by next week."

"This is important."

"More important than a three-hundred-million-dollar lever-aged buyout?"

"Actually, yes."

He stopped typing. "What's going on?"

I took a deep breath. "I've been feeling sort of odd lately. Achy in my abdomen. Just kind of—off."

"You should see a doctor." He started typing again.

"I will. Because. . . I'm pregnant."

Silence.

"Rob?"

Silence.

"Rob?"

"I'm processing . . . Are you sure?"

"I just took a home test. It was positive."

"Shit."

"I know this wasn't exactly in the plans yet, and I've got to admit, I was pretty shocked at first too, but now that I've had a little time to digest it—"

"Shit!"

"Right now, that response isn't exactly helpful."

"There goes the Newport house."

"What Newport house?"

"The one we were going to buy once we'd paid off our student loans."

"Rob? For God's sake!" My throat tightened. "There will be

plenty of time to buy a house and cars and go on vacation and all that crap. And we'll still have two incomes. I'm not going to stop working. But we're having a baby! Aren't you at least a little bit happy about it?"

"You shouldn't tell them at work."

"They're going to notice."

"Eventually, yeah. But you have your review coming up. If they hear about this they might think *mommy track* and—"

"Can you come home? It would really help if we could talk about this."

"We are talking about this. Talking more isn't going to help. I've got to do those acquisition briefs, and . . . shit! I cannot fucking believe this."

He stayed late at the office to finish his brief. When he got home, I was asleep.

A month later, my abdomen stopped feeling achy. My breasts, which had gotten bigger, returned to their normal size. To his credit, Rob accompanied me to the ultrasound and held my hand as the doctor pointed out the peanut-shaped mass that had stopped growing and had no heartbeat.

"More common than most people realize," I remember the doctor saying. And: "Won't affect your future odds of conception."

Also to Rob's credit, he held me as I cried that night and drove me to the D & C the next day. But three months later, when I asked him if I thought we should start "trying," he looked at me as if I were insane.

"We got lucky last time," he said.

"You call a miscarriage lucky?"

"This is not a good time for a baby."

"When is a good time for a baby?"

"Maybe never."

We spent the next year discussing and debating (never arguing) whether or not to have children. And then he left me.

"It's become increasingly clear that we want different things out of life," he said. "That's never going to change."

A year later, he married a secretary from his office. Not his own: that would have been tacky, and Rob was not a tacky man. She became pregnant almost immediately.

And so did I.

---

Eric is surprised to see me in the waiting room.

"I just wanted to make sure everything went okay," I tell him.

He sinks into the chair next to me and buries his face in his hands. "I couldn't do it."

In an instant, my anxiety turns to despair. "But when we talked on the phone, you said you had no reservations. You talked about altruism . . ."

He slumps back in the chair and stares into space. "I don't mean I couldn't do it from a moral perspective. I mean, I just . . . I guess I was more uninhibited when I was I was twenty-three."

Now I get it. "Oh! So you mean—oh."

This is awkward. But at least hope is not lost. He just needs to get in the mood, that's all.

I lower my voice. "You want me to run to the store? Get you some, um, magazines?"

"They had magazines," he tells me.

"I've got a portable DVD player at home," I say. (Do I have time to drive up and back?) "I could buy you a movie . . ."

"They had movies," he says. "A whole shelf of them. One for every . . . predilection. And if I'd been anywhere else—really, it would have been fine. Easy. But the room, it smelled like, you know—"

"Oh God."

"No! Not that. It smelled like a doctor's office. Antiseptic. And kind of desperate. If desperation had a smell. And I could hear people walking by and the nurses on the phone." He shakes his head.

"You want to go for a walk?" I ask. "Then try again?"

The lab would need an hour, an hour and a half, maybe, to wash his sperm. My appointment isn't until three o'clock. There is still time.

He shakes his head. "I'm really sorry, Laura. I don't think it will make any difference."

I swallow hard. Attempt a joke. "So when you say, 'It's not you, it's me . . .'"

He snorts. "Oh, yeah. It's definitely me."

"Let me buy you lunch, at least. And then you can decide."

# Wendy

Looking back, so many things are funny—but not really.

Like: From the first time Darren and I slept together, two months after we started dating, until the day we got married, two years after college graduation, I had at least four pregnancy scares and was just so, so, *so* relieved when they turned out to be false alarms.

Like: For years I blamed our lack of sexual chemistry on my fear of pregnancy. Then, once fertility became an issue, I blamed our lack of sexual chemistry on the pressures of pregnancy.

Like: Now that we've got two kids and there's neither the fear nor the pressure of pregnancy, we don't have sex at all.

Ha ha. Funny, right?

---

The summer between my freshman and sophomore years of college, Darren came to visit me at my parents' lake house in northern Michigan. We were sleeping in separate rooms, me with my sister and him with my brother. We hadn't seen each other for over a month, and while our relationship, even at the beginning, was based on more of an emotional than a physical connection, we were nineteen and in love, and a month is a month.

Three days into the visit, we went for a walk after dinner. Down the street, a path led away from the lake, into the woods. We were about ten minutes down the path, talking and hugging and kissing and laughing, when it hit us: at last, we were alone. It was unlikely that anyone would be showing up, given that the mosquito-to-human ratio was somewhere in the neighborhood of ninety-to-one.

We rolled around on the mossy ground, the possibility of discovery only adding to our excitement. This was passion. This was love. *This* was what everyone was always making such a fuss about.

It wasn't until the very last moment that we realized that Darren hadn't brought a condom.

"Do it," I urged.

And he did.

I had just finished my period. Surely I couldn't be ovulating. Right? *Right?*

By the time we got back to the cabin, our arms and legs and Darren's butt covered with mosquito bites, I was convinced that I was pregnant and my life was over.

"What will we do?" I asked him over the phone a week later.

"There's nothing to do," he told me. "You're probably fine."

"What will we do?" I asked him two weeks after that, when my period was officially late. Granted, my period was late as often as not, but this time it felt different.

"What do you want to do?" he asked.

"I don't know."

Keep the baby. Give up the baby. Have an abortion. Each option terrified me in its own way.

"I'll stand by you no matter what," he said.

And just like that, I could breathe again. Everything was going to be okay. Darren loved me. I loved him.

The next day, I got my period.

"Thank God," Darren said.

"I know. We'll never do that again, huh?"

"Well . . ."

I laughed. "You know what I mean. As soon as we get back to school, I'm going on the pill."

"You sure?"

"I'm sure." I'd told Darren my concerns about the pill—including that it might affect my fertility down the line—but I couldn't go through this again. I'd barely slept in a month. As it turned out, even being on the pill didn't stop me from worrying about pregnancy, but at least the later scares were less intense.

That night on the phone, I said, "When you said you'd stand by me no matter what—it means a lot to me."

"I meant it."

"I know you did."

He took a deep breath. "And someday . . . years from now, after college . . . someday you'll be pregnant for real. And we'll be happy about it. And . . . I kind of can't wait for that."

---

Five years later, we got married. Another four and a half years after that, I switched from the pill to a diaphragm. I didn't dare going straight from the pill to pregnancy: too much risk of multiple births.

Finally, after six months, I packed away birth control altogether. At first, we told ourselves we weren't really "trying." We simply weren't preventing. After two years of "not preventing," we started trying for real: first the ovulation charts, then the ovulation predictor kits. My cycles were irregular. They always had been.

"It'll happen," Darren told me.

"I'm sorry," I sobbed one night. I did a lot of sobbing in those years. Even more than now, I mean.

"For what?"

"If you'd married someone else, you'd be a dad by now."

"There is nobody else. Never was, never will be. And anyway, we don't know that's it's because of you. It could be me."

We both knew he was just saying that to make me feel better, which somehow made me feel worse.

Darren went with me to the fertility specialist, a woman that my gynecologist had recommended without mentioning that she, unlike most of her patients, was pregnant.

"We'll have to test you too," the doctor told Darren, resting my patient file on her enormous belly.

"That's fine," he said.

"But I know it's me." I sat on the examining table, arms crossed over my paper dress. "My ovulation . . ."

"It's standard procedure." The doctor placed her clipboard on the counter. "It's entirely possible that you both have issues. It's not uncommon."

She waddled over to the examining table and flipped up the stirrups. "If you haven't ejaculated in the last couple of days, you can do it right now," she told Darren over her shoulder.

He blinked at her. "Here?"

She smiled. "Down the hall. In a bathroom. There are magazines. Or your wife can go with you. Whichever makes you more comfortable."

Comfortable? Was she kidding? Suddenly the paper dress and stirrups didn't seem so bad. I checked Darren's face. He looked mortified.

"Or you can do it at home," the doctor told Darren. "As long as you follow proper protocol and tell us ahead of time that you're coming in."

The clinic was a half hour from our house, forty-five minutes from Darren's office. He'd taken the morning off to be here.

"I'll just . . . I'll do it now." He stood up. I've never seen him look so dazed.

The doctor proceeded with the exam, which was more uncomfortable than I expected. When she was done, she tossed her rubber gloves into the metal trash can and told me I could get dressed.

"I'll have the nurse bring you a specimen cup," she told Darren.

"You want me to go with you?" I asked, yanking on my underpants.

When he shook his head, I felt relieved. And then I felt rejected.

He must have noticed my expression, because he said, "If I do this alone, I can pretend it never happened."

He wasn't gone long—five minutes, maybe a little longer. We walked out of the office without saying anything. When we reached the parking lot, I took his hand. "I'm sorry you had to go through that."

He squeezed my hand. "It's worse for you."

He was right; it was worse for me. After five humiliating minutes in the restroom, Darren was off the hook. His sperm motility was so bad and his count so low, there was no medical procedure in the world that would make the slightest difference.

My problems, though: those could be investigated and addressed through exploratory surgery, hormone shots, intrauterine insemination, and, finally, in vitro. But I'm getting ahead of myself.

Darren chose our first sperm donor, a tall, athletic, educated six-footer with light brown hair and blue eyes.

"Just like me, only better," Darren said, forcing a smile.

"No one's better."

He rolled his eyes.

We tried taking the cheap route first—an intrauterine insemination in the doctor's office. When that didn't work, we emptied our checking account and took out a big chunk of our savings for one failed in vitro attempt and then another. I cried a lot. Darren began spending more time on his computer. He slept farther away from me in the bed.

He suggested adoption.

"I want my own baby," I blurted—and then immediately wished I could take it back. Instead, I tried to dig myself out. "I mean, with adoption—it's just such a long wait. And so expensive. And you can't control what the mother did when she was pregnant or what kind of genetic issues you're dealing with . . ."

"I get it," he said.

The bank had run out of our tall donor's sperm. When I asked for Darren's input on a new donor, he said, "I don't care. You pick."

I found another six-foot-tall man, this one blond with green eyes, but the clinic told me that his remaining vials had been reserved for the families that had already used him and might want more children.

I thought of Darren, and my heart hurt. He's the one I really wanted to father my children. The closer the donor matched him, the better.

"Do you have anyone who's five foot eight?" I asked the cryobank. "Brown hair, blue eyes. Really smart, likes math and science?"

I paid two hundred and fifty dollars for sperm from a medical student identified only as Donor 613.

"Last chance," I told Darren. "If this doesn't work . . ." I couldn't even bear to finish the sentence.

When my pregnancy test came up positive, I left a message on Darren's voice mail.

He didn't call back.

# Laura

We are mostly silent during the fifteen-minute drive from the fertility clinic to the restaurant, and it isn't until I've parked the car and turned off the ignition that Eric realizes where I've taken him—and why I spent so much time fiddling with my GPS.

"Hooters?" His mouth hangs open.

"I considered a strip club," I admit. "But this was closer. Also classier, at least in relative terms."

He continues to gawk—and we haven't even left the car yet. Maybe this wasn't such a great idea.

"We can go somewhere else, if you'd rather," I say. "If you're not, um . . ."

"A boob man?"

"Right."

He bursts out laughing and opens the door. "I like boobs just as much as the next guy. Let's eat."

Aside from the well-endowed (naturally or otherwise) girls in white tank tops and orange hot pants, Hooters resembles the count-less chain restaurants that Ian and I frequent on the weekends, with scuffed wood floors and pine walls decorated with sports ban-ners. Outdated music plays a touch too loudly over the speak-ers. Big-screen TVs dangle from the ceiling and sprout along the walls, flashing images of baseball, boxing, soccer, track, and even shuffleboard.

"I don't suppose you have a children's menu," I joke to the pretty hostess, who is much too short to be carrying breasts that size.

"We do!" she chirps. "Plus kids eat free on Sundays!"

We follow her through the half-full dining room. To my sur-prise, I am not the only female customer, though the clientele defi-nitely skews toward men in their thirties and forties, the majority dressed casually in T-shirts and shorts, with a few sporting ties. Most of the men appear more fascinated by the televised baseball than by the girls in orange hot pants.

Our table, set with plastic orange glasses, a chunky wood con-diment dispenser, and our very own roll of paper towels, is near a wall; I stand aside to allow Eric the seat with the better view. The hostess hands us laminated menus, instructs us to have an amazing lunch, and scampers back to her stand.

"You bring a lot of clients here?" Eric asks, opening his menu.

"Just the really important ones. And only when I can't get a table at Applebee's."

He shakes his head and smiles. "This is officially the weirdest day of my life."

Our waitress introduces herself by sitting sideways in a spare chair at our table and writing her name on a cocktail napkin: *AFTON* ♥. I didn't even know Afton was a name, but no matter. For my purposes, she is perfect: tall, thin, and busty (of course), with shiny black hair and big brown eyes.

"I'll have an iced tea," I tell her.

"Just water," Eric says, working so hard keep his eyes off of Afton's chest that he seems to be focusing on her forehead. Nearby, a guy built like a bouncer buses tables.

"How about a beer?" I suggest. "You should have a beer."

"I'll have a beer," Eric tells Afton's forehead.

She flashes us a big smile, stands up, and bounces away. The back of her tank top reads *Delightfully tacky yet unrefined*.

"I'm going to have to come here more often," I joke, scanning the menu, which features man food: chicken wings, burgers, seafood.

"No veggie burgers," I say. "Sorry."

"They've got grilled cheese. Good enough." Eric shuts his menu.

"Why are you a vegetarian, anyway?" I ask.

He shrugs. "Because eating meat is unhealthy, bad for the environment, and cruel. Why are you a carnivore?"

"Omnivore," I say.

A new waitress, this one blond, appears at the table and sits in the seat Afton vacated.

"Hi!" Her smile is very, very white.

"Hello."

"I'm right next door." She gestures to a table full of men. "Holler if you need me!" She takes out a pen and writes her name below Afton's on the cocktail napkin. *CAYLA*.

"No heart next to her name?" I say to Eric once Cayla leaves.

"I'm kind of hurt," he says.

Afton delivers our drinks and settles back into her chair, crossing her shapely legs. Eric orders his grilled cheese. I go for mahi mahi tacos. Afton playfully suggests we order chicken wings. We playfully tell her no. Well, I do, anyway; once he's done ordering, Eric keeps his eyes firmly fixed on the paper-towel dispenser.

"Well?" Eric asks once Afton leaves and he can look up again. "Why do you eat meat?"

"Just because," I say.

He raises his eyebrows. "Impressive reasoning. That the kind of argument you present in court?"

"I'm not a litigator. I don't go to court."

"Did you want to be a litigator?"

"Oh, no. I dislike conflict way too much."

He takes a swig of his beer. "Why law, then?"

I shrug. "Why not law? I got out of college with a liberal arts degree. American literature. Not the most marketable major in the world. I spent a couple of years in advertising. The money was terrible, plus I didn't really get the point. You know, putting all that effort into something that ultimately just annoys people."

"Unlike lawyers."

"Oh, for God's sake. We're not all ambulance chasers. I mainly practice estate law. Wills, trusts, that sort of thing. I help people plan for the future so their heirs can avoid conflicts later on. I like working, feeling productive. For the most part, I take a lot of satisfaction from what I do. And I certainly appreciate the financial security."

In a corner of my brain, I consider that I am defending my career choice to a college-educated, med-school-dropout Costco checker.

I rip open a packet of sugar and dump it into the iced tea. No artificial sweeteners for me, not while I'm trying to get pregnant.

Afton comes by again and sets a few wrapped packets on the table. At first I think they are condoms (the last thing we need right now), but when I pick one up, I see it is a hand wipe. There is writing on the back of the package. *Bartender: pharmacist with limited inventory.*

I check another package. *Does the name Pavlov ring a bell?*

And a third. *Insomnia is nothing to lose sleep over.* Obviously, that one is for me. I rip the package open.

On the overhead speakers, a Rolling Stones song gives way to Madonna's "Like a Virgin."

"Tell me about your music," I say, cleaning my hands. "What was it like?"

Eric chooses the Pavlov wipe. "Acoustic. Rhythm-based. Kind of like Jason Mraz only . . ."

"What?"

"Not as good." He half smiles.

"I bet you were better than you give yourself credit for."

He raises his eyebrows. "Want to know what the bloggers said?"

"What?"

"That I was kind of like Jason Mraz only not as good." This time he full-smiles. I can't help but grin back.

He drinks some more of his beer, puts the bottle on the table, and picks at the label. "Your other pregnancy. I don't know if it's any of my business. But was it . . . mine? I mean, from my, uh . . ."

For a moment, I don't understand what he is talking about. "Your . . . oh! No. It was before that. I was married. Briefly. Three years. The year before our divorce, I got pregnant, but it just didn't . . . take. I was eleven weeks along."

"That must have been hard."

"It was. For me, anyway. My ex-husband never wanted the baby. He was afraid it would have a negative impact on my future earning potential."

"He didn't really say that."

"He really did. But he wasn't—it's not that he was a bad guy. On paper, we were a perfect match. But it turned out that wasn't enough. Oh, look! Lunch is here."

When Afton puts our baskets of food on the table, her breasts come within a foot of Eric's face. Silly girl: she must assume he's paying. She has barely left when yet another girl in orange hot pants, this one a green-eyed brunette with a girl-next-door appeal, balances on the edge of our spare seat.

"Aren't those mahi mahi tacos good?" she asks me. "Those are the only kind of seafood I like. That and tuna." She takes out a pen and adds her name to the cocktail napkin. *SENECA* ♥. Yes, we got another heart.

I catch Eric watching her as she trots away. I smile. Everything will be just fine.

---

Back in front of the shiny building, I don't offer to accompany Eric up the elevator to the clinic. I'd rather not distract him from the fresh memory of pretty Seneca.

Once he disappears through the front door, I circle around to the lot and park under a tree. I call the clinic and review the situation with the receptionist, who says she can push my appointment back to four o'clock to allow them time to wash Eric's sperm.

I turn on my car to leave—then I turn it off again. Twenty-five minutes later, Eric comes out of the building, walks over to a small blue car, and drives away.

I dial the clinic.

"This is Laura Cahill. Just wanted to confirm my appointment for this afternoon. Will the donor semen be washed and ready?"

"Hold on a moment please, Ms. Cahill."

After several minutes that feel like several hours, she gets back on the line. "Everything's on schedule. See you at four."

# Vanessa

When I get home, Eric is sitting on the couch, reading and listening to his iPod.

I put my purse on the side table by the door. I can't even look at him.

"How was it?" I ask.

He doesn't answer.

I force myself to look at him. "Well?"

"Huh?" He blinks at me. Turns off his iPod.

"How was it?" I repeat. My voice shakes.

He closes the book. "Awkward."

"And is she . . . when will it get put in?"

"It's done. At least I assume it is. She had a three o'clock appointment, but there were some . . . issues. With my donation. When I left they told me she was coming in at four instead. She has better odds this way, using fresh—you know."

It's done. All day, I'd been hoping he'd change his mind—and if he didn't, that she'd back out. But it is done. Over.

Wait a minute.

"What kind of issues with your donation?"

He leans back and looks at the ceiling. "My first try didn't work. I just—it wasn't happening. So Laura and I grabbed something to eat, and the next time it worked."

"You and Laura—what?"

"We got some lunch. No big deal."

"You mean at a restaurant?"

"Well—yeah."

"Like a date."

He scowls. "No. Not like a date. We were both hungry, that's all. And she appreciates what I'm doing for her and her son, so she bought me lunch. Also, she paid me for the donation. Three hundred dollars. If you want me to use that money to take you out, I will."

"Don't you think it's kind of funny?" I say, my voice rising. "You couldn't get off the first time you tried, but after going out to lunch with Laura, you were fine."

"We went to Hooters."

Did he just say . . .

"What?"

"Hooters. She took me to Hooters."

"Is she gay?" That would be awesome.

"No. At least I don't think so. She just thought it might help get me in the mood. Which maybe it did, or maybe it was the beer."

Laura. Hooters. Sperm. Beer. This keeps getting better and better. But I can't get pissed. At least, I can't let him see that I'm pissed. I said he could do this.

I say, "You said her odds are better this way. What are they?"

"Since the sperm was fresh, she's got about a twelve percent chance of getting pregnant. If it's frozen, it drops to six."

"And if it doesn't work this time, is she going to . . . are you going to . . ."

"There was enough for three tries. They were inserting one to-day and freezing two other vials."

Eric's sperm is in a freezer. If I pay Laura what's-her-face three hundred dollars, will she sell it to me?

He says, "It's over. Just forget about it, okay?"

*Part 3*

---

JULY

# Wendy

The children claw at the glass slider like a couple of cats lusting after a sparrow. But it's not a bird they want, it's the swimming pool.

"Why can't we wait for the swim 'structor outside?" Sydney asks, brown eyes fixed on the small patch of blue. Her sunscreen hasn't quite soaked in yet. If she sees her white face in the mirror, she will pitch a fit.

Still, she and Harrison look seriously cute. They are wearing the bathing suits my mother gave them for their sixth birthday last month. Hers is navy with white-and-yellow daisy appliqués. His looks like an American flag. My mother also gave Harrison a white rash-guard shirt, but he refuses to wear it.

"You can't be in the pool without a grown-up, and I'm not going in yet." I've told them that at least four times in the last half hour. The both love the water and beg to swim even when the air and water are much too cold. I think of Eric Fergus. Laura said he surfs.

"We won't go in till the 'structor gets here," Harrison lies. Or maybe he thinks he's telling the truth. As I look through the glass, our yard looks sunny, cheery, inviting—assuming you enjoy running on concrete and playing with gravel, as Harrison does. Open the slider, though, and harsh, hot reality would blast you in the face.

It is a hundred and nine degrees in North Scottsdale. According to the news, it's a hundred and eleven on the southern, slightly lower side of town. If I were the optimistic type—which, obviously, I'm not—I'd be grateful for those two degrees, but what does it matter? I can take it up to a hundred and four, at least for short periods of time, but anything above that makes me loony.

When the doorbell rings, the children race out of the kitchen to the front door. I follow, reknotting the oversize scarf I've tied around my waist. As a swim cover-up, it's half fabulous, falling all the way to the floor and completely covering my cellulite-dimpled legs. The exposed half of my swimsuit isn't too bad: green-and-blue floral, with a low V-neck meant to draw attention to my boobs and away from everything else. Still, I'm self-conscious about my flabby arms. Plus, it's been several days since I've shaved my armpits.

I love the young swim instructor on sight, if only because she's unapologetically fat. No flattering V-neck for her! A high-necked, green-and-black racing suit flattens her chest and highlights enormous shoulders. Gray gym shorts reveal chunky thighs. Her long yellow hair hangs in a thick, stiff braid down her back. A whistle hangs from a cord around her neck.

"HEY! YOU MUST BE WENDY! I'M SAMANTHA! FROM SWIM SAFE!"

Clearly, this is someone accustomed to holding conversations outside. Or perhaps underwater.

She holds out her hand and proceeds to crush mine.

"Nice to meet you," I grunt through the pain.

She strides into the living/toy room (sometimes I think of it as

the Living Toy Room). Sydney and Harrison back up, semifright-
ened brown eyes stuck on Samantha, half smiles fading fast.

Hands on generous hips, Samantha grins at the wreckage of the
room. "HEY! I GUESS YOU GUYS LIKE LEGOS!"

Harrison nods, just a tiny bit.

"This is Harrison." I put a hand on his bony shoulder. "And
Sydney." She sidles over to me, snuggles against my arm.

Samantha claps her hands. The kids and I flinch as if a gun has
just gone off. "YOU GUYS WANNA SHOW ME THE POOL?"

Showing Samantha the pool turns out to be just that: standing
next to it without going in. When Harrison dips a toe into the soupy
water (ninety-three degrees, last I checked), Samantha turns up the
volume even more.

"HEY—DUDE! DID I SAY YOU COULD GO IN YET?"

Unused to having anyone but me yell at him, Harrison draws
his foot out of the water.

"They gotta understand they can't go in whenever they feel like
it," Samantha tells me. Maybe she's lowered her voice, or maybe
I've just gotten used to it.

"It *is* hot out here," I say. It is also five minutes into the forty-
dollar, half-hour lesson.

"Safety first," Samantha says. Her deep brown skin isn't even
damp with sweat. I don't have to ask whether she's grown up in
Arizona. Natives develop a lizardlike resistance to the heat but
turn blue at the edges and put sweaters on their pets whenever the
thermometer drops below sixty.

She crosses her arms over her flat chest. "They can float?"

"Yeah, sure. They've had lessons every summer since they were
three. But Harrison will only swim underwater, and Sydney will
only swim above it. You know—dog paddle. She's afraid to put her
head under."

"Hmm." She narrows her eyes, smiles a little. "We'll take care
of that."

"When can we go in the pool?" Sydney asks.

"Any second," I say. Sweat bathes my entire body. I can't wait to escape into the air-conditioning and then, once SAMANTHA has left, I will join the twins in the pool.

"*DUDE!*"

At the sound of Samantha's angry voice, Sydney stumbles backward, her face tight with fear. She hasn't even touched the water. I no longer like this Samantha person, no matter how fat she is.

"*LEAVE THAT ROCK ALONE!*"

Oh. She isn't shouting at Sydney. She is scolding Harrison, who has followed her instructions to stay out of the pool. Instead, he plucks at a pile of river rocks lined up to look like a stream at the edge of the lot.

"*THERE COULD BE A SCORPION UNDER THERE!*"

I touch the side of my face. I think she has injured my eardrum. "Can you start the lesson now?"

"This is part of the lesson. Safety is rule number one."

"Right," I say. "But they've only got five more lessons, and I was hoping they'd learn their strokes this year." Which will be difficult if they stay on land.

She narrows her blue eyes (which are already pretty narrow from a lifetime spent squinting in the sun), picks up the whistle, and—ouch! This time I think she really has injured my eardrums.

At the sound of the whistle, Harrison scurries across the yard like a puppy sniffing raw hamburger meat.

"WHEN I BLOW THE WHISTLE AGAIN, I WANT YOU GUYS TO JUMP IN THE POOL."

"Sydney won't jump in," I tell her.

Samantha ignores me and picks up the whistle. "ONE! TWO!"

I sprint for the slider. The whistle burns my ears, but not as badly as last time. Behind me, I hear one splash.

There is a brief pause, after which Samantha yells at Sydney. "NO! YOU CAN'T JUST CLIMB IN! WHAT IF YOU FELL?

WHAT IF SOMEONE PUSHED YOU? YOU GOTTA KNOW WHAT IT'S LIKE TO GO UNDER! YOU GOTTA BE ABLE TO GET OUT!"

I escape into the house before I hear Sydney's reply.

The thermostat is set at eighty degrees, but all that sweat makes me shiver. A pile of pool towels sits on a kitchen chair. Damn—I meant to take them outside before the lesson. There's no way I'm going out now, though, not while Samantha is going *mano a mano* against Sydney. There's no doubt that Sydney will win, that I will have paid forty dollars to have her spend thirty minutes sulking on a pool chair rather than jumping in the pool. But that doesn't mean I want to hear about it.

I mop my face and chest with a Cinderella towel and glance through the slider just in time to see Samantha scoop up Sydney, step to the edge of the pool, and—no! She can't possibly be planning to—!

The slider muffles the splash, but there is no barrier in the world thick enough to mute Sydney's screams once she comes back up. She sounds more angry than frightened. No, she sounds more furious than terrified. No, she sounds like she is going to rip Samantha's head off.

A dark shape moves underwater; Harrison has wisely retreated to the bottom of the pool, just as he does when I'm not paying anyone to teach him otherwise.

Samantha turns her head slightly. Is she really smiling? Because she threw my six-year-old into the pool? Sydney's wail continues like a car alarm. She treads water with swift, jerky strokes. Her wet hair falls in dark ringlets around her red face.

Samantha says something, but, miraculously, Sydney is so loud that I can't make out the words. Sydney's scream has always been unusually shrill, but today she is in rare form. Samantha checks her watch. I know what she's thinking. *She can't keep this scream up forever.*

Ha! Sydney's scream endurance in unmatched by any child I've ever encountered. True, even she will eventually wear out, but there are a mere twenty minutes left to the lesson. She is just getting started.

Harrison swims a lap underwater—then two, three, four, five before popping up for a quick sip of air and going back down.

I've just poured myself a glass of iced tea when the doorbell rings. I leave the drink on the counter, retighten the scarf around my waist, and pick my way through the LEGOs. When I see Lane Plant looming, shirtless, in the doorway, I reflexively take a step back.

Lane Plant is a big, dark, hairy man, with heavy eyebrows, a perpetual five o'clock shadow, and a virtual rug on his chest and back that the whole neighborhood gets to see on a regular basis since he walks around shirtless from May through October. Today he's wearing shiny blue gym shorts, leather flip-flops, and the sandalwood cologne that he's worn for as long as I've known him and that I've always liked in spite of myself.

"Sorry to, um . . ." He clears his throat. "I was doing some work in the backyard, and I heard, you know—someone was screaming. Just wanted to make sure that, you know. Everything okay?"

No one has ever accused Lane of being articulate.

"Everything's fine." I make myself smile. "The kids, um—swim lessons. Sydney, she's doesn't like—she's afraid to go underwater. So the swim 'structor—I mean instructor—threw . . . pushed . . . she threw her in."

So maybe I shouldn't make fun of Lane's inarticulateness.

"That might work," Lane says.

"But it probably won't."

He doesn't smile. Lane never got my jokes. (Was that even a joke?) Even in the old days, when Sherry and Lane and Darren and I used to sit around drinking margaritas, Lane never laughed at a single thing I said.

"Otherwise, how are things?" he asks, still standing in the doorway. Do I have to invite him in? No, I don't think so.

"Good," I say. "Same."

"Good." He nods.

"Thanks for stopping by. For checking."

"No problem." He smiles, and it changes his whole face, makes him almost handsome. He should smile more often.

I smile back, and we hold each other's eyes for about two seconds more than is comfortable. Finally, he holds up a hand in a wave. "Catch you later."

"Sure thing."

He heads back to his house.

When I close the door, my heart is racing and I'm sweaty again. I wish, for the ten-thousandth time, that Darren would get another job and we could move far, far away from Sherry and Lane Plant.

Back in the pool, nothing much has changed. Sydney's siren scream continues unabated. Harrison shoots back and forth underwater like a tadpole. It may be my imagination, but it seems like Samantha's resolve has been dented. Her hands have left her hips and hang helpless at her sides. She slumps, just a little bit.

After a couple of minutes, Samantha blows her whistle, long and hard. Shocked, Sydney stops screaming for several heartbeats before covering her ears and wailing with renewed fury.

Harrison swims a couple more laps along the bottom before hauling himself out of the pool. Dripping, he crosses the concrete, ignoring Samantha as she shouts, "DUDE! WHERE YOU THINK YOU'RE GOING? DUDE! WE GOT TEN MINUTES LEFT!"

Harrison and I face each other through the glass slider. I grab a towel and pass it to him. He wraps it around his shoulders and sloshes into the kitchen.

"I gotta pee."

A minute later, the toilet flushes. Harrison tramps back out, still trailing pool water.

"There's water on the floor," I say.

"Dodie did it."

He hauls the slider open. If Samantha was weakening before, she has renewed her resolve.

"YOU CAN SCREAM ALL YOU WANT, SYDNEY. BUT YOU KNOW WHAT? YOU'RE GONNA LEARN TO GO UNDERWATER! I'M GONNA HELP YOU! AND THEN YOU'LL REALLY LEARN TO SWIM."

Harrison pauses. He half turns to me. "Samantha needs to use her indoor voice."

I throw my head back and laugh. Harrison giggles. I open my arms, and he steps back into the house, right into my embrace. I kiss the top of his wet, dark head.

"I love you so much. You know that?"

"I know," he says.

# Vanessa

Sofie Sanchez sits on the floor behind my desk, stacking the little paper cups that Melva and Pammy use for mouthwash. Sofie is supercute, even though her pink T-shirt has a big orange-juice stain on the front and her thick, dark hair needs a trim.

"Look, Nessa!"

I turn around just in time to see the paper-cup tower tumble. Sofie smacks the ground.

"You want to make the bottom bigger," I say.

The waiting room is empty. I join Sofie on the floor, where I help build a better paper-cup base. Then we start in on the second layer, slightly smaller than the first.

When we get to the third layer, she says, "It's a wedding cake!"

Ugh. It does look like a wedding cake. Just when we were having such a good time.

My left hand is still bare. In a moment of complete stupidity, I told Eric I didn't need a diamond. A plain wedding band would be fine. Of course, that was back when I thought that engagement led to marriage—and before I realized that even saying the word "wedding" would make Eric go, "I'm just getting used to the idea of being engaged."

I point to the stack of paper cups. "I think it looks more like a sand castle."

"Hello?"

Someone has come into the office. I scramble off the floor and smile at Kristin Minahan, who is ten minutes early for her eleven o'clock appointment. Kristin is about my age, pretty and preppy, with a gold band and big-ass diamond on her left hand.

"Sorry, Kristin. I didn't hear you come in."

"That's okay. Looks like you're busy." Kristin smiles and wiggles her fingers at Sofie. Sofie plants her face in the carpet.

"Shy," I mouth.

"She one of Dr. Sanchez's?"

"The youngest. The other two are at camp this week, and their nanny is in Mexico for the month."

I don't tell Kristin that Dr. Sanchez offered to pay me extra to watch Sofie at work. I said no even though I could use the money. It made me think of Eric's nanny comment and made me feel weirdly offended. But then, everything to do with Eric feels weird these days.

I pull out Kristin's file. "Your information still the same? Address, phone, insurance?"

"Yes, except . . ." She touches her belly.

"Yeah?"

"I'm pregnant." She smiles, and her face turns pink. "We haven't told many people. It's only two and a half months, so until I hit the third-month mark . . ."

"Right." My face feels tight, tense.

"But I figured I should let you know. I can't have X-rays, of course. I'm not sure if it makes any difference with the cleanings."

"I'll tell Pammy."

"Thanks." She exhales and her smile grows bigger.

I know I'm supposed to say something, ask her how she's feeling or tell her she looks amazing. But all I can think is: *She got pregnant right when Laura Cahill did*. If Laura Cahill did.

"Were you trying for long?" I blurt, though it's none of my business.

Kristin isn't offended. She shakes her head. "First try."

"Good for you," I say. "Congratulations."

---

There is a 12 percent chance that Laura Cahill got pregnant that day that Eric did his . . . thing. And if that didn't work, she still had two more shots at a 6 percent chance each. So that means she has a, what? Twenty-four percent chance of being pregnant? That can't be right. Because if the first time didn't work, she'd go back to zero, and . . .

Crud. All those times when my high school math teachers said, "Pay attention because you'll need to know this someday." Turns out they were right.

"How are you feeling?" I ask Kristin as she sorts through magazines on a wall rack.

"Little nauseous," she says. "But not too bad. I'm just so tired. No matter how much I sleep, it's never enough. Good thing it's summer vacation, or I'd be napping on my desk." Kristin teaches second grade.

I spend the rest of the morning playing with Sofie and obsessing over whether or not Laura Cahill got knocked up. With Eric's child. Finally, I decide it's stupid to torture myself. When I get home, I'll call her and find out.

---

That night, I'm about to hang up when Laura Cahill answers her cell phone on the fourth ring. *"Eric?"*

She sounds way too excited to be getting a call from our home number. I almost hang up, but then she'll just call back, maybe even try Eric on his cell, and I don't want him to know I called. He's on his way home from work now—I just talked to him. I've got at least twenty minutes before he walks through the door.

"Um, no. It's Vanessa. Eric's . . . fiancée." I'm sitting on the couch, clutching a pillow.

"Oh. Hello." She no longer sounds way too excited. There's a lot of static in the background.

"Hi. I . . . um . . . Are we on speakerphone?"

"Bluetooth. I'm in my car."

"Oh. Good. I wanted to be sure you weren't in your office with anyone listening . . ." *Just say it.* "Are you pregnant?"

It takes her forever to answer. I know she hasn't hung up because the static is still really loud.

"I don't know," she says finally.

". . . When will you?" Without meaning to, I hold my breath.

"A couple of days."

I exhale. I hope she can't hear me.

"So I guess that means . . . that first time. In April. It didn't . . ." I have a flashback to that awful day on the beach, waiting for Eric to come out of the restaurant.

"No," she says. "It didn't."

"So you, um, tried again?"

"Yes."

"Once?"

"Twice."

That means it's all gone. If this time didn't work, it's all over.

"How long till you know?" I squeeze the pillow.

She takes so long to answer, I think she's going to ignore the question. Finally she goes, "I don't know. A few days. Maybe a week."

"Can you call me when you know?" I ask. "On my cell. I just—I need to know. It's not that I don't want . . . I just need to know."

Again, she is quiet for a long, long time. When she speaks, it sounds like she is even farther away or deeper underwater. "If it's positive, I'll call you. Otherwise, you can assume it didn't take."

"Thanks." I would've liked a call either way, but this is better than nothing. "I'll give you my cell number?"

"Sure."

"And you'll call me? If it's positive, I mean?"

"Yes."

I rattle off my phone digits, realizing as I do so that she's driving and can't possibly be writing them down.

#  Laura

It's stupid to cry. Worse, it's dangerous, given that I'm in the thick of rush-hour traffic, stuck behind a shiny cream Lexus SUV with an irritating habit of speeding up and then jamming on the brakes.

I lied to the girlfriend. The fiancée. I do not need to wait a few days or a week to learn whether or not I am not pregnant. I already know that I'm not.

I don't normally put much stock in intuition, but from the time I drove home from my last clinic visit until yesterday morning, when enough time had passed to take a home pregnancy test, I felt certain that it had been unsuccessful. Two more tests wait in my bathroom cabinet. For another week, I'll continue to lay off alcohol, ibuprofen, and sushi until the second pee stick confirms what I already know.

My tears dry up several exits before I get off the freeway. By the time I pull into my garage, my face, as reflected in the rearview mirror, just looks tired. I am tired.

In the kitchen, Carmen is dredging fish fillets in cornflake crumbs.

I force myself to smile. "Halibut?"

"Tilapia."

"Fresh?"

"Frozen. Sorry."

"No, no—it's okay. Make sure you take some home for your dinner, Carmen."

Ever since Ian's unfortunate discovery that the food chicken and the animal chicken are the same thing in different forms (one being a live form, one dead), Carmen has been cooking a lot of mild fish—which Ian will only eat if it's been dredged in crumbs and pan-fried. He won't touch salmon or ahi or shellfish. Beef is out, too, because "Cows are cute and they have feelings."

Last week Carmen grilled turkey burgers. Several bites in, Ian asked, "Is turkey the food the same as turkey the animal?"

I pretended not to hear him, and he ate the entire burger, but I know it's only a matter of time before we're living on bread and cheese—especially since next week Carmen is flying to El Salvador to visit her children.

Tonight, still reeling from Eric's girlfriend's phone call, I don't really care what I eat. It was a huge disappointment, of course, having the test turn out negative yesterday. However, one thought saved me from total despair: *I can ask Eric for more.*

A couple of days ago, I even sent him a casual e-mail: *Just came across some pictures of Ian (attached) when he was little & thought you might get a kick out of them . . .*

I thought he'd write back and ask whether I was pregnant, which would give me the perfect opening to make my next request. But I haven't heard from him. After my conversation with the fiancée, I doubt I ever will.

If only I had gone with in vitro from the beginning, instead of

waiting until the third try. It was foolish of me to do the first insemination, when the sperm was fresh and my odds were greatest,
without so much as a hormone injection. I had such an easy time
getting pregnant with Ian, and lately my cycles had been so regular,
my ovulation so predictable. Getting Eric Fergus to agree to a donation seemed like the biggest hurdle—no, the only hurdle. I thought
my body would take care of the rest.

The sounds of an inane children's program drift into the kitchen.
I follow the noise down the hallway and into the office. The blinds
are drawn, the lights off. Ian lies on his belly, chin on hands, glazed
eyes fixed on the flickering screen.

"Hey, buddy."

He turns his head to say, "Hi, Mom," before returning his attention to the show.

"Can I have a hug?"

He pushes himself up from the floor, gives me a quick squeeze,
and then resumes his position on the carpet.

I put my handbag on the desk and step over Ian to the window,
where I pull a cord to open the venetian blinds. Ian flinches at the
light but keeps watching his moronic show.

"Are you still in your pajamas?" I ask.

He checks his oversize T-shirt and baggy boxers as if seeing
them for the first time. "I guess."

"It's after five o'clock." I raise my voice to be heard over the
laugh track.

"Lazy day." He shoots me his most irresistible smile.

"You've had several lazy days."

"It's summer."

"Did you rake the chicken coop like I asked you to?"

The smile wavers, just a bit. "I forgot."

"You need to check your list. First thing every morning." Ian
has a whiteboard in his room; his daily responsibilities are in the
top left corner, in red ink. For a while, the system worked.

"The coop is starting to smell," I say. Actually, there's no "starting" about it; the coop stinks, especially in the summer heat.

He rolls onto his back. "Can't Carmen rake the coop?"

"No! Carmen cannot rake the coop!" Suddenly, surprisingly, I am angry. I scan the desk and the floor before spotting the remote control on a chair.

When I click off the set, Ian abandons his irresistible-child routine. "Mom! I was watching that!"

"Did you make your bed this morning?"

"Carmen did it."

"What about the piano—did you practice?"

"I'll do it later."

"No, you'll do it now." My voice warbles.

Ian stares at me like I'm a stranger before getting off the floor and stalking out of the room.

"Get dressed first," I call after him. He doesn't answer.

My hands shake; my face burns. I almost feel the way I did after my hormone shots. A nurse had me practice jabbing an orange, and then she showed me how to stab myself in the thigh. I didn't mind the sharp burn so much, but the flushing and jitters that followed worsened my insomnia and left me feeling anxious.

In the kitchen, Carmen heats olive oil in a large frying pan and avoids my eyes. She heard me yell at Ian.

"Please don't make Ian's bed tomorrow," I say.

She throws three tilapia fillets into the pan. When they hit the oil, they sizzle. "I tell him. Two time. But he no do it, and it look messy."

"I know. But we have to stop doing so much for him. He needs to learn."

My voice must sound funny because Carmen turns and touches me on the arm. "You okay?"

The gesture makes my eyes fill. I blink back the tears.

"Just tired," I say.

"Tomorrow I make you pasta," she says. "No fish."

I laugh, and a tear bubbles from my eye. "Pasta sounds wonderful. Thank you, Carmen." After a pause, I add, "You're good to us."

Ian, dressed at last, in gym shorts and an old T-shirt, settles himself at the piano, shuffles his sheet music, and begins to play. Badly. At first, I think he's hitting the wrong keys on purpose, but his stiff posture and the concentration on his face makes me think otherwise.

His piano teacher said that he showed an unusual natural musical ability. Presumably, he received that from Eric Fergus, along with his easygoing charm and slacker tendencies. Natural ability is of no use without practice and perseverance.

Eric Fergus. Who goes from medical school to Costco?

Ian continues to pound the piano. I cross the room, place my hands on his shoulders, and kiss the top of his head, breathing in his little-boy smells. He tilts his face back. I kiss his nose. He smiles, as incapable of staying mad at me as I am at him.

Out of nowhere, I wish I had a partner—not just so I could avoid all of the donor sperm issues, but so I could talk about how wrenching this baby quest has become. How I want another child like Ian more than I've ever wanted anything.

Eric Fergus doesn't have a child to call his own—by choice, presumably—but he does have Vanessa. I can't get her voice out of my head, the tension when she asked, "Are you pregnant?"

She wanted me to say no; that much was obvious. Her happiness is directly correlated with my disappointment. So, yes, I could ask Eric Fergus to make another donation, and I think he'd agree. But whether or not the pregnancy succeeded, his donation would compromise his relationship. Just because I've shied away from marriage doesn't mean everyone else should.

"Dinner is ready." Carmen places a platter of fish, a spinach salad, and some roasted potatoes on the counter.

As she packs up her things and prepares to leave, Ian and I fill our plates with food and take them to the outside table. It's a bit warmer than ideal, but after a day in a temperature-controlled, fluorescent-lit office, I like to spend a half hour with grass, trees, and, yes, chickens. They rush to the front of the coop and squawk.

"You can't come out," Ian tells them. "There are owls and coyotes."

I don't ask whether he let them free-range today. If he says no, I'll have to scold him, and we've clashed enough for one day.

We eat without talking for a while, Ian taking the tiniest bites of his fish. He is getting as bored of it as I am.

Finally, I say it. "You know how I was trying to have a baby?"

"Yeah."

"It didn't work."

He nibbles at his fish and says nothing.

"I've been thinking about it," I continue. "I'm glad I tried. And that we met your donor. But I think it's time to give up on this baby thing. We're a family, you and me. I love you so much. So, I'm sorry if you're disappointed, but you're not going to have a brother or sister." It is an effort to hold back tears, but I need to stay strong for Ian. He's wanted a sibling for so long.

He drinks some milk and places the glass just so on the table. "Okay," he says finally. He jabs his spinach salad—which he likes even less than regular salad—before poking some more at the fish. When he speaks again, his voice is light.

"Can we get a puppy?"

I blink at him. "You want a dog?"

He grins. "Yeah. Wouldn't that be cool? When Carmen and I went to the mall yesterday, we went into the pet store, and they had this awesome dog. It was white with blue eyes. It was like a husky or something. But mixed with something else."

Later, when he's in bed, I dial Eric's home number one last time.

When a female voice answers, I say, "This is Laura Cahill. I just thought you'd like to know the test results. They were negative."

She is quiet for a while. Finally, she says, "Thank you."

The line goes dead.

"You're welcome," I whisper.

# Wendy

At ten o'clock in the morning, the thermometer outside the kitchen window reads one hundred and two degrees. For two months, it has been over a hundred every day, and we can expect the streak to last into October. It's like this every year, though sometimes the crippling heat starts in April. For the millionth time, I ask myself why we—no, why *anyone*—lives in Arizona. However, as Darren so kindly pointed out the last time I bitched about the heat, I used to say the same thing about Chicago whenever the temperature dropped below zero.

Since seven A.M., the children have been in the television room, glued to a succession of shows featuring unnaturally perky preteens who are pretty much guaranteed to be in treatment for either drug addiction or anorexia or both before their eighteenth birthdays. Sydney sits on the couch, surrounded by silver Pop-Tart wrappers, while Harrison lies on the crumb-encrusted carpet, an open box of crackers near his feet. In the summer, I let the children make their own breakfasts.

Of course, I'm tempted to let them watch television and eat junk food all day. I often do. Approximately seven hours into any television marathon, though, they snap. All of the misbehavior they've stored up comes pouring out in a tsunami of tears and tantrums. Taking the twins out in public is about as relaxing as walking around with a grenade in my pocketbook, but sometimes staying home is worse.

The phone rings: it's my mother.

"Twenty-seven days till they go back to school," I tell her. "Not that I'm counting. It's just that the kids are so sick of being cooped up inside."

"Who starts school in the middle of August? I don't understand why they have to go back two weeks before the rest of the country."

"Arizona is not like the rest of the country."

"Amen to that." My mother is not what you'd call a desert person. "What's your weather like today?"

"It's five bazillion degrees out right now," I say. "But we're supposed to get a monsoon later. That should drop us to about four bazillion degrees for a couple of hours, so maybe the kids can play outside."

"You ever use that Barnes & Noble gift certificate I gave you for your birthday?" she asks.

"No," I say. "Good idea."

When I hang up the phone, I feel the familiar pang of missing my mother. We didn't take our usual trip to Michigan this summer. Darren couldn't get the time off, and the flights were expensive. Plus, after the four horrific hours we spent in the Detroit airport last year when our plane was delayed by storms, the TSA has probably added Harrison's name to the terrorist watch list.

"Want to go to the bookstore?" I ask the kids.

This deep into their hypnotic state, it takes them a moment to register the question. At last, Harrison says no and Sydney says yes.

And then they reach a kind of consensus when Harrison says yes and Sydney says no.

"I'll buy you cookies at the café," I tell them. Once again, bribery works its magic. I hurry them into clothes before they have a chance to reconsider. I grab a frozen bottle of water, and we're on our way.

At the strip mall, every shady spot is taken, so I park my minivan in the full-on glare, knowing that when we return the interior will be somewhere in the neighborhood of what it takes to cook a turkey. By then, the frozen bottle of water will be mostly thawed. I will use it to douse the children before they climb into their car seats. The droplets will evaporate, saunalike, as I race back to our air-conditioned house.

Like I said, Arizona is not like other places.

In the children's section, Sydney falls to her knees in front of a shelf of chapter books while Harrison makes for a rounder. He tugs a stuffed *Where the Wild Things Are* creature off the display. Some things should really be left at two dimensions.

"I'll buy you each a book," I tell him. "But no toys."

He ignores me. Since he isn't actively destroying the thing, I sidle over to Sydney, who has pulled a book off the shelf and is frowning at the page.

"The picture books are against the wall over there. Or maybe you want to try an easy reader?"

At the end of kindergarten, both of the twins were at the sound-out-the-words stage of reading, which Mrs. Stick-up-her-Rath said was "within the acceptable range," but that "many of the students are up to level-three readers." She encouraged me to spend at least forty minutes a night reading with each child. After some discussion, Darren and I agreed that he would read with Sydney after dinner every night, and I would read with Harrison. And then we both pretended we'd never had the conversation.

Still, in my (semi) defense, at eight o'clock every night, I send the children to bed and tell them they can "read" for a half hour. They flip pages and pretend to understand the words. They are calm. They are quiet. So what if they don't know what they are reading? They haven't even started first grade, for God's sake.

Now, at the bookstore, Sydney ignores my easy-reader suggestions and continues to frown at the text-heavy page. Fifteen feet away, Harrison has dropped the *Where the Wild Things Are* monster on the floor and has moved to a stuffed Runaway Bunny.

Sydney turns the page, "reads" a little more, and shakes her head. "I don't like this one." She shoves the book back on the shelf and pulls out something with a black cover clearly intended for older girls.

"Wendy? I thought that was you!"

I turn around. "Oh! Hi, Mary . . ." *Think, think, think . . .* "Jane."

It's Mary Jane from scrapbooking, wearing shorts, a tank top, sneakers, and an expression that looks way too relaxed. I look around for her children, whom I've never actually met but could probably recognize from their perfectly trimmed photographs.

"Your kids here?" I ask.

She shakes her head. "Day camp. Up at my church. Nine to three, four days a week. They *love* it. They play on the playground in the morning, before it gets too hot. Then there's crafts inside and sometimes a movie, then after that they go back outside for some water play."

"Is it just this week?"

She shakes her head. "It goes till school starts."

My pulse quickens. "Do you have to belong to your church?" For three weeks of freedom, I'll convert to pretty much anything, if necessary.

"I don't think so. I'll e-mail you the information, if you want. I'm pretty sure there are still some openings."

We chat a little more, and then Mary Jane wanders off to the romance section while I say a silent prayer, thanking God for keeping my children quiet and nondestructive for that five-minute stretch. Sydney sits Indian style at my feet, her chin resting on her knuckles, her eyes fixed on a print-heavy page. She giggles. If I didn't know better, I'd really think she was reading. Still smiling, she turns the page and glances up at me.

"Can I get this?"

"You can only get one book," I say. "So why not pick out an easy reader?"

"Easy readers are boring."

"No they're not!" (Yes, they are.)

"I like this one." She holds it so tight, the spine threatens to break.

"Fine." I'll save my battle strength for Harrison, who is going to want one of those stupid, overpriced stuffed animals. "But it's going to be years before you can actually read it."

"I can read it now. It's about a body switcher."

A body switcher. Lovely. Why doesn't anyone write books about ponies and pioneers anymore?

I say, "So read some of it to me, then." I'll pretend to be impressed by her fake reading. Then I'll buy her the book along with something for Harrison and get the heck out of here.

Sydney narrows her dark eyes at me before turning her attention back to the open page:

*"Don't freak out: It probably wasn't you I woke up with on that stormy night last July. Well, unless you're about five foot four, with pretty brown eyes and long, dark hair. Then it might have been you. (You might want to rethink that white-blond streak in your hair, by the way. It makes you look like a skunk.)"*

Leaning over Sydney, I check the text. It can't be—but it is. Sydney is really reading—slowly, haltingly, but she is doing it.

"Oh my God, Syd. But how . . . At the end of the year Mrs. Rath said you were just sounding out the words. She said she had you try a level-two book, and you couldn't do it."

"I didn't like Stick-up-her-Rath."

"Sydney!"

"That's what you called her to Daddy."

Oh, shit. I've really got to be more careful.

"So you could read all along, but you just didn't tell anyone?"

"I guess."

*"Stop throwing those on the floor! Are you here with an adult?"* Fifteen feet away, a bookstore employee scolds Harrison, who made it his mission to empty the rounder while Sydney was reading. Sydney was reading!

"Can I get the book?" Sydney asks.

"I didn't do anything," Harrison tells the employee. "It was Dodie."

Sydney gets the book, of course. And, when he threatens to throw a tantrum, I abandon my no-toys injunction and buy a big stuffed Eric Carle–styled ant for Harrison.

———

At home, I make the children peanut butter sandwiches (with jelly for Syndey and marshmallow fluff for Harrison; no crusts for either), which they hardly touch because they are so full from the oversize chocolate chip cookies I bought them at the Barnes & Noble café. Never one to let food go to waste, I finish the sandwiches. I'd already eaten the crusts. Then I microwave a piece of pizza because the other stuff didn't register as food.

Once the kids are resettled in front of the television, I call Darren.

"Sydney can read," I announce.

"Really? That great." He sounds insufficiently impressed. His computer keys rattle in the background.

"No, Darren, I mean she can *really* read."

"I know. You said that. I'm happy."

"I'm not talking picture books. I took the kids to the bookstore and Sydney picked up this book . . ." The saga feels less dramatic in the retelling. I leave out the bits about Harrison and the stuffed animals.

"That's awesome," Darren says, sounding less than awestruck, computer keys continuing to click, even when I tell him that Sydney outshines every kid in her kindergarten class, even the ones who went to tutors.

"You could stop typing and listen to me," I say. My jaw is tense.

The clicking stops. He sighs. "I'm just trying to get some work done. I'm listening."

Suddenly I have nothing else to say, except, "Will you be home regular time?"

"Yeah."

"Okay, see you then."

My laptop sits on the kitchen desk. I turn it on, open my e-mail program, and compose a note to Laura Cahill.

**Subject: Success?**

Hi Laura,

I've been thinking of you. Did the IUI work? Fertility treatments are no fun, but hopefully it was worth it.

Things are okay here. It's very hot (of course) but summer vacation is giving the kids lots of time for books. Sydney is already reading advanced chapter books. We are very proud of her. How old was Ian when he began to read?

Wendy

Later that afternoon, I receive her reply.

**Subject: RE: Success?**

Hello Wendy,

Unfortunately, I did not get pregnant despite two IUIs and one IVF. Your children are lucky to have each other, but I'm sure you already know that. I would love to introduce them to Ian someday, though I understand if you'd rather not. But please keep in touch.

Warmly,
Laura

P.S. Without any instruction, Ian surprised me by reading when he was four! As of his last test, he was reading at a sixth-grade level. I can't keep enough books in the house.

———————

I brace myself for a wave of irritation. Of course Ian learned to read when he was four. But instead I feel a surprising kinship with Laura Cahill. There are so many ways to be lonely. Laura's loneliness is different from my own, but it is there, no doubt about it.

# Vanessa

Eric acts like the whole thing at the clinic never happened. I wish I could do the same, but even after I find out that there's no baby on the way, I can't stop thinking about that little blond boy. Even worse, every time I see a kid with streaky blond hair, I wonder, *Could that be his?*

"Do you ever think about him?" I ask Eric, breaking the silence on yet another Friday-night drive to his mother's house in Glendale.

"Who?"

"The boy."

"What boy?"

"Ian."

"Oh." He pauses. "No."

"How do you feel about him?" I press.

He shrugs. "I don't."

"What is that supposed to mean?"

"I'm indifferent." He glances in the rearview mirror, flicks on the blinker, and changes lanes.

Later that night, he doesn't sound so indifferent when he's checking his e-mail.

"Oh my God." He's on the bed, leaning against some pillows, the laptop balanced on his knees.

"What?" I've just doused a Q-tip in eye makeup remover. My hand jerks, and the gel splatters.

"Nothing."

"It's obviously something."

"Just—I haven't checked my e-mail in a while and . . ."

"What?"

"Laura Cahill sent a couple of pictures. Of her son when he was little."

I yank a couple of Kleenex from the box on the back of the toilet and wipe away the spilled gel. Eric is waiting for me to ask to see the pictures, but I'm not going to do it. I'll just make myself crazy. Maybe if I can pretend to be *indifferent*, eventually I'll start to feel it.

He's still staring at the laptop. "This is so weird. He looks like . . ."

"What?"

"Nothing."

He expects me to press him. Does he look like you? Like your brothers? Or your nephews, maybe? What a shock that shared genes *make people look alike*.

Instead, I say, "But of course, you're indifferent."

"No. I mean, yes. I am. It's just—this picture. It's weird."

I am not going to ask him who the picture reminds him of.

"Everything about this experience is weird." I snap the top back on the eye makeup remover and squeeze watermelon-flavored paste onto my toothbrush. I really wish he'd start buying mint.

I turn the water on high and scrub my teeth till my gums bleed.

# Laura

When the doorbell rings, I fish my American Express card out of my purse and yank open the slightly sticky front door, assuming our pizza has arrived. As such, it takes me several moments to compose myself when I discover Eric Fergus, in a T-shirt, shorts, and flip-flops, standing there instead.

Since my conversation with his fiancée, I've thought about calling him countless times and actually started to dial twice. My internal battle isn't about Vanessa's right to happiness versus mine, but rather her right to happiness versus Ian's, and in that, it's no contest. Ian says he wants a dog, and maybe he does, and maybe—probably—I'll break down and get him one. But someday he may feel lonely, even with a dog, and then it will be too late.

"I'd say I was in the neighborhood, but I wasn't," Eric says, smiling shyly. Smiling like Ian.

"No, I wouldn't think you would be. But it's good to see you."

Eric's car, a beat-up blue Ford Focus, sits at the curb. My mother instinct kicks in: is that little car really safe to drive in Southern California traffic?

Although it is after six o'clock, the sun still glares and the temperature hovers above ninety. Eric's face glistens with perspiration. He holds something in his hands. "I wanted to show you this. I would've just e-mailed it, but I don't have a scanner."

I shove my credit card in my front pocket, and he hands me a photograph of Ian at three or four wearing overalls, sitting on a curb. My initial reaction is confusion—and fear. What is he doing with an old picture of Ian? And why is it in black and white?

And then it hits me. "This is you?"

He shakes his head. "My father."

"Oh my God."

"This is me." He hands me another picture, in color this time, of a preschool-aged blond boy on a tricycle. It is not Ian, but the resemblance is uncanny.

I say, "I have a picture of Ian that looks just like this. Even the posture and the expression. Only he's not in a driveway, he's in a park. Oh! Of course. You got the pictures I sent."

He nods. "Vanessa wasn't too—you know. When I told her I was coming here. But . . . I guess I wanted to see your reaction. If you thought Ian looked as much like my dad as I do."

I nod. "It's eerie."

I don't mean to stare so intently at Eric, to examine the line of his jaw, the shape of his eyebrows, the color of his hair, but I can't help it. This is what Ian is going to look like someday. And if I have another child—if Eric has come to tell me he will donate despite his girlfriend's objections—he or she might look like him as well.

He reaches into a pocket and hands me a third photo, this one of four children on a beach. "This is me later, when I was about Ian's age. I'm the one on the end."

He didn't have to tell me that. Eric is the child in the photo who looks most like Ian, though by then he could no longer pass for his almost-twin. I feel a weird stab of disappointment.

"Your brothers and sister?" I ask.

"Uh-huh."

I search the faces for hints of my son. Maybe there's something around the eyes over here, maybe something around the mouth there.

A car, as small and beat up as Eric's, parks behind the Ford Focus. A guy in a red shirt climbs out, balancing an insulated square.

"Have you eaten?" I ask Eric.

In the kitchen, I place the pizza box on the stove and rummage in a cabinet for paper plates. "Sorry the house is such a mess. My nanny is away for a few weeks, and everything pretty much falls apart without her."

My brain whirs as I try to find the words to explain Eric's presence to Ian—and, perhaps more importantly, the best way to revisit the donation issue. On the first count, I am too slow.

"Are you going to help my mom try to have a baby again?"

At the sound of Ian's voice, I spin around and begin to blabber. "Ian! Buddy. Eric's here. Say hi to Eric."

Eric opens his mouth and looks from Ian to me. He looks at my stomach. "So, I guess that means . . . it didn't . . . you're not . . ."

It hits me, right in the gut: his fiancée didn't tell him that the insemination failed. Which means he has not come to offer another donation.

"It didn't," I say. "I'm not."

He bites his lip. "I'm really sorry."

"Yeah, me too."

I fumble with the pizza box, annoyed to note that my hands are shaking. "Who wants pepperoni pizza?" I chirp, my voice sounding like a stranger's.

"I do!" Ian says.

Eric says nothing, and I remember, too late, that he is a vegetarian. If he tells Ian that pepperoni comes from an animal, I'll . . .

"Thanks, but I'm not hungry," he says.

I flash him a smile filled with gratitude just as he adds, "Plus, I don't eat meat."

―――――――

While I boil water for macaroni and cheese and set the table (taking clean dishes straight from the dishwasher), Ian takes Eric out back to see the chickens. The initial shock having passed, I feel anxious about his presence and its implications for the future. If he didn't come to talk about a donation, why is he here? Is he looking to have some kind of role in Ian's life? And if so, is that a bad thing?

With shocking regularity, people—some I hardly know—will ask me why I don't date. I tell them that my son is my number one priority: I have neither the time nor the desire to have a man in my life. The time part is true, and desire is something I rarely contemplate, at least during my waking hours. But the primary reason I have avoided a relationship is because the odds are so high that it wouldn't work out. I'd encourage Ian to form an attachment to a man, only to watch him walk away. Or—and this is just as bad—to have me send him away.

Better to have loved and lost? I think not.

Still, when I look out the window and see Ian next to the man who contributed half his DNA, both bent forward next to the coop, gazing at the chickens with wonder, I can actually feel my chest loosen and fill with warmth. Eric Fergus came over here on his own accord. Maybe there's room in his life and in his heart for a little boy—within limits, of course. A supervised visit every few months. An exchange of photographs.

I stir the macaroni. When I look out the window again, Ian appears upset—angry, even. I rush out of the kitchen and into the backyard.

"Just not fair!" Ian says, hands clenched into fists at his side.

Oh my God. Is he talking about my failed pregnancy attempts?

"That's a stupid law," Eric says, with equal ferocity. At least they seem to be on the same side of . . . whatever.

"It's retarded," Ian says.

"Don't say 'retarded,'" I call out. It's awful how kids throw that word around.

Eric and Ian look surprised to see me.

"But it is retarded that we can have chickens but not roosters," Ian says. "It's sexist and discrimination."

It's really, really hard not to laugh. "Roosters crow," I say. "No one wants to listen to them."

"I wouldn't mind," Ian says.

"The neighbors would."

"You might be surprised," Eric says. "They might actually like it. Shades of the country and all that."

"Well, it's against city regulations, so we won't have a chance to find out."

"That's retarded," Eric says. He catches himself. "Sorry."

Ian laughs. And then, before I've had a chance to decide whether or not to chastise him again, he says, "My mom wouldn't let us have roosters anyway because they'd have sex with the chickens."

"No. I said we couldn't have them because they're noisy and aggressive. And also because we don't want—or at least need—the eggs fertilized."

"Same thing." Ian grins at me, though clearly his performance is intended for Eric's benefit.

I consider pulling Ian aside, but sometimes the best way to extinguish bad behavior is to ignore it.

"I'll go check on the mac and cheese," I say.

Eric, having apparently forgotten that he is not hungry, puts away two big bowls of Annie's organic macaroni and cheese. Ian, having digested the idea that pepperoni is not just meat but mystery meat, downs one bowl. They both drink milk and nibble baby carrots, which they slip under their gums to make orange fangs.

So this is what it feels like to have two children.

I eat two slices of pepperoni pizza, sip a small glass of Chardonnay, and feel like I am three thousand years old.

After dinner, Ian asks Eric if he likes video games. I fully expect Eric to say video games are fun but he really has to be heading home. Instead, the two boys—that is how I'm thinking of them—scurry off to the den. Soon I hear battle sounds and laughter.

When I became pregnant for the first time all those years ago, back when I was married, I felt certain Rob would be a good father, despite his misgivings. He was solid. A good provider. Responsible. I imagined him teaching our child things: skiing, maybe, or how to use a hammer. (Was Rob good with tools? I can't even remember.) I pictured family vacations and holiday mornings.

Never, though, did I imagine Rob just hanging out with our child. Laughing. It's not that Rob was humorless—he had a dry wit—but he wasn't . . . fun. Of course, I'm not a barrel of laughs either, so it's not surprising we seemed so well matched.

I wonder if parenthood has taught Rob to live in the moment the way it has me. Somehow, I doubt it, though I hope for his children's sake it has.

There is whooping down the hall. "I creamed you!" Eric shouts.

Clearly, Eric does not need any assistance on the carpe diem front, though his goal-setting skills could use a little work.

When I go in at nine o'clock to tell Ian to get his pajamas on, he begs for more time, but Eric takes the cue. "I gotta hit the road," he says, standing up. He holds his hand out sideways, and he and

Ian do that front-slap, backslap, knuckle-bump thing peculiar to the male sex.

"Later, dude," he tells my son.

"Later," Ian says, wondering, I am sure, just how much later that means. In a month? A year? Never?

I walk him to his car. "Thanks for coming out."

He jingles his car keys. "I hope it's . . . I didn't mean to . . . was this okay?"

"Yes. Absolutely."

"Cool." He turns toward the car.

"Eric?"

He turns back.

"Would you consider donating more of your sperm?"

He blinks once. "Yeah. Sure."

"Okay, then."

# Wendy

Nothing says "first day of summer camp" like a hundred and five degrees in the shade and a seven-foot-long gopher snake in the backyard.

"How many weeks is camp?" My mother has called to wish the kids good luck. I haven't told her about the snake, which we've sighted four times in the past week.

"Three," I say. "And then they'll be back in school."

Harrison and Sydney take turns talking to Gammie. Sydney says, "My pink dress . . . no . . . no . . . I dunno, for my birthday."

"Have you bought their back-to-school clothes yet?" my mother asks when I get back on.

"There's no summer-weight stuff left in the stores," I say. "I bought a bunch of sale stuff at Target in May, but it's already kind of small."

"You want me to check the stores here?" she offers, as I knew she would.

"That would be great," I reply, as she knew I would. She grabs a pencil, and I rattle off current sizes.

"If you lived here, we could shop together," she says, as if for the first time. "When your sister and Jade were here last month, we had such a lovely time at the stores. We even went out for high tea, did I tell you that? Jade looked so adorable."

"Mm." I thought I was done hearing about all the lovely and adorable things my adorable four-year-old niece did on her last lovely visit.

When Harrison yanks open the slider, I tell my mother I'll call her after I drop off the kids.

I chase my son into the already-hot yard. "Inside! Inside!"

He ignores me. Or maybe he takes that as a challenge. In any event, he sprints for the wash, which was a stream for about twenty minutes following yesterday's monsoon but is now back to being a dry, rock-lined drainage ditch. My pulse quickens when a shadow twitches against the rocks, but it's just a branch of the mesquite tree, quivering in the wind.

I scan the concrete, gravel, and wash for the snake, but there is no sign of him. Her. It. Ever since Harrison heard Darren say that gopher snakes are not dangerous—in fact, by claiming the territory and depleting the rodent population, they help keep rattlesnakes away—Harrison has been intent on seeing the reptile up close and personal. I, in turn, have been even more uptight than usual, and that's saying something.

"I'm going to count to ten!" I yell. I saw another mother do this recently, and I couldn't believe it worked.

"One . . . two . . . three . . ."

I get all the way to nine and eleven-sixteenths before Harrison gives up on the snake and trots back into the kitchen, where Sydney is nibbling on a cookie. (Not the most nutritious breakfast in the world, but are Fruit Loops any better?)

Five minutes later, they are buckled into their car seats. Two brand-new beach bags (one pink, one green), stuffed with sunscreen, swimsuits, towels and lunch boxes (one Disney princesses, one a medley of hideous sci-fi action heroes), snuggle on the chair next to me.

"Who's excited about camp?" I chirp.

The twins are silent (there's a first). I flip on the radio and back out of the garage, singing tunelessly along with Gwen Stefani.

I, for one, haven't felt this lighthearted since . . . well, since the first day of kindergarten, when everything was fresh and new and they hadn't yet begun a battle of wills with Mrs. Rath. Camp will be different. And if not, at least camp will be shorter. By the time the counselors have exhausted all attempts at controlling the twins, it will be time for first grade.

We are halfway down the block when I spot the dead snake in the road. I slam on the brakes. Fortunately, there is no one behind me.

"Is it our snake?" Sydney asks.

As always, I check the tail first. "No. This one's a rattler."

"Cool!" Harrison says.

I press the accelerator and drive around the lifeless reptile before Harrison can decide he needs a closer look. My heart races. Is this some kind of bad omen? No. As far as I'm concerned, the only good snake is a dead one.

Waiting outside the preschool building where the camp is held, I spot Mary . . . oh, hell, was it Beth or Ann? I start to walk toward her (Mary *Jane,* that's it)—but when I see that she is talking to a couple of moms from the twins' kindergarten class, I stop in my tracks. Something tickles my arm: a fat black ant crawls toward my elbow. I shriek and flick it onto the pavement.

"Don't hurt it!" Harrison yells, falling back on the ground.

Next to me, a mom I don't know chuckles. "Boys and bugs."

I smile at her, thinking, *Three weeks from now, she won't meet my eyes.*

Just then, the camp director opens the door. She looks young and eager enough to be in high school. Her dark hair is cut in a bouncy bob, her eyes are big and brown, her mouth is painted cherry red.

I say, "Are you Miss Rossi? I'm Wendy Winder. We talked on the phone?"

"Yes!" she trills, leaning down to talk to the children. "*You* must be Sydney! And Harrison! We are going to have the most glorious time together!"

I half expect a bluebird to land on her shoulder.

"Mom," Sydney whispers, her brown eyes fixed on the young woman with the bright red lips.

"What?"

"It's Snow White!"

It's going to be a good three weeks.

# Vanessa

## 8

Eric waits until we're pulling into the grocery-store parking lot to drop the bomb.

"So I told Laura I'd donate again." He puts the car in park and turns off the ignition.

I feel like I've been punched in the stomach. "Please tell me we're talking blood."

We're really quiet for what feels like forever, and then he goes, "No. But it could be worse. At least it's not a kidney."

I want to scream, *This is not funny! A kidney would be better than this.* Instead, I get out of the car, cross the parking lot, grab a cart, and head into the store.

I pick out bananas while Eric sorts through the summer fruit and comes back with a plastic bag of plums because they're on sale. Then I get tomatoes and he gets lettuce. Then we head for the cereal aisle.

Just when I think we're not going to talk about it anymore, Eric goes, "You can go with me if you want. It might make you feel more a part of the process." He plucks a box of Honey Nut Cheerios off the shelf and drops it in the cart.

My hands clutch the cold plastic handle so hard, they hurt. "You're asking me to come into the bathroom with you. At the doctor's office. And, and . . ." I'm about to say something really crude, but next to us, a mom pushes two little kids in one of those carts with a plastic car on the front.

One of the kids is blond. Streaky blond. Could he be another one of Eric's kids? How many are out there?

"Only if you want to come." Eric strolls down the aisle until he finds his favorite granola.

"I don't want to."

"That's fine."

He's sounding all casual, but he's looking way too fascinated with Cream of Wheat.

I push the cart closer to him, but I can't get past the woman with the car cart. A chubby hand reaches out of the passenger side and plucks a sack of chocolate cereal. If the mother notices, she doesn't say anything.

"It's not fine," I tell Eric. "Nothing about this is fine."

"Whatever you want to do," he says.

"It's not what *I* want to do! It's what I want you to *not* do!"

The mom with the car cart stiffens, but at this point, I don't give a crap. I'd throw my engagement ring at Eric, but, oh yeah—he never gave me one.

I go, "Do you even think about how many hundreds of children you could have running around? Does that not even bother you?"

He shakes his head. "I only did it five, six times, and my—" He shoots a look at the lady with the car cart. "It wasn't exactly a fast seller. Wendy Winder, the one with the twins, she bought her vials three years after Laura, and I wasn't even her first choice. Man. If there were a Big Lots for this kind of thing, that's totally where my guys would've ended up."

"It's not funny, Eric."

He sighs. "I told Laura I'd do this for her."

Hearing her name makes me snap. "Fine! Then you can go jerk off for Laura—or you can marry me. Take your pick, Eric!"

"*Excuse me.*" The mom straightens the car cart as her child rips open the plastic cereal sack. Little brown pebbles spill over the hard floor. They crunch under the wheels of her cart.

At last, Eric meets my eyes. "Tell me you don't mean that."

I say nothing.

# Wendy

Six hours. That's how much time I have until I have to pick up Harrison and Sydney. *Six whole hours.* I love summer camp!

Over the summer, I developed a long mental list of the things I would do once I had time. Organize the closets, join a gym, sort the toys, shampoo the upholstery. Instead, I head over to Target, where I browse the books and housewares, the shoes and plants. And no one bothers me! There are plenty of little kids there with harried mothers. I ignore them all. After an hour or so, I leave with a new fall purse, long pants for Harrison, and a whole bunch of food that we may or may not need.

Out in the vast parking lot, the air is hot and my minivan is hotter. I have no choice but to go straight home. That's okay: the house is empty!

Back in my kitchen, I sing an old Tiffany song while I put the food away. *"I think we're alone now. There doesn't seem to be anyone a-rou-ound."*

Upstairs, I prepare for a shower, then decide to take a bath instead. When was the last time I took a bath? I can't even remember. With Harrison and Sydney around, I can't even manage a ten-minute shower without someone pounding on the door.

The cold tap turned up full force, tepid water spills from the spigot into the oversize, soap-scum-coated tub. If I want my water chilly in August, I'd have to add ice cubes. Tepid is fine.

I've just stepped into the tub and am contemplating how much I hate my cellulite-ridden body when I hear the phone ring. I hesitate. Could it be the camp calling? So soon? The kids were perfectly healthy when I sent them off less than two hours ago, without the slightest sniffle or fake stomachache. If Snow White is calling to say that Sydney is crying or Harrison hit someone, what am I supposed to do? Rush down to the church and yell at them?

And then I remember: I was supposed to call my mother back. She's probably curious to hear how the drop-off went. Ah, well—another half hour won't make any difference.

I turn on the jets and position a folded towel beneath my head. Eyes closed, I enjoy the sensation of pulsing water on my soft flesh. I haven't felt this relaxed in . . . maybe forever.

*Six hours alone, Monday through Thursday.* I am going to be one clean mother.

I don't know how long I soak. A half hour? Forty minutes? When I finally haul myself out, I set to work on my hair. The desert air is so dry, there's maybe a ten-minute window in which to blow-dry. The instant I turn the dryer off, I hear the phone ringing, once, twice—and then it stops.

I grab the first clothes I find—a red T-shirt that is a little too big, and denim shorts that are a little two tight—and hurry down the stairs, irritated at whoever called, even if it's my mother. Two months I've been with the kids 24/7. *Two months.* Does anyone really begrudge me my six lousy hours?

When I see the red number five blinking on the answering machine, my irritation turns to fear. My mother wouldn't call me that many times.

*"Mrs. Winder? This is Tammi in the St. Stephen's day camp office."* Her voice quivers. *"We have your Harrison here. He's been stung by a scorpion. On the playground. We think—his counselor thinks it was a bark scorpion. He's in a lot of pain, and, and—I'll try your husband."*

Next is Darren. *"Wendy? Wendy?"* There is a click, and a dial tone.

The third call is Darren again. *"Wendy? Pick up. Are you there? Are you there?"*

Fourth call: *"Wendy. Lane Plant here. I just got off the phone with Darren. Asked me to see if you were home. I thought I saw you drive up earlier, but I just rang your doorbell, and there was no answer."*

The fifth call is from Darren again, but I don't bother to listen to what he says. Instead, I grab the phone and dial his cell number with shaking hands.

"Where were you?" He sounds like he's been crying. Darren never cries.

"In the bath, I didn't hear—"

"Harrison's been stung by a scorpion."

"I know! Is he—"

"The traffic. It took me so long to get to the church. We're at the hospital. Just got here . . ."

Harrison is with Darren? Then why can't I hear him screaming in the background? Oh my God oh my God oh my God . . .

I say, "But what happened? Where was he stung? I don't understand how he—"

"Meet me at the ER. Scottsdale North." The line goes dead.

I need to find my keys. Where is my purse? Did I bring it in when I came back from Target? Did I take it upstairs? Maybe I left it in the car. *Where is my goddamn purse?*

I am crying and stumbling and I think I might pass out. *Where are my keys?* I need to calm down. I need to function. I need to breathe.

Harrison. Oh my God. I've told him to watch out for poisonous insects, begged him not to turn over rocks. Bark scorpions. Those are the bad ones, right? Rarely lethal to adults, but to small children . . .

*Oh my God.*

The doorbell rings. I think it might be Darren, coming to pick me up—forgetting for an instant that he's already at the hospital; he just told me that—so I open the door, and there's Lane Plant, big and dark and hairy as ever but looking gentle. Looking like a friend.

"Darren called me."

*"Harrison,"* I sob.

"I know."

Lane drives me to the hospital. We don't even discuss it—he just puts his arm around me and ushers me to his pickup truck. It takes us almost half an hour to get there. I cry the whole way.

He finds a parking spot near the emergency room entrance and walks me across the scorching pavement and through the automatic glass doors. Darren isn't in the waiting room, so Lane tells the receptionist who I am, and she tells us to take a seat. It is cold inside, so cold. I wrap my arms around myself. My teeth chatter.

"You okay?" Lane asks.

I shake my head.

Finally, Darren comes down the hall and into the waiting room. I stand up, terrified, trying to read his face.

"Is he okay?" My voice cracks.

He looks at Lane and then back to me. "They gave him antivenin. He's going to be okay."

"Oh, thank God." The tears, which I'd kept under control since we got inside the hospital, burst out in full force.

Lane says, "That's great news" or something like that, and then he leaves.

Darren and I stand a few feet apart, and I want him to hold me so badly, but he's got this stony look on his face and I figure he's mad that I didn't answer the phone. I'm mad at myself too. I should have been here from the start.

Darren leads me into a tiny room, where Harrison lies on an examining table, curled in a fetal position, pressing an ice pack to one hand. A nurse tells us she'll check back, and she leaves us alone.

"Mommy," Harrison whimpers.

"Oh, baby!" He usually scolds me when I call him baby, but this time he drops the ice pack, locks his arms around my neck, and holds on tight. He smells of boy sweat, dirt, and rubbing alcohol.

"It hurt so bad," he says.

"My poor baby." I run a hand up and down his spine.

"I wasn't gonna kill it," he whimpers. "It didn't have to sting me."

I laugh and cry at the same time. "Big meanie. Was it really a bark scorpion?"

"Yeah. I mean, I'm pretty sure. It was under a rock and there was this leaf kind of covering it. So I moved the leaf. And that's when it got me."

When he sniffles, I lean back to get a tissue from my purse, but he holds on tight, and we stay that way until the doctor comes in. He checks the swelling on Harrison's hand and tells us he wants him to stay for a few more hours.

"Can you pick up Sydney?" I ask Darren. "She'll be done at three."

"Sure." His face is hard. The doctor is still talking to Harrison, so I say, "Be right back," and guide Darren into the hallway.

"I'm sorry," I say. "That you couldn't reach me. I was so thrilled to have the whole day to myself, and I know this sounds awful now, but I went to Target and then I took a bath. I heard the phone ring once, but—"

Darren keeps his eyes on the wall when he speaks. "You know, going through all this today—getting Harrison at school, and he looked so scared, then driving here and working so hard to keep it all together . . . for the first time in a long time, maybe ever, I felt like I was his father."

"You are his father."

He looks down the hall, toward the waiting room. "And then you walk in here with Lane."

"But . . . I thought you called him."

"I called Sherry. It was the only thing I could think of. But he answered the phone."

"But what difference does it—" His expression stops me. Suddenly I feel cold all over, like when I first got to the hospital, before I knew that Harrison was going to be okay.

"I know what happened," Darren says.

"But how—"

"Sherry told me. Lane told her. I've known all along."

There are so many things I should say, but the shock is so great, I can't even think. I close my eyes. "I'm so sorry."

When I open my eyes, Darren is gone.

# Laura

The day before Eric's donation appointment, I call his cell number to confirm. I don't know what he's told his fiancée about his plans. Frankly, it's none of my business, and I'm fine with that.

He doesn't answer, so I leave a brief message, with instructions to contact me immediately if he needs to reschedule. Timing is much more flexible this time around. With in vitro fertilization, there's no statistical difference between using fresh or frozen sperm. As such, I've encouraged Eric to make his donation as soon as possible so his sample will be in the bank, so to speak. On top of that—though I wouldn't say this to him—the sooner he donates, the less time he will have to rethink his decision.

For the rest of the day, I focus on the contested will of a man who left behind one young wife, two older ex-wives, and nine children, one of whom, the second wife's only child, received nothing: no money, no property, not even a memento.

"If he'd even made a little effort," the forgotten daughter said when she hired me. "Remembered my birthday when I was growing up or come to see my kids when they were born. Then I wouldn't be doing this. It's not about the money. It's that he just threw me and my mom away like we were trash. And I want to make him pay."

And so, while we agreed it was not about the money, we were suing the estate for a ninth of the assets—which, as it turned out, was not a lot. Three families require considerably more upkeep than one.

As I put together my brief, it hits me: now that Ian has met Eric Fergus, might he feel abandoned later in life? I put the thought out of my mind (where it is sure to fester until the instant I try to sleep that night).

That evening, Ian and I dine on cheese tortellini (which I overboiled myself) while he tells me about his day at sports camp. He doesn't like spending the whole day at camp, but until Carmen gets back, we have no choice.

"Did you do those multiplication problems in that workbook I bought you?" I ask.

"I forgot."

"I'd like to see that workbook completed before you go back to school."

"Uh-huh."

"We can work on it together after dinner."

"'Kay."

But after dinner, he sits down at the piano instead, playing so beautifully—and so long—that I forget all about the workbook until I'm lying in bed at two o'clock in the morning, agonizing over the potential repercussions of introducing Ian to his donor.

From there, my brain segues to concerns about in vitro fertilization. (Do the low odds justify the high expense? Might the hormone shots do more harm than good?)

When I get to worrying about Ian's somewhat shaky grasp of the multiplication tables, it comes as a welcome relief. I can work with him after school, and if he still has problems, I will hire a tutor. At last, this is something I can control.

Around two-thirty, I fall into a dream. I'm in a dark tunnel. White bird feathers swirl around. Ian is somewhere ahead of me, but I can't catch up.

When my alarm goes off at six o'clock, I'm left with a sense of crushing fatigue and general anxiety. At work, my computer greets me with an Outlook reminder: *8:30 a.m.—Eric clinic.* I hit "dismiss" and turn my attention to my in-box, which was empty when I left last night but now has more than twenty messages. I'm not even halfway through them when Marissa buzzes me:

"You have a call? From a place called . . . let me check . . . Orange County Center for Reproductive Health? It's about a missed appointment?"

As I dial Eric's cell number, I tell myself, *He must have forgotten.* Or, *Maybe he got stuck in traffic.* Or, *He couldn't get the day off work.* But wouldn't he have called me, then?

*He changed his mind.*

His phone rings two, three, four times before voice mail kicks in. He doesn't even have a personalized message, just a robotic voice reciting the number. I take a deep breath and make myself sound as pleasant as I can manage.

"Eric! Hello. This is Laura Cahill, calling in regards to your appointment at the clinic this morning. Sorry you couldn't make it— something must have come up. I hope everything's okay. In any event, there's no problem with rescheduling. You can still go today— or switch to later in the week. Whatever's best for you. Anyway. Call me. Thanks."

When I haven't heard from him by the end of the day, I call the clinic to see if, by any chance, he turned up later in the day or called to make another appointment. No on both counts.

On the drive home, I try his cell phone again, only to hear four rings followed by that robotic voice.

"Eric, hi. Laura Cahill again. I hope you received the message I left this morning . . ."

I keep my cell phone on during our dinner (leftover overcooked cheese tortellini); while I help Ian with his math workbook; and for the pre-bedtime half hour we spend in companionable silence, reading in the living room.

After Ian goes to bed, I try Eric's cell number once more. And then I call him at home. I have no intention of getting into any awkward or hostile exchange with the girlfriend. If she answers, I will ask for Eric. If she insists on voicing her opinion of our agreement, I will reiterate my request.

The girlfriend does not answer. Neither does Eric.

Time and insomnia only serve to stoke my anger. When I call his cell number from work the next morning, I expect the four rings, the robotic voice. I clear my throat and prepare myself to say, once again, that he has missed his appointment. That we can still reschedule. That I would appreciate the courtesy of a phone call.

"Laura. Hey."

At the sound of his voice, my throat seizes up.

"I. You. Hi."

"Hey," he says again. "You at work?"

"Yes."

"Awesome."

There is nothing awesome about my work—unless you consider the stability, the respect, the pay . . . yes, okay. My work is awesome.

"So." I clear my throat again. My allergies have been awful this summer. "You missed your appointment yesterday."

"The . . . oh . . . yeah . . ." The way he says it, you'd think I was asking him to recall some decades-old event.

"Would you like me to reschedule?" I ask.

"Thanks," he says. "But—yeah. I don't think so."

"You don't want me to make the call? Or you've changed your mind about donating?"

"Yeah. That."

"*Which one?*" I can't believe this guy got into medical school.

"The, um. The second. The thing is—I think you and your son are awesome. And I'd really like to help you out. But I—can't."

"Actually, you can. We've already seen that."

"Well, yeah." He forces a laugh. "That Hooters lunch actually helped with the, um, mechanics. But, ah—right. The whole thing is causing a lot of problems on the home front. But it was nice to meet you."

"It was *nice to meet me?*"

"Yeah. And your son. Ian's awesome."

Stunned, I am silent—but not for long.

"Why did you show up at my house last week?" I ask.

"'Cause of that picture that you sent me. I told you."

"I don't think that's the real reason."

"Well—yeah. It was. I mean . . . it was just kind of shocking, you know? To see how much Ian looked like my dad when he was little. And like me too, I guess. And I just kinda . . . I wanted to see him again."

"You can't do that," I say. "Just show up unannounced. Play with the chickens. Eat pizza with us. Play video games with my son. You can't promise to do something and then not do it. You can't do that to my son!"

"I didn't actually eat any of the pizza," he says.

"That's not the point."

"Yeah, I know. I was just . . . I was making a joke."

"It wasn't funny," I say.

"You seemed okay with it," he says. "When I came to the door."

"I'd called you the week before," I say. "To tell you that I hadn't gotten pregnant. To ask if you'd help me out again. But your girl-friend got so upset that I let it drop. When you came to our house, I thought it was because you were coming to say you'd do it. That she'd said it was okay."

"It wasn't okay."

"Yeah. I get that. But what I don't get is why you didn't confer with her before making the decision or why you didn't at least call me to say you'd changed your mind."

He sighs. "Plans change."

"Plans change? *Plans change?* That's the best you can do?"

He sighs again, longer this time. "I don't know what you want me to say."

"It's not about what you say that matters, Eric. It's about what you do. You seem to believe that if you don't commit to anything, you won't get older. You'll stay twenty-three forever. But you know what? While you're pissing your life away, time is passing, and there's nothing you can do to stop it. You've had every advantage, every opportunity. You could have done anything with your life, Eric. Anything at all. And instead you've just grown up to be this, this— macaroni-and-cheese-eating man-boy!"

He is so quiet that at first I think he'd hung up in the middle of my outburst.

"I guess that's all, then," he says at last.

"I guess it is."

# Vanessa

If Eric really loved me, he wouldn't show up at my office on Pizza Day, asking if I wanted to grab something to eat. He would know that I already had plans. He would know that the last Thursday of every month was a big deal because before Dr. Sanchez's wife got sick, she used to take the orders, buy the pizza, pour the soda, and make everyone laugh. And that it's really cool and sweet and sad that Dr. Sanchez has kept Pizza Day going because it's a way he can feel connected to her.

If Eric really loved me, he would know all this because I've told him every last Thursday of every month for as long as I've worked here.

At a quarter after twelve, Melva, Pammy, and I are sprawled on the waiting room couches, hoping to catch a glimpse of the Domino's delivery guy that Melva calls Hottie Van Hotness. Hottie V. hasn't shown since the spring, and we're starting to think that he got a new route or a new job. Which might be good for him but would suck for all of us.

When the door opens, we all sit up straight and smile . . . only to have Eric walk in. Weird. Back when I worked at Sears, I used to get all hot and happy whenever Eric popped in and asked me if I wanted to grab some coffee or whatever. But now it feels awkward. Like, he's not here because he couldn't stop thinking about me but because we almost broke up a few days ago. It's also awkward because Melva and Pammy—but especially Melva—think he's a total douche.

"What are you doing here?" I say. Which is so not the right thing to say but it's what pops into my mind.

"Uh, hi." He laughs. Kind of. "Good to see you too."

"I didn't mean . . . it's just, you know. The last Thursday of the month."

He gets this look on his face like he's trying to remember a name. Then he goes, "Oh, yeah. I guess it is."

Melva stands up, sighs really loudly, and heads down the hall, toward the bathroom. I told Melva and Pammy all about our latest fight and how Eric was going to donate again. And even though he chose me over that woman, they still agreed that it was total crap that he even wanted to do it.

"Do you think he might do it and not tell you?" Pammy asked.

At first I was like, no way, Eric never lies. But then I remembered that he never told me about donating in the first place, which was kind of like lying. So now I wonder how well I really know him.

It's too bad that Melva is in the john, because Hottie Van Hotness is on duty.

"We haven't seen you in a while!" Pammy says, springing off the couch and reaching for the cardboard boxes.

Hottie V. has dimples, cut cheekbones, tan skin, shiny black hair, and a body that looks like it's never seen a pizza, at least from the inside.

"Guess you need to order more pizza," he says.

"Sounds good to me." Pammy manages to put the boxes on the receptionist counter without taking her eyes off him.

Dr. Sanchez comes out of his office and hands Hottie a credit card. When he sees Eric, he goes, "Oh."

"Hey." Eric shoves his hands in his pockets.

Hottie gives Dr. Sanchez back his card and also a slip to sign. He says bye and leaves and I'm thinking, *I didn't get to flirt with him, and Melva didn't even get to see him, and Eric ruined everything.*

It is so weird to feel this way about Eric. I guess I am still mad.

Pammy and I go to the storage room to get the paper plates and soda cans.

"It's not a big deal," she says, her voice low. "If you want to take off and have lunch with Eric."

"It is a big deal. And anyway, I don't know that I even want to."

She raises her eyebrows.

"Yeah. I know."

Melva comes out of the john.

"You missed him," I say.

"Eric? Good."

"Uh-uh. Hottie."

Her eyes bulge. "Shit!"

"Shhhh!" Pammy and I both giggle.

"Can't we call Dommy's?" Melva says. "Say he forgot to give us our crushed red pepper packets or something?"

In the waiting room, Dr. Sanchez and Eric aren't laughing. Dr. Sanchez stands above Eric, arms crossed. Eric's on the couch, elbows on knees, hunched forward. When he sees me, he stands up. I don't know what to say. There's plenty of pizza, but it's not really mine to offer, even if there's anything without meat.

"Guess I'll see you at home," Eric says.

"Oh!" All of a sudden I want him to stay. Instead I go, "I'll walk you to your car," and follow him out the door.

"Thanks for coming by," I say. "It's just, you know. Pizza Day."

"Right." He leans forward, gives me a superfast kiss on the mouth, and gets in his car.

Back in the office, everyone is sitting and chewing. Melva's got one partially eaten crust on her plate already and is halfway through her second piece. I snag a piece of sausage pizza and a Diet Coke and sit at the end of the couch closest to Dr. Sanchez.

Pammy holds her can of Diet Sprite up high. "To Rosie."

"To Rosie." We all toast the ceiling.

Dr. Sanchez takes a long drink of his Sprite. He doesn't look happy, exactly, but he looks like his mind is in a better place than most days, at least.

Melva chows down on her second piece of pizza and then goes to the counter for two more. Everyone's quieter than usual.

Pammy goes, "It was nice of Eric to stop by. I'll give him that."

Melva snorts and plops back down on the couch, balancing her paper plate. "You couldn't pay me to have that guy's baby."

---

Since it's Eric's day off, he's at the apartment when I get there.

"You didn't look real thrilled to see me today."

"I was just—I didn't expect you, that's all."

"You used to like it when I showed up. You know, back when you were at Sears."

"That was different. There were so many people there. And it was in the mall."

"And Dr. Sanchez wasn't there."

"Huh?"

"He has a crush on you."

"That is ridiculous."

Eric shakes his head.

"What happened when I was in the back, anyway?" I ask.

"Dr. Sanchez told me that I was an asshole."

"He did not."

"He said, 'You need to treasure what you have.'"

"Yeah, because his wife died. Not because he has a crush on me."

"And then he goes, 'If you can't see how amazing this woman is, you're a fool and you don't deserve her.'"

"He really said that?"

"He's hot for you, babe." Now he's grinning. Like it's real. Like it's funny. Like it's something that he wishes would happen.

Suddenly I'm mad. "You'd like that, wouldn't you? If you could just pass me on to someone else so you don't have to feel guilty about dumping me?"

He says no, but he says it too fast.

"I'm right, aren't I?"

"Just because I said that your boss has a crush on you, that doesn't mean that I—"

"If you don't want to marry me, Eric, say it. Be a man and *just say it*!"

My ears buzz and my breathing is loud. The air around me feels thick and sour.

Finally, Eric speaks. "I don't want to marry you."

And then he leaves.

# Wendy

It was just one time.

I would say it didn't mean anything, but of course it did. It always does, even if it's with the man you've been with since you were eighteen years old. In that case, it can mean: I still love you. Or: You mean everything to me. If it's infrequent enough or strained enough, it can mean, I'm staying with you because it's the right thing to do. Or, Maybe this will help.

It was just one time.

***

The doctor told us to have sex. Darren and me, that is. After two weeks of daily hormone shots to stimulate my ovaries; after an additional trigger shot to make my eggs drop; after thirty-six hours of tender breasts and a cramped abdomen; after shaking with fear (and cold) in an outpatient room as the doctor slipped a catheter far, far inside me, his eyes on a black-and-white ultrasound screen as he harvested two, three, four eggs; after I'd slipped back into my clothes while Darren sat hunched in a visitor chair, playing a game on his cell phone, that's when the doctor told us.

"Studies indicate that intercourse before implantation increases the odds of success."

I said, "What?"

Darren looked up from his phone.

"Something in the seminal fluid sends a signal to the uterus to prepare for implantation. That's the theory, anyway."

"But Darren's sperm count . . ." I didn't need to finish. The doctor knew our story.

"Doesn't matter," the doctor said. "The reaction is to the seminal fluid, not the actual sperm."

"That's—wow," I said.

Lips tight, Darren went back to his game with renewed concentration. I hoped the doctor would think he was at least checking e-mails or something.

"You might feel a bit sore from the egg harvesting," the doctor told me. *Egg harvesting.* God, I hated that phrase. It made me feel like I'd fallen into a sci-fi movie.

"But we've got three to five days until the embryos will be ready for insertion," the doctor continued. "If you can have intercourse once in that time, good. Twice, even better."

Once the doctor left, I couldn't even look at Darren. For a long time, we had sex only when the doctor told us to. Ever since we'd been told it would never make us a baby, we hardly did it at all anymore.

"Ready to go?" I asked the floor.

Darren slipped his phone into his pocket. We left without speaking.

Two nights later, I put on my very best XXL T-shirt and worked hard to seduce my husband: "We might as well get this over with."

"Give me twenty minutes." He was watching television in the living room.

I nodded and retreated to the bedroom, where I read a magazine. When a half hour had passed and still no Darren, I went back to the living room.

"Now?" I asked.

He looked at me and then at the floor. "I don't think so."

"What do you mean?"

"I just . . . can't."

I swallowed hard. "Of course you can. You always have before. You don't have to like it."

He shook his head. "Sorry."

The next morning I tried again, waking early so I could get him before he was fully conscious. No dice. He recoiled from my touch and scrambled out of bed.

"I don't want to do this."

Tears spilling down my cheeks, I said, "Am I that repulsive?"

"You don't need me to have a baby. Why do you need me for this?"

Just like that, my sadness morphed into anger. How dare he? I was doing this for both of us. Had the situation been reversed, I would have gladly used an egg donor—and for the sake of my future children, I would have chosen a tall blond woman with a really fast metabolism. Now it was all about Darren's stupid male ego. That's what had made the infertility treatments so awful, even more than all the painful physical stuff.

When Darren left for work, about forty minutes earlier than he really had to, my anger slid back into sadness and then landed with a thud on self-pity. I was unlovable. Unsexy. Infertile. My own husband didn't want me.

I almost didn't answer the doorbell, but I did. When I saw Lane Plant standing there, in a T-shirt and paint-stained jeans, I thought: *I shouldn't have answered the doorbell.* At least he was wearing a shirt, for once.

Lane said, "I'm painting the eaves. Darren said I could borrow his tall ladder."

I burst into tears.

Had the situation been reversed, had Darren rung the Plants' doorbell to borrow something, only to be met by a tearful Sherry, he would have backed away in terror, mumbled some apologies, and fled to the safety of his own home. Emotions make Darren squirm.

But Lane wasn't Darren. Without hesitation, he took me into his big hairy arms. Without hesitation, I threw my head against his chest and let my tears soak his T-shirt. He smelled like sandalwood—I don't know the brand of his cologne, but it must be pretty popular because I'll catch a whiff of it every now and then, and it always makes me shudder with shame.

He closed the front door. Not because he had any plans to seduce me but because the air-conditioning was leaking out. Or maybe because he didn't want his wife or another neighbor to see me crying.

On the couch, I blabbered the miserable details of my miserable life, my miserable marriage. He didn't say much, just stroked my back and said, "Mm." And, "Ah, no."

Finally, I told him about the hormone shots. The egg retrieval. My failed seduction.

"I'm disgusting," I said.

"Don't say that."

"It's true. My own husband . . ."

"You're a beautiful woman." His hand touched the back of my head.

"I'm not."

"You are. Beautiful. Sexy." He ran his hand through my hair, pulled my head to his chest.

"Then why won't he . . . won't he . . ." His chest was so warm. So strong. It smelled so good. That aftershave . . .

"Any man would want you. Any man."

"My own husband . . ."

His mouth on mine felt sweet, friendly. I tasted toothpaste plus something sugary. Cereal, probably. Maybe a piece of fruit. And then his mouth was on my ear, murmuring, "Sexy. Hot. So hot." And still it felt friendly.

We kissed for a long time. I hadn't kissed like that since high school. His breathing grew heavy, his touch more insistent. I knew what was coming. Of course I did. And I could have said no. I could have stopped. I knew it was wrong.

And yet.

A baby. I wanted a baby so very, very badly. This could make the difference.

Is it better that I made the decision to sleep with Lane Plant from a place of clinical rationality? Or would it be more forgivable if I'd been driven by love or even lust? Does it even matter at this point?

———————

Rather than asking Darren to pick us up at the hospital, Harrison and I take a taxi. When we get home, Sydney is munching Cheez-Its in front of the television while Darren, of course, is stationed at his computer. But instead of playing Sims or World of Warcraft, he just stares at his home page, a compilation of news and sports and weather. I don't think he's really seeing anything.

"Harrison wants to know what happened to the scorpion," I say.

Darren looks at me for just an instant and then trains his eyes on his lap.

"The doctor thought that was really funny." My voice is flat. "Harrison said he hoped no one killed it because it wasn't the scorpion's fault. I told him the scorpion probably just ran away."

"It's dead," Darren says. "The teacher saved it so we could see if it was a bark scorpion, but I forgot to take it with me."

"That's okay."

Darren glares at the computer screen. He jabs at his keypad, pulling up a Fantasy Football site.

"I'm sorry," I say.

His face is so tight, his lips are turning white.

"It was an emotional time," I say. "I was hurt. And angry. I'm sorry."

He doesn't look at me.

"I wanted a baby. So much."

Finally, he speaks. "No matter whose baby it was?"

"I thought you were okay with a donor. At first, anyway. I know you didn't love the idea, but adoption just—" All of a sudden I realize what he just said.

"Oh my God. You think Harrison and Sydney are . . ." And just like that, I see it too: the thick, dark hair. The brooding eyes. The quick tempers.

"There's no way," I say, even as I try to picture Ashlyn and Brianne Plant, steeling myself against a resemblance. "The doctors would have known when they implanted the eggs." (Would they have? Twenty-four hours later?) "I didn't get pregnant before that even with hormone shots and IUI, so there's no way . . ."

Hormones. I'd taken plenty before the egg harvesting. Could I have dropped more eggs afterward?

"I don't think it's possible," I say. When he doesn't respond, I add, "We can get a paternity test, if you want. Just to make sure. It would be easy because . . ." Because I have the number of the clinic that has already analyzed Eric Fergus's DNA. But Darren doesn't even know about Eric: just one more dirty secret.

"It doesn't matter anymore," Darren says. "Not really."

That's when I know: I've lost him.

# Laura

Ian doesn't even like Axel—with complete justification, I might add. The one time he came over to our house (a quid pro quo situation following a six-hour swim and playdate at Axel's house, followed by dinner at Islands), he threw LEGOs at the cat and talked incessantly about poop. Chickens, humans, cats: no one's excrement potential went unmentioned.

In addition to making fart noises in the classroom, Ian once told me, Axel has been known to whisper an inappropriate word to the girls.

"Which inappropriate word?" I asked.

"I don't want to say it."

"What's the first letter?"

"*B.*"

As there's a lot you can do with a *B,* I probed further. "What's the second letter?"

He looked up in the air, considering. "*U.*"

Now I was really confused. "Whisper it."

His eyes widened.

"It's okay," I told him. While I disliked the idea of encouraging my son to repeat an obscenity, I needed to know just how badly this Axel kid had corrupted him.

He leaned forward and said, in a stage whisper, "Boobies!"

"It's spelled *B-O-O*," I said. "Not *B-U*."

He frowned. *"B-O-O-B-I-E-S . . .?"*

"Yes."

"That's how you spell 'boobies'?"

"Yes."

*"B-O-O-B—"*

"Enough, Ian."

He pressed his lips together and looked at the ground. "Sorry for being inappropriate."

"It's okay."

"And for saying 'boobies.'"

Because of this conversation, when Axel's mother called one evening last week to see if Ian could spend a long weekend at their house on the Colorado River ("His sister's bringing a friend too"), I felt confident saying that I didn't think Ian would be comfortable spending three nights away from home but that I'd ask him.

"Sure, I'll go," he said.

"But you don't like Axel," I reminded him.

"He's okay."

"You said he's inappropriate."

"He's better this year."

"The River is four hours away. If you're unhappy, I won't be able to come get you." (I'm bluffing, of course; I'd gladly drive to the desert to pick him up, if he so much as hinted that he wanted to come home.)

"I want to go," he said. "Axel said they have a boat."

"It'll be hot there," I said.

"I want to go."

I've left work early to pick up Ian from sports camp. He's all ready when Axel's family arrives at one o'clock, the four of them plus his twelve-year-old sister's friend stuffed into a dirty, black, boat-pulling SUV. I haul Ian's duffel bag down the sidewalk while he races ahead.

Axel's mother, Terri, a busty blonde with power shoulders and tanned, meaty thighs, bounces out of the passenger seat. The boat sticks out into the street. An image flashes through my mind: our local teenage chicken-hitting driver zipping around the curb and colliding with the boat. The idea shouldn't please me, but it does.

"Laura!" When Terri embraces me, I have no choice but to hug back even though we are cordial acquaintances at best.

"Thanks again." I take a step back. "For taking Ian. He's really looking forward to it."

"No, thank *you*! For letting him *come*! 'Cause Axel would drive us *crazy* if his sister had a friend along and he didn't!"

Next, Axel's red-faced, hefty father gets out of the car.

"Hot!" Pete says. "Ninety-seven degrees. Says my thermometer. And the River? It's gonna be, what? Twenty more'n that? Whooh!"

"Better you than me," I joke, though I'd gladly spend a weekend in the Sahara if it meant I could be with Ian.

I pass the duffel bag to Pete. He straddles the trailer hitch, pops open the back window, and shoves the bag next to a bulky Coors cooler.

I gesture at the cooler. "You don't drink while you're driving the boat, do you?" I try (and fail) to project a casual tone.

"'Course not." He grins and gives the duffel bag one more pat before slamming the window shut. He doesn't meet my eyes. He is lying.

Ian has settled and strapped into the third row of seats, next to Axel, too far from the door for me to kiss him.

I lean in next to Axel's sister, who is singing along to whatever is playing on her iPod.

"Have fun, buddy," I say to the back row. "Call you tonight."

"'Kay." He barely even looks up, too engrossed in the spare Nintendo Axel has brought along.

I stand in my driveway until the SUV and boat are out of sight, thinking, *I have entrusted my child to people who drink beer while driving their boat. I have entrusted my child to people who named their son Axel.*

———————

By the time I realize I should have gone back to the office rather than working from home, it is too late. Between Carmen and Ian, I am almost never alone in the house, and the quiet, empty space only serves to amplify my loneliness. Last night I dreamed that Carmen called from El Salvador to say she wasn't coming back. I awoke in a cold sweat. At least tomorrow is a workday; overtime will be my salvation.

For now, though, it's just me and the chickens. And the cat, of course, but he's asleep underneath my bed and not much in the mood for conversation. I work on my laptop until six o'clock, when I figure enough time has passed for Ian to have arrived at the River. Terri's phone number is affixed to my refrigerator (also listed on my computer and programmed into my cell).

"Laura! Hey!" Children yell and laugh in the background. At least, I think they're happy sounds.

We exchange pleasantries (they stopped at Taco Bell for an early dinner; it's hot in the desert), and then she calls Ian.

"Hi."

"Hey, buddy! Having fun?"

"Yeah." Do I detect any uncertainty in his voice?

"What have you done so far?"

"We just go here. We're going for ice cream later."

"Fun!"

"Yeah."

"I miss you. I love you." My voice catches.

"I love you too."

"Call me anytime," I say. "If you want to talk, or . . ." I catch myself before I can say *if you want me to come get you.*

When we get off the phone, I pull some leftovers out of the fridge for the chickens—last night's pasta salad, made from a kit.

The doorbell rings.

Face pleasant but stern, I open the door, prepared to say thanks, but I don't want your magazine subscriptions, contracting services, candy bars, or religion.

"Hi," Eric Fergus says.

I am not prepared to say anything.

"Can I come in?"

I step out of the way. He passes the threshold and pauses, looking around.

"He's not here," I say.

"Oh." He shifts his weight. "Then I guess I—"

"Have you eaten anything?" I blurt.

It's Eric's idea to eat outside with the chickens, and it isn't until I've set the bowl and plates on the table that it hits me: my yard looks like crap. I mean that literally. There is chicken crap on the walkways. Chicken crap around the patchy grass. Even chicken crap on a lounge chair.

What the chickens haven't crapped on, they've largely eaten. We have no weeds, true, but we don't have much of a lawn left either.

"The chickens were a mistake," I announce.

Eric, who has just opened the coop, stops throwing pasta at the greedy birds. "No, they weren't."

"They were supposed to teach Ian responsibility," I say. "But he doesn't clean up after them. And they were supposed to be calming.

That's what everyone said—nothing more soothing than hanging out with your chickens. But what's soothing about witnessing the slow destruction of my yard?"

Eric chucks pasta into the coop. "They're cool. It's like you're living on a farm or something."

"But I'm not. That's the thing. We're not on a farm. Ian is not growing up in some rustic, homey paradise with a laid-back earth mother. Instead he's just got me and my commute and my endless insomnia. I think the chickens were supposed to make up for all of the things I couldn't give him. A father. Brothers and sisters. A normal life."

"Who's to say what's normal? I grew up with two parents, two brothers, and a sister. And look how I turned out."

He isn't joking or looking for argument: he says it as a statement of fact. And then he goes back to chucking pasta.

"If I open a bottle of wine, will you have some?" I ask.

"Sure."

He follows me into the kitchen, puts the pasta bowl into the sink, and leans against the counter as I stick a corkscrew into a bottle of Merlot that someone from work gave me for Christmas.

"Does this mean you're not going to use a different donor?" he asks.

I stop my twisting. "No. I could keep going with the IVF . . . but it's so expensive. We weren't even able to afford a cheap vacation this summer. Plus, the doctor said . . ."

I swallow hard and twist the corkscrew violently, push down, and pull up. The cork releases with a satisfying pop.

"What did the doctor say?" Eric asks, twenty seconds after I assumed we'd dropped the conversation.

"He said I'm probably just too old. That I could try using a donor egg or a surrogate, but considering how many failed attempts I've had, the odds of me becoming pregnant are so slim that it would be foolish to keep pushing my body this way."

Eric says, "I'd like to donate again. That's part of the reason I came here. To tell you that."

I take a deep breath and exhale every shred of hope I'd been carrying around. "It's too late. It wouldn't work. And I . . . I just can't go through that again."

I pour the wine into two big glasses. I give one to Eric and take mine, along with the bottle, out to the shabby backyard.

The wine smells and tastes vaguely musty. I try to remember who gave it to me. A case of regifting, perhaps?

Eric and I sit at the teak table. I scoop some supermarket-bought Cobb salad onto his plate, trying to minimize the bacon.

"Do you date?" he asks.

I freeze, salad servers poised over my plate, and search for the appropriate words for this kind of situation—the only problem being, of course, that hardly anyone has ever been in these circumstances before.

"You're a lovely man," I say. "But given our . . . connection . . . in addition to the age difference, I don't think it would be wise to pursue any kind of a romantic relationship."

He chuckles. "I wasn't asking you out. I was just curious."

"Oh! Right. Of course. My apologies." My face burns. How could I have possibly have thought . . .? "No. I don't. Date, that is."

"Why not? I mean, you're . . . you know."

"What?"

"Attractive. And I'm sure that if you wanted to go out with someone, you could find an age-appropriate man who hadn't fathered your children."

"You didn't father my child. Exactly."

"Semantics," he says.

"Right." I sip my wine. Look at the chickens.

"You didn't answer my question," he says.

"That's correct." I hold his gaze.

"I'm just curious," he said. "You say you wish you had those things for Ian, a father, siblings . . ."

"I didn't say a father, specifically."

"Actually, you did."

"Really?"

"Are you gay?" he asks.

"No!"

He raises his eyebrows.

"I didn't mean it like that," I say. "From what I've seen on the donor sites, lesbians—the sperm donation route generally works out really well for them. They've got it all, the partner, the kids. They even get to choose which of them carries the baby. What I meant was, a woman can be straight and still feel she's better off without a man. That she's better off alone."

"But why?" He is relentless.

"You missed your calling," I say. "You should have been a lawyer."

"I've never heard the law referred to as a calling." He takes a bite of his salad, swallows, and grabs his napkin. "Is that bacon?"

I shrug. "I tried not to give you any . . ."

He jabs at his salad and flicks away the bacon bits like bugs.

"Why did you drop out of medical school?" I ask.

He looks up, shocked.

"You're not the only one who can ask questions," I say.

He sips some wine and considers. "You answer my question, I'll answer yours."

"Fine," I say. "But you've got to understand, you're not the first person to ask me why I don't date, though I appreciate your not tacking on some variant of 'you're not getting any younger.'"

"No one really says that."

"Sometimes they do. And sometimes they just imply it," I say. "Anyway. My parents divorced when I was thirteen. My father remarried almost immediately, which makes me think his second wife was the reason for the breakup, though I didn't really get that till I was much older."

"Did your mother remarry?"

"Eventually. When I was in college. But during high school, she dated more than I did. Not that that was saying much, but still. I remember how it felt, her getting all dressed up to go out with some guy. Leaving me behind. Like this stranger was more important than I was. More worthy of her time. I'm not going to do that to my kid."

"But what if you found a guy who really cared about Ian?"

I shake my head. "Question asked and answered. Your turn. Why did you drop out of medical school?"

"Because my father died."

Once again, I feel a pang for the biological grandfather Ian will never know—even though the biological grandfather he does know has so little interest in him.

"Were you and your father close?" I ask.

"Yeah. I guess. I mean, I've got two brothers and a sister, so it wasn't like the one-on-one thing you have with Ian. But yeah—he was the best. And when I got interested in medicine, that's when we really bonded."

"He was a doctor," I say.

Eric nods. "When I was studying for the MCATs, and then when I started medical school . . . I'd save up stuff in my head. You know, to tell him. Or questions to ask or whatever. Then once he was gone—I just couldn't focus. So I dropped out and starting playing music. I always thought I'd go back. But six months went by and then a year. And I just—couldn't face it. Everything about medicine, even thinking about med school, reminded me of him. It was just too painful."

He stops talking and drinks some wine. His eyes glisten.

"I'm sorry," I say.

He nods.

"But your music . . ." I say. "Maybe you should give it another try."

He snorts. "I didn't quit medical school to pursue a music career. I pursued a music career because drinking too much and playing guitar in bars was all I could handle at that point. And by saying I was all about my music—people respected that. They left me alone."

He pauses. "That's not entirely true. Music . . . that was always the thing that made me happy. But then I cut a CD that no one wanted, and I started reading negative stuff that people posted online. And the whole starving artist thing . . ." He shakes his head. "At first I thought, once enough people heard me play, things would really take off. But it didn't work out that way. And by the time I stopped, music had lost its magic for me. I can't even remember the last time I picked up my guitar."

"You cut a CD? Is it on iTunes?"

He snorts. "No. But every once in a while one'll pop up on eBay for like a dollar." He takes another bite of his salad and drops his fork. "Bacon! Ugh!"

I smile. "When did you become a vegetarian?"

"Junior high school. This kid next door was in the agriculture program at our local high school, and he had a pig. Daisy. Not the most original name, but whatever. Anyway, I went to the school with him a couple of times to hang with Daisy, who was really pretty cute. And clean. And smart. And then, at the end of the year, my parents bought one-eighth of Daisy and stuck her in the freezer."

"Ew," I say. Now I don't want to eat the bacon.

"And the thing is—Daisy had a good life. She wasn't dirty and crowded like factory farm animals are, all doped up with antibiotics. But she had a name."

"So you're saying I shouldn't chop up Red or Rusty and serve them with Marsala sauce?"

"I wouldn't recommend it."

"So back to your career . . ."

"Uh-uh." He holds up a finger. "You already snuck in an extra question with the vegetarian thing. My turn."

"But—"

"Was your ex-husband an asshole?"

"No. Of course not."

"Of course not?"

"I wouldn't marry an asshole. Rob was . . . not nice, exactly, but ethical. Reliable. We had the same career goals, the same life goals. We shared a lot of interests. We were extremely compatible."

"That's hot," Eric says. When I don't react, he adds, "Sorry."

I shrug. "It was a long time ago. So what about you and Vanessa. Are you compatible?"

"Not really."

"Share common interests?"

"None."

"Career goals, life goals . . ."

"I don't have any goals, remember?"

"Well then," I say, trying to lighten the mood. "Perhaps you share that with her."

He shakes his head. "She has life goals. Marriage, children . . ."

"Maybe you're just not right for each other," I suggest.

"Oh. I know we're not right for each other." He drains his wine.

"You just don't want to hurt her."

"It's too late for that." He picks up the bottle and splits the remainder between us. "But enough about me. My turn to ask a question. Yes?"

"Shoot," I say.

He takes a long drink of wine. I think: *He won't be able to drive home.*

He looks up at the pink-tinted sky and grins. "What about sex?"

"*Excuse me?*"

"Ian's what, eight? Add nine months for your pregnancy. Are you saying it's been nine years since you . . ."

I clear my throat. "Of course not." I gulp my wine and scan the stupid yard for the stupid chickens.

"Of course not *what*?"

"Of course it hasn't been that long."

He leans forward and rests his chin on his knuckles.

"Have you eaten any meat at all since becoming a vegetarian?" I say.

He snorts. "Nice try. Does this mean—what? You have a shadow life, a secret lover? Maybe a married man?"

"No!" My tone is harsher than I intended. He straightens.

I say, "Nothing like that. Over the years I've attended a number of legal conferences. And there were a couple of occasions . . . it didn't mean anything. Neither of the men—there were two, a couple of years apart—neither was married."

"How many years ago?" Eric asks.

"I don't remember."

"Of course you do."

He's right. "Five years ago," I say. "The last time." I swallow the huge lump in my throat, but it won't go away.

Around us, the air fills with the sounds of scratching chickens, crickets, and the waterfall of distant traffic.

Eric says, "A week after my father died, I ate a hamburger. In-N-Out. Double Double."

"Did you like it?"

"Best thing I ever tasted."

The wine is gone and my head is swimming. We herd the chickens back into the coop and carry our dishes inside. While we're loading the dishwasher, Eric's hand brushes my arm, startling me with an almost electric charge. I move my head and the walls sway, just a tiny bit.

I say, "When my husband left me—it was his decision, not

mine—he said that he had never loved me. He didn't say it to be mean, he just thought I should know because it would help me to better understand his actions. That's why I don't date. I'm not going to let anyone else make me feel that bad, ever again."

Eric opens a couple of cabinets until he finds a glass, which he fills with tap water. He takes a long drink and stares at the wall. Finally, he speaks.

"I was so afraid that if I became a doctor I'd screw up and hurt someone. Make a wrong diagnosis or prescribe the wrong medicine. That I'd tell someone everything was fine only to find out when it was too late that they had cancer or something, and were going to die because of me."

He finishes his water and puts the glass in the dishwasher.

He says, "And the other thing that scares me is the idea that I'll get stuck in some job that I hate, doing the same thing for thirty years just so I can pay for a car, a house in the suburbs, a week at the beach. My God. Is that all there is?"

I touch his hand. "Not necessarily. Sometimes there are chickens too."

He laughs. His smile is really beautiful. I drop my hand and cross to the refrigerator, though I can't remember what for.

"Are you okay to drive?" I ask.

"Yeah."

"Then . . . you should probably go."

"Do you want me to go?"

"No." We look at each other from across the kitchen.

"Then I'll stay," he says, his voice not much louder than a whisper.

# Wendy

Two weeks after Harrison's scorpion sting, I pull up in front of Tara's stucco house for my scrapbooking meeting only to see Sherry Plant's SUV parked at the curb. I try to work up the old indignation—how dare she hone in on my group?—but shame overwhelms me. Sherry was a lousy friend, but that doesn't excuse my betrayal. And nothing excuses my betrayal of Darren. I pull away from the curb and head home.

Darren and the kids are at the kitchen table, eating pepperoni Bagel Bites. Harrison turns, and in a flash I see Lane Plant in his eyes. Has Sherry noticed the resemblance? Has she been looking for it all these years?

"You had a call," Darren tells me. "From a genetics counselor."

The DNA test. I didn't think the results would come in this fast.

"The number's on the counter," Darren says, refusing to meet my eyes. "She left her cell."

Outside, the air is hot and heavy, the not-yet-setting sun searing the yard. So maybe we shouldn't have bought a house with a west-facing backyard.

I sit at the table, the plastic chair scorching my legs, and dial the genetics counselor. She answers on the first ring. Blood rushes through my ears with such force, I'm afraid I won't be able to hear, but I catch the most important words: *Eric Fergus. Biological father. Ninety-nine-point-nine percent probability. Ian Cahill. Biological half sibling. Ninety-nine-point-nine.*

Lane Plant is not my children's father. I'd been impregnated by a complete stranger. The news comes as such relief, I burst into tears.

When I manage to compose myself, I go back into the house, only to find the kitchen empty. The children are watching television. Upstairs, Darren is on the computer. When I place a hand on his shoulder, he tenses. I fight the instinct to take my hand away.

"It's not—his," I say. "It was the donor. A man named Eric Fergus. I have some things I need to tell you . . ."

I'm terrified that Darren will be angry at me for keeping Eric Fergus a secret, but as I tell him about Eric and Laura and Ian, he barely registers any emotion. Somehow, that's even worse.

"I think we should move," I say.

When he doesn't respond, I say, "It's not working here. *We're* not working. But maybe we can be happy somewhere else. We could go to Michigan, live near my parents. They'd help with the kids, give us more time for each other."

His face twitches. I can't read him. Could I ever? I think so, but it was so long ago.

I say, "If we've got any chance of working things out, we've got to leave. Don't you agree?" Cautious, I take my hand off his shoulder, touch his cheek.

"Yes." He brushes my fingers lightly. And then he reaches for his computer mouse.

———

Days later, Harrison and Sydney throw fits when we tell them we are moving to Michigan. Well, when I tell them. Darren just sits there as Harrison kicks and Sydney screams. They don't want to leave Arizona. They'll miss their house, their pool, their school.

"You hate school," I remind them.

"We might hate the new one even more!" Sydney shrieks. I can't argue with the logic, even as I think, *How much worse can it be?*

"We'll get to spend time with Gammie and Pop-Pop," I say. "We'll even get to live with them until Daddy comes out."

That last bit is directed at Darren, a reminder that he's coming too. As soon as he finds a job in Michigan, we'll be a family again. Or: we'll be a family at last. If I say it enough times, maybe it will make it true.

"I'll miss my friends!" Harrison says (yells).

"What friends?" I say, by which I mean: "Which of your friends will you especially miss?" I swear I do. Instead, it comes out sounding like: "You don't have any friends." Which I'd never say.

Fortunately, Harrison takes it at the first meaning. "Dodie."

Dodie. Uh. Amazing how much you can despise someone who doesn't exist.

"He can come with us," I say.

Harrison shakes his head. "He lives here."

"I can ask his mother."

He shakes his head. "He doesn't have a mother."

"His father, then."

"His father will say no."

"I bet he'll come with us anyway."

I try to catch Darren's eye—to share a moment, a smile, something. But he is far away, deep in his head.

"I don't want to go without Daddy," Sydney says, more a whine than a shriek.

"Daddy will come out soon. Right, Daddy? Right?"

# Laura

Eric doesn't exactly sneak out after our night together, but he might have if the jangle of his keys hadn't woken me. It is early, just the slightest shades of gray creeping around my blinds. Even the chickens are still asleep.

"Sorry," he whispers, seeing me stir.

"It's okay. I had to get up soon, anyway." Is he apologizing for something besides waking me?

He tugs his T-shirt over his head and carries his shoes and socks into the bathroom, closing the door with the faintest click. My clothes lie in a puddle next to my bed. It isn't like me to leave them there, but then, nothing I did last night was like me. I can't remember the last time I slept so well.

Once I pull on yoga pants and a T-shirt, I head to the kitchen to start the coffee. While it brews, I poke around in the cabinets and refrigerator, pulling out everything vaguely breakfastlike: cereal, granola, yogurt, fruit, juices, English muffins. Should I let him help himself or offer to serve him? It has been so long since I've been in this situation.

Eggs! Of course! I should scramble some of our home-laid eggs!

Hands shaking, I yank open the refrigerator and pluck two brown eggs from a bowl on the top shelf. As I turn around, Eric walks into the kitchen, startling me. I drop the bigger of the two eggs, which smashes on contact, bright yellow fanning out from the delicate brown shell.

Eric yanks some paper towel from the mounted roll near the sink. "Let me help you."

I put the unbroken egg on the counter and join Eric on the floor with my own wad of paper towel.

"We've got plenty more eggs." We are so close, I can smell the now-familiar faint vanilla musk of his skin.

"Thanks, but I should get going." Eric pushes himself up from the floor and scans the room for a trash can.

"Under the sink," I say.

He throws away the paper towel. I wait for him to move out of the way before I pitch mine.

"You want some coffee?" I ask, trying—and failing—to meet his eyes.

"Thanks, but I'm good." He shoves his hands in his pockets and shifts his feet. "Thanks," he says again. "For last . . . for dinner. And—you know."

"Right."

At the front door, he finally looks at me and starts to say something before changing his mind.

"It's okay," I tell him, not sure I believe it myself.

He nods, brushes my arm, and drives off into the pale gray morning.

As I drink my coffee and eat my cereal (I lost interest in the eggs), I wait to feel hurt, cheap, and abandoned. Neither of us pretended that our encounter was anything more than a once-off; for that I am grateful. Guilt at having bedded another woman's boyfriend nibbles at my conscience, but they aren't married and clearly never will be.

All in all, it is a night best forgotten. I know Eric Fergus is gone from my life forever. Why, then, do I feel . . . hopeful? Is it just the reward for a deep, dreamless sleep?

Finally, it hits me. After all that time and money spent tracking Eric down, after all the pain and expense of undergoing artificial insemination . . . I just may have gotten pregnant the old-fashioned way.

I pour the rest of my coffee in the sink and make a note to pick up some folic acid on the way home from work—or maybe even on the way to work. I've got plenty of time, after all.

# Vanessa

It is just barely daylight when he comes home. Six o'clock, six-thirty—something like that. The sound of his key wakes me up. I didn't think I'd sleep, but I guess I did.

I think, *He came back.*

But for how long?

I'm afraid to get out of bed. Afraid to look at him. To hear what he's going to say. I was stupid to push him like that. To test him. Stupid to think that would make him love me.

He is in the doorway. I can feel him. Hear him breathing. My face is wet. I feel like a little girl again, lost and alone.

I clutch at the bedspread and look up. He looks so sad. And older, somehow.

He opens his mouth.

"No," I say.

He waits for me.

"I don't want you to say it. Whatever it is, I don't want to know."

He closes his mouth. Closes his eyes. Nods.

*Part 4*

OCTOBER

# Wendy

My body forgot how cold Michigan could be in the fall. I'm wearing a bulky sweater over a thick turtleneck and chain-drinking coffee in my parents' kitchen, and still I can't stop shivering.

"How are you going to handle January?" my mother asks, handing me a section of the paper.

"I'll be used to it by then. Not sure about the kids."

"Children are adaptable."

In truth, I'm not so worried about how the kids and I will handle a Midwestern winter. I'm more concerned that we will still be living in my parents' house. The children—and my parents—believe that Darren will move out as soon as the Arizona house sells because that's what I told them. I didn't tell them that there are very few jobs for aerospace engineers in Michigan. I certainly didn't tell them that the day we put the house on the market, Darren said, "I'm not sure I want to be married to you anymore."

But as long as I don't think about what comes next, I'm okay.

I sip coffee and open the newspaper. Cold or no, this is my favorite part of the day. The kids are in school, having eaten a nutritious breakfast (that I didn't cook). My dad is running errands. My mother and I are just hanging out, chatting. Everything feels right—even as I know that moving in with my parents at this stage of my life should feel very, very wrong.

It's just temporary.

Dodie didn't come with us. The day we left, Harrison spent an hour in his bedroom, saying his good-byes, and then, forlorn, he walked out to the front yard and slumped on the stoop.

"Dodie can hang out with Daddy until the house gets sold," I said. In the house, there would be more imaginary people than real ones, but then, maybe there always were.

---

An hour before school lets out, my cell phone rings.

Without bothering to say hello, my new friend Pat starts talking at her usual double speed.

"Gus wanted to know if Harrison could come over after school to look at his new Pokémon cards. He bought a whole bunch with some of the Target gift cards he got for his birthday because he only had like three thousand cards and that wasn't enough. But anyway they could do homework together, if they have any, and Sydney can come too, so Tillie doesn't drive me crazy."

"They'd love that," I say. "I'll have to get them kind of early, though, like four-thirty. My sister is flying in from Texas."

Harrison has a new best friend. Gus is much nicer than Dodie and also has the distinct advantage of being real. Gus is loud and twitchy and given to intense obsessions (Pokémon) and aversions (any food that has touched any other food). Gus's mother, Pat, is my new best friend—the first I've had since Sherry Plant. Astonishingly enough, Gus's twin sister, Tillie, is one of Sydney's *two* new best friends, the other being a My Little Pony fanatic named Kaleigh. Three is always a bad number, and I have a feeling things won't end well, especially since Tillie keeps asking Sydney to choose between My Little Pony and Polly Pocket.

But that's just one more thing I try not to think about.

"So nice you found a family just like yours," my mother says when I get off the phone.

Luckily for the rest of humanity, there is no family exactly like mine, but Pat's comes close-ish. A couple of years older than me, she went through similar infertility torture before becoming impregnated with donor eggs fertilized with her husband's sperm. Weirdly enough, Tillie and Gus look more like Pat than her husband. Maybe that's why it doesn't seem to bother her that they don't carry her DNA.

Does Darren feel closer to our children now that he knows that half of their genes come from a man I've never met—and never want to meet? Of course, it might be easier for him to leave us if the children were the product of my infidelity.

When our Arizona house sells, we will use the money to buy something in my parents' school district. It will have to be small or a fixer-upper or both for us to afford it. The Arizona real estate market took a real hit in the years since we bought. If Darren hasn't found a job in Michigan by then, he will rent an apartment near work and visit us for holidays and occasional long weekends.

That's the official line, anyway.

――――――――

"How'd it go?" I ask Pat when I show up at four-thirty. Her house is a mess, but it always is, and it doesn't seem to bother her.

She shrugs. "All four are still alive, so I figure I've done my job. Your sister who's coming—is she the one with the perfect kid?"

"That's her." I roll my eyes. "Her husband is out of town for a couple of weeks—some business thing in China—so Tracey and my niece Jade are flying in from Texas. Tomorrow they're going to the museum because Jade wants to learn more about the Impressionists."

"Impressionists? How old is she?"

"Four."

Pat howls. For the moment, at least, I feel like everything is going to be okay.

"Oh!" she says. "I keep meaning to tell you. Gus and Tillie's piano teacher says she has openings. I'll give you her number."

Once we've said our good-byes and the kids are strapped into their seats, I say, "Your cousin Jade will be at Gammie and Pop-Pop's in about an hour. Promise me you'll be good? And you'll play with your cousin?"

"Four's little," Sydney says.

Harrison kicks the back of my seat. "Before, you said she was three."

"She was three. Now she's four."

"She told us she was four," Sydney tells her brother.

"Did not."

"Did so!"

"If you don't fight, you can have Oreos when we get home," I say.

---

An hour later, I'm helping my mother set the table when a siren goes off outside.

"Is that a car alarm?" I ask.

My mother is already heading for the front door. "Jade's here!"

When she opens the door, the sound gets louder and clearer. It is a child, after all, a brown-eyed, brown-haired, red-faced bundle of fury. As my sister attempts to unstrap her from the back of my father's car, Jade flails and wails, her piercing scream starting to

form words. Specifically: NOOOOO! And: DOOOOOOON'T.
And: I-I-I-I-I HAAAATE YOUUUUU!

Harrison and Sydney scramble down the stairs and out to the
front lawn, where they stand gawking at their powerful niece and
their obviously unbalanced aunt.

"Stop it, Jadey! I said, stop it! Ow! You kicked me! Stop it!
You're embarrassing yourself. Can't you see you're embarrassing
yourself?" Tracey looks like she is going to cry.

I check my mother's face for shock but find none. "Is she always
like this?" I murmur.

"She's just tired," my mother says. "All children throw tantrums when they're tired. Or hungry. Or—well, all children throw
tantrums. It's part of growing up. When you were little . . ." She
smiles and shakes her head.

"What?"

"You've always been emotional," she says. "Which is a wonderful thing. That you don't bottle it up"

"You always said I was a good child."

In the driveway, my sister has taken a step back from the car
and appears to be on the verge of tears. "I'm going to count to five,
Jade Elizabeth. One . . . two . . ."

"Should we do something?" I ask my mother.

"Oh, no," my mother says. "We shouldn't make a fuss. That'll
just embarrass your sister and make Jade think she's having an ef-
fect on us."

I can't believe it. Jade is a monster! Here I've been thinking I
was the only one with temperamental children when . . . wait.

"Mom, when you said I was emotional . . . I know I cried sometimes, but . . . I wasn't like that, was I?"

My mother laughs. "Oh, Wendy, that little girl's got nothing on
you. There was a time, you were maybe four, when your nursery
school teacher said we might have to institutionalize you." She
laughs some more.

"That's not funny," I say.

"You're telling me! I thought it was something I'd done or not done. But gradually things got better."

"I was a horrible child," I say, still stunned.

"Not horrible," she says. "Just emotional. Look! Jade's out of the car! Jadey, dear, look where you are! You're at Gammie and Pop-Pop's house!" She hurries to the driveway and takes the little beast in her arms.

Here I thought I was just a bad mother. Now I know: it's all in the DNA. Eric Fergus's wimpy little genes didn't have a chance against mine. Not a chance.

# 2
## Laura

It was absurd to think I might be pregnant—no, to believe, deep down, that I was. Hormones and IUI and in vitro couldn't get the job done. Why would a one-night stand?

I cried the day I got my period in the ladies' room at my office, my hands plastered over my mouth so no one would hear my sobs. Once my breathing calmed down, I washed my face and left early so I could pick Ian up from school. On the concrete outside his classroom, I gave him a quick kiss on the head (anything more demonstrative would embarrass him).

"I've got big news, buddy."

"What?"

"We're getting a dog!"

That was over two months and countless hours of research ago. Today is the big day: a goldendoodle in Colorado named Mae West is giving birth, and we've got dibs on one of her puppies.

When I get home from work, Ian is sitting at the kitchen table, surrounded by his homework, while Carmen stirs something creamy and garlicky on the stove.

She says, "A package come for you today." She motions to a brown padded envelope on the counter.

Without looking at the envelope, I say, "Three girls, one boy."

Carmen claps her hands. To my surprise, she's at least as excited about the dog as Ian. Even more exciting for Carmen: her son has applied for a U.S. work visa, and I've assured her I'll do everything I can to help. After all these years, they can finally be a family again.

"Did Mae West have her puppies?" Ian asks.

I nod. "The boy is ours. Eight more weeks and we can get him."

He looks out the window. "Do we really have to get rid of the chickens?"

"Sorry, buddy. But we really do."

A dog means no chickens for the simple reason that he might kill them. Ian argued that we could keep them apart, but when I reminded him of the hit-and-run incident, he relented. Fortunately, it only took several phone calls to find a taker for the birds: Axel's family. His mother thinks chickens will teach Axel responsibility. I didn't disagree, at least out loud.

Now Ian walks to the glass slider and stares out at the smelly coop, the ravaged yard. Before spring, I will ask the gardener to re-seed the grass. A year from now, we'll be cleaning up dog poop instead of chicken crap. It will be like the chickens never happened. Instead, we will be just another family with a dog. A happy family with a dog.

I smile.

Ian announces, "I'm going to go practice my guitar." At the end of summer, Ian begged to switch from piano to guitar. I didn't really believe him when he said he'd practice every day, but sure enough, every afternoon he shuts himself into my office, which affords him greater privacy than the living room.

"Homework done?" I ask.

"Yes."

"Put it away, then."

As he shoves the papers haphazardly into his backpack, I think, *He's just like his father.* And then I put the thought away. A part of me wishes we'd never met Eric Fergus, but Ian has stopped talking about him, so I think he is at peace with the situation. At least he doesn't have to wonder about his donor anymore. He knows exactly who he is.

I pick up the padded envelope. No DNA test this time. The return address is an apartment in Arkansas. I may not have gotten another child from Eric Fergus, but thanks to the Internet, I've managed to buy his CD.

"I'll be in my room," I tell Carmen.

# Vanessa

## 3

It's Friday night, and Eric and I are on a study date at Starbucks. Which seems weird. It is weird. But nice too. We've both gone back to school. Eric is working on a PhD at UCLA in immunomicrobiology. Or microimmunobiology. Something like that. I might be missing a syllable. Anyway, he's able to use a lot of the stuff he learned in med school, so he says he's ahead of the game.

As for me, I'm learning about computers. It all started in August, when Dr. Sanchez called me into his office as I was about to leave one day and asked, "Vanessa, do you know how to use Excel?"

I said no.

"How about Word?"

No again. If this had been a job interview, I would have been out the door.

Dr. Sanchez said, "How would you feel about taking classes to learn them? You're smart. You'd pick it up in no time."

He said he was spending way too much time on billing and paperwork nights and weekends, when he really just wanted to be with his kids. He said he knew I could handle the extra responsibility. Next semester, he'll pay for an accounting class. And after that, he'll promote me to office manager.

So I'm looking at more education, more responsibility, and more money. Any one of those things is enough to make me scream with happiness. But what meant the most was having Dr. Sanchez call me smart.

At Starbucks, Eric and I have a table for two along one wall. I really want the couch and coffee table, but the people there don't look like they're ever leaving. Our table has just enough room for two laptops and two beverages. My laptop is new. It was the cheapest I could find at Best Buy, but it works.

I'm creating an Excel spreadsheet for my Computer Basics course and drinking a pumpkin latte with whipped cream. Eric doesn't drink coffee, so he got this nasty chai stuff. He's better than me at concentrating, but we knew that. Here's Eric: bent forward, iPod in his ears. He squints at the screen, making little faces now and then, after which he starts typing like crazy. Then he stops and squints at the screen some more.

Here's me: "I don't know about this pumpkin latte. It tastes like pumpkin pie, and I guess that's the point, but I'm not sure pumpkin and coffee really go together."

He doesn't react at all, and at first I think, *Wow, his concentration is amazing.* But then I remember the iPod and wonder, not for the first time, whether he uses it to block me out. And then I think, again not for the first time, that I have to stop thinking this way, always looking for the negatives.

At the next table, two teenagers are sharing a big slice of cheesecake. The glass display case looks a little picked over, but there are still giant cookies, blondies, brownies, and muffins. Chocolate: that's what my pumpkin latte needs.

I touch Eric's arm. He looks up and turns off his iPod.

"You want something to eat? I'm getting a brownie. Or we can share."

"I'll get it for you." He starts to stand up.

I press his shoulder. "No, you're working."

"So are you."

"I'm ready for a break."

Eric doesn't get that part of the reason I want the brownie is that it means I can get out of my chair. We've been here for over an hour. It's been a nice date, but I had a long day and now I kind of just want to go home and watch trashy television. Or even do some more schoolwork without all these distractions.

The barista is super good-looking—talk, dark, and handsome, just like I always liked men before I met Eric, who's really handsome, don't get me wrong, he's just not tall or dark. But, anyway, the barista manages to pick the biggest brownie out of the case without taking his eyes off me. And he keeps smiling. His teeth are really white. He has dimples. He's probably gay and just looking for a good tip.

I drop my eyes and tell myself that it's nothing, me checking out some random guy. But it's been happening more and more, noticing guys other than Eric. Holding their eyes too long. Smiling too much. All I can think is that it must be payback. Eric cheated on me. Just thinking that sentence makes me feel nauseous. I don't want a one-night stand, not really, but maybe it would make things even.

"You want this heated?" The barista, still smiling—God, he's hot—holds out the brownie.

"No," I say. "Thanks."

I pay him and put the change back in my purse rather than in the tip jar.

I have to move Eric's nasty chai drink to fit the plate on the table. "You want to take a break?" I ask. "And talk?"

"Um, sure." That means no, but whatever.

He hits a couple of keys on his computer and takes the iPod buds out of his ears. He smiles at me. Sort of. And looks attentive. Sort of.

"Have some." I nudge the plate toward him, realizing as I do so that a few months ago he would have just taken a chunk of the brownie without me having to offer it.

"How's your assignment going?" he asks, pulling a corner off the brownie.

Why am I being so weird in the head? Things are better than they used to be. He's interested in me, in what I'm doing.

"It's kind of boring, but kind of not. It's—I think I'm getting the hang of it. And it'll be really cool to be able to use it at work. To set up patient records and stuff."

"Awesome." He takes another piece of the brownie.

"How's your essay?"

He shrugs. "It's—you know."

"Right."

I try to think of something else to say, but I just can't. Eric sips his chai and looks at me.

"I guess we should get back to work," I say.

He smiles. "Yeah. I guess." He puts the iPod buds back in his ears. Before hitting the play button, he says, "Thanks for getting the brownie."

"You're welcome."

At the counter, the hot barista waits on a chunky teenager. He smiles at her just like he smiles at me. She laughs. He laughs. He hands her a pastry, and she drops some change in his jar.

# Wendy

4

"Everything I've read says you should put all your experience on your résumé, not just paid work, but I'm not sure that wiping butts and being the tooth fairy count as transferable skills," I say into the phone.

"Actually, I was always the tooth fairy," Darren says.

*Was.*

It is just after eight P.M. in Michigan, seven in Arizona. I am sitting on the bed in what was once my room, then became a guest room, and now, to my simultaneous delight and horror, has become my room again. The walls are beige. The rug is beige. The bedspread is white. My mother's approach to interior decorating has never been what you'd call adventurous.

I say, "I told the kids I was going to get a job. At first Syd got all upset because she didn't think anyone would pick her up from school. I told her Gammie or Pop-Pop would pick her up if I couldn't, and she said, 'I want Daddy to pick me up.'"

*Silence.*

"They miss you, Darren."

"I miss them too."

I almost say, *And I miss you,* but I can't bear the thought of having him say nothing in response.

I say, "I was thinking. Maybe you can read to them at night. Over the phone. Sydney still likes being read to, even though she can do it herself. And that way—it's something they can look forward to every night. Make them feel closer to you."

"Okay," he says.

"Jade's dad does that. Reads to her over the phone. It's the only time she's quiet all day. My sister lost it at dinner. Just started screaming at the top of her lungs because Jade wouldn't stop whining. My mother sat there eating like nothing was wrong."

"And your father?"

"Took his plate and went into the den. He used to do that when we were growing up. I just never realized why before. But, anyway. I think they're better," I say. "The kids, I mean. Maybe because they're playing outside more. Or maybe it's just that they're getting older. They're not even the worst-behaved kids in class anymore."

"Who is?"

"Harrison's best friend, Gus."

Darren laughs—not loudly, but I'll take it.

"Anyone look at the house?" I ask.

"Some people came back for the second time today. Think they're going to lowball, though, if they offer at all."

"And . . . any job leads?" I try to keep my tone casual.

"No."

"But . . . you're looking. Right?"

"Yeah."

*It never hurts to look.*

I say, "Will you . . . I hope . . . please give me another chance,
Darren."

After a beat, he says, "I am."

From two thousand miles away.

I exhale. I hadn't even known I'd been holding my breath.

I say, "Harrison's learning a new song on the piano. Did I
tell you?"

# Laura

My brother Mike calls one evening, and it's not even my birthday. Immediately, I think: *He's getting another divorce.* Or maybe something happened to one of our parents.

"Is everything okay?" I ask after his hello.

He laughs. "I believe the proper response is, 'So good to hear from you.'"

"So good to hear from you. Is everything okay?"

"Everything's great. Shereen and I were just talking about Christmas."

It takes me a moment to remember that Shereen is Mike's latest wife. She's Indian. She has two little girls. She works at the university with Mike as . . . something.

"Do you have any plans?" Mike asks.

"For Christmas? Uh, yeah. I was thinking about putting up a tree. Buying some presents, baking cookies, that kind of thing. Pretty radical."

"Ha! You're going to bake cookies or Carmen is?"

"Shut up!" I laugh. "I can make cookies! Well, I can slice and bake them, anyway."

Ian gets up from the kitchen table and holds up his completed homework. I give him the thumbs up.

Mike says, "In that case, if you're going to be around . . . tell me if this doesn't work for you because I completely understand . . . but Shereen said she really wants to meet you. And I want you to meet her and the girls. Your weather is nicer than ours in December, so we were thinking . . ."

Suddenly, I get it. "You told her I live eight miles from Disneyland, didn't you?"

He sighs. "Shereen knew already, but Lily and Amelia just found out. They are relentless. There will be no peace until they visit Cinderella's castle and the Tiki Room and whatever else they've got going on there."

"In that case, yes. Of course. Come. Ian and I will go with you. The park is really pretty at the holidays and we can battle the crowds together."

Ian is slipping—well, shoving—his papers into his backpack. At the sound of his name, he looks up.

"Uncle Mike," I mouth.

"He's coming?" Ian asks.

When I nod, he says, "Yes!" and punches the air for emphasis before heading to my office to practice his guitar.

"Shereen really does want to meet you," Mike says.

"I really want to meet her too."

"And the girls. Oh my God, Laura, you're going to love them. They are so smart. And funny. And exhausting too, but . . . I can't believe what they've brought to my life."

For a moment, I am speechless.

"You always said you didn't want children," I say at last.

"I didn't! That's what's so crazy. Maybe I just wasn't ready. Or maybe I hadn't found the right woman and the right children. It doesn't even matter that the girls aren't mine because . . . they are mine, you know?"

I smile. "I know."

We are quiet for a moment.

"So . . . see you at Christmas?" he says.

"I can't wait."

# Vanessa

Eric is taking me out to dinner. Not to his mother's house or a picnic on the beach, but to a restaurant. A real restaurant, with cloth napkins and heavy menus and waiters. This can only mean one thing.

Eric is going to dump me.

He's been so quiet, lately. Even more than usual, I mean. And every time I catch him looking at me, he's got this sad expression on his face. Even when he smiles, he looks sad.

I will not cry.

I will not make him feel bad.

This is for the best. I know it is. For both of us. If I were a stronger, better person, I'd do it myself. I'd set him free. But I just can't. I love him too much.

He looks so handsome tonight, in a white button-up shirt, blue jeans, and black shoes. He looks like, I don't know. An indie film-maker or something. I think of the women who will fall in love with him when he's free. And then I stop because it makes me want to cry.

I will not cry.

He holds the driver's-side door open for me. We're taking my car because his tires are bald and it would be so uncool to have him dump me and then get a flat. He doesn't say much except to give me directions to a restaurant we've passed a hundred times. A hundred times I've said, "I'd like to go there sometime."

So I guess dinner is his final gift to me. If I'm lucky, he'll wait till dessert to dump me, because I'll probably never get to go here again.

They've got valet parking. I say, "We can park on the street," but Eric says, "No, I've got this," so I let the valet open my door and hand him my keys.

I know I look good, and not just because of the way the valet checks me out. I bought a dress special for tonight. Simple, black, low-cut, but not too short. I want Eric to realize just what he's losing. But I think he already knows. He already feels bad.

*I will not cry.*

We get a table with a water view. I start to cry.

"What?" Eric takes my hand over the table.

"It's just—I love you." The sobs come full force now.

"I love you too." He smiles with no sadness at all.

I take my hand away and dig through my purse, but there's no tissue. Damn. If only this place had paper napkins, I could blow my nose. I sniffle hard, gagging a little on my snot.

Eric reaches for my hand.

A busboy pours waters. A waitress asks us if we want something to drink. I say I'll have a Diet Coke because if I drink alcohol in this state, I'll really lose it. Eric says give him a minute, he's not sure yet.

I ask him why he didn't order anything to drink, and he says he wants to know whether or not to order champagne, and then he pulls out a ring. Gold. With a diamond.

He goes, "I didn't do this right last time. I'm sorry. You deserve better. You probably deserve better than me too, but Vanessa . . . will you be my wife?"

I go, "What?"

The ring looks kind of familiar.

He says, "Will you have me?"

I go, "You mean, marry you?"

"Yes."

"But—you already proposed. And then, like—unproposed."

"Yeah, I know. And that was really uncool, so . . ." He looks around. "Do you want me to get down on my knee?"

He totally wants me to say no.

I say, "Yes." Then, "No, of course not. Eric, it's just—I'm confused. Where did you get that ring?"

"It's my mother's. Because Angie got one of my grandmother's rings and Kara got the other, so my mom thought it was only fair."

"I can't take your mother's ring, Eric. That's creepy."

"She wanted you to have it. Seriously. But if it makes you feel better, I can just buy you your own ring."

"It would."

"It won't be as big. The diamond, I mean."

"I don't care." The waitress is by the next table. I hold up my hand and she comes over.

"Cosmopolitan," I say. "Please."

Eric says, "I thought this was what you wanted."

"It was. It is. But only if you want it too."

"I do."

"I mean getting married. Not just getting engaged. I mean a wedding. And being husband and wife. And . . . having babies together."

He says nothing.

"Eric?"

He nods. And says, "Yes."

His mother's ring sits on the table between us for a little while, then Eric slips it back into his pocket.

"I'll get you a different ring," he says.

"Okay."

# Wendy

The phone rings at eight o'clock: right on time. My parents have retreated to the den. They have taken to watching a news program after dinner. I'm starting to think they're less intrigued by current events than desperate to find an oasis of calm.

"Daddy!" Sydney runs into the kitchen.

"Get your jammies on so you're ready for him." I reach for the kitchen phone. "Hello?"

"Hey." He sounds tired.

"You eat dinner?" Yesterday he skipped it.

"Cereal."

"That's not dinner."

"I know. But I didn't get to go to the store, so . . ." He sighs.

"My mother made kielbasa for dinner. And, get this. Harrison ate it."

"No way."

"Way. I think it's because of Jade. He saw the way she wouldn't eat anything but pasta and decided that was a baby way to act."

"What about Sydney?"

"She took a bite. And then spit it out and said she felt like she was going to puke, so could she please have something else?"

"At least she said please."

"I considered it a victory."

"Your sister get off okay?"

"Yeah, my dad drove them to the airport this morning. He made them leave like three hours before the flight. My mom cried, but I think they were tears of joy. It's kind of quiet around here now."

"You say that like it's a bad thing."

I considered. "Jade's a good kid. And she really is kind of brilliant. She's just . . . high-strung. And so spoiled. Tracey and I actually had a really good talk last night. She asked me for parenting advice."

Darren made a little noise.

"Did you just laugh?" I ask.

"No." He's a terrible liar.

"I told her what I've done and said she should do the opposite."

"We have good kids," he says. *We.*

"Yes. We do."

There is so much to say in that instant that neither of us says a thing. But I am not ready to hand him over to the kids yet.

"Any news from your boss?" I ask. Darren has proposed the idea of telecommuting, at least on a trial basis.

"He said he's going to talk it over with human resources. I thought that was promising."

"It is. And if he says no . . . if you can't get anything out here . . . we'll come back. If you want us."

I hold my breath until he speaks.

"We'll figure something out," he says.

I exhale. I'm not really sure what he means by that, but if it isn't good, at least it isn't bad.

The house shakes: Harrison is coming down the stairs. He

comes into the kitchen holding the copy of *Chronicles of Narnia* that Darren had delivered from Amazon. His pajama bottoms show his skinny ankles; I realize with a start that we've been here long enough for him to have gotten taller.

"Where's Sydney?" I ask Harrison. "She was supposed to be getting her pajamas on."

"SYDNEY!"

"I could have done that. Don't yell. Gammie hates it when you yell."

Yelling works, though; in a moment Sydney comes running down the stairs in a pink *Beauty and the Beast* nightgown.

"DON'T START WITHOUT ME!"

"DON'T YELL," I yell.

The phone is cordless. The children follow me into the living room and settle on opposite sides of my mother's gold brocade couch. Unfortunately, a streak of chocolate runs along one arm. Fortunately, Jade did it.

Sydney hugs her favorite pink kitty, Harrison the book. I push the speaker button and place the phone on the couch between them.

"They're ready for you," I say.

"Chapter four," Darren says. He begins to read.

Sydney closes her eyes, the better to picture Narnia. Harrison clutches his book and stares longingly at the phone.

I stand there for the longest time, just looking. Just listening.

Darren and I will work something out. We have to.

# Vanessa

"Furlough day," Kyla Sanchez tells me. It's a Monday morning, and she's hanging in the waiting room, reading a celebrity magazine.

"Huh?"

"The teachers don't make as much money as they used to, so they get extra days off." She shrugs. "Works for me."

"Where are your brother and sister?"

She turns the page. "Home with Michelle."

"Who's Michelle?"

"Not Michelle. ME-shell. ME." Kyla rolls her eyes. "She has a total thing about how you say her name. She's our new nanny, housekeeper, whatever."

"So how come you're here?" I ask.

"Because it's Take-Your-Daughter-to-Work day."

"Really?"

She grins.

I slap a hand over my mouth to keep from laughing. When I can talk normal, I go, "What happened to your old nanny?"

"Got another job. With a baby. More hours." She holds up the magazine. Inside, two beautiful women, one skinny, one curvy, wear two identical leopard-print dresses. "Who do you think wore it better?" Her palm hides the vote tally.

I point to the curvy woman.

"I thought so too." Kyla moves her hand. Our pick lost the vote by five percentage points. "It's 'cause the other one's thinner."

I go, "Boys like curves."

"Not the boys I know."

"That's because they're still babies. Wait till they get older. And *you* get older. You're gonna be a knockout."

She flushes and looks down, but I know I've said the right thing.

And then she says the wrong thing—or maybe the right thing at the wrong time. Right when Dr. Sanchez comes out of his offices, she goes, "Do you have a boyfriend?"

"Yes. Good morning, Dr. Sanchez."

"Are you going to marry him?"

"You shouldn't ask personal questions," Dr. Sanchez tells her.

"No, it's okay," I say. It's not okay at all, but I don't want Kyla getting into trouble.

"I don't know," I tell her. "I used to think so, but now . . ." I shrug. "It could go either way." Since our awkward dinner, Eric hasn't mentioned marriage again, and neither have I.

"My dad has a girlfriend," Kyla announces.

He turns bright red. *"Kyla."*

What? Dr. Sanchez is seeing someone? I should be all over this, like, I can't wait to tell Melva and Pammy at lunch. But instead it just makes me . . . sad. Like he's betraying his wife. Or maybe I'm just worried about the kids. It's bad enough that they keep having to adjust to new nannies. But to bring someone into their lives who might not love them enough?

"I'll be in my office," he mutters.

"He's weird," Kyla says.

"Your father is the least weird person I know," I say.

"You oughta get out more often." She holds up the magazine to a spread of an up-and-coming young female star. "You think she's pretty?"

"Not as pretty as you."

She rolls her eyes but can't hide the smile tugging at the corners of her mouth.

I grab a legal pad. "I gotta go over the day's schedule with your dad. When I come back, I'll find some work for you."

"No rush."

Dr. Sanchez pecks at his keyboard so hard, I'm afraid he'll break it.

"My apologies for my daughter's behavior." He doesn't look up.

"Nah. I love Kyla."

He squeezes his eyes shut. When he opens them again, they're shiny.

"She's something," he says, his voice soft. "When I think . . ." He stops. Clears his throat. Forces himself to look at me. "Okay. So. Root canal at nine-thirty—is that right?"

"Yeah. Though it's Mrs. Meyer, and she's usually late."

"Well, I hope she's on time today. We've got those implants scheduled for this afternoon . . ." He taps his desk with a pencil. "Do you think it's normal? The way Kyla is so interested in clothes and movie stars at this age? That she's asking to wear makeup?"

"Of course it's normal."

"She's twelve!"

"Exactly. She's twelve. Almost thirteen. Right on schedule."

He nods. "And after Mrs. Meyer . . . some checkups?"

"Two of them. They should be quick. Might even be able to squeeze them in when Mrs. Meyer is still in the chair. You know, if she's late."

"Which she will be."

"Yeah, she will."

"I don't have a girlfriend."

Oh. My. God.

"It's none of my business if you do." It comes out sounding bitchy. I don't mean it to.

He drops the pencil. Drums his fingers on the desk. "I signed up with Match.com. A couple of months ago. There've been a few lunch dates." He clears his throat again. And again.

"That's good. Isn't it?" I don't sound convincing.

He shrugs. Looks down at his hands. "I just figured it's . . . time. But there's been no one. That I've met. Who I want to see again, I mean. Certainly no girlfriend."

"It takes time," I say, for lack of anything better.

He nods and makes a funny noise, like a half grunt. Then he goes, "Computer class still going well?"

"Yeah. Awesome."

"Glad to hear it. Okay then." He stops drumming the desk and pats it, which is code for "We're done here."

Back at my desk, Kyla is opening drawers.

"What you looking for?" I might've been annoyed, but there's only boring stuff in the drawers: pens and Post-its and extra forms. I keep all my makeup and McDonald's toys in the filing cabinet.

"Pictures of your boyfriend."

"You won't find any."

She shuts the door and leans back in my chair. "You got any in your wallet?"

I shake my head. Long ago, I had a snapshot of Eric that I kept in my wallet. Just a casual shot of him playing guitar. Then one day he saw it and got kind of weird, like, "Who do you show this to?"

I was all, "No one" (which wasn't true)—I just liked to look at him every now and then.

He said, "In case you forget what I look like?"

That was the end of the wallet photo.

Kyla goes, "My dad said your boyfriend's short."

"He's not short. He's average. Your dad's just tall. And why did you ask me if I had a boyfriend if you already knew?"

"Because when I asked my dad why he didn't go out with you instead of those skanks he met online, he said it's because you have a boyfriend. So I wanted to see if maybe you'd broken up."

"He went out with skanks? You shouldn't say 'skanks.' It's not a nice word." Wait a minute. "You know, Kyla, when your father said that, like, if I didn't have a boyfriend . . . I don't think he meant . . ."

"Yuh-huh."

"He was just saying that."

Kyla raises one eyebrow. She smirks. Then she goes, "You got any nail polish around here? I could use a mani."

---

I don't tell Melva and Pammy that Dr. Sanchez has joined Match .com, and I definitely don't tell them what Kyla said. It's just embarrassing. For him, I mean. And so obviously not true. But I feel like I have to tell Eric. Not telling him would be keeping a secret.

"It's probably true," he says.

"Of course it's not true. Don't you think I would have noticed?"

"Noticed what? Dr. Sanchez is an upstanding guy. He's not going to look down your shirt."

"He can't look down my shirt. He makes me wear scrubs, remember?"

Eric shakes his head. "The kind of guy he is, if he was into you, he'd go out of his way to act like he wasn't. So the fact that he acts as if he doesn't like you probably means he likes you."

"That makes no sense."

"Actually, it does."

My face is hot and I can't look at Eric. So weird. I should be mad at him right now because he's pushing me away. And yet . . . and yet . . .

He says, "Do you . . . If there were no us, I mean. Would you . . . would this be a good thing?"

Eric knows me so well. Better than myself, sometimes. Damn it. There's no point being anything but honest with him, though it takes a long time to find the words.

"I'm not sure. It's kind of weird. Really weird." I pick at my thumbnail. Thanks to Kyla, it's hot pink. "I'd need to be really careful, not to mess things up with my job, you know. But, yeah. I guess if I were single I'd be curious to see where things went. Whether I just like him for his children or if there's anything there. Which there probably isn't."

"But there might be."

". . . There might be."

"And if there's nothing with him, would you be curious to see what else was out there? Who else was out there."

"Maybe." I swallow hard. "Yes."

I look up slowly, terrified that I'll see relief in his eyes. Or joy at finally getting his chance at freedom.

I can't believe it. He is crying. He's not making any noise, but his face is drenched. All of a sudden I'm crying too. I cross the room and throw my arms around him, bury my face in his chest, soak his soft T-shirt with my tears.

"I love you," he whispers. "You've got to know that."

"I love you, too."

"But . . ." he says.

"I know. You don't have to say it. I know."

# Laura

Now that the chickens are gone, Ian is eating meat again (though not poultry). We have just finished devouring our beef Stroganoff when the phone rings. According to my machine, the number is unknown. I answer anyway.

"Laura? This is Wendy Winder."

Wendy Winder! I never thought I'd hear from her again.

"The kids and I are staying in Michigan," she says. "Living here, actually. I don't have my computer, or I would have just e-mailed you."

"Did something happen? Did anyone else contact you?" How ironic if someone finally came up with a vial of 613 sperm. For an instant, a pang of hope shoots through me—but then I realize that it's too late. It's over.

"No, nothing like that. It's just—remember how you asked if my kids had natural musical ability?"

"Oh, right. Ian's switched to guitar," I say just as he points to my office to let me know he'll be practicing. "He started two months ago, and his teacher says it sounds like he's been playing for at least a year."

Unwelcome, a vision of Eric Fergus flashes through my mind.

"Really. That's—yeah. Nice. Anyway. I signed my kids up for piano. They've been taking lessons for three months now."

"And?"

"They're awful. Terrible. No talent whatsoever. With years of practice, they might be average. My parents—we're staying with them—they have a cat? And every time Harrison or Sydney so much as sits at the piano, the cat runs for the door and starts crying to be let out." She laughs.

"Maybe if they tried another instrument," I suggest.

"Oh, no, I'm going to make them stick with the piano, at least for a couple of years, because it's good for them to learn about music and it keeps them out of trouble for a half hour a week. But what I wanted to tell you was, don't assume that the things that make Ian special come from the donor. Maybe he gets his musical ability from you. Or one of your long-lost relatives. Or from nowhere at all. The stuff that makes our kids who they are—some of it comes from the mother and some from the father. But most of it—who knows? They just are who they are."

I say, "Funny. I guess I've reached the same conclusion. I just never put it into words."

"Are you in touch with Eric Fergus?" she asks.

"No." A faint pain flares in my chest. "You?"

"God, no. So after that last IVF, did you ever . . . try again?"

"No. I thought about it, but . . . no."

"Sorry."

"Me too. But—it's okay."

"Do you still have his e-mail?" she asks. "I'd like to send him a note. Thanking him. For what he did. For what he gave me."

After I give her the information, we say our good-byes without any pretense of staying in touch or of being family. I still wish I could have met Wendy and her children. I may always miss the reunions that never were, but I like knowing that they're out there.

Besides, shared blood doesn't make a family. I should know that better than anybody. Carmen is more of a grandmother to Ian than my mother will ever be. And he couldn't be more excited about meeting his new cousins if they were actually related. The two of us are not alone in the world, after all.

Guitar music spills around the edges of the closed office door. Ian hits a wrong note, says, "Ugh!"

Love washes over me with so much force it makes me dizzy. I need to see Ian's face. I need to hold him.

Beyond the closed door, he laughs and says something I can't understand. It is new, this habit of talking to himself.

The doorknob is cold in my hand. I push the door open slowly, carefully, just enough for a peek. The computer is on, music playing. Some music program or video, maybe?

"Try it again," the man on the screen says. For an instant, I am impressed by the interactive nature of the program. And then it hits me. Blood rushes to my ears.

"Eric?" I swing open the door. "What are you doing talking to my son?"

On the other end of the Skype call, Eric Fergus sits on a couch, a guitar in his lap. He looks stunned.

"Oh, crappus," Ian mutters.

Eric says, "I . . . I . . ."

"It's my fault," Ian says. "I told him you said it was okay if we talked. But that you didn't want to talk to him."

"It's not okay?" Eric says.

"Who initiated the contact?" I demand.

"In English?" Ian asks.

"I did," Eric tells me. "I tried to Skype you a couple of weeks ago, but Ian answered, and we got talking about music. It's really awesome that he's taking guitar."

"Why didn't you tell me Eric called?" I ask, trying and failing to catch my son's eye.

Ian sits hunched over his guitar. "You told me we were never going to see Eric or talk to him again. So I figured you'd say I can't Skype him."

"You can't Skype him," I say.

On the screen, Eric Fergus sits hunched over his guitar.

"Eric." I try to get him to look at me. "*Eric.*"

He peeks up through his shaggy hair. Wendy Winder is right: our children are themselves and nobody else. But damn, if Eric doesn't look exactly like my son right now.

"I don't really know you," I say. "Not really. You could be a complete psychopath."

"I'm not."

"But you *could* be."

"But I'm *not.*" Now he's looking straight at me, with a slight frown.

"If you want to see my son—and, bear in mind, he is *my* son, not yours—we'll need to draw up an agreement. Make it clear how often you can talk to him and what kind of behavior is and is not acceptable. You can't just call him whenever you feel like it."

"I'm not trying to be a father to him," Eric tells me. "I wouldn't even know how. I just thought I could be, like, a family friend."

"We're writing a song together," Ian tells me.

Out of nowhere, tears fill my eyes. "*You can't hurt him,*" I tell the computer screen. "You can't make him care about you and then just disappear. That's why I did things the way I did."

Now I am crying. Really crying. Shit.

"Maybe . . . you want to talk about this later?" Eric asks. "In person?"

My vision blurry from the tears, I nod. And then I find the "end call" button and click it. The screen goes blank.

"Don't hide things from me," I tell Ian, knowing this is just the beginning. The older he gets, the less he will belong to me.

I go to my bedroom to collect myself. Alfredo, sprawled across my pillow, twitches his tail when he hears me enter. Who says I sleep alone?

I lie down for a while, curled around the cat. Maybe I even doze off. For once I don't dream. When I get up, it is a half hour until Ian's bedtime. I rinse my face with cold water and push the slider to the backyard. The teak table and chairs are still there, but now, instead of looking at the chicken coop, they oversee a patch of lonely dirt.

The moon slips up above the hillside behind my home. Just as I think, *Everything is going to be okay,* the sounds of guitar music slip out of the house and into the night. I leave the dark yard and go into the living room, where Ian sits on the couch, holding his guitar.

I'm about to speak when something moves in the corner of my eye. Eric sits at the piano bench.

"Hi," he says. "You said we could talk."

"Was that you? On the guitar?" I ask, too shocked to say anything else.

He shakes his head. "Ian's amazing."

I nod. Should I be happy? Angry? What? "You play piano?" I ask.

"Since I was five."

"You want to hear our song?" Ian asks.

The music starts. For once in my life, I'm just there in the moment, not planning or analyzing or worrying but just feeling the tones of the piano and the strum of the guitar.

When they finish, I say, "That's beautiful."

Eric stands. "Sorry if I . . . I guess I should have called first. I'll go."

Ian opens his mouth to protest, but then thinks better of it. He crosses the room to Eric, who holds up a fist. They bump knuckles. Ian looks at Eric. He looks at me. And then he heads off to bed.

"That's how we say good-bye on the computer," Eric tells me, and while I don't love the thought of my son punching my monitor, I understand the appeal.

In the doorway, Eric says, "When I Skyped you, it was because I thought you might be pregnant. From—you know."

"I thought so too. But I wasn't."

"I know. Sorry."

I say, "I bought your CD."

"Really?"

I nod. "You're good. Really good. So much better than you give yourself credit for. I keep listening to it, over and over, and I hear new things every time. And it just . . . makes me angry."

"Why?"

"Because if I had that kind of talent, I'd never walk away from it. I'd just push and push until—" I shake my head. "Sorry. It's your life. And . . . I'm glad you're playing again."

"I'm not with Vanessa anymore," he says. "Not that that—means anything for us. I just thought you'd want to know. If it affects the way you feel about allowing me into Ian's life, I mean."

I start to make a lame joke about how he can see Ian as long as he promises to never have another girlfriend, but I decide to let it go. For a moment, our silence feels awkward. When he opens his mouth, I expect him to say good-bye.

"I can't believe you got rid of the chickens."

I burst out laughing. "We didn't need them anymore," I tell him.

"But they were really cool."

"Yeah. I guess they were."

He crosses the room and stops a foot away from me. His eyes are so blue. Nothing like Ian's. Or mine. Or anyone I've ever known.

He holds up a fist. We bump knuckles.

"A family friend," I say. "Sure you're ready for that?"

He grins. "As ready as I'll ever be."

*what came first*

---

READERS GUIDE

# Discussion Questions

1. What did you think of Laura, Wendy, and Vanessa when they were first introduced? Did you sympathize with one character more than the others? Did your opinion of the women change as the novel progressed?

2. What was your reaction when Vanessa didn't get an engagement ring for her birthday from Eric? Did you feel like her anger was justified? Were her expectations in the relationship reasonable? How would you have reacted in that situation if you were Vanessa?

3. On page 16 Wendy says that when she and Darren were trying to become pregnant the very idea of being childless sent her into a depression and she states, "How could I ever lead a full life without a house full of little people to call my own?" How do you feel about this statement? Do you think it is possible for a person to lead a full life without children of her own?

4. Discuss the differences between Laura's and Wendy's parenting style. Do you think one of them parents better than the other? If so, why? What sort of parenting style do you think is most effective?

5. After Eric learns that his sperm donation gave life to Laura's son Ian he tells Vanessa, "He's not my child. He was conceived with my sperm, but he's not mine" (page 113). What do you think about this statement? Do you think that a sperm donor is only a donor and should not be called a "father"? What should a donor's role be, if any, in a child's life?

**6.** When we are first introduced to Wendy's children, Wendy is adamant about not wanting the school psychologist to label them with having behavioral issues. Yet throughout the novel, she desperately seeks to find a reason for their unruly actions. Why do you think this is? What sorts of labels do adults frequently place on children? How does this affect their childhood?

**7.** How did you feel when Eric decided to meet Laura and then redonate his sperm? Did you understand his decision? Do you think Vanessa should have been given an opinion in the process?

**8.** During Wendy's scrapbooking party, Wendy remembers Sherry saying that she thought Wendy was being selfish for using a sperm donor. Sherry goes on to state that to get pregnant by a stranger instead of adoption shows that "it's all about you and your ego that you have to have a kid with your genes" (page 190). Do you agree with Sherry? If you were Wendy, what would you have said in response?

**9.** How did you react to Wendy's confession that she slept with Lane? At that moment did you think there was a chance that Lane was Harrison and Sydney's father?

**10.** Why do you think Eric chose to get back in touch with Laura and Ian? Do you think he wanted to donate again? Do you think his feelings for Laura and Ian were sincere?

**11.** Throughout the novel, the story moves among the perspectives of Laura, Wendy and Vanessa. What knowledge do you gain by the story being told in this format? Did you find that this style provides you with a better understanding of the characters?

**12.** What did you know about IUI and IVF prior to reading this novel? Have your thoughts about the process changed after reading about these women?

**13.** Discuss the title of this novel. In what ways does it relate to the story and its characters?

**14.** Imagine what the lives of these characters are like after the novel. What role will Eric play in Ian's life? What will become of Vanessa and Eric's relationship? How about Wendy and Darren's relationship?